THE SEA OF LUCIDITY

THE SEA OF LUCIDITY

Book One of
THE ELDORMAAR

DAVID MACKAY

Cover design by Melanie Moor. Melli M Designs

ISBN: 9798711762959

At The Point Of Forever Literary Creations

www.atthepointofforever.com
www.theeldormaar.com

CHAPTER ONE

Sunlight danced among the trees, casting ghostly shadows through the old forest. All was quiet, save for the whisper of the breeze. Immersed in his thoughts, paying little attention to his surroundings, he followed the track alongside a small stream winding its nomadic journey through the ancient woodland.
At a bend in the trail, he slowed to a halt.

A short distance ahead, an old man with a dog shuffled slowly past the wooden footbridge spanning the stream.

Sighing his irritation, he carried on walking. He wasn't in the mood for conversation. Today, more than any other, he craved the peace and solitude of the forest. He quickened his pace. Passing the old man without slowing, he offered a brief greeting.

'It's a fine day.'

His gesture met with silence. Annoyed with himself for wasting his breath, he glanced back over his shoulder.

If the old man was aware of his presence, he was choosing not to acknowledge it.

He walked on for several minutes deliberating the exchange. Something about it didn't feel right. He'd never seen anyone in this part of the forest before. The elderly stranger might be lost, disorientated, and in need of help.
Turning in frustration, he made his way back along the track.

Arriving back at the footbridge, his mood swung from frustration to bemusement. The old man and the dog were nowhere to be seen. Scratching his head at the bizarre twist, his bemusement quickly turned to annoyance. With the realisation his efforts had been in vain, he turned again and resumed his course.

Troubled by the chance encounter, he pondered the old man's odd manner and sudden disappearance. Failing to find any logical explanation, he became lost in contemplation. When he came to an unexpected fork in the path, it dawned on him that he too might just have lost his way.

He scanned his surroundings. None of this looked familiar. The forest he thought he knew so well suddenly looked very different. So which way should he go? Spurred on by the prospect of exploring new ground, he considered his options and made his decision. He'd walked only a short distance when, detecting a change in the air, he came to a sudden stop.

As the breeze dropped away, everything fell very still. The trees now stood statuesque, as if watching on in silent conspiracy. The bright sunlight shimmered with a peculiar, hypnotic haze. As if held in suspended animation, the old forest waited in quiet expectation.

He watched the trees on either side of the glade, seeking sign of movement or some clue as to what was happening but found neither. Hoping to break the spell that appeared to have captivated the forest, he took a tentative step forward. A broken branch cracked beneath his feet. His heart raced as an uncomfortable feeling washed over him. Was he being watched?

Glancing warily over his shoulder, he took a few further hesitant steps forward. His gaze darted from side to side. Try as he might, he just couldn't shake the feeling.

As his mind wrestled with the notion, a sudden movement in the trees caught his eye. He held his breath and waited. He saw it again. From nowhere, a gust of wind rushed through the trees, rousing the branches to life. The flurry lasted only a matter of seconds; the wind receded as quickly as it had appeared, leaving a gentle breeze in its wake. A wood pigeon noisily heralded a return to normality and, high above the treetops, a lone buzzard swooped in the sunlight.

With a shake of his head, he glanced at his watch. 1.45 pm. Only fifteen minutes had passed since he'd left his truck at the edge of the forest. It felt longer; so much longer.

The peculiar event played on his mind as he left the clearing. Back once more among the trees, the path came alongside a stream, much wider than before. Was it the same stream? He could only hazard a guess; his usual infallible sense of direction had apparently deserted him. He hoped it was a temporary glitch.

At the sight of a rocky outcrop, his mood lightened. He now sensed a strange familiarity with his surroundings. The path wound its way up the rock formation and, as he neared the top of the climb, he was drawn towards the thundering sound of falling water.

The narrow ledge came to an abrupt and precarious end. Peering over the edge of the precipice, he watched the water tumble onto the rocks far below. Had he been here before? He couldn't say for sure.

With his curiosity rekindled, he took one last look at the waterfall and retraced his steps along the ledge. Climbing to the top of the outcrop, he re-joined the track and continued on his way.

Troubled yet again with the unnerving sensation of being watched, he glanced repeatedly over his shoulder, each time expecting to see someone emerging from the trees behind.

There seemed little doubt about it.

He was being watched. He was being followed.

CHAPTER TWO

Venturing further into the forest, he wondered again if he'd strayed into uncharted territory. And yet it seemed unlikely, for so many reasons, not least the undeniable feeling he'd been here before.

At a bend in the stream, the track left the water's edge and climbed steeply through a stand of pine. The stream would eventually lead to safety, he was convinced of it, but with the lure of a viewpoint proving too good to resist, he turned his back on the water and began the climb.

As he neared the top of the rise, he felt a cool breeze on his face. Leaving the cover of the trees, he reached the brow of the hill and, shielding his eyes from the bright sunshine, looked down in astonishment on the valley below.

From where he stood at the edge of the forest, the land rolled gently downhill to meet a great river forging its way through a sweeping expanse of lush green meadowland. At a turn in the river, next to a large wooden bridge, stood a cluster of stone huts. Struggling to comprehend his discovery, he counted the huts, a dozen at least. He saw people moving among the dwellings. Smoke rose from a great wood-stack piled high at the centre of the settlement. What was this place? And, more importantly, how had he come to be here?

A group of figures left the settlement and crossed the bridge. He counted five of them, carrying what looked like long wooden spears. Once across the river, they began the modest climb up through the bracken. They were heading straight for him.

He threw himself to the ground. Panic set in as he gauged their progress. They were getting close. He had to get out of here. A branch snapped loudly behind him. Spinning round, he realised he had taken too long to plan his retreat.

His followers burst rowdily from the forest; three bearded men with bushy, tangled hair, their upper bodies draped in grey furs. Jumping to his feet, he turned to run, only to find his way barred by the five from the bridge. The tallest of them, a grizzled character with a beard that reached down to his waist, passed his spear to a comrade, broke rank, and strode towards him.

'Morusk, my friend.' He clasped him firmly by the shoulders. 'We thought you lost. Where have you been?'

Freed from the man's grip, he stepped back in bewilderment. Glancing at them one by one his trepidation slowly receded with a startling realisation. He recognised them. He knew them all. His response was staggered, his words came slowly. Barely recognising the sound of his own voice, he searched for sense in the confusion.

'Kruff… I don't know… I don't know what happened.'

'You've been missing. Gone six days and nights you were. We feared the Raiders had taken you.'

'We followed you in the forest, Morusk.' Another of the men interrupted. 'You were acting strangely, like it wasn't really you.'

'Stuc… I…' He wanted to respond… he wanted to explain,

but he couldn't find the words.

'Tengk was keen to use you for arrow practice, until we got closer and knew for certain it was you.'

'Could have been a trap,' Tengk sneered defiantly. 'A Raider ploy. Lucky for you Stuc was with me. Otherwise…'

'We haven't seen you since the hunt, Morusk,' Stuc interrupted again. 'Where have you been these last six days?'

'Enough talk for now,' Kruff ended the discussion bluntly. 'Our friend looks weary. Let's get him home.'

The short walk down to the settlement was fraught with confusion. Had he really been missing for six days? If so, where had he been? And why could he remember nothing about it? This was home, these were his kinsfolk. And yet something wasn't right. He knew it. Tengk's watchful stare suggested he knew it too.

'You look like a man in need of a drink, Morusk.' Kruff's voice focused his attention. 'We broke open the casks of the sloe berry ale, night before last. It's a fine brew, I reckon you'll be impressed.' Kruff's expression grew sombre. 'The beacon fire is lit. Carn Cull and his men are on their way from DunTreshen. We must feast and drink a while in their honour. The Raiders attacked there three days ago, much of the settlement was burned to the ground. They lost several of their kin.'

An uneasy silence followed. Kruff waited a few moments before continuing. 'Carn Cull wants revenge, he says it's time to stand up to the Raiders threat; to take them on and hunt them down.'

'Reckon we should have no part in it, Kruff,' Juuk countered. 'Stay out of the Raiders' way an' most likely they'll stay out of yours.' His assessment brought murmurs of agreement from the others.

'Maybe,' Kruff nodded. 'That was the way things used to be, but I'm not so sure anymore.'

'An' if we refuse Carn Cull,' growled Tengk. 'What do you think will happen then? Man like that would think nothing of cutting our throats while we sleep!'

'That's for sure.' Kruff sighed. 'He's ruthless at the best of times. Let's keep on his good side, for now.'

It seemed to Morusk that everything had been turned upside down. Approaching the bridge, he felt the knot in his stomach tighten. Glancing anxiously at the others, he saw the suspicion in Tengk's stare. Lifted by the warm greeting he received on his return to the settlement, he tried to push his concerns aside. Something had happened to him, something had changed, and he suspected the answers were to be found back in the forest. An opportunity to return there would present itself soon enough, he may only have to wait a few hours. After the feasting and drinking when everyone was either asleep or too drunk to notice, hidden by darkness, he could make his way back into the trees.

With his kinsfolk gathered round, making themselves busy with the preparations for the feast, he took a seat by the great fire. Stuc ambled towards him, a wry grin on his face and a pitcher of ale in each hand.

'Reckoned you'd welcome one of these.'

'You'd reckoned right, old friend.' Morusk drank thirstily. 'Kruff was right,' he smacked his lips in appreciation. 'This is a fine brew.'

Stuc snorted his agreement as he raised his pitcher. 'Sure is, and this is the first of many. Drink up, Morusk. I've a feeling it's going to be a long night.'

CHAPTER THREE

Three pitchers of the sloe berry ale later, four riders crossed the wooden bridge and entered the settlement of DunTreggan.

'Looks like Carn Cull's crew have started to arrive.' Stuc rose from the fireside. 'I'd say that's Tal leading, and Brodar, but I don't recognise the other two.' He swung an arm in invitation. 'On your feet, Morusk, let's go hear what they have to say.'

They joined the conversation just as Kruff welcomed the DunTreshen riders.

'Carn Cull and the others will be here by nightfall,' Tal replied as they dismounted. 'But he sent us in advance to introduce new allies.' He gestured to the man and woman accompanying them. 'They bear grim news from the north. The Raiders' threat now blights every corner of the land.'

The tall stranger stepped forward and offered his greeting. 'I am Terek of the Brochen Eyne, and this is Ava.' The dark-haired woman nodded silently as the man continued. 'We rode south from our homeland, seeking new alliances, to rid these lands of the Raiders once and for all.'

'DunTreggan bids you welcome.' Kruff gestured towards the fire. 'We must await the arrival of Carn Cull before we discuss what can be done. Until then, eat, drink, rest by the fireside.'

'This Raiders business will be the end of us all.' Stuc hissed his disapproval as Kruff walked away.

'I hope not.' Tal turned to them both. 'Morusk, it's good to see you safe and well. We'd heard you were missing following a hunt.'

Morusk nodded in response, he had nothing to say. He couldn't remember what had happened, or where he had been. Stuc snorted his annoyance.

'The lazy oaf went exploring, leaving the rest of us to the hard work, skinning and preparing the beasts. Still, that's Morusk for you, always wandering in the forest.' He pointed an accusatory finger. 'I honestly don't know what you find so interesting in there, my friend.'

'There's more to the forest than firewood and places to hide.' Morusk replied vaguely.

'Only if you have a vivid imagination.' Stuc glared disapprovingly. 'And when you want to avoid doing your share of the work.'

Laughter echoed around the beacon fire of DunTreggan as it cracked loudly, its searing flames reaching ever higher into the darkening sky.

CHAPTER FOUR

Morusk stared blankly into the flames. He was troubled, driven to distraction by the compelling urge to return to the forest. Something wasn't right. Why was he finding it so difficult to accept the word of his kinsfolk? Something strange was going on. He appeared to be the only one aware of it, and he was certain the answers lay in the forest.

Drawing his attention away from the fire, his gaze settled on another reason for his unease. The woman from the Northlands eyed him suspiciously. She'd been watching him constantly since her arrival. Her position by the fire, directly opposite him, appeared no coincidence.

Her quiet demeanour unsettled him. She'd barely spoken a word to anyone, leaving all the talking to Terek. Perhaps it was their custom. Contact with the elusive inhabitants of the mountainous lands was rare indeed, with most knowledge of them restricted to legend and folklore. Many a tale had been told of the Brochen Eyne in taverns and around campfires, but tonight all talk round the beacon fire of DunTreggan was of the Raiders.

The hooded riders were now sweeping north in new offensives. The cause for their increasingly brutal attacks was unknown. They offered no dialogue, gave no reason. Their origin and purpose remained a mystery.

The clamour for answers around the fire was slowly giving way to a steely determination, a need to join forces and face the threat head-on. Morusk paid little attention to the discussions.
As serious a threat as the Raiders were, he had more pressing things on his mind. He needed to get back to the forest. He had to do it soon. He had to do it alone, unseen. How was he going to do it under the fierce scrutiny of the northern woman's watchful stare?

Inexplicably drawn to him, she had sensed his presence the moment she had entered the settlement. They called him Morusk; there was something unusual about him, something different, something only she seemed to have noticed. She watched him studiously. He was troubled, that much was obvious. He was clearly uncomfortable with her attentions; it didn't matter. The more she watched him, the more she became convinced of what she must do. She had to get him away from here. And she had to do it soon.

CHAPTER FIVE

Watching the trail impassively, they waited silently at a fork in the river, their hooded forms barely visible in the encroaching darkness. Longswords and hatchets readied, skeletal fingers gripping the reins of their spectral mounts, they sniffed the air. The scent was strong; their prey would soon be in sight.

The DunTreshen riders, led by Carn Cull, were almost at their journey's end when it happened. The desperate warning shout from a stricken scout came too late. The Raiders appeared suddenly from the darkness, charging at the riders, driving them backwards into the river. With no warning and no time to prepare, their cause was a lost one. Those that didn't meet their end by drowning in the melee of flailing men and horses were savagely cut to pieces on the riverbanks. It was over in minutes; the attack as swift as it was deadly.

With the brutal ambush over, the Raiders regrouped a short distance away, callously assessing the carnage. The river was tinged with crimson red. There was no movement, none had survived. And yet traces of the scent were still evident. There were others… not far downriver.

Driven by the incessant craving to eradicate their quarry, the hooded riders gathered pace in pursuit of their cause.

CHAPTER SIX

Sitting alone in his hut, Morusk contemplated his next move. He couldn't delay any longer. The men from DunTreshen still hadn't appeared. Their late arrival would lead to a night of drinking, feasting, and long-winded strategic discussions. It might be daybreak before the chance to return to the forest presented itself. He couldn't wait until then, and besides, it would be easier to carry out his plan under a veil of darkness. It was time to go; he had to leave now.

A knock at the door disturbed his thoughts.

'Morusk?' It was Stuc. 'Are you in there?' He held his breath. Another knock... louder this time. 'Open up, Morusk.' As the knocking became more persistent, he gave up his pretence and unlatched the door. 'There you are.' Stuc pushed past him. 'They were thinking you'd gone missing again, but I knew you'd be here. You were supposed to be fetching more ale.' He pointed accusingly. 'What happened?'

'I just needed to get something.'

'Doesn't matter. Kruff and a few of the others are riding out with Tal and Brodar to look for the DunTreshen group. They're late, something must have happened to them. Either that or they got lost in the dark. You'd hardly think that was possible with a fire that big to guide them.'

Morusk quickly considered his options. 'Are you going with them?' He asked more in hope than expectation.

'And waste valuable drinking time?' Stuc shook his head. 'Kruff says we've to stay here. We're to keep watch.'

Morusk nodded quietly. His plans were back on hold. They left the hut and made their way back towards the beacon fire.

'What do you make of the northerners?' Stuc quizzed. 'The big fellow seems friendly enough, but the woman is strange, she's hardly said two words to anyone.'

Morusk sensed an opportunity unfolding. 'Maybe she's just overawed by the new surroundings. Take her another ale. Reckon that'll help.'

A grin flashed across Stuc's face. 'I reckon you're right. Why don't we both go talk to her and the Northman? See what truths there are in the legends?'

Morusk hid his satisfaction. 'You go ahead. I'll talk to Kruff and the others before they ride out, then I'll come join you.'

'Now that's a plan I can work with.' Stuc grinned. 'Don't be long though,' he taunted. 'I might just drink all the ale.'

With Stuc's attentions focused elsewhere, Morusk doubled back to the hut and went inside. Holding the door ajar, he watched the riders thunder across the bridge and merge with the night. The moment he'd been waiting for had finally arrived. This was his chance. With Kruff and the others gone, and an inebriated Stuc keeping the northern woman occupied by the fire, he would be able to make his return to the forest.

Like a thief in the night, he moved quietly among the huts to the river's edge. Avoiding the risk of being seen on the bridge, he opted to wade across. Moving swiftly, spurred on by the cold water, he soon reached the other side and from the shelter of a small copse of alder trees he looked back across the river. The beacon fire blazed brightly, enveloping the settlement in its warming glow. Smiling at the thought of Stuc entertaining the woman from the far north with his drunken chatter, he stepped from the cover of the trees.

'Going somewhere?'

Caught off guard, he wheeled round as she stepped into view. He couldn't believe it; she'd followed him. 'I… I thought you were at the beacon fire?'

'I was. Your friend is a tiresome drunk. I left him there. I'd prefer to take a walk. Looks like we had the same idea. Want some company?'

'I was planning on going alone…'

'I know you were,' she countered. 'Where did you plan to go?'

It might have been an unintentional move, but she now blocked his way to the forest.

'No business of yours,' he muttered, brushing past her. 'Just something I have to do… Alone.'

Grabbing him by the arm, she pulled him to a halt. 'Not the forest,' she hissed. 'Believe me, you don't want to be going there, not now.'

He pulled free from her grip. 'Why not?' Frustration welled inside. His plan was foiled, his opportunity gone. He looked back towards the settlement.

'Not there either,' she said solemnly. 'We need to go. We must leave this place, quickly.'

'Go where? What's going on?'

'There's no time for explanations, you have to trust me. We must go now; we must make for higher ground.' She took a few paces before turning to him. 'Did you see the old man in the forest?' He stared blankly in response. 'The old man,' she repeated impatiently. 'The old man with the dog. Did you see him in the forest?'

Struck by a sudden moment of clarity, his words tumbled out freely. 'Yes, I saw him... How do you know about that?'

'We can talk about it later,' she held his stare. 'If we survive.'

CHAPTER SEVEN

Instinct told him to follow. They gained height quickly. Once clear of the bracken-clad slopes they continued the climb through a scattered stretch of pine woodland until, with a sudden change in terrain, the pace finally eased.

Cursing the jabbing pain in his side, he stumbled awkwardly up the scree. When she came to a halt beneath a rocky crag, her attention seemed focused on the valley below. Looking down, he saw a group of riders galloping at breakneck pace towards the beacon fire. Following closely behind, a band of hooded riders, outnumbering them by three to one, closed the distance between them ominously. By the light of the crescent moon, Morusk watched on helplessly as the terror unfolded.

He saw the flash of steel as the hooded riders caught up with their quarry, savagely scything through them, their longswords swinging back and fore. The desperate pleas for help echoed loudly, bringing DunTreggan's inhabitants running from the fireside. In the hope of saving their kin they were brutally cut down, shown no mercy by the blades of the invading horde. Fleeing desperately, many were driven into the river and drowned beneath the thundering horses, whilst others ran ablaze from the burning huts. Several of them made a futile attempt to reach the safety of the forest, only to find their way barred by more of the hooded horsemen. Swarming from the trees, they rode down the slope towards the burning settlement, crushing all who stood in their path.

Having watched as much of the senseless slaughter as he could stomach, he turned to find her standing by his side. He eyed her suspiciously for a moment before speaking. 'Raiders?'

'Yes.'

'You sensed they were coming. And you knew they were in the forest? How could you know that?'

She shrugged her shoulders. 'Intuition. Let's go.'

'What about them? Is there nothing we can do to help them?'

'What would you suggest?'

The cause was a hopeless one. He knew there was nothing they could do. His frustration boiled over. 'They are being torn to pieces down there. You don't seem to care.' He cast her an accusing glare. 'And you somehow knew it was coming.'

'I did what I could.'

Her measured response took him by surprise. He felt the sting of regret. Though she chose not to show it, he could tell his comments had angered her.

'We have to go,' she repeated. 'We need to get higher.'

With his options further limited, the decision to follow was a simple one. Evasive as she was, she might just be his best chance of finding answers; of clearing the confusion that fogged his mind. And so, aware of the poignancy of his actions, he turned his back on DunTreggan and continued the climb into darkness.

Hidden by the gathering clouds, the moon slipped from view. With the screams of terror and cries of despair left far behind, the mountainside fell eerily quiet. By the time he caught up with her, crouched in the shelter of an overhanging ledge, the rain had begun to fall. Choosing his words carefully, he offered an apprehensive apology.

'I'm sorry about what I said back there. You lost one of your kin tonight. Terek. Was he your...?'

'An acquaintance,' she replied coldly, 'nothing more.' She brushed her hair back from her face and looked up into the night sky. 'We are out of danger, for now. The rain is going to get heavier. There is a cave not far ahead, we can shelter there.'

He followed in silence and a short while later, as the downpour intensified, they reached the cave and went inside. It was cold and cramped. He didn't care. It was dry and he desperately needed to rest. She took a fur from her pack and handed it to him. Offering his thanks, he stretched out on the floor of the cave, every muscle aching from the rapid ascent. She tossed a small water pouch his way. He drank thirstily.

'It seems you're a lot better prepared than I am.'

Her stone-faced expression gave nothing away. 'Seems that way.'

'Do you think anyone survived that attack?'

Her face was just visible in the half-light of their sanctuary. 'We survived. There may be others.' Sipping her water, she eyed him warily. 'I expect you have questions.'

'That's an understatement. But so much has happened, so many things I can't make sense of. I'm not sure I'd know where to start.'

'Best start at the beginning. What's your name?'

'Taro Brook,' he replied. His words sounded strange. As if doubting the sound of his own voice, he said it again with more conviction. 'My name is Taro Brook.'

If she was surprised by his response she chose not to show it. 'Not Morusk?'

'I thought it was. Back there at the settlement, the others, they recognised me. I felt like Morusk but...'

'What about now?'

'I'm not sure.'

'You seemed sure of who you were when I asked your name.'

'I know who I am. It's just... This is all really confusing.'

The inquisition continued unabated. 'What were you doing in the forest?'

'It's a ranger's business to be in the forest,' he replied. 'Farnwaar Forest is under my watch.'

Her eyes flickered with interest. 'A woodsman?'

'That's one name for it.'

Nodding her approval, her tone changed. 'I knew you were troubled, and that you suspected something was amiss. Your determination to return to the forest made it obvious.'

'You mentioned the old man in the forest,' he interrupted. 'How did you know about that?'

'He has been seen before,' she replied cagily. 'By others.'

'I'm not sure I understand. How did you know I'd seen him?'

She brushed his question aside effortlessly. 'Event repetition; a simple explanation. I sensed something bad was imminent. I had to do something.' She paused momentarily, as if passing judgement on her actions, before continuing. 'We were in danger. It was acceptable intervention, given the circumstances.'

He shook his head. 'I don't know what is going on, but you can't honestly expect me to believe that I am two different people?'

'I don't,' she replied calmly. 'You are the same person experiencing different perceptions. It is a simple concept. The sooner you accept it, the easier things will become for you.' Turning her back to him, she lay down and pulled a fur over her shoulders. 'I speak the truth,' she said quietly. 'Your presence here is the only proof you need. It will be light soon. I suggest you get some sleep.'

Lying in the gloom of the cave, he listened to the falling rain. Her words played repeatedly in his mind. As unlikely as it seemed, her interpretation of events was at least plausible. What other possible explanation was there? 'Just one more question,' he whispered, unsure if she was still awake. 'Assuming everything you say is true, how is it that the Northlanders know so much about this strange phenomenon?'

'They know nothing of it, Taro Brook. I am not from there. I am a Drifter, just like you.'

CHAPTER EIGHT

He woke to the sound of footsteps in the scree. A splintered beam of bright sunlight pierced the gloom of the cave. Sitting up quickly, he saw that he was alone. As he clambered to his feet, she appeared at the cave entrance.

'I see you are awake at last.' She held out an apple. 'I'm afraid the breakfast menu is limited. But it's a beautiful day.'

Gathering his thoughts, he stretched, took a drink of water, and then followed her outside. Scanning the slopes below, he saw no movement and no sign of life. With the valley bathed in warm sunshine it was hard to believe the horror that had taken place during the hours of darkness.

In the distance the old forest stretched as far as the eye could see, its sprawling mass covering an area many times greater than he had ever imagined. It looked so different, yet the urge to return there remained, stronger than ever. The sight of it held him captivated. The colours danced in the hazy distance. The forest seemed alive.

'Let's go.' Her prompt focused his attention. 'It's a short climb to the ridge.'

He watched her as she began the ascent. Tall and slender, she moved effortlessly, her long dark hair flowing in the breeze. Black swirling markings adorned her bare arms. He'd never seen anyone like her before. Her bewitching presence seemed almost other-worldly. Looking back, she motioned him to follow, her dark eyes scrutinising his every movement. Switching his thoughts quickly, he averted his gaze and followed her lead.

The climb steepened noticeably. Reaching the ridge, he found her waiting by a large conical stack of white stones.

'The Cairn of Scaraven,' she announced. 'An exquisite landmark, don't you agree?'

With a momentary glance at the cairn, he then gauged the surrounding landscape. To his left the ridge faded into the distance, merging with the hazy sunlight. Directly ahead, a towering mass of white rock loomed ominously, whilst to its right, the summit path wound its way upwards amongst the rocks and crags. Far below them, a vast expanse of water glistened in the sunlight. 'Impressive enough.'

She sat on a rock by the cairn. 'We should rest here a while.'

He sat down next to her. He needed answers and there seemed little point in putting it off any longer. Throwing caution to the wind, he began with what seemed as good a question as any.

'Where are we going? Where are you leading me?'

Her response was blunt and to the point. 'Higher ground. To safety.'

'Okay. I understood the logic of that when we were further down the mountain, but do we still need to go higher? I'd hoped to be on my way back to the forest by now.'

She eyed him closely as she considered her response. Feeling the weight of her stare, he scratched at his chin.

'It suits you better, in my opinion.'

'What do you mean?'

She drew a finger slowly down her jawline. 'Clean shaven. Your bone structure is not best complimented by a beard.' Sensing his bemusement, she continued. 'Morusk is bearded, but when you arrived at the cave last night your appearance had changed. Perhaps I should have mentioned it sooner. It didn't seem relevant until now.' Shifting her gaze, she quickly changed subject and pointed back down the mountain. 'You can't go back down there, not yet. The valley will be crawling with Raiders looking for survivors.' She shook her head. 'The forest too. You can't go back. Not until it is safe.'

Swayed by the conviction in her voice, he relented. 'Okay, I bow to your judgement. But when will it be safe?'

Content that her argument had convinced him, her gaze returned to the ridge. 'I don't know, Taro Brook. Soon, I hope.'

A silence enveloped them. Whilst he didn't doubt the sincerity of her actions, he had his suspicions. Why was his safety so important to her? Where was she leading him? And what of the bizarre chain of events that had led him here to this strange place? Far from making things any clearer, her explanation in the cave had caused only further confusion. His jumbled train of thought drew to a sudden halt.

'You told me things last night,' he began cautiously. 'None of which made any sense. What did you mean when you said you were just like me? You said we were Drifters?'

'And that is what we are. I am not from the Northlands, and I do not belong here. And yet, here I am. Just like you. We are the same.' Her tone lightened. 'We call ourselves Drifters, Taro

Brook, for it is a name that fits us well. You drifted from your world, your reality, call it what you wish, and you found yourself here.' She gestured to the surrounding landscape. 'Your home world; DunTreggan; this mountain. They are all one and the same, your perception of them being the only difference.' She hesitated for a moment before continuing. 'You used the word phenomenon; a fact, occurrence or change perceived by the senses of the mind.' Her stare wandered once more along the ridge. 'But fear not, you will soon drift back to what you perceive as normality.' Brushing the dust from her black leggings, she got to her feet. Shielding her eyes from the sun, her expression lifted. 'Good, there he is. He is coming now.'

Taro Brook clambered quickly to his feet. Following her gaze along the ridge, he saw a figure moving steadily towards them. The newcomer's sudden appearance put him instantly on edge. 'Who is that?' he asked nervously.

'Do try and keep up, Woodsman.' She frowned her disapproval. 'It's Scaraven.'

He glanced at the stack of white stones. 'The Cairn? It's named after him?'

'Yes, it is.'

Taro Brook watched as the approaching figure came into focus. An old man, wearing a faded jacket and flat-topped hat. A little, old man, moving at a pace that belied his apparent years. He turned to her. 'You've been watching,' his suspicions nagged again. 'It's as if you were expecting someone. How did you know he was coming?'

'Intuition, Taro Brook.' She shrugged. 'Intuition.'

CHAPTER NINE

Scaraven was, without doubt, the strangest character Taro Brook had ever set eyes on. Watching as the two strangers embraced, the old man standing not much higher than her waist, Brook tried in vain to guess his age.

Wearing a shabby jacket bleached white by the sun, the new arrival moved excitedly towards the cairn, his boots scuffing noisily on the rocks. Wisps of white hair poked out from under his peculiar yellow hat; a flat-topped oddity patterned with strange cryptic symbols. His weathered face sported a white drooping moustache and little pointed beard. It seemed a happy face; a face fixed with a permanent grin.

'Aha! There it is!' The newcomer chuckled jovially. 'The Cairn of Scaraven. Splendid!' Patting the stones fondly, his attention switched quickly to Brook. 'And who do we have here?' He clasped his hands together in delight. 'What weary traveller rests his aching limbs by the Stones of the Messengers?'

She bridged the awkward silence with her introduction. 'Taro Brook; a ranger from Farnwaar Forest. Also known in some parts as Morusk of DunTreggan.'

The old man quickly bowed his head. 'DunTreggan,' he sighed. 'A sad business. A sad business indeed.' Looking up, he caught Brook's eye. 'My sorrows for your loss, Morusk of

DunTreggan. Still, you survived, eh? And there will be others too. And where there are survivors, there's hope. And so, the cycles go on.' With a twitch of his nose, his beaming grin returned. 'A woodsman, eh? Splendid work, Sir. Splendid work indeed. A guardian of the forest. A Jack-in-the-Green, no less.'

Half closing one bushy-browed eye, he looked Brook up and down. 'You're a big fellow for a hobgoblin… if you don't mind me saying so?' Without waiting for an answer, he thrust a hand forward in greeting. 'Delighted to make your acquaintance, Master Brook. Absolutely deeelighted! Messenger Two Cups, at your service.'

He shook the old man's hand. 'Two Cups?' Brook frowned. 'She said your name was Scaraven.'

'It is.' she countered matter-of-factly.

'Ahaa! And so, Master Brook, you are not the only one to be known by more than one name, eh?' The old man chuckled. 'Two Cups will do just nicely.' Dropping his pack to the ground, he began rummaging inside. 'Two Cups by name, two cups by nature.' Producing a tarnished metal flask topped by two mugs, he grinned widely. 'Who's for tea?' Removing the mugs, he frowned momentarily. 'Ah! You appear to have me at a disadvantage.'

'It's okay,' she cut in. 'Taro Brook and I can share.' She rolled her eyes towards him questioningly. 'I'm sure he won't mind?'

'Guess it's okay with me.'

'Splendid.' Two Cups busied himself with pouring the tea. 'Silver Birch Leaf. The finest brew I know. I think you'll be suitably impressed.'

'I can vouch for it.' Taking one of the mugs, she offered it to Brook.

'You can go first.'

'As you wish.' She took three quick sips of the tea and handed it to him. 'Try some, it's really good.'

'Tea from a birch tree?' Holding the mug to his nose, he was surprised to find the aroma far from unpleasant.

Two Cups snorted his amusement. 'Not just any old birch tree, my friend. The Silver Birch of Dipper Mill Forest. The leaf picked at precisely the right moment; by moonlight as the silver birch gleam ghostly pale like lost souls in limbo.' Raising his mug, he toasted his tribute to the brew. 'Bottoms up, Woodsman!'

Taro Brook supped the tea cautiously. It tasted good.

'I think there's some bread in here somewhere.' Two Cups searched the contents of his pack. Dividing a small loaf into three pieces, he passed them round. Taro Brook hadn't realised just how hungry he was. The Messenger studied him closely. 'So, a woodsman, eh?' He gave a wry grin. 'Yet, I see no axe, no saw. I trust all is well in the forest?'

Brook took a moment. 'No trouble at all. All was fine, until yesterday.'

Two Cups pondered his response. Snapping his fingers suddenly, he jumped excitedly to his feet. 'You came through the Harlequin Forest?'

'Harlequin?' Brook frowned. 'If you mean the great forest, I know it by another name, but yes, I did, and I plan to return there sometime soon.'

'Time is irrelevant, my friend.' Two Cups scoffed dismissively. 'A pointless commodity by which fools who know no better even though they should, attempt to measure quantities of their existence. Tell me, Woodsman, do they practise such folly where you come from?'

Brook nodded, unsure quite where the conversation was going. 'I don't worry too much about time. The sun rises in the morning and sets in the evening. Not much more needs to be said.'

'Splendid answer, Woodsman. I couldn't have put it better myself.' Two Cups beamed his approval, smiling at Brook as if he'd just rediscovered a long-lost friend.

Supping his tea, Taro Brook listened as the two strangers chatted.

'So, Scaraven, what news from the east?' she asked cautiously.

'The news from the east?' He smacked his lips. 'Not good. Not good at all. It saddens me to say that Enntonia is once again in turmoil. Politics! A bad business. Worse still, the Dragon Slayers have returned, and trouble is never far behind them.' Pausing, he refilled his mug. 'The Scribe of Bog-Mire Towers, Token ScriptScratcher, had kept us well informed, but the first snows of winter came early and since then we have heard no more. Those winged messengers are good enough in fair weather, but when winter comes, they are useless. They turn tail and make for warmer climes.' Snorting his disgust, he took a noisy slurp of tea and wiped his whiskers. 'And to think they call them progress. We messengers who move on foot may take a little longer, but at least we ensure the message gets delivered.' His discontent noted, he gulped down another mouthful of tea.

'What kind of messenger are you?' Brook asked cagily. 'To whom do you carry news?'

'To anyone and everyone.' The old man smiled. 'There is always an ear eager for news of one form or another. Indeed, today, have I not found another pair of ears? A traveller keen to hear the wise words of a Messenger?' Taro Brook nodded in quiet agreement. It seemed like the right thing to do. The old man studied him closely before continuing. 'Remind me again. What did you say your name was?'

'Taro... Taro Brook.'

'As in the cards?'

'No, no T.'

A look of shock flashed across the old man's face. 'What? No tea? Are you sure?' He grasped the flask tightly.

'No T,' repeated Brook. 'There's no T at the end of Taro.'

Two Cups puzzled for a moment before his grin returned. 'Ha! You had me worried there. For a moment, I thought you meant no tea.' He turned his empty mug upside down for effect. 'What a thought. It doesn't bear thinking about.' Putting the mugs back on the flask, he rose from his seat and, with a contented sigh, pulled his pack onto his shoulder. 'We must be on our way, my friends.'

'On our way?' Brook echoed warily. 'Where?'

'West, Woodsman. We must head west.' As if reading Brook's thoughts, the old man spoke solemnly. 'I know you want to return to the forest, but you can't go back there. It's not safe, not yet.'

Brook looked at them both in turn. 'So you both keep saying. When will it be safe? I need to get back. People will be looking for me if I don't return soon.'

'Have no fear,' smiled Two Cups. 'You will return there soon. And believe me,' he winked mischievously, 'when you do, it will appear as though you'd never been away.' The old man patted the cairn once more and, with stick in hand, set out along the path.

Brook glanced sideways to her. 'Do we follow him?'

Silently nodding her instruction, she began walking. With his doubts further fuelled, Taro Brook followed grudgingly.

Progress was slow in the warm sunshine and by the time he reached the crest of the ridge where he found them waiting, his shirt was sticking to his back. Taking in the view, he wiped the sweat from his forehead. The ridge was narrow, only a dozen paces at its widest. White and silver rock sparkled in the sunlight. A path picked its way through the crumbled quartzite to the base of an imposing stone tower, fifty strides wide, perhaps three times as high. Brook gazed up at the great slabs of rock in wonder. Layer upon layer of gneiss, sandstone, and quartzite. To the left of the tower stood another peak, perhaps four times as high, littered with staggered pinnacles and craggy towers. A path wound its way upwards through the crumbling rock. On the right of the path the mountain tumbled away dramatically in a vertical drop. Beyond the summit, the white ridge stretched far into the distance before becoming lost in a haze of sunshine and mountains.

'Behold the crags and tors of Krechan-Bhann.' Messenger Two Cups made his dramatic announcement.

Taro Brook surveyed the scene with a mix of awe and trepidation. 'Are we going up there?'

'Safest place.' Two Cups snorted. 'As accomplished as those damnable Raiders are on horseback, this route is far beyond their reach.' He patted Brook's arm encouragingly. 'Besides, it's really not as bad as it looks.'

'But where are we going? Is there no other way?'

'We are headed west, Woodsman. Our route takes us through the crags and tors, along the great White Ridge to the Black Glass Traverse. An encounter with the Pinnacles of Sorrow then awaits and, beyond that, the enchanted Pass of TorisDuan. With luck on our side, we will finally arrive at the Firth of the Last Crossing and our journey's end, Sumarren.' He grinned at Brook's expression. 'Well, you did ask!' With a chuckle, he was on the move again, his stick tapping mystic rhythms on the rocks.

Feeling her presence at his shoulder, Taro Brook turned to her. 'Sumarren?' he questioned. 'Any particular reason?'

'He always makes for Sumarren.' she replied cryptically. 'Perhaps this time he will actually get there.'

A short distance ahead, the Messenger drew to a halt. 'Come, Sanna,' he bellowed. 'Tell me your news as we walk.'

'Sanna?' Brook scowled. 'I thought your name was Ava.'

'It was, back there.' For a fleeting second her face softened with the first tangible trace of a smile. 'Let's go, Taro Brook, we'd best not keep him waiting.'

CHAPTER TEN

The survivors of the savage attack on DunTreggan picked their way sombrely through the smouldering remains. With their leader Kruff among the fallen, the responsibility for taking charge of the gruesome task had fallen on Juuk, one of the settlement's elders.

He'd advised Kruff not to consider standing with Carn Cull against the Raiders. Surveying the scene of carnage, he realised the futility of his warning. It appeared their fate had already been decided.

'I think we are about done.' Stuc approached dejectedly. 'We've been through the huts several times but found no more survivors. We've assembled the bodies by the fire as you asked.'

Juuk nodded. 'Then let's get on with it.' Rising to his feet, he clasped his kinsman on the shoulder. 'Still no sign of Morusk?'

Stuc shook his head. 'No.'

'He may still be alive. Don't give up hope. Come, let's do what must be done.'

'Are we doing the right thing?' Stuc asked hesitantly.

'The right thing under these circumstances. There are so few of us left, we simply don't have the manpower to dig graves for so many, and you've seen the remains. Let the fire cleanse them, their memories will remain true.'

'And then we leave?'

Juuk frowned. 'I fear we must. This place can no longer be called home, not after what has happened.' Grim-faced he turned and strode towards the beacon fire. 'Assemble the others, Stuc,' he shouted. 'Let's get this done.'

CHAPTER ELEVEN

A group of hooded riders watched from the trees at the edge of the forest as the flames of the funeral fire gathered pace. Faint traces of their prey still remained, poisoning the air. Some still lived, hidden from view. They were not among those gathered at the fire. Turning their mounts away from the scene, the phantom-like figures moved back into the forest to re-join their ranks. The survivors of their attack were spared, for now. Used as bait, they would lure the others out into the open.

Nothing would halt the relentless pursuit of their objective, the eradication of all Drifters.

From the safety of the boulder fields high on the far side of the valley, Morusk watched as the Raiders moved into the forest. 'They are leaving. I think we can go back down now.'

'It may be a trap.'

He turned to her. She looked different in the daylight, less sure of herself. Hardly surprising, given the circumstances. The horrors they'd witnessed would strike fear into the coldest of hearts. The hours following the attack had passed slowly on the mountain. Sleep had evaded them. With the first light of dawn, the Raiders' presence in the valley began to dissipate and slowly, one by one, DunTreggan's survivors began to emerge from the ruins. Plagued with a sense of guilt for leaving them to their fate, Morusk had watched them carry out the search for bodies, all the while keeping his eyes on the lingering Raiders. They were now gone, and he had waited long enough.

'It may be a trap,' he sighed, 'but I must join my kin by the fire.' Stepping from cover, he held out his hand. His recollections of their desperate escape from the attack were jumbled. She had intercepted his planned return to the forest, he remembered that much, but the rest was a blur. One thing though was certain enough; her intervention might just have saved his life.

'The hooded savages will pay for what has happened. One day, we will make this right. Come, Ava. You are not alone. Let's join the others.'

CHAPTER TWELVE

Taro Brook's suspicions were growing. With so many unanswered questions surrounding his predicament, as intriguing as they were, there was much about his new companions that troubled him, things that just didn't add up. The flask belonging to the enigmatic Scaraven puzzled him greatly. Messenger Two Cups, as he preferred to be called, had poured countless mugs of tea from the flask since their first meeting at the cairn, yet its contents seemed no nearer an end. Eager as he was to ask the question, Brook held his silence, knowing how ridiculous his words might sound.

Perched on a rocky ledge in the shadow of the crags and pinnacles, Brook looked back at the great stone tower. It had proved far less of an obstacle than he'd expected. Having clambered without difficulty or any great effort over the initial overhanging slabs, they'd picked up a narrow track which had bypassed the main thrust of the climb and led them back on to the crest of the ridge. Deciding against raising the subject of the flask, he chose another avenue of questioning.

'So, what really happened to me back there at the settlement? Was it some kind of time-shift?' Feeling instantly uncomfortable with such a suggestion he attempted to give his words credence.

'I mean... hundreds of years ago, our ancestors would possibly have lived like that... At least, my ancestors would have.'

Messenger Two Cups was quick to respond. 'Come now, Woodsman, we have already discussed the folly of time, have we not? Time is irrelevant.' He waved a finger in the air. 'The simplest explanation to an unusual occurrence is, more often than not, the correct one. I read that once somewhere, very fitting indeed.' He drew another slurp of tea. 'Simply put, you became aware of another existence. Which leads to the assumption that you, my friend, have a gift.'

'A gift?' It hardly seemed the most fitting description.

'Yes, indeed,' beamed Two Cups. 'Would you agree, Sanna?'

'It appears that way.' she agreed candidly.

Taro Brook challenged the suggestion vigorously.

'An interesting concept, but I have my doubts. How can I possibly be two different people, in two different places, at the same time?'

The Messenger spluttered a mouthful of tea down the front of his jacket. Wiping his whiskers, he chortled with delight. 'Pardon my amusement,' he wheezed, 'but there are an awful lot more than two of you.'

'How many?'

The old man quickly sprang to his feet, waving his tea mug animatedly. 'Too many to fathom, my friend. Worry yourself not with numbers; they can be as useless a commodity as time.' Rubbing his little beard thoughtfully, he pulled his pack onto his shoulder. 'Let's be on the move. We can talk more as we walk.'

Sanna followed closely behind as the Messenger continued his explanations. 'So, Woodsman, imagine that I were to ask your name. How would you respond?'

'Taro Brook.' he replied, casting a glance back to Sanna. She'd followed the very same line of questioning.

'Splendid!' Two Cups continued. 'So, you are Taro Brook, and yet you must concede that you are also Morusk of DunTreggan?'

'I suppose so,' Brook agreed grudgingly. 'I appeared to be... back there.'

'Appearances can often be deceptive, but not in this instance. Two men, two different worlds, yet inextricably linked.' Drawing to a halt, Two Cups looked up inquisitively. 'Make any sense so far?'

Brook shrugged. 'Some, I think.'

'Excellent!' Two Cups continued walking. 'I suspect that Morusk will be completely unaware of your presence. He may have experienced some moments of confusion but will have passed them off without further consideration. However, I'm afraid things will appear quite different to you now,' he paused. 'I'm guessing by your expression that you'd already figured that much out.' He grinned as Taro Brook nodded his agreement. 'And it is only the beginning, Woodsman. You are many. So very, very many.'

With the scale of his plight becoming ever more apparent, Brook put his hands to his head. He didn't want this; he didn't want any of it. Why was this happening to him?

'Fear not, Taro Brook.' He turned in response to her words. Her expression was one of genuine reassurance. 'You are not alone.'

'Indeed you are not,' fired Two Cups indignantly. 'Let's take a moment to gather our thoughts.' He reached into his pack. 'More tea?'

They'd come to a stop at the foot of a steep climb up through the crags. Watching the old man thirstily drain another mug of tea, Brook grappled with the enormity of what he'd been told. 'If what you say is true, how is it that I only ever feel like me?'

'Perfectly natural, I assure you.' Two Cups smiled. 'There is a danger in over thinking, my friend. Accept what comes naturally. When I asked your name, you responded without hesitation, am I right?'

'Yes.'

'Then there is no doubt. The very essence of life is the awareness of who you are and your perception of everything around you.'

Brook quietly pondered the profound statement. It made sense and yet he began to wonder if his questions were helping his understanding of things or were only making things more confusing. 'What about the old man in the forest? The old man with the dog.'

Messenger Two Cups' grin widened. 'Old Breck? Did you see him?'

'Yes, I saw him.'

Two Cups clapped his hands together gleefully. 'Wonderful. How is the old fellow?'

'He didn't say much. In fact, I don't think he was even aware of me.'

'And so it would be. Old Breck is what we call an Indentation. Appearing blissfully unaware of those around him, he wanders happily through the forest. He is always there, yet very few are lucky enough to ever see him.'

'If he is always there, how is it I've never seen him before?'

Two Cups wagged a finger knowingly. 'Call it your awakening, Taro Brook. Did you see anything else? Did you notice anything strange happening in the forest?'

'Yes, I...'

'Stop right there.' Two Cups put his hand in the air. 'Don't say any more. Let me guess, the forest appeared held in the grip of some form of enchantment? Everything stood still?'

'Yes,' Brook's suspicions spiked again. 'How could you know that?'

'A simple deduction based on experience.' Two Cups shrugged dismissively. 'Your arrival here is no accident, Woodsman. We just have to work together to figure out the purpose of it.'

Taro Brook had no intention of staying in this strange place any longer than was necessary. 'I'm not interested in finding that out,' he countered. 'I'd rather our efforts were concentrated on getting me back home as soon as possible.'

The Messenger pulled thoughtfully at his whiskers. 'Perhaps we can come to a compromise. Would it be fair to suggest you need our help?' Taro Brook wasn't quite sure how to respond. Two Cups was quick to acknowledge his reluctance. 'I appreciate your uncertainty. For all you know, we could be lying to you, deceiving you.'

'I didn't imply that. I'm just a bit unsure about everything.'

'Indeed, and it is understandable. Let me be honest with you. I don't believe in coincidences; I think we were destined to meet.' He offered his hand. 'We are not trying to deceive you, Taro Brook, far from it. Will you take a leap of faith? Will you accompany us?'

Spurred by the directness of the old man's request, Brook cut to the chase. 'Why? What is it you want from me?'

'Straight to the point,' Two Cups grinned. 'I like that. Let's call it mutually beneficial. I believe you may be able to help us. In return, we can help you gain a better understanding of your predicament and ensure your safe return to Farnwaar Forest.' He thrust his hand forward again. 'What say you, Taro Brook? What say you?'

Brook's response mirrored his confusion. Accepting the handshake he immediately questioned the motive behind the offer. 'You want me to help you? Seriously?' He almost laughed at the absurdity of it all. 'How do you think I can help you? I can barely get my head around any of what has happened to me. I don't even know where I am. Where are we?'

Messenger Two Cups cleared his throat. 'We can discuss other matters in due course. First, let me endeavour to help you make more sense of things.' He rubbed his hands excitedly. 'Imagine an infinite number of bubbles in an enormous vat of sparkling wine. Suppose we imagine each bubble to be a world; a reality all of its own. With me so far?'

Brook nodded. 'I think so.'

'Splendid! So, let's say that in one of these realities there is a forest ranger called Taro Brook from Farnwaar Forest. Yes?' His eyebrow twitched in anticipation. Brook nodded again.

'Excellent! Now we must accept that there is a Taro Brook in every one of these bubbles, in every one of these realities. However, here is the twist. In every world he is a different person; he has a different name, different personality, and his existence follows a unique set of circumstances in each world. An infinite number of realities; an infinite number of you, Taro Brook.'

'It is a lot to comprehend.' Sanna offered her support.

'Indeed it is.' Two Cups snapped his fingers. 'And whilst you ponder that, let me explain a little about where we are. These countless worlds constantly come into contact with one another and, as a result, their fabric can become worn or thin. At these points of contact, tears may occur; breaches as we in the know like to call them.' He jumped to his feet. 'These breaches are all around us. It is through them that we Drifters are able to pass from one reality to another and you, my friend, encountered one in the Harlequin Forest. That is how you passed from your world to another.'

'At the cairn. Is that how you appeared so suddenly?'

'Indeed.' Two Cups grinned. 'Yet it is no trick, no illusion. You achieved the very same feat in the great forest.' Pushing back his hat, he scratched at his forehead. 'Now, as to where we are. Overspills have formed great bridges spanning the gaps between worlds. We stand on one now; the Krechan-Bhann. It stretches far beyond the limits of comprehension and from it, gateways lead to an infinite number of worlds.' Puffing out his cheeks, he blew a whistle. 'Well, there you have it.' Grasping the flask, he refilled his mug. 'Thirsty work.'

Taro Brook rubbed at his eyes. The scale of information was staggering. And far beyond the realms of his understanding. It did, however, reinforce his earlier doubts. 'I really don't see how I can be of help to you. I accept that something happened in the forest and your theory may or may not be right.' He hesitated as a frightening thought struck him. 'If what you say is true, what will happen if I am unable to find another of these so-called breaches? How will I get back home?'

'Worry not, Taro Brook,' Sanna cut in. 'It will happen again, I assure you. It is simply an act of perception, of opening your mind to the possibility. Having experienced it once, you will again.' She crossed her arms placidly. 'Take my word. I speak from experience.'

'Indeed,' echoed Two Cups. 'And as for how you can assist us, we can discuss that further along the way, that is, if you will accompany us?'

They waited patiently, studying him closely as he battled with his thoughts. He was no nearer to understanding what was happening, or why. If anything, he was becoming more confused by the minute. Infinite worlds; infinite different versions of him. The possibilities were staggering; the thought of facing them alone, daunting. 'You will try to help me get back home?'

'Absolutely!' grinned Two Cups.

'The journey you described, it sounded as if it could take a long time. I want to go home as soon as possible.'

'And so you shall, Woodsman. Remember, the concept of time means nothing here.'

Taro Brook looked up at the towering mountain. 'It looks a long way to the top.' He spoke with an air of resignation. 'The sooner we get started, the sooner I get home. Let's get on with it.'

CHAPTER THIRTEEN

Token ScriptScratcher, the Scribe of Bog-Mire Towers, sighed and put down his quill. Peering over his rounded spectacles, he frowned at the silhouetted shape of the figure seated in the far corner of his cluttered study. Having blown out the candles, the stranger waited silently in the shadows. The slim slither of moonlight creeping through the shuttered window did little to lift the gloom.

Token's mood matched the feel of the room. He didn't like the look of his uninvited guest, the sooner he was gone the better. Only then could he attempt to repair some of the damage caused by this night's dark business. With another heavy sigh, the Scribe returned his attention to his work. Blowing gently on the ink, ensuring it was dry, he carefully rolled the parchment tight. Holding it for a moment beneath a tilted candle, he pressed the seal of Bog-Mire Towers firmly into the hot wax and held it out at arm's length. The task was complete. 'It is done. Now, be on your way.'

As the hunched figure got to his feet, the chair dragged noisily on the flagstone floor. Lurching awkwardly across the room, he snatched at the scroll. Dragging the point of his knife across the seal, he tore it open.

'What are you doing?' Token hissed.

'Checking your handiwork. Ensuring you've followed your instructions. You could have written anything. Can't trust anyone these days.' Quickly scanning the script, he nodded his approval, and handed the scroll back. 'Seal it again, and be quick about it.'

Token ScriptScratcher did as he was asked. He had considered the idea of such deception but was now glad he'd decided against it. 'There, it's done.'

'Much obliged to you, Scribe.'

Token swallowed uncomfortably. 'There was no need to wait,' he said shakily. 'I would have dispatched it myself by messenger, the moment it was done.'

The hooded figure glowered menacingly. 'The orders of the High Council were clear. I was to wait while you carried out their demands. Once stamped with the official seal, I was to deliver the parchment, personally.' A line of drool hung from the corner of the twisted mouth. The figure smiled a gap-toothed grin. 'Farewell, Scratcher of Scrolls, I must take my leave. I have urgent business to attend to.'

Token held his breath until the door swung closed. Shaking from the ordeal, he clutched the corner of his desk to steady himself. 'Dark days.' he muttered quietly. Dark days when such unsavoury characters were acting on behalf of the High Council. Token had at first refused to take any part in the proceedings. The stranger had arrived after nightfall, which in itself was highly irregular, and when Token had read the orders of the Council, he was appalled. He would write no such summons. Under no circumstances would he dishonour the seal of Bog-Mire by associating it with such evil.

The sharp point of a sword had swung his judgement. It was clear the High Council would have no hesitation in appointing a new Scribe, one more accommodating to their wishes, should anything unfortunate happen to him. Few now doubted the depths to which the once great Council would stoop in order to achieve their goals. The visit of their dubious envoy, and the orders he carried, were a further damning testament.

But perhaps all was not lost. Token ScriptScratcher could still stem the tide. He could send word; send a warning of what was unfolding. He gathered his thoughts. The deed was done, there was no point wishing otherwise. The scroll was on its way. He had to act quickly.

Moving hastily to his quill and ink, he readied another parchment, and began writing. The quill scratched noisily across the paper. A sound that would normally fill his heart with joy, did little to slow his racing pulse. He must send word immediately.

The fate of Enntonia depended on it.

CHAPTER FOURTEEN

Taro Brook eased himself warily to the edge of the narrow ledge and looked down. Struck by a sudden wave of dizziness, he retreated quickly. Clinging to the rock nervously, he steadied his racing heart and continued climbing.

The ascent had begun gently; the path winding its way aimlessly among the small crags. Steepening sharply, it had led them to the foot of a seemingly impenetrable slab of vertical rock. Their progress continued via a series of great stone chimneys, each the height of thirty men or more. Despite his initial reluctance, he was now enjoying the climb. The rock offered a secure grip; hand and footholds were plentiful. The enclosed feeling of the stone chimney gave a welcome, if false, sense of safety. Standing on the ledge, the brief blast of exposure had given a stark reminder of the reality of his situation.

Messenger Two Cups led the way, chatting constantly. When not discussing the joys of rock climbing, the prospect of great adventures that awaited them, and the delights of fine tea, he was either chuckling and snorting in appreciation of his observations or quietly muttering to himself in some strange incomprehensible dialect. Taro Brook marvelled at the old man's agility, and his ability to talk incessantly whilst negotiating such a difficult climb.

Approaching the crux of the ascent, as the great notch in the rock narrowed, the moves became increasingly difficult. Straining as he reached for holds, Brook slowly but surely clawed his way upwards. Clambering on to a jagged shelf, he found Two Cups waiting, a wry grin etched on his face.

'Aha! There you are. Excellent! I need you to lead the next section of the climb. It's rather tricky for a chap of my limited stature. One of the many perils of having a backside too close to the ground.' He snorted his amusement. 'Not to worry though, with you leading, and Sanna behind me giving a helpful shove, I'm sure we'll manage eh?' He leaned in close. 'Between you and me, it gets a bit airy from here. If this doesn't get your blood pumping, then nothing will.' With a chuckle, he got to his feet as Sanna appeared at the ledge. 'Splendid! We can be on the move again.' Pulling a rope from his pack, he handed it to Brook. 'It will be of no help to you,' he warned, 'but I'd be grateful if you'd drop it down to me when you get a chance. Lead on, Woodsman.'

They watched him as he climbed.

'He is growing in confidence, Scaraven.'

'Yes, he is. His resolve is strengthening. Tell me, Sanna, how much does he know? What did you tell him before I joined you?'

'Very little, enough to ensure he followed.'

'Excellent.'

'I didn't realise who he was. Not until we were high in the mountain.' She frowned as she watched Brook move precariously above. 'Do you really think he can help?'

'He came through the Harlequin Forest,' Two Cups smiled reassuringly. 'You know the prophecies; we must put our trust in the writings of the Seer Magister.' Looking up, he grinned widely. 'Great climbing, Woodsman,' he bellowed. 'Your prowess on the mountain is the envy of many a goat.'

Glancing down, Taro Brook saw them locked in discussion. What were they talking about? His break in concentration almost cost him his hold on the mountain. As the Messenger shouted his words of encouragement, Brook lost his footing. Fumbling frantically for grip, he began sliding down the rockface. Pushing himself instinctively against the rock, he managed to slow his descent and regain a secure hold. Gripping the rock tightly with his grazed hands, his heart thumped loudly in his chest. Another shout came from below.

'Isn't it exhilarating? I told you this would get the old pulse racing.'

With the Messenger's laugh echoing loudly, Taro Brook pushed himself onwards and upwards. With adrenalin coursing through his veins he safely negotiated the rest of the pull without any further problems. With his limbs trembling, he reached the safety of the ledge, secured the rope, and dropped it over the edge. Easing himself into a sitting position he watched the wisps of cloud racing across the blue sky.

Moments later Messenger Two Cups' grinning face appeared. 'Great climbing, Woodsman. I don't think I would have managed it without you leading.' Taro Brook had his doubts. The old man showed little sign of exertion. As Sanna climbed into view, Two

Cups clapped his hands encouragingly. 'Onwards, fellow travellers. Not far to go now.'

Traversing the rock-strewn terrain, they came to a natural staircase of boulders. Climbing to the top, they were rewarded with a breath-taking view along a wild and exposed ridge, dotted with vertical towers and jagged pinnacles.

'The eastern summit ridge,' announced Two Cups with satisfaction. 'There are caves in the crags just short of the summit. We can rest there during the hours of darkness. Take care on the way, friends.' With a wave of his stick, he led the way, pronouncing loudly that a well-deserved and somewhat overdue cup of tea awaited them along the ridge.

CHAPTER FIFTEEN

Elfin Fingle hurried up the spiral stairway, his boots echoing noisily on the stone. Reaching the landing at the top of the stairs, he caught his breath and tapped briskly on the wooden door.

'Come in, Elfin,' the voice commanded from within. 'Quickly!'

Elfin burst into the room. His mentor did not like to be kept waiting. 'You rang for me, Scribe?'

Token ScriptScratcher looked up from his desk, a worried look etched across his face. 'Yes, Elfin, indeed I did. I need you to ride into town.'

'At this late hour?'

'I'm afraid so. I regret calling you from the fireside on a bitter night like this, but it is an errand of the utmost importance.'

'I am here to serve.' puffed Elfin proudly. 'What is it you require from town?'

'I need you to find Harbinger Talus.'

Elfin drew a sharp breath. 'The Harbinger? Really? He will not take kindly to being called upon at this hour.'

'I am well aware of what his mood will be, and it is of no concern to me. We are faced with a situation of the greatest urgency and he must be prepared to do his duty along with the rest of us. You know best where to look. When you find him, accompany him to the Western Gate. I will meet you both there, thirty turns of the sand from now. Mention nothing of this to anyone other than Talus himself. Go now, Elfin, and make haste.'

With a nod, Elfin pulled the door closed behind him and hurried downstairs. An errand to town at this late hour was most unusual. The wintry conditions would make it all the more unpleasant. The fact he was going looking for the Harbinger only made it worse. A few moments later, as he crossed the cobbled courtyard, there was more on his mind than the cold wind biting at his face.

The snow started to fall as he galloped his pony along the tree-lined approach to town. Crouching low in the saddle, hood drawn, he braced himself for the task ahead. The Scribe had given no indication of what was going on but, if the Harbinger was to be involved, it must be a grave state of affairs indeed.

Harbinger Talus eyed the room from his seat in the corner of the Twelve Bells Tavern. A solitary individual, he was well used to being on his own. Luckily, he liked things that way; company didn't tend to come looking for a man of his profession. He had often been told his reputation preceded him, he found such statements very fitting. Taking a slog of ale from his pitcher, he scowled his contempt at the busy tavern. It was getting noisy, it would soon be time to leave and seek a quieter refuge, but he was reluctant to move; it was cold out there tonight.

Gossip raged through the room like wildfire. A city on the point of financial ruin, a corrupt government, and there, standing by the fireside, gathering anxious looks from the revellers, another worrying cause for unease. A group of dishevelled individuals, half a dozen in number. Dangerous looking they were, glances darting shiftily around the room, watching, waiting for trouble. If it didn't come to them, they'd most likely go looking for it. Talus sighed his disgust. He knew who they were, he knew what they were. His focus moved across the room as the tavern door swung open.

A cloaked figure, small in stature, entered, accompanied by a burst of wind and a flurry of snow. Talus watched as the figure pulled back his hood and brushed the snow from his green cloak. As he scanned the room, his gaze settled on Talus. Resigned to the fact his plans for the evening were about to change, the Harbinger drew another mouthful of ale as the new arrival approached his table.

'Harbinger Talus, I'm glad I've found you.'

'Take a seat, you look cold.'

'There's no time. I bring an urgent message.'

'Urgent it may be, young fellow, but if you'll take my advice, you'll sit down. As you won't have joined me for my wit and jovial company, I'm guessing bad news has brought you here; news best kept to ourselves. So, let's not draw any more attention than is necessary, eh?' Nodding to the bench, he snapped his fingers in the air. 'You'll have an ale?'

Elfin Fingle felt torn. Ale sounded good, yet time was of the essence. He compromised. 'Best make it a half.' The warmth of the crowded tavern offered welcome respite from the snow. Following the bitterly cold ride to town, Elfin's search for the Harbinger had already taken him to three taverns and a card house. Gulping thirstily at his ale, following Talus' stare, he peered over his shoulder towards the fire.

'Dragon Slayers,' growled Talus, hawking a spit to the sawdust floor in disgust. 'Look at them. How the mighty have fallen.'

A woman, dressed in similar garb to the others, had joined them at the fireside. Her eyes searched the room warily. 'Still,' Talus continued, 'I suppose their fall from grace ain't much different to that of the great land they once served.'

Elfin shrugged. Enntonia was in disarray, that much was beyond doubt, but now hardly seemed the time to be discussing its sorry decline at the hands of an inept High Council steeped in corruption.

Harbinger Talus took a mouthful of ale, belched crudely, and wiped his mouth with his sleeve. 'So, envoy of Bog-Mire. Tingle, isn't it? What brings you away from your fireside book and slippers on a foul night like this?'

Elfin cleared his throat bravely. 'It's Fingle, and I am here with a summons.'

'I'd guessed as much at the sight of you in a place such as this, Tingle,' grunted the Harbinger. 'A summons from Bog-Mire then, from the Scribe of the Towers himself, I'll wager. How is the old bookworm?'

Rising from the table, Elfin finished his ale and thumped his tankard down firmly. His patience with this night's work was wearing thin. 'You can ask him yourself, Harbinger. We are to meet him at the Western Gate. My name is Fingle, and we are already late.'

Talus drained his pitcher and rose purposefully from the bench. 'Western Gate it is.'
He scowled once more towards the group gathered by the fireside. 'I was thinking of moving on anyway. The clientele in this place ain't what it used to be!'

CHAPTER SIXTEEN

Standing on the steps of the Central News Agency, Tybor Barkal looked out across the sprawling mass of Sahropa. Held captive in a blanket of hazy smog, the city baked under the glare of the hot afternoon sun. Barkal had a thumping headache. He'd probably had too much to drink the night before, but the noise and the fumes weren't helping. An hour from now he would be back in the Boneyard Bar enjoying a cold beer; he'd feel better then. Flicking his unfinished cigarette to the ground, he stamped on it, and entered the building. He needed to stop smoking. He'd already promised himself that when he got a new employer he would quit once and for all. If everything went to plan, it wouldn't be long now.

Taking the elevator to the fifth floor he walked along the corridor passing the bustling main office. Telephones rang, voices chattered loudly. The air buzzed with anticipation, news in the making. Tybor Barkal had no time for the whole concept. Far as he was concerned there was no such thing as news. Ignorant masses were being drip-fed information; information those in authority wanted them to believe in order to maintain their control. Brainwashing for the civilised, that was Tybor Barkal's opinion, but then he knew what he was talking about. For the last few months he had been playing his part in it all; a cog in the machine. Not for much longer though. He rapped on the door and went inside.

Fara Lane shot him a frown as she looked up from her desk.

'Oh, it's you.'

Barkal pulled the door closed behind him. 'Nice to see you too,' he returned sarcastically. 'Always a pleasure.' Taking the padded envelope from his jacket, he tossed it on to her desk. 'A delivery from our mutual friend, the Senator. He wants it on prime time this evening, said you're the woman to get it done. Guess you'll be hearing from him, that is if you haven't already?' The look on her face suggested the latter. With his task completed, Barkal was ready for that beer. 'No offence,' he quipped, 'but I'm hoping I won't be seeing you again, at least, not in person. I'm hoping to get myself fixed up with some new employment.'

Her mocking laugh stopped him in his tracks. 'Let me guess,' she rose from her desk. 'Senator Sobek has told you he won't be needing your services anymore. One more errand, two at most, then you'll be done. You'll be free to go. Am I right?'

Barkal felt his cheeks flush, both with embarrassment and annoyance.

'And you believed him?' She shook her head. 'You really don't look that gullible, Barkal. Don't you think he tells all his hired hands the same thing? Believe me, when you get tangled up with someone like Sobek, there is no last job. There's no end to it.' Her expression changed suddenly; her smile appeared almost genuine. 'Take the word of someone who knows.'

Barkal felt the dread sink to the pit of his stomach. Maybe he wasn't going to be able to quit smoking after all.

'How did you get involved with the Senator anyway?' she eyed him quizzically.

'Guess I'm easy led,' he replied. 'Started by just helping a friend out, delivering packages. Easy money.'

'Money,' she sighed, 'the root of all evil. Money and fame, traps us all in the end.'

Her reaction surprised him. Fara Lane, journalist, television news broadcaster, and producer. Her exploits in the world of media had not only made her a star in her home city, but one of the most recognised and respected faces in the nation. Was she merely just another one of Sobek's pawns? If Fara Lane felt she couldn't escape his control, what hope was there for him?

Shaking his head despondently, Tybor Barkal grumbled a quick farewell, shut the door behind him, and headed for the elevator. His head thumped worse than ever. He desperately needed that beer.

CHAPTER SEVENTEEN

By the time Token ScriptScratcher arrived at the four rounded towers of the Western Gate, the snow was falling heavily. The ornate steel gates, rusted and overgrown, gaped open as if abandoned in great haste. The crumbling stonework of the towers and flanking walls cried of neglect. Once a sight to behold, the Western Gate of Enntonia's ruined state was synonymous with the city's fall from grace.

The Scribe of Bog-Mire took shelter in one of the old sentry posts and waited for them to arrive. They were late. Harbinger Talus would have been reluctant to move quickly at this late hour, but his stubbornness would have found its equal in Elfin Fingle's dogged determination. They would be on their way; they would be here soon. Token found some comfort knowing he could call on such reliable accomplices to help his cause.
Stamping his feet to keep the chill at bay, he checked the contents of his pack. Two scrolls, both hastily prepared and sealed with the mark of Bog-Mire. One for Harbinger Talus, detailing the instructions for his task, the other, to be delivered by the Harbinger, carried grave news, a grim résumé of the night's events. Its recipient would know best what must be done.

The full moon appeared through a momentary break in the snow shower. His horse whinnied in the cold. Moments later,

Token heard them approaching, their arrival strangely muted by the thick blanket of snow which now covered the ground.

Their moonlit exchange was quick. Harbinger Talus broke the seal and read his instructions, raising an eyebrow in interest. 'That sly old fox, eh?' He handed back the rolled-up parchment. 'Burn it on your return to the Towers, Master Scribe. I have my orders. I'd best be on my way. It's a foul night for a horse ride.'

Token ScriptScratcher held the reins as Talus mounted up. 'You will make haste, Harbinger. I cannot divulge the content of the scroll you carry, suffice to say the fate of many rely on our actions this night.'

'Worry not, Scribe,' assured Talus. 'You know the saying as well as I, bad news travels fast.' Turning his mount, he tipped the brow of his hat in parting gesture. 'Fare ye well, ScriptScratcher. And you, Master Tingle.'

As they watched him fade from view, Elfin clenched his fists in annoyance. 'It's Fingle!'

'What did you say?' Token turned to him.

'Oh, nothing.' The snow began to fall again, and the moon slipped once more from view. 'Where is Talus going?' Elfin rarely questioned official business but on this occasion his curiosity had the better of him.

'Not here, Elfin. We must return to Bog-Mire before the weather deteriorates further. I will tell you more when we get there. Dark days lie ahead, and I fear we may not be safe out here in the dead of night.'

The fire in the drawing room of Bog-Mire Towers cracked loudly. Stretching his legs, Elfin Fingle warmed his feet as he drained the last of his hot chocolate. His shirt was stained with butter which had dripped from the toasted muffins Mrs Burrows had prepared for them on their return. Save for the light of the fire and the two candles burning on the mantelpiece, the room was in darkness. Shadows danced on the back wall, their ghostly movements putting Elfin even less at ease. On the far side of the fire, Token ScriptScratcher lit his pipe and settled back in his favourite armchair.

'Fetch the bottle of brandy, Elfin. These old bones of mine are not suited to running late-night errands in such cold conditions.'

Elfin glanced out the window as he poured the brandy. The snow was still falling heavily, whipped up in frenzy by the howling wind. With their glasses filled, he retook his seat and waited tentatively as the Scribe took a long draw on his pipe.

'History, Elfin,' he began. 'This place is steeped in it. It oozes out of the very fabric of Bog-Mire. Stored within these walls are countless scrolls, parchments, books, and maps. Centuries of history; documentation of past ages, all recorded for the benefit of future generations. Tales of great monarchs, rulers of tyranny, and brave leaders of men. Heroic deeds, great battles won, bloody battles lost. Sordid accounts of blackmail, deceit, and treachery. Some telling of prosperity, some of hard times, and, in the midst of it all, governments, good and bad.' Pausing for effect, Token sipped at his brandy and puffed again on his pipe. Rising slowly, the smoke hung lazily above his head, as if waiting for him to continue.

Spellbound, Elfin sat by the fireside, his heart beating ever faster.

The Scribe leaned forward, frowning over his spectacles. 'But the tale I must now tell, is the darkest one of them all.'

Elfin shifted uneasily in his chair.

'Dragons!' scowled Token. 'The Black Wing. Devils straight from the jaws of damnation. Not since ages have they prowled the fair lands of Enntonia; not since the Great Wizard banished them.' He raised a clenched fist in the air. 'But tonight, under cover of darkness, a visitor came to Bog-Mire, and a desperate individual he was. He carried with him orders from the High Council. I was forced at the point of steel, a treacherous blade, to carry out those orders.' He thumped the arm of his chair angrily. 'I scratched dark lines on that parchment, Elfin, the darkest lines imaginable. I can only pray our actions in the aftermath have some small measure of success.' He shook his head slowly. 'And so, I wrote under pain of death. A summons it was, sealed by wax with the mark of Bog-Mire Towers, as all official Council orders must be. A summons, Elfin.'

Gripping the arms of his chair tightly, Elfin Fingle found his voice. 'A summons to whom? And where have you sent Harbinger Talus? Whom does he seek?'

'By now, that summons will be in the foothills of the Terra Hydra, on its way to the Basilisik Mountain.'

Elfin's jaw dropped open. 'No!'

'Yes, Elfin, I'm afraid so. By my hand those fools in the High Council may have sentenced us all to a terrible end.' Token ScriptScratcher slumped back dejectedly in his chair. 'The High Council has summoned the Black Wizard Osfilian, effectively freeing him from his mountain prison.'

As he drew slowly on his pipe, the Scribe's gaze settled on his young assistant. 'Our hopes now rest with Harbinger Talus. He rides west to the Breach of Krechan-Bhann. He rides in search of Scaraven.'

CHAPTER EIGHTEEN

Sitting at the entrance to the caves, Taro Brook switched his attention from his grazed hands to Messenger Two Cups. The old man was sitting cross-legged on a large boulder. Motionless, he appeared held in some kind of trance. He hadn't moved in quite some time.

'What is he doing?'

'Listening.'

'Listening to what?' Brook turned to her. 'I don't hear anything.'

'There is no need to whisper, he will not hear you. His mind will be focused on things far from here. He is listening for news.'

'What news is he hoping to hear?'

'He will be hoping that all is quiet. I have heard a phrase on my travels,' she continued. 'No news is good news.'

'I've heard it too.' Taro Brook considered asking more about her travels, and where it was she came from, but decided against it. The answers to his questions seemed to lead only to further confusion. He was still coming to terms with her change of name. Best keep things simple. He turned his head back to the view. The sun had dropped beyond the summit peak. The evening light danced on the vast expanse of water far below, stretching as far as the eye could see.

'The Sea of Lucidity,' she followed his gaze. 'And there, on the horizon, Eldormaar. The realm of the Seer Magister.'

The distant, shimmering landform appeared to float above the surface of the water. Taro Brook shared his observations. 'It must be a trick of the light.'

'It is no illusion,' she replied firmly. 'Eldormaar lies at the edge of forever. You could sail for all eternity and never reach it. It is said that none may set foot there unless the Seer Magister himself decrees otherwise.'

'Who, or what, is this Seer?'

'I know only of him through the words of Scaraven. Centuries ago he left these shores for the last time. Eldormaar became his final resting place.'

'Long time ago,' mused Brook. 'Just a legend then?'

'Scaraven talks of him often as though he were still alive. He is said to have possessed great powers, so anything is possible, but perhaps only his writings live on.'

'It makes for an interesting tale.' Brook conceded, happy to give the possibility no further consideration. Calmed by the peaceful seascape and captivated by the wondrous imagery of this strange land, his mood lightened. Turning slowly, he met her stare. She held his gaze for a moment before turning her eyes to the sea.

'You have a strong presence, Taro Brook. The kind I could easily find in a crowd. I was drawn to you at the beacon fire of DunTreggan. A strong connection between us may yet prove useful.'

Feeling a sudden tinge of embarrassment, he cleared his throat. 'I was certainly aware of you, but I had no idea what was going on.' He was even less sure now.

'Understandable,' she nodded. 'It was a new experience for you. You were Morusk of DunTreggan. Only a small part of your own awareness lingered, manifesting itself in your desperate need to return to the forest in search of answers.' She faced him again. 'When we drift into another reality, we become someone else. And yet some parts of us remain present, subconsciously making the other person do or say things without them really knowing why. To others around them it would appear that they are acting out of character.'

'And what about when you drift back?' asked Brook, again grappling with the bizarre concept. 'How much of it do you remember?'

'Very little,' she replied. 'Often, nothing at all. How much do you remember of Morusk?'

Brook scratched thoughtfully at his chin as he pieced the jumbled fragments together in his mind. 'Come to think of it, hardly anything. I remember the Raider attack vividly, and our climb up the mountain but, before that, all I can remember was walking in the forest. I thought I was lost, then I saw the huts and the men and... that's all I remember.'

'Then you have your answer. Sometimes I remember strange sights and sounds, or unfamiliar faces, but without full memory and awareness I have no way of knowing just how often it happens.'

'Why do you do it?' The words tumbled out of his mouth before he had the chance to judge their merit.

'Why did you do it?' She frowned. 'I don't think either of us chose it. It just happened to me one day. I was lucky, Scaraven was close by and came to my aid.'

'But to continue doing it? Is it by choice?'

'It keeps happening, there is nothing you can do about it. But I do know from experience that it gets easier once you accept it. Scaraven calls it a gift, that's why I chose to help him.'

'You make it sound as though Drifters have a purpose.'

'We do, Taro Brook.'

A panicked shout interrupted their discussion. 'Can someone help me down from this confounded rock? My leg has gone to sleep.'

A short while later, having rescued Two Cups from his predicament, they watched patiently as he fumbled with his flask.

'Did you hear anything?' she asked warily.

'No, I didn't, but I'm worried.' His nose twitched as he stroked his whiskers. 'Mark my words, there's trouble afoot. I can feel it in my bones.' He swallowed a mouthful of tea. 'It may require further investigation, but for now, we can talk more.'

'I told Taro Brook about the Seer Magister.'

'Oh, did you now? Excellent.' The Messenger's gaze became distant. 'You know, I still miss the old fellow. Imagine just packing up like that and taking off to live on an island.' He snorted his amusement. 'A floating island, of all things.'

Taro Brook shared his astonishment. 'You knew him? The Seer Magister?' He looked at her in bemusement. Had he misheard her? 'Sanna said he left these shores centuries ago.'

'What?' The Messenger appeared genuinely puzzled. 'My goodness, is it really that long ago?' He took another slurp of tea and quickly regained his composure. 'Of course I knew him. He was the greatest tutor a young wizard could ever wish for. And I was his finest pupil.'

Brook drew a breath in surprise. Just how old was this strange character? Would it be rude to ask outright? Would he even get a straight answer? He decided against trying. 'So, the Seer. Is he still alive?'

The Messenger's whiskers twitched with interest. 'Well now, that is a good question. He may well be, but having confined himself to his island retreat, we can never know for sure. His writings live on though, and they are a great source of guidance, and that is why we must make for Sumarren.'

'Why?'

'Sumarren was the spiritual home of the Seer Magister for many centuries. He and his followers studied there before he set sail for the island, and it is there that I will find the answers to questions that trouble me. Great standing stones, adorned with countless ancient writings, surround the sacred gardens and somewhere beneath the remains of the wondrous structure lies a treasure trove of scrolls and parchments holding the key to many prophecies still untold.'

Brook was fast becoming enthralled with the tale. Whether it held any element of truth seemed irrelevant. 'You say that you studied with the Seer,' he probed. 'Have you not been there before?'

'Yes, yes, on many occasions, but we are constantly faced with new threats and new challenges. New questions arise, questions requiring answers. My recent attempts to reach the beloved old place have proved unsuccessful.' The old man grinned wryly. 'Trouble is, I always seem to get side-tracked, but not this time.' Clicking his tongue, he raised his mug. 'I have a particularly good feeling about this. Let us toast to a successful journey.'

Daylight faded rapidly, and not long after, following a short discussion on the many varied intricacies of tea leaf preparation, Messenger Two Cups fell asleep. Slumped in a sitting position, he dozed noisily. A varied selection of snorts, sighs and strange mutterings emanated from beneath his hat which had slipped forward and now covered his eyes.

'Is he really a wizard?' whispered Brook.

'I don't know,' she replied. 'He talks of it now and again. Does it matter?'

'I don't suppose so. It's just... I've never seen one before. To be honest, I don't believe in such things.'

She shrugged. 'We should let him sleep. Let's take a walk.' She led them a short distance up the ridge to a flat shelf of rock. The sky sparkled with a myriad of stars. 'Look there,' she pointed. 'The constellation of the Eight Bears.'

Not being much of a stargazer he was unable to draw any real comparisons to the night sky from home, but the sight was impressive, nonetheless. Stealing a fleeting glance sideways, he wondered if his present company was causing him to see the beauty in things. Tired from the day's climb he lay down on the rock and stretched out his legs.

Watching the stars, he pondered the many questions that still remained unanswered. Right at that moment, they hardly seemed to matter. A feeling of contentment washed over him and, as his eyelids flickered in harmony with the twinkling of the stars, Taro Brook fell asleep.

CHAPTER NINETEEN

Procrastinator Vardoger gazed in wonder at the magnificent white city. He never tired of the view from his official chambers. Situated high above the city, they did more than just offer a fine viewpoint; they were a constant reminder of his elevated position of authority. The city sparkled in the sunshine. A breath-taking maze of marble and glass, sweeping its way gently downhill to meet the shimmering ocean. The city of Craton, the jewel in the Confederacy crown.

Turning his attention from the view, Vardoger's eyes settled on Kalina Tronn as she entered the room. Tall and curvaceous, his personal aide and confidante was a raven-haired beauty of impeccable taste and standards. A woman who excelled at everything she did, Kalina was much more than just his professional colleague. She was one of the many beautiful women on whom he could call when affairs of the heart took precedence over affairs of state. Whilst not intending to lead anyone on, or to play one against the other, he had little choice. It was not that being faithful held any fears for him; in truth, the concept was an appealing one. His dilemma was simple. In order to choose one of these beautiful women to be his long-term companion, he would have to make a decision... something Procrastinator Vardoger was completely incapable of doing.

He watched her as she crossed the room. A vision of perfection, she was his favourite, by a long way. Why couldn't he just let her know how he felt?

'Your visitors have dined and rested, Procrastinator,' she smiled. 'Do you wish to speak with them again before they take their leave?'

'If you think it would be beneficial, Kalina. Show them in, at your convenience.'

'Of course, Procrastinator. I'll be right back.'

He watched her leave the room. Perfection personified. He turned to the window, his thoughts drifting to the subject of having to choose a dinner companion for the evening. Decisions; why was life so complicated?

The moments passed in a blur. He turned back to the room as the door opened. Kalina showed the three men to the conference table. Pouring brandy from a crystal decanter, she distributed the filled glasses. 'Let me know if there is anything else you need, Procrastinator.'

'I will, Kalina. Thank you.' Transfixed by her beauty, Vardoger watched her leave then turned his attention to his guests. Before him sat representatives from the three largest oil and gas producing corporations in the Confederacy. Raising his glass, he addressed them confidently. 'Delegates, I propose a toast. To your safe journey home and to future good health and prosperity.' Having attended to the formalities he took his place at the head of the table. 'And so to business.' He cleared his throat. 'I have given a good deal of thought to your presentation this morning and I think it has substance. I would therefore be willing, at some point in the future, to go before the Supreme Assembly, requesting their consideration in the respect of the raising of a motion in support of further deliberation of your proposal.' He tapped a finger on the desk. 'However, at this stage, I would like to go over the main points again, if you would indulge me?'

The three men exchanged a worried glance. 'Forgive us, Procrastinator,' the silver-haired man began, 'but we were hopeful that in the event of our proposal gaining your support, you would take it to the Assembly for immediate consideration.'

Vardoger rubbed his fingertips together. 'Delegates, as I am sure you are aware, the Supreme Assembly always has a full and busy schedule ahead of it. Government of the Eight States is no small task, and we must proceed with the programme armed with no small amount of diligence, whilst at the same time following, at the very least, some degree of order. Many are the motions presented to me, and although the majority of them have varying degrees of worth, it is only fair that they are dealt with in chronological order.'

He paused for effect. 'Of course, there are, on occasion, mitigating circumstances. If a case can be made for an exception to the rule, the Supreme Assembly has within its remit the power to make allowances for such occurrences. Especially if it were deemed that it was in the best interests of the Confederacy to do so.' He tapped the desk as if to emphasise his point before continuing. 'And so, to your proposal. The formation of a syndicate, a gathering of the oil corporations. A novel idea I must say. Brave new ground is it not? Are we tired of the endless cut-throat nature of business, gentlemen?'

'We believe it is the way ahead.' Silver-hair agreed.

'Yes,' chimed another, a slippery looking character too young in years for a position of such power. 'We can take collective decisions concerning new explorations whilst at the same time setting realistic targets and price structures. We can involve the smaller independent producers, thus ensuring an equal spread of profits throughout.'

'It is time to end the fuel price wars,' chorused the third, 'and the bitter competitiveness that has held us all back in recent years.'

'With the backing of government, this syndicate can achieve great things.' Silver-hair added enthusiastically. 'You just need to look at our first proposal for evidence of the possibilities.'

Vardoger sighed as he eased back in his chair. He found the whole thing hard to believe. These corporations had been at each other's throats for decades. At one point, several years back, the Supreme Assembly had even been forced to get involved, an occurrence it did not want to be repeating. It was one thing to sit idly by, snatching huge chunks of revenue from these oil-rich barons, but having to work for the money was a different proposition altogether. Vardoger glanced at the clock on the wall. Time was slipping by. His focus would soon have to shift to the delicate matter of choosing a dinner companion for the evening. He would ask Kalina to help; her input would be invaluable as always. It was time to get this meeting wrapped up. Sitting forward, his diplomatic skills crunched into gear.

'Very well, I believe your intentions to be honourable. So, to your first proposal, as you call it. Will it work?'

'We believe so, Procrastinator. With us all working together towards a common goal, we believe anything to be possible. The infrastructure is already in place. The procedure is straightforward enough.'

'But to do it on the large scale you propose, the costs are going to be astronomical.'

'Working collectively, Procrastinator, financing the project will not be a problem. A fraction of combined profits would fund the entire project.'

Vardoger raised an eyebrow. An opportunity too good to miss may just have presented itself. 'Well, I must say I am impressed. If you were to allow me some time to work on how best to present this idea to the Supreme Assembly, I think, with some political leaning, we could make this work. The Assembly would no doubt require some recompense in altering its busy schedule. Did you have some figure in mind to oil the wheels? If you'll pardon the pun.'

The three men looked at each other in surprise. 'Procrastinator,' Silver-hair again took the mantle of main spokesperson. 'It appears you may have misunderstood the nature of our pitch. We, as a syndicate, would be making no profit from this venture. We feel that having taken so much from the desert lands throughout the decades it was time to give something back to the people of these lands. The desalination of the Dead Lakes could change those people's lives forever. We had assumed, perhaps naively, that the Supreme Assembly would fully endorse such a plan without delay. We had assumed that it, like us, would not want any financial gain from such a venture.'

Vardoger fought back the urge to laugh. Managing to disguise his reaction as a cough, he cleared his throat. 'Of course, I understand perfectly.' He paused to regain his composure. 'I suggest therefore that I put some thought to the way ahead and present your proposal to the Supreme Assembly at the first available opportunity.'

'An excellent motion, Procrastinator. We will await news of your deliberation. Thank you for your counsel and for your hospitality.'

As the door closed behind his guests, Vardoger poured a large glass of brandy and slumped down on the couch. What a tiring day. He found it hard to believe that the warring oil giants were planning to work together. He didn't see their arrangement lasting long. It had little chance of working. Even if the corporations themselves genuinely wanted to make it work, they needed the approval of the Supreme Assembly and they would have little or no hope of gaining that. With the present arrangement returning a healthy revenue, the Assembly would prefer things to stay just as they were.

The secret to the sustained success of the Assembly was simple. Representing all Eight States, it faced an unenvious task. Believing that people, in general, feared change, the Assembly changed little, and the majority of the population stayed relatively content.

This underlying principle of rule was the main reason behind Vardoger's rapid climb through the ranks of government. Nowhere in all the Eight States could there be found an individual more suited to the task.
He had struggled most of his life with his indecisive nature. It had been the cause of great personal torment. His childhood had not been a happy one, his family and friends always ready to make fun of him. His father had often told him that he would make a great politician due to his inability to give a straight answer. In recent years they'd shared the recollection together fondly.
The young Vardoger had fallen into politics by mistake rather than by design, but once noticed by his peers, his ascent of the ladder of power was swift. The Supreme Assembly had come calling for him. He was the answer to many of its problems. Someone in the chain of command, filling the vacuum between the Assembly and the demands of the forty-six Houses of Representatives, each filled to the rafters with bickering local governors. A human shield whose constant refusal to make decisions or to proceed with policy suggestions, would slow the process of governing down to the point where they would rarely need to be called to action.
They were so taken with their new recruit they created a new post and title especially for him. Procrastinator Vardoger; Chief Policy Advisor to the Supreme Assembly. In Craton, capital city of the Confederacy of the Eight States, anyone wanting legislation brought before the Supreme Assembly, had to go through him. And they would have to be prepared for a long wait.

He re-filled his glass and moved to the window. As he gazed down on the city, his thoughts returned to the visit from the oil delegation. There was something refreshing about their plans. To make things better for others at the expense of personal gain was an intriguing idea. It was the kind of thing that would have appealed to him a long time ago, before his life had become so comfortable. The proposal was revolutionary; to provide fresh drinking water to the people living in the most inhospitable part of the Confederacy. It could save thousands of lives.

Draining his glass, he returned to his desk. There was little point in dwelling on the idea. The Assembly would have no interest in it when there was to be no financial benefit to the Confederacy coffers. The tribes of the desert lands had existed without the luxury of fresh water for generations, they would continue to do so. Perhaps though, as the idea had caught his imagination, he would present the case to them anyway. There would be no harm in doing so and perhaps he would feel better for trying to support such a noble cause.

Assembling the documents from the meeting, he slipped them inside an official folder, and filed it in a bureau behind his desk. Present the idea to the Assembly? Yes, he thought he might do just that. Then again, perhaps he wouldn't.

He closed the bureau and locked it. Either way, there was no need to rush into anything.

Kalina entered the room as he turned from the bureau. 'Is there anything else I can do for you, Procrastinator?'

'I'm not sure, Kalina. My thoughts are unclear. It has been a trying day.'

'Might I suggest a drink to unwind? And dinner perhaps?'

'You might be right,' he nodded. 'I was going to ask your thoughts on that very subject.'

'I would be happy to join you,' she smiled. 'If you preferred not to dine alone? I wouldn't want to intrude.'

'Kalina, you wouldn't be intruding. Not at all. That sounds marvellous.'

'It would be my pleasure. Would you like me to make a reservation?'

'I think that would be beneficial.'

She hesitated for a moment. 'Is there anywhere in particular you would like to dine?'

Procrastinator Vardoger stared back blankly. 'Oh, I don't really have a preference, Kalina. You decide.'

CHAPTER TWENTY

Taro Brook opened his eyes and took in his surroundings. Bright sunlight filled the cave. Feeling well-rested, he made his way outside. Sanna greeted him with a mug of tea.

'I trust you slept well, Woodsman?'

'Yes, thanks.' He scanned the rocky landscape. 'Strange thing is, I remember falling asleep under the stars, up there on the ridge. When did we come back down to the cave?'

'You don't remember walking back down?'

'No, I don't.'

'That is strange.' Her expression gave nothing away.

As he pushed the subject from his thoughts, he became suddenly aware of the old man's absence. 'Messenger Two Cups, is he gone?'

'Something was troubling him. He didn't say what it was, and I thought it best not to ask. But he said he will re-join us soon, further along the ridge.'

'And he left his flask behind?'

'Yes, which suggests he won't be gone for too long.'

Brook took a seat on a boulder. 'The old fellow appears genuine but tell me, can he truly be trusted?'

'I trust him with my life, Taro Brook. With all of them. You must come to your own conclusion.'

'Fair answer.' Brook took a mouthful of tea and tried to lighten the mood. 'Do you know how old he is?'

'I've never asked. You know how he feels about the concept of time. Does it matter?'

'No, I was just asking out of interest.' His attempts at conversation were floundering badly. 'He claimed to be a pupil of the Seer Magister,' he persevered, 'and yet you say the Seer left these lands centuries ago. How is that possible?'

'All things are possible. Have you not yet come to accept that?'

Though the evidence for such a claim was mounting, Taro Brook was still struggling to come to terms with it. 'So, do you think he is a wizard?'

'I still say you think too much, Woodsman. I'd never considered it, but if he is centuries old and is still in such good shape, it would be logical to assume that he holds some degree of magical power.'

Quietly digesting her response, Brook cast his gaze back down the shattered ridge.

'We should be on our way,' she prompted. 'The mountain awaits.'

The view from the summit was breath-taking. The Sea of Lucidity sparkled in the morning sunlight. Far in the distance, Eldormaar shimmered mysteriously, floating somewhere between sky and sea. The white ridge stretched out endlessly in front of them, leading the eye towards a vista of countless mountain peaks.

To their right, the land fell away sharply for several hundred feet, culminating in gentle sloping valleys littered with boulders and highlighted by sparkling areas of water.
On their left, only a few paces away, the ground beneath their feet appeared to tumble directly down to the sea far below.

Halfway along the narrow ridge they stopped for a rest. The contents of the Messenger's flask seemed no nearer an end. Passing a filled mug to him, she eyed him closely.

'I expect you want to know more about the cause of the Drifters.'

He wasn't entirely sure he did. 'If you expect me to be of any help, it would be useful.'

'Our purpose is simple,' she began. 'Harnessing our ability to drift from one reality to another, we try to prevent dark agents from carrying out their acts of mayhem.'

'Dark agents?'

'Acts of random chaos are often mistaken as naturally occurring events,' she continued. 'But the truth is, they are planned and executed by these agents who are present in all worlds, taking many different forms. You have recently witnessed them at work.'

'The Raiders?'

'Yes,' she nodded. 'In Morusk's world, they take the form of hooded skeletal riders.'

'The attack on DunTreggan.' He mouthed the words quietly, at the same time trying to push the graphic images from his memory. 'These agents... they are everywhere?'

'Yes, and often found in positions of power, where they can inflict the most damage. They will be present in your world, you will have seen them, watched them in action without even realising it. In many worlds they are already in control.'

'How do you recognise them?'

'That is the challenge. We use many different approaches in our attempts to identify and expose them. Our efforts to thwart them are not always successful and it can be a difficult, painstaking process. Our intervention must be minimal; the effects of too much interference could be catastrophic.'

Taro Brook took a deep breath. 'Sounds like an impossible task.'

'We have many resources to draw on for assistance,' she countered, 'one being the writings of the Seer Magister.'

'What do you mean?'

'Scaraven has discovered links between many such events and prophecies written by the Seer. He believes that further investigation and translation of his works could prevent some acts of devastation being carried out.'

'So that is why we make for Sumarren?'

'Yes,' she rose to her feet, 'and we should be on the move again.'

Taro Brook voiced his thoughts as they walked. 'So, your theory is that this Seer has foreseen such events?' His expression poured scorn on the very idea. 'I don't believe it's possible for anyone to predict the future. Too far-fetched for me, I'm afraid.'

She gave a sarcastic laugh. 'You continue to astound me, Taro Brook.' Drawing to a stop, she placed her hands on her hips. 'After all that has happened, you are still a prisoner to your ignorance.'

Stung by her response, he jumped boldly to his defence. 'You're entitled to your opinion, but I think you should know that I intend to leave this place and return home at the first opportunity.'

'Understandable,' she replied calmly, unfazed by his outburst. 'I too felt the same way at first, but things change, and as we are being candid with each other, it's only fair that I share something with you. It may change your thinking.'

He doubted it very much. 'What is it?'

'I'm not sure Scaraven would be pleased with me for sharing such information at this early stage, so I'd appreciate it if you kept it between us?'

'Fair enough.'

'There's a reason Scaraven, Messenger Two Cups as he would have you call him, is so excited by your arrival. He believes you have a part to play in the unfolding of a mystery he has been trying to unravel.'

'What do you mean? Was he expecting me?' Brook eyed her suspiciously. 'Did he send you to meet me?'

'No, he did not. I knew nothing of you. Yes, I was drawn to you at the fire of DunTreggan, I sensed your presence, but I did not know why. We survived the attack, and we met up with Scaraven. None of it was planned.'

'Then how would you explain it? Coincidence?'

'There's no such thing as coincidence,' she corrected him. 'We prefer to call it synchronicity.'

'Okay,' he sighed. It seemed like she had an answer for everything. 'Let's say I believe you. This mystery, how can either of you possibly think it involves me?'

'Scaraven recently received news of a stranger's arrival at Sumarren. Crossing vast oceans and sailing for countless new moons, this envoy from the frozen northlands of Nallevarr carries with him a scroll. It was found in caverns beneath ancient ruins there. Despite their best efforts, the people of Nallevarr succeeded in translating only part of the scroll, instructing them to journey with it to Sumarren, where a follower of a great visionary would offer further translation.'

'Scaraven?'

'It appears so.'

Taro Brook hesitated. 'I still don't see why you think I could be involved.'

'We must first reach Sumarren. Once there, if Scaraven can successfully translate the scroll, your part in it all will become clearer.'

'But what makes either of you think I have a part to play?'

'There seems little doubt about it,' she replied. 'Scaraven had already uncovered part of a prophecy he suspects is connected to this. It is written on the great stones at Sumarren. It tells the believer to watch and wait for the Man of the Trees, for he will come through the Harlequin Forest, heralding the arrival of answers from the Frozen Lands.'

A silence grew between them as Brook wrestled with her words. He was still struggling to come to terms with his strange predicament. Was he now expected to believe in the existence of seers, wizards, and age-old prophecies? Worse still, in a prophecy that mentioned him?

A shout interrupted his contemplation. Looking along the ridge, he saw Messenger Two Cups waving his stick in greeting.

A lone figure moved silently among the ancient standing stones. Lifting his head to the stars, a smile flashed across his weathered, bearded face.

The Man of the Trees would soon be here.

With the sound of the waves breaking gently on the shore, the figure turned away from the moonlit water, walked under the great stone archway, and entered the ruins of Sumarren.

CHAPTER TWENTY-ONE

Tybor Barkal drained his glass and signalled for a re-fill. Striking a match to his cigarette, he pushed his way through the crowded room towards the exit. The noise in the Boneyard Bar made telephone conversation difficult and this call was one he couldn't ignore. Stepping into the glaring sunshine, he pressed the phone to his ear, and answered grudgingly.

'Barkal! Finally.' The grating voice sent a familiar shudder down his spine. 'I thought you were never going to pick up.'

'Senator Sobek.'

'Glad to see you made that delivery on time. Did you see the news last night? That Lane woman has a talent for unearthing great stories. Imagine her finding out about my generous donations to the city charity funds? And to think I'd tried to keep it all anonymous. Still, I suppose good publicity can do someone in my position no harm at all.'

'I don't watch the news. But I'm sure it showed you in a great light. Hardly surprising, given the circumstances.'

'I'd no idea you were so cynical, Barkal. I thought you'd be happy to be playing your part.'

He quickly seized the opportunity to air his concerns. 'Yeah, about that. You said one more job, and our arrangement would be fulfilled. Do you stand by that?'

'Why? What's the problem? It's a bit late in the day to be developing a conscience. I wouldn't let something like that get in the way of earning easy money if I were you.'

'Let's just say I feel like a change.'

'Well, if that's how you want it. I need people I can rely on. But keep the next few days free. I have plans in place, plans that include you. It's too late to make changes at this stage, so stay sober. There's no room for error. Payment for yesterday is waiting for you at the usual place. Stay by the phone, I'll be in touch soon.' The call ended abruptly.

Barkal felt less than convinced. Would Sobek stick to his word? One more job and he'd find out. Throwing his half-smoked cigarette to the ground, he stubbed it out with his boot. Half was a good start. Maybe in a few days he'd be able to quit for good. Maybe, maybe not. He'd just have to wait and see. Muttering his discontent he pushed his way back inside the Boneyard Bar.

Three beers later he left his favourite haunt and made his way across the city. Sahropa appeared busier than ever. Avoiding the bustling streets, he boarded the cross-land train. Staring out at the endless mass of concrete as it trundled by, he wondered if he would ever realise his dream of leaving the city. He longed for the peace and quiet of the countryside; he'd never been there but he'd heard all about it. Days like today made him yearn for it more than ever and though he didn't suppose it would ever actually happen the thought of it alone was a welcome distraction.

By the time he reached his destination his thirst had returned with a vengeance. The Ice Bar had obvious Sobek connections and didn't rate highly on his list of favoured hangouts. Situated close to the city's financial sector it attracted the wrong sort of company for Barkal. His dislike for the money men was nothing personal, he just didn't understand what it was they did. But the bar was run by an old friend and had recently, rather conveniently, become the place to collect his dubious earnings.

The bartender grinned his acknowledgement as Barkal approached. 'Well, someone looks in need of refreshment.'

'You got that right, Jeb. How's business?'

'It's paying the bills, Ty. How about you?'

'I've had better days.' He took a mouthful of beer.

'Talking of paying the bills, there's a package through the back for you. I'll go get it.'

Barkal scanned the room with disinterest. The two scantily clad dancers in the far corner were doing their best to hold the attention of the dozen or so mid-afternoon drinkers. It appeared they were failing miserably. Moments later, Jeb returned and pushed an envelope across the bar top.

'This was delivered a couple of hours ago. Another errand completed for Sobek?'

'Right again.' Barkal nodded as he tore open the envelope. Jeb whistled his appreciation at the sight of the cash bundle.

'Now, there's a sign of a happy employer.'

Quickly flicking through the notes, Barkal pushed the money back into the envelope and slipped it inside his jacket. It was a lot more than he'd been expecting for simply delivering a package to the news agency. His reaction didn't go unnoticed.

'Ty, for a man who just came into a lot of money, you don't look very happy.'

'I'm starting to feel a bit uncomfortable with the whole thing, Jeb. Don't get me wrong, I appreciate you putting a word in for me, and the money is good; maybe too good. I'm just not sure it's for me anymore.' He patted his jacket worryingly. 'It's a lot of cash for delivering a package to the CNA place, and the payments are spiralling. Every job I do for Sobek, the amount goes up. Feels like I'm getting hauled in deeper than I'd like.'

Jeb dismissed his fears with a grin. 'You worry too much, Ty. So, the cash incentives are increasing, so what? It shows that Sobek values your contributions. Nothing wrong with that, is there?'

'I don't know. Feels like maybe my silence is being bought.'

'Look, we all know Sobek has his shady side but he's a politician, what do you expect? Money talks, it's the way of the world, you know it, same as I do.' He waved a hand across the room. 'Look at this place, do you think I'd have managed to get it up and running without a financial helping hand?'

'Yeah, but at what cost? Doesn't your conscience ever bother you? I spoke to Fara Lane today at the news place. Turns out she's in league with Sobek too. She reckons once you get tied up with him there's no way of getting out.'

'Fara Lane?' Jeb scoffed sarcastically. 'What's she got to be complaining about? News reporter of the year, three years running! Did she get to those dizzy heights all by herself? Bit hypocritical to be complaining about it now, and besides, if Sobek wasn't buying her services someone else would be. That's how it works, everyone is answerable to someone and if you ask me it's no big deal. Just keep on doing what you're asked and count the money as it rolls in.'

Tybor Barkal was unconvinced. 'I'm glad it's all working out for you, Jeb, I really am. But I just don't think I'm cut out for it. Far as I'm concerned, I'm going to hold Sobek to his word and make my next job for him my last.'

'Your call, old friend.' Jeb smiled as they shook hands. 'And I wish you well with it. See you soon,' he winked casually. 'I'll let you know when your next payment arrives.'

Watching his friend leave, Jeb's smile vanished quickly. His need for pretence was over. Tybor Barkal's fears were well founded. Fara Lane was right. Once you got hooked up with Senator Sobek, there was no way out. Jeb knew that better than anyone.

CHAPTER TWENTY-TWO

... Troubled yet again with the unnerving sensation of being watched, he glanced repeatedly over his shoulder, each time expecting to see someone emerging from the trees behind. There seemed little doubt about it. He was being watched. He was being followed.

Hans Rugen stared blankly at the screen of his laptop computer. The cursor blinked impatiently, as if waiting for him to continue. Rugen's problem was that he had no idea what to write next. Initially he'd wondered if he was suffering from writer's block, but he now suspected the cause of his dilemma was much simpler. His latest idea for a novel, which at first had seemed so full of promise, now appeared to be going nowhere.

The telephone burst into life. He answered the call, thankful for the distraction.

'That you, Rugen?' The voice belonged to Mitchell Egberts, editor of the local newspaper.

'Hello, Mitch. How's things?'

'All good. I got your email with your first chapter, I just finished reading it.'

During a conversation the previous weekend, Rugen had shared the idea for his novel with Egberts and, for reasons beyond his comprehension, had agreed to let him see a rough draft of his opening chapter. Never before had he taken such an ill-advised step and only now was he realising how much he regretted it. He broke the awkward silence tentatively.

'So, what do you think?'

'I'm going to be honest with you, Hans. It's a load of nonsense. There's not a lot to it, is there? A man walking in the woods, thinking he's being followed. Who by? Who is following him?'

'Well, I haven't got to that part yet.'

'There's a lot of detail about the forest in there, but I skimmed over most of it. I think you need to get to the point. Where is the story going?'

Rugen sighed. 'It's padding, Mitch. And you're not alone. I think everyone skims over the finer details to some extent.'

'Right!' Egberts sounded far from convinced. 'What happened to the old man and the dog? And the trees standing still? What's going on there?'

Rugen groaned dejectedly. 'Look, it's my mistake. I should have waited until I had written more before I let you read any of it. I honestly don't know what I was thinking.'

'Okay, carry on then. Write some more. Send it to me as soon as you can, and I'll let you know what I think.'

'I really think it would be best if I wait until it's finished,' Rugen replied flatly. 'I appreciate your interest, Mitch, I really do, but you seem kind of impatient.'

'Finished? How long will that take?'

'Well, it's difficult to prejudge these things.'

'Right!' Egberts went quiet for a moment. 'Okay, just send me another chapter, soon as you can. I want to know who is following.'
The call ended without further debate.

Deflated by the conversation, Rugen wandered slowly back to his study where the laptop cursor continued to blink impatiently. Despite being well known for his abrasive manner, Mitchell Egberts' stinging indictment had seemed unfairly excessive. Rugen knew he'd made a big mistake in letting anyone view his work at such an early stage and yet he had to concede that he agreed with much of what Egberts had said.
Rugen himself had no idea where the story was going.

CHAPTER TWENTY-THREE

Procrastinator Vardoger strolled along the tree-lined avenue leading from the Supreme Assembly buildings. Housing Craton's rich and powerful, the glass-fronted, white marble structures dazzled in the bright afternoon sunshine. Following a lengthy business lunch, Vardoger had declined the services of his driver. Exercise was important, he reminded himself, and the fresh air would do him good. Besides, he had a lot to consider following his hastily delivered presentation to the Assembly's special committee that morning.

He had been scheduled to speak on a matter of trivial taxation, a long-standing dispute with the seaport authority regarding unpaid taxes. With no semblance of a resolution in sight, at the very last minute, Vardoger had found himself instead fumbling through the documentation presented by the oil and gas delegation. After a slow and unassertive start, he had delivered his unrehearsed pitch with a surprising degree of enthusiasm.

The same could not be said of the reaction of the committee. Their response was as he had suspected it would be. With no obvious financial benefit, they saw no sense in granting the wishes of the energy syndicate.

Congratulating the Procrastinator wholeheartedly on his oration, the committee chairman had closed the discussion, declaring that, for the time being, things should remain just as they were. Walking in the sunshine, Vardoger couldn't help but wonder if he had done his best to support such a noble cause.

From over his shoulder he heard someone call out his name. Turning, he saw Jarl Sere, Chief of Internal Committee Affairs, hobbling awkwardly behind him. Drawing to a halt, Vardoger waited patiently for the old councillor to catch up.

'Procrastinator,' wheezed Jarl. 'Thank you for waiting. Oh, what it is to be old and withered.'

Vardoger helped his elder to a wooden bench shaded by trees.

'What can I do for you, Jarl?'

'Sere, will suffice. I see no need for titles out here, my friend. I wanted to congratulate you on your speech this morning. I found it most invigorating.'

'It's a shame the rest of the committee didn't share your view,' replied Vardoger wistfully.

'Pompous fools,' the old man grinned, 'every one of them. Don't get me wrong, I know the system well, and I've been every bit as stubborn as the rest of them throughout my years in the Assembly.' He paused to stifle a yawn. 'However, it seems my advanced years have pricked my conscience somewhat. And I am interested to learn how someone like your good self, relatively young and in a position of comparative luxury, can come to have such a keen interest in a matter of humanity.'

Vardoger looked at him blankly. 'I honestly don't know. Believe me, I am as surprised as you are. I thought it would be little more than a passing interest, but it seems the Dead Lakes have caught my attention.'

Jarl Sere smiled. 'And so they should, Procrastinator, so they should. I must say I find it encouraging that a colleague with many years of service ahead of him has found such a cause to believe in.'

'Vardoger, please,' he offered, 'as we are being informal.'

'Of course.' The old man smiled as he rose from the bench. 'I do have some thoughts, Vardoger,' he said, leaning on his stick, 'if you would be interested in hearing them?'

'You have? Yes, yes I would.'

'I'm glad. Whilst sitting in council, it occurred to me that there might be a way round this whole thing, a way for this ambitious proposal to come to fruition.'

Vardoger raised an eyebrow in interest. 'There could?'

'Yes, I believe so. As noble and enjoyable as your speech was, I think it was probably completely unnecessary.'

'I'm not sure I follow.'

'Let me explain. In theory, to forge ahead with their plans for the desalination of the Dead Lakes, the only legislation the oil syndicate would need from the Supreme Assembly would be a granting of permission from the Department of Environment. Once the wheels were set in motion, all resulting revenue and taxation issues would be dealt with as and when the need arose.' He winked mischievously. 'And we both know how slowly the wheels of government can turn, don't we?'

Vardoger looked at him in astonishment. 'You honestly think it could be pushed through that easily?'

'Officially, I'd have to point out that rules are rules, and procedures should always be followed. However, speaking off the record, I think it only fair to draw your attention to other options that might be available to you.'

Vardoger eyed his colleague carefully. 'Are you suggesting that someone skips procedures?' he asked warily. 'And that they push through the relevant documentation without mentioning it to the Assembly?'

Jarl Sere scratched his greying beard thoughtfully. 'As for them not being told, I think it's a little late for that. However, in my experience, members of the Assembly remember little of what they discuss from one week to the next. In my opinion, all you would need to do is find someone in a prominent position in government, someone who believed the proposal to be a worthy one.' he grinned widely. 'And of course, it would be beneficial if this individual were familiar with someone who could assist in obtaining the necessary documentation from the Department of Environment. Perhaps someone in Internal Affairs?' With a casual wink, Jarl Sere patted Vardoger on the shoulder. 'I will let you deliberate further in peace, Procrastinator. I must not take up any more of your time. I'm sure you have many pressing things to deal with. I bid you good day.'

Calling out his thanks, Vardoger began the process of calming the turmoil in his head. Systematically dissecting the conversation, he came to a startling conclusion. It could work. Jarl Sere's suggestion made perfect sense. All he needed was someone bold enough to do it; someone decisive enough to make it happen. Continuing with his afternoon stroll, he wondered where in all of Craton he would find such a person.

CHAPTER TWENTY-FOUR

As twilight approached, the sharp-edged scree underfoot gave way to smooth slabs of rock much darker in colour and with an almost reflective quality. Stopping to look down on a tree-lined valley far below, Taro Brook felt the Messenger's presence next to him.

'The Valley of the Lost.' Two Cups' tone was sullen.

'How did it come by such a name?' Brook queried. 'It looks so peaceful.'

Two Cups snorted. 'Looks can be deceptive. Believe me, it is well named. One day, a disorientating mist appeared suddenly. In error, I lost my bearings and descended from the ridge. I was wandering down there for days until the mist cleared.' The Messenger's frown was quickly replaced by his beaming grin. 'But thankfully the escapade ended well. Let us hurry on, my friends. We must reach the Black Glass Gap before darkness falls.'

Walking a short distance ahead, Sanna led the way as they moved across the slabs. The Messenger's expression suggested he had things on his mind.

'Tell me, Taro Brook,' he winked casually, 'what do you think of our enchanting companion?'

The directness of the question was unexpected. 'Well... she seems nice.'

'Nice?' Two Cups scoffed his response. 'There is no need for such bashful denial. She is an incredible woman. We couldn't wish for a finer companion on a journey such as ours.'

Taro Brook nodded. 'She probably saved my life. I'm obviously grateful for that, but conversation with her can be difficult. Where does she come from? I don't feel comfortable enough to ask her.'

Two Cups chuckled heartily. 'Very perceptive, young fellow. Even if she were to confide in you, I very much doubt you'd believe her. But let me divulge a little. I'm sure she won't mind, and it could save you both from an awkward situation later.' He gestured ahead. 'Our friend hails from a distant world. She is a direct descendant of the Ra-Taegan, a tribe of fierce warriors who were sworn followers of a Sun God.' He pointed a finger animatedly at Brook. 'Be glad she is on your side, my friend, for that sword she carries would separate your head from your shoulders in a blink of an eye. Whilst she appears a peaceful soul, those markings on her arm are a calling, some say the mark of the Sun God.' He drew a breath for effect. 'And I wouldn't like to be the one who crosses her.' With his finger, he slowly motioned a cutting gesture across his throat, all the while grinning at Brook's startled reaction.

A short while later, as the last of the fading sunlight slipped from view, they came to a halt at the base of a great wall of obsidian stone. At the top of a series of steps gouged into the stone, a large crack in the rock beckoned.

'The Black Glass Gap,' announced Two Cups as he began the climb. 'We can rest here until daylight returns. It would be folly to attempt the Black Glass Traverse in darkness.'

Moonlight pierced the gloomy veil of the cave. As Messenger Two Cups poured the tea, Sanna brought him up to speed with their discussions of the day.

'Excellent,' he slurped at his tea. 'You have done well.'

'I can take no credit,' Brook shrugged. 'Sanna has the difficult task in dealing with my endless questions.'

Two Cups snorted his appreciation. 'And so it should be. What use is a good teacher without a willing scholar eager to ask questions, eh?'

Sanna silently nodded her agreement. Taro Brook was still finding it difficult to come to terms with what the Messenger had told him about her. He couldn't help but wonder if the old man had been entirely honest with him. Short of asking her outright, something he definitely didn't have any plans to do, he knew he would just have to wait and find out.

'And now, my friends,' Two Cups drew a breath. 'I have news to share and a story to tell, one that concerns us all. Sanna, you will already be familiar with much of what I'm about to say. Woodsman, I trust you will continue to listen well and learn fast.'

'I'll do my best.'

'I don't doubt it for one second.' The Messenger toyed thoughtfully with his whiskers. 'The writings of the Seer Magister are becoming ever more relevant,' he began. 'The Man of the Trees has arrived.'

His gaze settled on Brook and stayed for a moment, causing him to shift uneasily. Seemed he still wasn't comfortable with being considered part of an age-old prophecy. Truth was, he just didn't believe it.

The Messenger drew his attention away and continued talking. 'And the traveller from the frozen lands awaits us at Sumarren. It is believed he carries with him a sacred scroll. Who knows what answers will be revealed in its translation, but of this much I am certain. We are on an adventure, an escapade predicted ages ago.' He paused to sip at his tea. 'Today, I heard a calling in the morning breeze and that is why I had to leave you. I was summoned to meet with a fellow messenger, a Harbinger, to give him his correct title. And grave was the news he bore from the land of Enntonia. Harbinger Talus carried with him the written words of Token ScriptScratcher, the Scribe of Bog-Mire Towers. Words penned in great haste, of that there was no doubt, and desperate words they were.'

'What news, Scaraven?' Sanna cut in. 'What has happened?'

The Messenger's expression darkened. 'Curses on them!' The anger in his voice was evident. 'The fools in the High Council have summoned Osfilian down from his mountain prison.' With a sigh of despair he pulled his hat forward and hung his head.

Taro Brook glanced uneasily in Sanna's direction. She kept her silence, and her thoughts stayed her own. Moments later, Two Cups lifted his head, pushed back his hat, and offered them both a broad smile.

'My friends, please forgive my outburst.' With a mouthful of tea, he quickly regained his composure. 'Of events in Enntonia, we know very little. Harbinger Talus carried few details. Token ScriptScratcher is carrying out further investigations and when the Harbinger summons me with further news, I may have to leave you again, and for that I apologise in advance. What we do know for certain is that, in their desperation, the High Council of Enntonia has committed an unspeakable act.'

He shook his head. 'It is a long story, fellow travellers. I should start at the beginning.'

Draining his mug, he looked at them both in turn. 'Enntonia, a land of towering mountains and sprawling forests, tumbling rivers and fertile farmland. On the coast of the Eastern Sea stands the city of Enntonia. This once great city has fallen on hard times and now I fear its people are in grave danger. I will speak more of this soon but first I must tell the tale of the Dragon Wars.'

Captivated, Taro Brook listened intently as the Messenger spoke.

'Many cycles of life ago, dragons roamed freely in the wilds of Enntonia. For the most part, encounters between people and the beasts were few and far between, the dragons' natural habitat being the foothills and forests of the Terra Hydra Mountains. However, with every new moon it seems man's bravery and stupidity grow in tandem. As the people spread out further into the countryside, staking claim to new land, the number of attacks and fatalities grew rapidly. Finding itself threatened, the dragon turned from hunted to hunter. And thus it came to be, the dragon had a new prey.'

Two Cups grabbed at the flask and refilled his mug.

'And so came the dawn of the Order of the Dragon Slayers. An assembly of the finest men and women in the King's Royal Guard. And their inception proved to be a great success, repelling the scaled monsters, driving them back to their mountain lair. It's fair to say that casualties were high, but then war does not come without its price. But the Slayers quickly became the pride of the land. The Order was given the royal seal of approval and brave fighters from all corners of the land were recruited to join the elite group, taking the place of those who fell in battle.'

Two Cups paused for a moment before continuing. 'But nothing ever stays the same for long. A new menace came to the land of Enntonia, an evil far greater than the scaled beast of the Terra Hydra. This menace was the Black Wizard, Osfilian. A sorcerer of great power.'

The Messenger's expression soured. 'Osfilian came to that fair land in the guise of a healer but his hideous appearance and strange healing methods quickly led to him becoming an outcast. The people shunned him. And right they were to do so, for he had come to them with evil in mind. The King, suspecting the healer's motives, ordered that he leave the city. Banished, Osfilian took refuge in caves near the Terra Hydra Mountains and there he plotted his revenge on the people of Enntonia. Dark were the days that followed.' The Messenger's words were now little more than a whisper. 'Hidden away in the caves, the fiend created a new monster. With his powers, he enslaved the dragons, and by the process of transmutation, spawned a new devil. The Black Wing, a dragon more deadly than any that went before, a beast intent on one thing alone. Destroying all that stood in its path.'

Two Cups' eyes widened as he recounted the events. 'Osfilian sent forth his new creation to wreak havoc on the land and its people. Never before had Enntonia faced such peril. The Order of the Dragon Slayers was its only hope. Men and women of honour; warriors prepared to die for the cause. They fought bravely, but their new foe was far too powerful. Even with a greatly accelerated recruiting process it quickly became obvious that their efforts to defeat the beast would be in vain. Panic filled the city's streets. Enntonia's days appeared numbered.'
Bowing his head, Two Cups fell silent.

Caught up in the tale, Taro Brook glanced across the cave at Sanna and back again. As if sensing his impatience, the Messenger lifted his head and continued.

'Often, when all hope seems gone, salvation comes to those who least expect it. When it appeared that all was lost, a stranger came to the city seeking counsel with the King. A quiet, unassuming figure, he introduced himself only as a servant of peace. Despite his doubts and fears, the King, in desperation, granted the stranger a private audience. The next morning he called a meeting of his closest advisors to tell them that, from that day forth, the stranger was to be known as the Defender of all Enntonia. Their noisy protests fell silent as the stranger entered the room. A quiet calm is said to have descended on the gathering as the stranger spoke to them all, assuring them the threat of the evil Black Wing would soon be quashed.'
Two Cups flashed a knowing smile. 'Yes, my friends, although they did not know it, the King and his entourage were being addressed by an old adversary of the Black Wizard. With the

blessing of the King, the stranger renewed his long battle with Osfilian, and in the hills and valleys of Enntonia, the two sorcerers waged their bitter war.'

'What happened?' Brook interrupted eagerly. 'What was the outcome?'

'I will not bore you with the details. To cut short a long story, the stranger triumphed. Osfilian was banished to the Basilisik Mountain, a prisoner only ever to be released by royal pardon. Only a king or queen of Enntonia, or in their stead, a governing High Council, would have the power to release him.'

'What of the dragons? The Black Wing?'

'With Osfilian's undoing, the Black Wing vanished. And since that day, dragons have never been seen in Enntonia again.'

'What about the stranger?' Taro Brook pressed. 'What happened to him?'

Reclining against the wall of the cave, Two Cups pulled his hat forward, once more covering his eyes. 'Legend has it,' he replied softly, 'that the stranger left those fair lands soon after Osfilian was banished to his mountain prison.'

Brook waited in anticipation as the silence lengthened. His patience waned quickly. 'The stranger. Who was he? And with no foe to fight, what became of the dragon slayers?'

No sound came from beneath the odd-shaped hat.

'Looks like the story's over.' Sanna unrolled the fur from her pack. 'He's fast asleep.'

CHAPTER TWENTY-FIVE

Charged with bringing order to Token ScriptScratcher's cluttered study, with his task complete, Elfin Fingle sat on the wooden footstool by the fireside and assessed the scene.

The Scribe of Bog-Mire had hidden himself away for two days, studiously poring over old maps and parchments. Elfin had never seen the room in such a state of disarray. It had taken him most of the morning to tidy up. Content with his efforts, he looked across the room. The Scribe sat quietly at his desk, quill in hand, staring blankly into space.

'The dragon slayers,' Elfin ventured quietly, hoping to engage his mentor's attention.

'What of them?' The Scribe answered without hesitation.

'I saw some of them in the Twelve Bells Tavern the other night, when I went to find Harbinger Talus. Why does he have such a low opinion of them?'

'Tell me, Elfin, do you often hear the Harbinger talk highly of anyone?'

'No.' Elfin had to concede the point. 'I don't suppose so, but he seems to hold them in greater contempt than anyone else.'

'And he is hardly alone in that. The once greatly revered Order finds little favour in Enntonia these days.'

'Why is that?'

Token ScriptScratcher put down his quill and reached for his pipe. Puffing out a circle of smoke, he watched it float lazily up to the wooden rafters.

'The Order of the Dragon Slayers,' he began slowly. 'Their fall from grace makes for a sad tale. Their sole purpose to defeat the dragon was, for many years, successful but according to accounts of the time, it was obvious that they had met their match in Osfilian's Black Wing. Without the aid of the wizard, the one known as the Defender of all Enntonia, I fear all would have been lost.' Token paused to draw on his pipe.

'Fortunately, that was not the case. Following the defeat of the Black Wing and Osfilian's banishment to the mountains, the King commanded that the Order remain in place to defend the land should the dragons ever return. I'm afraid this did them a grave injustice. As the years passed, it became clear that the threat of the dragon was long gone, and with no foe to fight, the Order lost its way. Their search for noble causes to support was a fruitless one. With the passing of the King, leaving no heir to the throne, governance of the land fell to the High Council. Judging the Order to be an unnecessary drain on treasury finances, they passed legislation which meant that all state payments to the dragon slayers must cease. However, as the Order of the Slayers could only be disbanded by royal command, it remained intact. Many of them continued to search for honourable means of income, but alas, times of peace are difficult for those trained in the arts of warfare.' Token frowned as he drew breath.

'Over time, the Order descended into anarchy. Some became bounty hunters and mercenaries; some became nothing more than common thieves and cheats. To put it bluntly, Elfin, in the eyes of most, the dragon slayer these days has little honour left. Perhaps that is why the Harbinger and many others talk so harshly of them.'

His expression softened slightly. 'I, however, must admit to having a certain amount of sympathy for them. The untimely death of the King left them victims of cruel circumstance.'

Placing his pipe down on the desk, the Scribe returned his attention to his work. Rolling the parchment, he commended Elfin on his diligent efforts. 'You have done an excellent job of tidying up. As it's a favourable day, you may take the afternoon off. Take the opportunity to enjoy the sunshine. I must take my leave; I have urgent business to attend to.'

Stamping the wax with the seal of Bog-Mire, he picked up his cloak and made for the door. 'I have an important meeting in town, Elfin, but you can inform Mrs Burrows that I shall be back in time for afternoon tea.'

The door closed behind him, leaving Elfin Fingle alone with his thoughts.

CHAPTER TWENTY-SIX

'So, Rugen, how is the new book coming along? I thought you'd have sent me another chapter to read by now.'

'It's only been a couple of days since we last spoke, Mitch.'

'Yes, I know, but I thought you writers churned work out quickly. I mean, you've got plenty of free time, it's not like a real job, is it?'

Hans Rugen held the phone at arm's length and bit his lip in frustration. Mitchell Egberts continued undeterred.

'What's the delay? It's your story. Don't you have it all planned out in advance?'

'No, not always,' Rugen corrected. 'I'm sure all writers are different, but I often find that many of my ideas come to life and grow as the process develops.'

'Really? Okay, whatever you say.' Egberts' tone was sceptical. 'You're the expert. Tell you what, I'll call you in a day or so for another update.'

Hans Rugen placed the telephone down on the desk and stared at the blank computer screen. It was almost noon, and he still hadn't switched it on. Gazing out the window of his study, he watched the trees swaying gently in the breeze.

The forest behind his cottage had been the inspiration behind his planned change of genre, but it appeared that the inspiration had gone. The tale of the walker in the woods was at a standstill; a fact he didn't see changing. Maybe he should just heed his agent's advice and stick to what he did best. His series of published crime thrillers had provided a very comfortable income, enabling him to purchase his new home; an idyllic setting to further nourish his creativity.

With a sigh, Rugen made his decision. He'd wasted enough time on a story that had no future. It was time to get on with some productive writing.

With a newly found sense of focus, he powered up his laptop. Fortunately, he had plenty of material already written for a follow-up crime novel. In only a matter of weeks his next book would be due with the publishers. His agent was beginning to get impatient.

So, it seemed, was Mitchell Egberts.

CHAPTER TWENTY-SEVEN

A chill hung in the early morning air. Far in the distance, beyond the jagged mountain peaks piercing a blanket of lingering cloud, the sky glowed with the orange hues of sunrise. Having wakened early from a troubled sleep, Taro Brook recounted the details of his vivid dreams as he and his companions climbed the track high above the Black Glass Gap. His restless night had not gone unnoticed.

'I saw that you were agitated.' Two Cups paused to take a breather. 'You say that these dreams began with a bearded figure walking among ancient standing stones?'

'Yes,' nodded Brook, 'under a moonlit sky.'

'And this figure, you say he appeared again in the dream?'

'Yes, when the dream jumped to the building in the snow-covered mountains.'

'Very interesting.' Two Cups toyed with his whiskers. 'Judging by your description, I am almost certain you saw the standing stones of Sumarren in your dreams. Remarkable, my good fellow, absolutely remarkable. And yet, I do not recognise this other building you mention. Describe it again.'

'At first, it was as if I was looking down on it from above. It stood alone, nestled high in the mountains. Inside, it looked like a grand banqueting hall. The timber roof beams were carved with symbols. The walls were covered with an array of weaponry; shields and spears; longbows and swords. There were also several wall hangings depicting battle scenes. And a long feasting table stretched almost the length of the room.'

'And at the far end of the hall,' Two Cups interrupted, 'you saw the wooden throne.'

'Yes, at least,' Brook hesitated, 'that was what it looked like.'

'And that was where you saw him again?'

'Yes, standing next to it, flanked by the two large white dogs.'

'And these dogs, you say they moved alongside you?'

'Yes, one on either side of me.'

'And then the bearded man spoke to you. Forgive my interruptions, Master Brook, but tell me again, what did he say?'

'He said he'd been waiting for my arrival, that ravens had returned to the chambers of the mountain king, and that the days of thunder were upon us.'

Messenger Two Cups clapped his hands together excitedly. 'This is incredible! Well remembered, Woodsman. This is fantastic news.'

'It is? Why?'

'The days of thunder are foretold in a prophecy of the Seer Magister. Alas, as with many of his writings, its meaning is not yet fully understood.' Two Cups fixed Brook with an inquisitive stare. 'The man in your dream, did he say anything else?'

'Yes. Just before he walked through an open doorway beyond the throne, he told me to make haste for Sumarren.'

Messenger Two Cups whooped with delight. 'Your abilities astound me, Taro Brook,' he beamed. 'Not only do you have a clear vision of the standing stones at Sumarren, but you are also then summoned there by none other than the envoy of Nallevarr.'

'Wait!' Sanna cut in. 'You think the stranger in Taro Brook's dream is the man from the frozen lands? The one that awaits us at Sumarren?'

'Indeed I do.' Two Cups grinned widely. 'Without any shadow of a doubt. It is another sign, my friends. We must continue our journey without further delay.'

They reached the top of the narrow track as the sun rose above the mountains. Ahead of them the terrain levelled; a dizzying expanse of smooth black rock stretching as far as the eye could see. Here and there, scattered patches of swirling mist floated inches above the shining surface.

'Behold! The Black Glass.' Two Cups motioned them on. 'Let us begin the traverse.'

Despite its glass-like appearance, the rock offered a secure grip. Brook's only problem was the glare of the reflected sunlight as it danced on the glistening surface.

'Best to avoid looking down,' warned Two Cups, noting his unease. 'Keep your eye fixed firmly on the horizon. The traverse is relatively straightforward but can become treacherous if one loses one's concentration.'

'Is it level all the way?' Brook shielded his eyes. 'How far to the other end?'

Two Cups chuckled his amusement. 'The duration of the traverse is best measured by the degree of difficulty you experience whilst crossing it. It appears to be flat, but we are dropping height steadily. And beware of that mist up ahead,' he cautioned. 'It looks harmless but can change quickly. Tread carefully, Woodsman, for the doorways to a countless number of worlds surround us.' He winked mischievously. 'I would regret most profoundly your untimely disappearance.'

Sanna offered her own words of advice as she passed. 'You will be fine, Taro Brook. Keep your eyes straight ahead and should you find yourself in unfamiliar surroundings, do not despair. I have every confidence you will quickly find your way back.'

Buoyed by her optimism, Brook let his mind wander to the Messenger's depiction of his dream. Had he really seen Sumarren and the stranger they believed was waiting there for them? He doubted it. Far as he was concerned, dreams held no true meaning or relevance.

Realising he was now surrounded by the mist, he drew to a sudden halt. With his visibility limited to no more than a few feet, he had lost all trace of his companions. Disorientated, berating his lack of concentration, he called out, but heard no response. The eerie silence was unnerving. He had to find them, but which way should he go? Should he wait for the mist to clear? Or wait for them to find him? The option of doing nothing didn't appeal. Deciding to take the initiative, he began walking.

Moments later, as the visibility began to improve, he saw daylight ahead. His decision to act had been vindicated. But his hopes were quickly dashed. Instead of seeing his companions waiting in the sunshine, as the mist dispersed, Brook found

himself in a snowbound forest. He shivered as his breath hung in the cold air. He scanned his surroundings nervously.
Where was he? And how did he come to be here?

Startled by a sudden burst of activity in the trees behind, he spun round to see a galloping horse bearing down on him. Throwing himself sideways to avoid collision, he caught a glimpse of the rider as the horse raced by. The sight of the hooded rider's skeletal face chilled him to the bone.
Scrambling to his feet, boots crunching loudly in the crisp snow, he made for the cover of the trees. His heart thumped loudly as he waited, anxiously fearing the worst. There was little doubt in his mind about the identity of the rider. What would become of him if it returned? He was in grave danger. As his panicked state heightened, his eyes settled on his footprints in the snow. He wasn't thinking straight. If the rider returned, his tracks would lead it right to him. He wasn't safe here.
Bounding from the trees, he hurriedly retraced his tracks, listening for the sound of the rider's return. Why wasn't it coming back? It must have seen him. Stopping abruptly, he stared down at the snow in astonishment.
On either side of his tracks, a trail of large paw prints mirrored his every step. He looked round anxiously. Was something other than the rider stalking him? His eyes darted nervously among the trees. He had to get out of here.

Picking up pace, he followed his trail until it came to a sudden stop. With one final anxious look over his shoulder, he plunged headlong into the swirling mist and left the snow-covered forest behind. Seconds later, the mist cleared, and he found himself in sunshine, standing once again on the shining black rock.

Sanna sat cross-legged as if in meditation. At the sound of his approach, she looked up from her thoughts and greeted him matter-of-factly. 'You're back.'

'Back? How long was I gone?'

'Not long.' She got to her feet.

'Where was I?' The Messenger's warning flashed through his mind. 'Another world?'

'I don't know. What did it look like?'

'It was a forest, in the snow.' Brook quickly described the scene.

Sanna shrugged her shoulders. 'It could have been anywhere.'

'I think I saw a Raider.' He shuddered at the thought of the rider. 'Do you think that's possible?'

'All things are possible, Taro Brook. Did it see you?'

'It must have, it rode straight past me. And yet didn't stop and didn't come back.'

'Then luck was on your side.'

An understatement. 'Was it an Indentation? Like the old man? He didn't see me either.'

'You think too much, Taro Brook. All that matters is that you returned safely, just like I said you would. Let's go, Scaraven will be waiting for us.'

As they walked, the sun continued its kaleidoscopic dance on the landscape. They found the Messenger sitting on a flat slab of rock, a mug of tea in one hand, and waving a small wicker basket in the other.

A broad smile lit up his face as he watched them approach.

'Ah! There you are. You returned safely, Woodsman. Well done, Sir. Now, is anyone hungry?' He emptied the contents of the basket. 'While I waited, I took the opportunity to replenish our supplies. Freshly baked bread, cheese, and oat biscuits.' He smacked his lips in anticipation. 'We must keep our strength up for the journey ahead.' Munching a mouthful of biscuit, he eyed Brook with interest. 'Tell me about your drift experience. What did you see?'

Brook had it in his mind to ask how the Messenger had come by the bread and cheese in such a remote landscape, but instead, he relayed the events of his short time in the snow-covered forest.

'Interesting.' Two Cups offered his thoughts in response. 'There would be cause for concern if the rider were as you suspected. Tell me, did you see anything else of interest?'

Brook hesitated. 'There was something,' he began warily, 'something strange, but probably just a coincidence.'

'Go on,' encouraged Two Cups.

'I saw large paw prints in the snow, two sets of them, beside my tracks. Yet I saw no sign of what could have made them.'

Two Cups snorted his delight. 'There's no such thing as coincidence, Master Brook. You dream of two snow dogs, standing guard by your side. You then see huge paw prints shadowing your own footsteps in the snow, and you call it a coincidence?' Grabbing hold of the flask, he hurriedly refilled his mug. 'Come now, Woodsman, even a man with an imagination as reserved as yours must concede this much. Two ghostly snow dogs watch over you, their purpose and origin remain a mystery for now, but of one thing I am more certain than ever. It appears you were meant to take a walk in Farnwaar Forest that day, and that you were meant to discover your new gift. It was no accident, and no coincidence. Synchronicity is at work here, my friend.' He fixed Brook with a determined stare, his eyebrows twitching for effect. 'Man's greatest wish is to know his destiny, Taro Brook. I believe you will know yours very soon.'

Tapping the ground enthusiastically with his stick, he urged them to make their preparations. 'Take as much food as you wish but leave the basket for another hungry traveller. Let us continue our quest for answers.' He grinned widely. 'Don't you just love an adventure? My belly is full, my heart is light, and my over-active sense of inquisitiveness nags at me constantly. Onwards, my friends, the Pinnacles of Sorrow await.'

CHAPTER TWENTY-EIGHT

'The thing I don't understand,' Elfin Fingle wiped the crumbs from his chin, 'is why the dragon slayers are still around. Dragons haven't been seen in Enntonia in ages, and Osfilian was banished centuries ago.'

Mrs Burrows tapped the table disapprovingly with her rolling pin. 'We'll have no mention of that name in my kitchen, Elfin. And what is this sudden interest in the dragon slayers? You shouldn't be concerning yourself with the likes of them. No good will come of it, you hear?'

'I saw some of them the other night in the Twelve Bells Tavern, when I met up with Harbinger Talus.'

'The Twelve Bells?' She threw him a look of disapproval. 'What were you doing in such a place? And with the Harbinger of all people.'

Elfin took another mouthful of freshly baked scone. 'In my defence, I was carrying out the Scribe's orders.'

'Don't be talking with your mouth full. It's rude!' She continued her lecture as she bustled round the kitchen. 'Honestly, I do wonder sometimes. Not that I'm one to question the word of the Scribe, but dear me, the Twelve Bells Tavern? What a place to be sending you to. And what business did he have with the Harbinger at such a late hour?'

'Urgent business,' replied Elfin, picking at his teeth. 'We had to meet at the Western Gate, something to do with the Harbinger going on an important errand...' Recalling his pledge of secrecy, he stopped mid-sentence and quickly changed the subject. 'These are delicious, Mrs B.' he smiled, helping himself to another scone. Munching greedily, his thoughts drifted back to the late-night conversation with the Scribe following their return from the Western Gate. What fate awaited them all, he wondered, if the High Council's envoy had successfully delivered the summons?

'Those slayers are bad news,' she continued. 'Cursed they are, least that's the way I heard it. The Defender himself cast a spell on them, that's what some folks say. Some kind of immortality they reckon, to keep them around in case the dragons ever return. Unnatural, that's what they are. Just plain wrong.'

A frustrated groan came from the armchair by the fireside as Mr Burrows stirred from his lunchtime snooze and moved wearily towards the table.

'Don't be listening to her, Master Fingle,' he yawned. 'That's nought but old wives' tales. Them slayers, untrustworthy as they may be, are no more unnatural than the scones you're devouring. There's a simple explanation why their Order still exists. Royal command decreed that every slayer's offspring be sworn to join the ranks of the Order, every generation same as the one before. They have no option, no choice. Some are even given no birth name, and instead are known only by number.' He smiled sympathetically in the direction of his wife as he helped himself to a scone from the table. 'There is some truth in your words, woman, I'll grant you. Them slayers are indeed cursed for it is a cruel existence they lead, and you'd do best to pay heed, Elfin, no good will come from any involvement with them.' Taking a mouthful of scone, he lumbered towards the door. 'You bake a fine scone, dear wife.'

As Elfin finished his scone and slurped down the last of his tea, Mrs Burrows gestured towards him with the rolling pin. 'Now then, Elfin, if the Scribe has given you some free time, I suggest you go and make the most of it. If you hang around here, that old husband of mine will only find chores for you to do.' She winked at him. 'Be off and have fun.'

Thanking her, Elfin hurried out into the afternoon sun.

CHAPTER TWENTY-NINE

Shielding his eyes from the sun, Procrastinator Vardoger scanned the barren wasteland. As their jeep trundled further into the desert he looked on in wonder as the towering Pyramids of Saa loomed ever closer. He had seen many photographs of the ancient structures but seeing them for real, at such close range, was an entirely different proposition. Marvelling at the sight, he turned to his guide.

'How old are they, Ta-nish?'

'Experts claim they were built around nine thousand years ago,' she replied. 'The identity of their creators is unknown, much like their purpose.' She pulled the jeep to a halt and lifted her gaze to the skies. 'The desert people consider them to be remnants left by the Star Gods.'

'A fitting description.' Vardoger agreed. 'Can we go inside?'

'The main outer chamber of the central pyramid is easily accessible,' she replied cautiously. 'But I suggest we continue with our journey. The settlement you wish to visit is still some distance away. Perhaps you can visit the chamber on our return trip.'

Vardoger nodded his agreement and as the jeep sped across the desert he recalled the chain of events which had taken him to the most inhospitable part of the Eight States. During dinner with Kalina, she had remarked on his new-found fixation with the proposed desalination of the Dead Lakes and the possible implications for the surrounding area. She had suggested that he take advantage of a week-long recess in government by taking a trip to the desert lands. Seeing things for himself at close quarters would give him a better understanding of the situation. On the other hand, it might bring his interest in the matter to an end. Either way it would help ease his burden of indecision regarding the proposal.

Following much debate, inner turmoil, and the usual helping of gentle feminine persuasion, Vardoger had agreed to the idea and so, the next morning after breakfast, Kalina had accompanied him to the quayside, ensured his passage on the ship, and bade him farewell.

Following the hastily arranged two-day voyage from Craton, Vardoger had found himself in the bustling town of Khensu, capital of the Dead Lakes State. As he disembarked from the ship, staring in confusion at the throng of people on the quayside, a dark-haired woman with piercing eyes had approached him, introducing herself as Ta-nish, his guide for the duration of his visit. Escorting him to his pre-booked accommodation, she informed him that they would be leaving early the next morning for the desert settlement of Kiva. She'd told him everything was arranged, his assistant Kalina Tronn had taken care of all the preparations.

Kalina, he smiled, what would he do without her?

As the jeep drew to a halt, his thoughts jumped back to the present. Switching off the engine, Ta-nish jumped down on to the sand.

'We are here.'

Vardoger looked all around. 'There are no buildings here. I thought we were coming to a settlement. There is nothing here.'

'This is Kiva,' she pointed to their left. 'Do not dismiss that which your eyes fail to see.' Two crumbling pillars of sandstone guarded a narrow entrance at the bottom of a great bank of sand. Vardoger looked hesitantly at his guide. She nodded in return. 'That is the entrance to the underground settlement of Kiva. And there, some of its inhabitants.'

Vardoger looked on in astonishment as a group of people began to emerge into the sunshine.

'They spend most of their lives underground to avoid the relentless heat of the sun,' Ta-nish continued. 'Do not be alarmed by their appearance.'

'Why? What do you mean?' As the people drew closer, Vardoger began to understand her warning. 'In the name of Craton,' he whispered. 'What is wrong with them?'

His guide moved closer. 'Do not be afraid,' she said quietly. 'No harm will come to you. I will act as your translator.'

'No.' Vardoger felt a rush of panic. 'We should leave this place now.'

'Stay,' she hissed. 'You wished to experience the wrath of the Dead Lakes Desert for yourself. Do not lose heart now.'

He watched in growing revulsion as the people gathered round the jeep. Their withered skin was cracked and blistered.

Several bore features almost beyond recognition. It was as if their faces were formed from melted candle wax.

'Mutants!'

'They are not mutants,' snapped Ta-nish. 'Their physical appearance, which you find so unsettling, is a result of the harsh environment in which they live.'

'The sun did this to them?'

'The sun is only part of the problem here. For generations, these people have been drinking the polluted water of the Dead Lakes. Their precautions are simply not adequate. Kiva is just one of the many underground settlements and, because of their ill-fortune, these people are shunned by the desert tribes and the inhabitants of Khensu.'

'This isn't possible,' Vardoger countered. 'We know nothing of these settlements, or their inhabitants. We have knowledge of Khensu, and several of the other desert townships. We know of their water shortages, and the need to improve things, but this is intolerable.'

Ta-nish shook her head. 'It comes as no surprise that you know nothing of them. These people are never talked about. They are driven underground and forgotten.'

Vardoger watched warily as a little girl approached, holding out her withered hand.

Ta-nish sensed his discomfort. 'She wishes only to greet you.'

Reluctantly taking hold of the girl's hand, he looked on in wonder as a smile softened her disfigured face. As Ta-nish spoke with several of the others in a strange tongue, the little girl led

Vardoger into the centre of the converging group. To his surprise, one by one, they began to kneel before him.

'What are they doing?'

'They are paying you their respects.' His guide looked on with growing interest as murmurs of anticipation echoed among the group. Pointing excitedly, they talked quickly in their strange language, all the while gesturing to Ta-nish. She nodded and held up her hand to call for quiet.

'What is it?' Vardoger asked warily. 'What are they saying?'

'You must first understand,' she began slowly, 'in spite of all their hardships, these people are a peace-loving tribe. They are deeply spiritual and very superstitious.' She paused, as if trying to choose her words carefully. 'They say your appearance bears a striking resemblance to one mentioned often in their beliefs.'

As if growing in courage, several of the group edged slowly towards him. One from the group gestured again at Vardoger and spoke to Ta-nish again in the strange language.

'What is he saying now?' Vardoger's unease grew.

His guide measured her words carefully. 'He says they would be humbled if the messenger of the Sky Gods would honour them by spending a short while with them in their underground home.'

Left speechless, Vardoger stared at her in wonder.

'There is nothing to fear,' she repeated. 'I will accompany you.'

Vardoger's journey underground moved him beyond words. The little girl held his hand as she led him through an unseen world far below the desert surface. The group following closely behind grew steadily larger as more joined the procession, some pointing and chattering excitedly, others content to follow in quiet awe of their unexpected visitor. Aided by sporadic shafts of sunlight from above, Vardoger's eyes slowly became accustomed to the dimly lit tunnels and caverns the people of Kiva called home.

Touched by the warm welcome he received from the people for whom life offered nothing but hardship and suffering, he couldn't help but feel embarrassed when his thoughts drifted to his own life, back home in the lavish luxuries of Craton City.

He asked many questions, and, with Ta-nish translating, he learned much from the people with the wax-like skin. When they returned to the surface, and the glaring heat of the desert sun, he knew that his experience had opened his eyes to a whole new world. As they exchanged their goodbyes, the little girl smiled and spoke for the first time.

Vardoger turned to his guide. 'What did she say?'

'Her name is Ketoh.' Ta-nish responded. 'She thanks you for coming. They look forward to seeing you again when you return with the gift of the Gods.'

'What in Craton does she mean by that?'

Shrugging her shoulders, his guide climbed up into the jeep. 'I do not know. Come, it's now time for us to leave.'

As they pulled away, he watched and waved as the people of Kiva slipped from view in the hazy distance. Feeling both shocked and moved by the visit, Vardoger quietly contemplated the little girl's words and the bizarre coincidence that his appearance would be perceived the way it had been by the desert people. For all his doubts, however, one thing was certain. Vardoger had never been surer about anything in his life. His visit to Kiva had convinced him further of the desperate need to bring the proposal of the oil and gas syndicate to fruition.

As they sped across the desert, Ta-nish broke the silence between them. 'You are a mystery to me, man of government. How is it that one who lives in such splendour in the sparkling city of Craton can find interest in the desperate plight of the people of Kiva? What is it that brought you here to the desert lands?'

'A sense of duty, I suppose,' Vardoger replied modestly. 'I am a man of government, as you rightly say.'

'Governments care for no one but themselves.' she hissed.

Undeterred, Vardoger briefly told her about the visit he had received from the fuel syndicate and their proposal to desalinate the Dead Lakes. Her mood changed quickly.

'Could this happen? Is it possible?'

'They assure me that it is possible, and I'm led to believe the process is relatively uncomplicated.'

Ta-nish struggled to hide her disbelief. 'If such a process exists, why, in a world two thirds of which is covered by seas and oceans, do thousands die every twelve moons from thirst or lack of safe drinking water?'

Vardoger could offer no response. He'd been struggling with the very same question for the past few weeks. An uneasy silence grew between them as they drove towards the setting sun.

A short while later, Ta-nish spoke again. 'We will soon be back at the pyramids. Do you still wish to enter the chamber?'

Vardoger rubbed his chin thoughtfully. 'I'm not sure. Do you think I should?'

'That is not my decision to make.'

'I appreciate that, but I would like your opinion.'

'A guide is trained to do as instructed. I am paid only to escort and translate, and to ensure your safety while you are here.'

Vardoger shook his head in confusion. He really wanted to see inside the pyramid, but a nagging doubt screamed caution. The thought of making a decision frightened him more than the prospect of entering the unknown. 'I can't decide.'

Ta-nish scowled her annoyance. 'If I were being paid extra to help you with your indecisive ways, I would be happy to help. However, as I am not…'

Vardoger slapped his hand down on the dashboard of the jeep. 'That's it! You may just have found the solution. We will have to confirm it on our return to Khensu, but I don't foresee there being a problem. If you'll make the decision for me, I'll recommend strongly that your fee is doubled.'

CHAPTER THIRTY

The dragon slayer known only as Twelve Seven Two woke from his fragmented sleep with a start. The bed sheet clung to his sweat-soaked body. Throwing it back, he rose from the bed and crossed the room. Wiping the windowpane with the palm of his hand, he looked out into the night. In stark contrast to his nightmares, the world outside lay quiet and peaceful. Pacing the wooden floor, he shivered as the images replayed in his head.

Dragons! Monstrous black beasts, the height of five tall trees or more. Alongside his fellow Slayers, he'd been locked in a losing battle against the winged demons. There was no hope against such evil.

Twelve Seven Two sat on the bed and put his head in his hands. The dreams were becoming more prevalent and ever more disturbing. Barely a night went by without nightmares filled with visions of the huge, fire-breathing monsters and the scenes of destruction left in their wake.

The dreams seemed so real. How could this be? Though born into the life of a dragon slayer, Twelve Seven Two had never faced the beast in combat. Neither he nor any of his comrades had ever even set eyes on a dragon. Hardly surprising, given that dragons hadn't been seen in Enntonia for centuries.

The night before last had seen the only break in the repetitive sequence. And whilst not disturbing, it had perhaps been the strangest dream of all. As part of a procession of Slayers, he'd walked the crowd-lined streets of the city, revelling in the adulation of the cheering masses. Twelve Seven Two sighed. Dragon slayers were despised by the people of Enntonia. Shunned and ridiculed, the Order was greeted with a hostile reception almost everywhere they went. If legends were to be believed, there was a time, long ago, when the Slayers were the toast of the nation but, like the winged beasts, those days were long gone and were not expected to ever return.

With no explanation to his troubled mind in sight, he crawled back under the covers. Closing his eyes, he hoped for a few hours of trouble-free sleep.

He hoped in vain.

CHAPTER THIRTY-ONE

"Man's greatest wish is to know his destiny. I believe you will know yours very soon."

Taro Brook pondered the Messenger's words. He'd been puzzling over them for what seemed like hours and was still no nearer an understanding to their meaning. Switching back to the present, he watched as the Messenger clambered down from the ledge.

'What did you hear, Scaraven?' Sanna broke the silence.

'Whispers in the wind, my friends.' Clearly distracted, he repeated his vague response. 'Whispers in the wind.' With a tap of his stick, he continued walking. Sanna glanced in Brook's direction. It appeared that, for the time being, no further explanation would follow.

They had been negotiating the descent of a steep-sided gully when Two Cups had announced that he must listen to the wind and, without further discussion, had clambered up the rocks to find a suitable place for meditation. Now, mumbling quietly to himself in his strange language, he continued down the track, inviting the others to follow with a wave of his stick.

At the bottom of the steep slope the ground levelled out to grassy moorland. The soft underfoot conditions made for pleasant walking. Taro Brook took the opportunity to further indulge his curiosity. 'You've told us about Osfilian being recalled, but you have not yet said what it could mean.'

Two Cups spun round swiftly. A frown etched his face. 'If Osfilian is free to do his worst, it could mean the end of all things for the people of Enntonia. And the implications could spread further still.'

'This place you talk about, Enntonia. Where is it?'

Two Cups waved a finger in the air. 'It is all around you, Woodsman. It moves constantly, as all other worlds do. The gateways to them are rarely found in the same place twice.' He snorted with delight at the sight of Sanna walking barefoot across the soft terrain. 'Aha, the spirit of the Dryad walks with you, Sanna.'

Brook looked at him questioningly. 'Dryad?'

'The Dryad; some say a female spirit of nature. A protector of the forests and the wild places. Perhaps with your new gift of perception you will now become more aware of her.'

A short time later they emerged from a copse of birch trees into a spectacular landscape dominated by a succession of tall weirdly shaped pinnacles of grey rock set amidst a sea of scattered boulders.

Brook stared at the scene in awe as Two Cups rummaged for his flask.

'The Pinnacles of Sorrow, Woodsman. Some say they are lost souls, watching over the fields where they fell in battle. Others would have you believe they are merely towers of basalt rock, left marooned when the land slipped many cycles of life ago.' The Messenger slurped at his tea. 'You can decide for yourself, but I caution you to take great care when walking among the pinnacles. It is my belief that they are the Gatekeepers, standing guard over the entrances to many different worlds.' He chuckled as he held out the flask. 'Have some tea, my friend. A short rest, then we must be on our way again. Negotiating the boulder field will be thirsty work.'

Messenger Two Cups led the way, humming quietly to himself. Taro Brook followed closely behind Sanna, who had put her boots back on to counter the rocky surface. On the few occasions they spoke, an eerie echo answered them, whispering repeatedly among the rock towers. Losing his footing several times on the strewn boulders, Brook opted to keep his eyes on the ground, instead stopping every now and again to marvel at the stone monoliths towering high above his head.

A short while later, he drew to a halt as the sound of falling rocks caught his attention. Moving towards the nearest pinnacle he heard another noise; the sound of rocks being dragged. He glanced ahead to where Two Cups and Sanna chatted, unaware of the disturbance behind. There was no need to alert them. There was no mist, no danger of them becoming separated. He decided to investigate the noise for himself.

As the sound grew louder, his vision suddenly began to blur. Seconds later, he was plunged into darkness.

Holding his breath, he waited for his eyes to adjust to the constricting gloom. Reaching out in desperation, his fingers touched cold stone on either side. Fumbling in the darkness, feeling his way gingerly, he took a few tentative steps forward.

Crouching low, he shuffled awkwardly along the narrow passageway in search of daylight and a way out.

CHAPTER THIRTY-TWO

Procrastinator Vardoger gazed in wonder at the interior of the pyramid chamber. The ancient walls were adorned with countless hieroglyphs, the strange symbols a reminder of a bygone age; secret messages left behind by a race of beings whose very existence was still shrouded in mystery thousands of years after their disappearance.

As his eyes grew accustomed to the half-light, his gaze settled on a small flight of steps leading down to an opening in the far corner of the chamber. With his curiosity aroused, he hurried across the chamber, descended the short stairway, and peered inside. At the far end of a cramped passageway, a small ray of light blinked invitingly. Squeezing himself into the narrow space, he crouched down. The walls closed in quickly as a wave of claustrophobia threatened to consume him. Resisting the urge to turn and flee, he waited for the feeling to pass, then made his way slowly along the tunnel towards the light.

At the end of the passageway, there was ample headroom for him to stand. A small section of the wall had fallen in, revealing slithers of daylight from beyond. Vardoger inspected the wall warily. It seemed to be much brighter on the far side of the wall than it had been when he'd left Ta-nish waiting by the jeep. Intrigued, he began moving the fallen stones, but he'd only removed only a few handfuls when another section of the wall gave way and fell backwards, blocking the light from beyond, leaving him shrouded in darkness.

Panic quickly set in.

His heart raced as he reached out in the darkness.

Which direction had he come from? Which way should he go? Left or right? One would lead back to the chamber, back to safety; the other would lead further into the inner depths of the ancient structure. He had to make a decision. Left or right? Which was it to be?

Racked by despair, Vardoger waited in the darkness, holding his head in his hands. He had to move. Waiting wasn't an option. He had to move, he had to do it now. Fumbling blindly, his hands reached out to find the walls of the tunnel. Crouching down, he spurred himself forward.

With a swelling sense of achievement, he saw a faint circle of light ahead, becoming larger and brighter with every step he took. Moments later, he stumbled free from the tunnel. With a rush of relief, he hurried up the steps, crossed the chamber floor, and marched quickly out into the warm evening sun.

'Finally!' Her voice interrupted his thoughts. 'I was beginning to think you had got lost in there.'

He turned to face her. She looked familiar and yet... Shaking the doubt from his head, he walked towards the jeep and climbed in beside her.

'Is everything all right, man of government?'

'Everything is fine, Ta-nish,' he replied. 'We should be getting back to Khensu; the day draws to a close and my ship back to Craton leaves early in the morning.'

Vardoger's guide eyed him warily as she fired the jeep's engine into life. His decisive response confirmed her suspicions.

All was not well with the man from Craton.

CHAPTER THIRTY-THREE

Messenger Two Cups and Sanna Vrai watched silently from the lengthening shadow of the rock tower. Despite their best efforts, their search had been in vain. They'd found no trace of Taro Brook. The breach through which he had slipped from view still eluded them.

Accepting defeat, they were faced with no alternative but to wait, in the faint hope he would find his own way back to safety.

The likelihood of such an outcome faded with every passing moment. Brook had returned from his previous drift in the snowbound forest almost immediately and, whilst that gateway had been clearly obvious to Two Cups and Sanna, with the daylight fast receding, their present predicament was one of great concern to them both.

Sanna scanned the surroundings anxiously.

'I just don't understand why neither of us can see it.'

'It is a strange one,' Two Cups replied, 'perhaps it's down to the influence of the Pinnacles.'

'How long should we wait?'

The Messenger frowned as he turned to her. He stroked his whiskers in contemplation. 'We'll wait until the sun dips behind the last of the pinnacles. I fear it would not be safe to stay any longer. If the gateway hasn't offered clues to its whereabouts by then, I'm afraid he will be beyond our help.' He whispered a further word of warning. 'One thing I do know for certain. By night, this place offers sanctuary to no one. We must leave before darkness falls.'

CHAPTER THIRTY-FOUR

Tybor Barkal watched the momentum of the media circus gather pace from his sanctuary in the Boneyard Bar. The giant television screen flashed with constant updates from the Central News Agency. The leaders of all the great nations were assembling in the city of Sahropa for a summit many claimed would herald a new dawn of peace, a forging of new alliances, and greatly improved international relations.

The opening ceremony of the World Peace Convention was still three days away but Barkal's interest in the whole thing was already waning to the point of complete boredom. In truth, he was distracted. He found it difficult to concentrate on anything whilst hanging around waiting for Senator Sobek to contact him. His arrangement with the statesman was really getting him down. He longed for the day when it would be at an end.

The woman behind the bar placed another chilled bottle of beer in front of him and grinned. 'I didn't think politics was your thing, Tybor.'

'It isn't, Sina,' he replied blankly. 'Politics does the same for me as television. It rots my brain and gives me nightmares. You'd be doing me a favour if you switched the damned thing off.' He gazed round the empty room. 'It's awful quiet in here today. Where is everyone?'

Moving from behind the bar, she pushed a pool cue towards him. 'I'm not complaining.' She prodded his arm playfully. 'Gives me the opportunity to give you another lesson. That is if you're up to the challenge?'

'Set it up,' he grinned. 'Loser buys the next beers.' He wandered across to the audio selection booth, keyed in his usual selection, and sauntered back towards the pool table. Taking a mouthful of beer, he made the decision to push all thoughts of Senator Sobek from his mind.

With good tunes pounding from the sound system, an endless supply of chilled beer, and the obvious womanly charms of his pool opponent to keep him occupied, Tybor Barkal came to the conclusion that, after a slow start, his day was definitely starting to pick up. Draining his bottle, he sighed contentedly. He felt better already.

CHAPTER THIRTY-FIVE

Lost in his thoughts, Procrastinator Vardoger stared blankly out the window of his private chambers. The city of Craton sparkled gloriously in the early morning sunshine.

'Is everything all right, Procrastinator? You seem somewhat preoccupied.'

Dragged back to his senses, Vardoger turned to apologise. 'Forgive my dreadful manners, old friend. What were you saying?'

Jarl Sere, Chief of Internal Affairs, rose stiffly from the chair. 'I hope you don't take offence at this, Procrastinator, but you don't appear to be yourself lately. Is there anything troubling you? Anything you'd like to talk about?'

Vardoger shrugged his denial. 'All is well, Jarl.' Wary of the old man's attentive stare, he offered his excuse. 'I'll admit to being somewhat distracted of late, but it has been a busy time since my return from the desert lands. Perhaps I am just tired.'

'Perhaps. You have been very busy, my friend. Indeed, your work schedule was something I wanted to discuss with you. That is, if you had a few further moments to spare?'

Vardoger waved a hand in protest.

'I'm afraid I am rather busy at the moment. There is still much to be done. Is there anything else you need from me to proceed with the matter in hand?'

Shaking his head in disappointment, Jarl Sere sighed. 'I believe all necessary documentation is in place for the desalination process of the Dead Lakes to begin.'

'Excellent. In that case, may I suggest we bring our meeting to a close?'

Vardoger's relief at avoiding any further inquisition was short-lived. With a gentle knock on the door, Kalina Tronn entered the room.

'Gentlemen,' she smiled. 'I've brought refreshments. I hope that meets with your approval?'

Lifted by her appearance, Vardoger's concerns eased. He crossed the room to greet her as she placed the crystal decanter and glasses on the table. 'Wonderful, Kalina, thank you.' Taking her by the hand, he glanced at the sparkling diamond ring on her finger and kissed her on the cheek. Kalina returned the smile before casting an anxious glance in Jarl Sere's direction. Smiling again at Vardoger, she then quietly made her exit.

Vardoger flushed with pride. He felt so blessed by the recent turn of events. His proposal of life companionship following his return from the desert lands had taken them both by surprise. The decision had been the easiest of his life but, whilst overjoyed by the outcome, the unusual nature of his actions were now beginning to trouble him. Something had happened to him; something had changed. He knew it, he suspected Kalina knew it, and it appeared Jarl Sere knew it too.

'She's a wonderful woman, Vardoger. You chose well for a life companion, but you must see that she is worried.' The old man's expression grew serious. 'It goes without saying that your new decisive streak pleased her beyond words when you proposed, but Kalina is concerned about you, as I am. You have a promising future together, but I fear you may be putting it all at risk with your recent assertive manner. I beg you, please don't let the Assembly find reason to remove you from your position.'

Vardoger eyed his colleague blankly. 'Whatever do you mean?'

'Come now, Vardoger. It's not only Kalina and I who have noticed the change in your behaviour these thirty days since your return from the desert. The Inner Chamber grows uneasy, my friend. They have little or no desire to retain the services of a Procrastinator who fails to procrastinate! Even I must admit to hesitation when using the title around you these days. You must find a way to curb your newfound drive and enthusiasm. If you don't, I fear your position could well become untenable.'

Vardoger's head spun. Yes, something had changed in his behaviour since his return from the desert, but he didn't know why.

Jarl Sere sensed his growing frustration. 'Vardoger, what in the name of Craton happened to you out there in the desert? Ten days from now, Kalina and you will become life companions under Craton law. Whatever has happened, you owe it to her to sort it out before your world comes crashing down around you.'

Shaken by his colleague's heartfelt appeal, Vardoger refilled the brandy glasses and walked to the window. Draining the glass in one mouthful, he watched the sunlight dance on the sea. His confusion slowly began to clear. The solution was simple. Why, he wondered, had it not occurred to him until now? Turning away from the window, he shared his conclusion.

'My friend, you are right, and I thank you most sincerely for your honest words of wisdom and support. Your concern is greatly appreciated. Yes, something did happen to me out there, what it was I do not know, but now that the process for the desalination of the Dead Lakes is under way, it is time to do what must be done. I must return to the desert lands.'

Stunned by Vardoger's response, Jarl Sere quietly nodded his agreement. Things were worse than he'd feared. Never before had he heard his colleague talk in such a decisive manner. Something clearly had to done, and if a return trip to the desert was what was needed to save his friend's political career, then so be it.

'If that is what you feel you must do. But can I ask why?'

'To be honest, the reason eludes me,' Vardoger frowned as he refilled their glasses. 'But this much I do know. I must return to the desert lands and revisit the Pyramids of Saa.'

CHAPTER THIRTY-SIX

As the sun dropped behind the great pinnacles, Messenger Two Cups rose from his quiet contemplation. 'Sanna, I'm afraid we must leave. Taro Brook is beyond our help, for now, at least.'

Nodding her agreement, she got to her feet. As she glanced towards the setting sun she saw a faint glimmer of light at the foot of one of the silhouetted rock towers. 'I see something, Scaraven. There may be an opening.' She broke into a run. As she neared the pinnacle, she saw the rock change appearance. 'I see it. I'm going through.'

With no time to join her, Two Cups shouted his words of encouragement. 'Take care, Sanna Vrai. We will meet again at the head of the Enchanted Pass.'

As she waved her acknowledgement, she disappeared from view.

Two Cups cackled his delight. 'Once more unto the breach!'

Packing his flask, he began his own progress across the rocky terrain.

As he moved past the rock towers, a sound of movement from behind brought him to a sudden stop. He was being followed. Turning to face his pursuers, he scowled his contempt.

Three deformed figures staggered into view. Bent and haggard, they dragged their contorted limbs slowly from the cover of the rocks.

'Stone ghouls!' It was time to make a hasty exit. Two Cups drew the small glass sphere from his pocket. Raising the orb above his head, he whispered his incantation quietly under his breath.

His three followers grunted in frustration as their quarry vanished before their eyes.

CHAPTER THIRTY-SEVEN

'Do you want the potion or not?'

'What? What did you say?'

'The potion. Do you want it?'

Sanna's eyes flitted quickly round the cluttered candlelit room before settling again on the old man's wrinkled face. Least, she thought it was a man; the haggard features made it hard to tell one way or the other. 'How much did you say?'

'Nine dragyr.'

'That seems excessive.'

'It's the going rate, and you've never complained before.'

'Mugwort grows freely on the hillside,' scoffed Sanna. 'Maybe I'll just go pick some myself, make my own salve and keep my money.'

'Fool!' The hook-nosed apothecary snatched the small bottle from the gnarled countertop. 'Mugwort alone does nothing for your ailment. Devil's Eye potion is a compound of many elements, none of which is easily come by. I've heard enough. There's plenty folks happy to pay fair price for my labours. Be gone and don't let your cursed shadow darken my door again.'
Sanna's protests died quietly in her throat as she felt the cold touch of steel on her shoulder. 'Escort this low-life off the

premises, Laris.' The hunch-backed figure disappeared amongst the overfilled shelves.

Prompting Sanna from behind with his blade, the unseen Laris ushered her briskly towards the exit and out into the night. Offering a derisory farewell of his own, he slammed the door closed behind her.

Resisting the urge to throw something at the steamed-up window, she turned away with a shiver. Snow lay thick on the ground; an icy wind chilled the night sky, whipping the falling flakes into a swirling frenzy. Collecting her thoughts, she gauged her surroundings. She stood in a narrow alleyway flanked on either side by overhanging, ramshackle timber buildings. Where was this place? Was Taro Brook here?

She eyed her dishevelled longcoat disapprovingly. The tattered knee-high boots, though long past their best, would at least be of some use against the weather conditions. Pulling up the hood of the coat, she set off through the snow in search of answers.

Turning right onto a wider lane she saw a group of drunken revellers spill out into the night from a noisy ale house. Drawn towards the bright light, the promise of a warm fire, and the lure of red wine, she stopped to examine the strange text on the weather-beaten, wooden facade. The free-flowing script meant nothing to her; the hand-painted depiction of the ten and two bells appeared obvious enough. Patting snow from her coat, she pulled back the hood and made her way inside.

Glancing round the crowded room, her attention settled on a group of rough looking individuals dressed in similar fashion to herself. Two of the men signalled their recognition in her direction. Her decision was made; it was time to find out her identity in this strange land.

'Ten Six Nine.' The burly unshaven man at the centre of the group barked his welcome as she neared the fireside. 'Glad you could join us.'

'General,' she barely recognised the sound of her own voice. 'On a night like this, it seemed as good a place as any.'

The others nodded as she glanced at each of them in turn. A fleeting look was all she needed; certain that Taro Brook was not among them she scanned the bustling tavern.

Her observations hovered for a moment on an odd couple seated in the far corner of the room. A small figure, with decidedly pointed ears, peered warily over his shoulder before returning his attention to his ale. Judging by the lingering flakes of snow on his green cloak he'd probably arrived only moments before her. His companion, a huge bulk of a man shrouded in black, cut a menacing figure as he leered in her direction and spat onto the sawdust floor.

'Drink up, woman.' The General thrust a bottle of wine into her hand.

Sanna held the bottle to her lips and drank thirstily.

'You all right, Ten Six Nine?' One of the men stared her way as he wiped beer froth from his greying beard. 'You seem a bit on edge.'

'Shoulder is hurting,' she replied without thinking. 'I didn't get my salve. Bit of a misunderstanding with Old Hunchback the herbalist.'

'You want to be careful with that Devil's Eye potion.' The General sneered. 'It's got damned potent hallucinogenic qualities; mixed wrong it can be lethal. Even at its safest it can induce disturbing violent visions.'

'And you don't want to start suffering from dreams and visions like Twelve Seven Two.' snorted Greybeard, bringing bursts of laughter from the others.

Sanna sensed the growing unease of the room. Anxious eyes watched their group warily.

'Where is he anyway?' roared the General. 'Have you heard his latest ridiculous predictions? Dragons, he says. The dragons are coming! And not just any old dragon either. Not according to Twelve Seven Two. These are big beasts, and blacker than night, he says. Can you believe it?' He chimed sarcastically. 'Centuries after they were last seen; dragons, here again, roaming the streets of Enntonia.'

Amidst the howls of laughter, Sanna gasped inwardly. She raised the bottle to her mouth and drank. Her initial response to the derision was a feeling of annoyance but this quickly gave way as the magnitude of her situation sank in. She had her answers. Her drift had taken her to Enntonia. And into the presence of a Dragon Slayer. Her mind raced. Her location was beyond doubt. Was Taro Brook also here? If so, under what guise would she find him?

'Well, I'll be damned.' The General's booming voice brought her back to the moment. Following his gaze across the room, she watched as the black-garbed man and little green-cloak made their exit from the crowded tavern. 'A Harbinger!' The General scowled. 'I thought I smelt trouble.'

'Looks like bad news for someone tonight.' added Greybeard.

'Reckon you're right.' The General winced. 'Won't bother us none though…' He flashed a grin. 'Who's for more drink?'

Turning away from the enthusiastic push for refills, Sanna seized the chance to make her exit. Merging with the crowd, she exited the ale house and stepped out into the night. Retracing her route through the snow, she found herself drawn towards a dilapidated timber house nestled in a side alley, tucked away from the main thoroughfare. Glancing over her shoulder to ensure no one was following, she pushed gently at the front door. It gave way easily and she moved quietly inside.

The dim lamplight from outside filtered through the grimy windowpane. Adjusting her eyes to the gloom, she studied the neglected interior. Broken furniture lay scattered across the floor. Dust-covered pots, pans and crockery were piled up in a cast-iron sink that looked more than ready to fall from its wall mounting. Mouldy wallpaper hung loosely from the damp walls. Screwing up her nose at the unpleasant odour of the room, Sanna crept silently among the debris and edged towards the wooden staircase.

A creaking step halted her progress to the upper level. She waited in silence for sound of movement from above, but none came. Spurred on by the growing suspicion she was not alone in the house, she moved quickly to the top of the stairs and made her way along the narrow passageway.

A door to her left stood slightly ajar; she looked inside. The room was empty save for a broken bed frame and rickety wardrobe.

Continuing to the end of the passageway, she stopped at a second door. This one was firmly closed. Holding her breath, she listened intently as her hand hovered inches above the door handle.

Her gut feeling had been right. From beyond the door she heard the sound of whispered voices, a man and woman in hushed discussion. Resisting the urge to invade their privacy she waited, but after only a few minutes, unable to fight the temptation any longer, she turned the handle and burst into the room.

To her astonishment she found that the room was empty. Where had they gone? The crumpled bedsheets showed signs of a hasty exit. Crossing to the window, she looked out to the street below. The snow was falling heavier than before.

Convinced that she hadn't imagined the voices, she paced the room in search of clues. Bending to inspect the fireplace, she ran her fingers through the cold ashes. A fire had been lit here recently. Her eyes settled on a small trinket on the wooden mantelpiece. Lifting it carefully she sat on the bed and examined the small metal identification tag. Tied to a thin black cord, the tag was no bigger than her thumbnail. The strange inscription on the metal seemed vaguely familiar and yet she could not say why. From nowhere, she felt a sudden wave of recognition. It seemed Ten Six Nine understood its significance.

Grasping control of her emotions, Sanna slipped the pendant inside her longcoat and made her way towards the door. As she passed an old mirror hanging loosely from the wall, she took a moment to gaze on her reflection. A faint trace of smile softened the troubled features as she ran her fingers through the shoulder-length blonde hair. Ten Six Nine had the appearance of a warrior, much like herself.

Nodding to the face in the mirror, she took the pendant from her coat pocket and placed it around her neck. With one last puzzled look around the room, she closed the door behind her.

An eerie silence greeted her in the passageway. As she made her way back towards the stairs she thought she saw the pattern on the tattered wallpaper change. A trick of the light? It had to be. Pushing the doubts from her mind she descended the stairs quickly to continue her search for Taro Brook.

The inexplicable events of the upstairs room were pushed further from her thoughts as she pulled open the door and looked outside. It was daylight, and the snow was gone. She had been in the house for only a short time, yet night had turned into day and although the air still held a chill, it was as if the seasons had changed in the course of only a few moments.

She ran back up the alleyway. The streets were deserted; everything was deathly quiet. Where was everyone? Turning towards the sound of galloping horses, she watched two riders approaching. Dragon Slayers.

'What is going on here?' She shouted as they came to a halt. 'Where is everyone?'

'Either locked up safe or they've run for their lives.' one replied.

'You need to come with us.' snapped the other.

'Why? Where are we going?'

'To the Eastern Gate. Where's your horse, Ten Six Nine?'

Sanna looked around in confusion. What was happening here? 'I don't know.'

'Then come with us,' offered the first, holding out his arm. 'Time is against us.'

The ride along the tree-lined Kings Highway to the Eastern Gate was fast and furious. The tall poplars passed by in a blur as Sanna's mind raced to keep up with the unfolding events.

Suddenly, from nowhere, a blood-chilling roar desecrated the forest. It was followed by the sound of trees being crushed, as if they were being snapped like giant matchsticks. They arrived at the Eastern Gate as another roar came from the trees beyond the great stone walls. Dismounting quickly, they joined the group gathered by the yawning iron gates. She recognised the men from the tavern amongst the group as they readied themselves with spears and swords.

'Slayers ready!' bellowed the General.

Yet another roar came from the forest, closer this time, as the ground rocked beneath their feet.

'The earth moves.' A Slayer gave voice to the group's fears.

'Hold steady.' The General shouted. 'Your destiny awaits. Here be dragons!'

The ground shook again. Sanna looked on in horror as a huge, black-scaled creature emerged from the forest. Standing three times the height of the great wall, its long neck reached high into the sky. Spanning its enormous wings wide, it thumped the ground and with its monstrous head raised high, the horned beast advanced towards the wall.

The Slayers were in disarray. 'That can be no dragon!' screamed one.

'To the Hells with destiny!' yelled another. 'Run for your life!'

'Hold steady, damn you!' The General snarled his commands.

Sanna turned to the man standing next to her. 'Why does he delay? A hundred men could not defeat that beast, let alone one dozen.'

'Oldest rule of the Order,' the man rasped. 'He waits because we never abandon one of our own.' He pointed beyond the wall. 'Twelve Seven Two is in there somewhere. He volunteered to scout the forest and hasn't come back.'

Sanna found herself pushing to the front of the group. It was obvious Ten Six Nine had strong feelings for the missing Slayer. As she neared the General, a shout stopped her in her tracks.

'There he is! There! It's Twelve Seven Two!'

Her heart jumped as she saw a figure running towards the iron gates. The gathering roared their support, urging him onwards.

As Twelve Seven Two neared the wall, just as his comrades dared to believe he might make it to the gate, he suddenly and inexplicably came to a halt and turned to look back to the forest.

'What is he doing?' Ten Six Nine screamed at the top of her voice. Sanna's emotions neared breaking point.

'Run, damn you!' The General vented his fury. 'Run!'

Sanna watched as Twelve Seven Two changed course. With the black monstrosity bearing down on him, instead of making for the gate, he raced towards the treeline.

'What in the Hells?' The General's face twisted. 'What's the fool doing? Twelve Seven Two, damn you! Make for the gate!' His command was drowned out by the roar of the beast as it ploughed towards its prey. Dropping its long neck low to the ground, its mouth gaped open. A forked tongue lashed out from between the great jaws and, as the beast moved in for the kill, Dragon Slayer Twelve Seven Two disappeared from sight.

Sanna lost all control of her emotions as Ten Six Nine screamed out in anguish.

'Where did he go?' The General bellowed. 'Did he make it into the trees?'

'He is gone!' A shout came for the group. 'The black beast has taken him.'

The scaled monster turned its attention towards the gate. Panic took hold as the General roared the instruction to retreat.

'We have no hope against this demon. Run! Run for your lives!'

Turning with tears in her eyes, Sanna forced Ten Six Nine to flee the scene. The Slayers scattered as the beast crashed through the walls of the once great Eastern Gate of Enntonia. The ancient structure crumbled and fell, crushed underfoot like a child's toy.

Sanna ran for the cover of the dense spruce trees. The sharp needles stabbed their protest as she brushed her way through the branches. Shielding her face with her arms, she pushed through the forest until the roaring of the beast began to fade far behind. As the trees thinned, she ran towards the daylight up ahead. Breaking free from the forest, she lost her footing and stumbled over the edge of steep drop.

Her fall ended abruptly, with her head hitting against a rock. Dazed and sore, she dragged herself into a sitting position.

Rubbing her eyes, she tried to focus. She saw a white-towered building, surrounded by trees. As she pain in her head intensified, she thought she saw a woman, dressed in white, walking towards her. As she slipped from consciousness, Sanna heard a calming voice, whispering words of assurance.

All would be well. She was safe now.

CHAPTER THIRTY-EIGHT

Token ScriptScratcher emerged from his rendezvous in the side street tearoom with a heavy heart and much to contemplate. Things were far worse than he'd expected. He had to return to Bog-Mire Towers at once. A parchment must be scripted and dispatched without delay.

He'd met surreptitiously with a clerk of the High Council who, shocked by recent events midst the corridors of power, had informed the Scribe of the true scale of the situation. As he spurred his mount homewards, Token couldn't help but wonder if his actions would be too little, too late.

On his arrival at Bog-Mire he hurried up the stone steps of the old bell tower and went out onto the rooftop balcony. Taking the small silver whistle from his pocket, he raised it to his lips and blew three times at short intervals. A raven flew into view and landed on the parapet next to him. Token hastily tied a black tag to its leg. As he clapped his hands, the raven took to the sky. He watched until it disappeared beyond the trees. The raven flew in search of Harbinger Talus. When it found him, Talus would know his presence was needed immediately at Bog-Mire.

Content that the summons was sent, Token left the balcony and made his way down to his study.

Quill in hand, he put ink to parchment. With painstaking detail he recorded the dark deeds of the High Council and despaired at the foolishness of mankind. Listing the facts as told to him by the clerk of the Council, he recalled the words of his long-departed father.

"It would be wise to never give power to those who seek it."

When the ink was dry, Token rolled the parchment and sealed it with the mark of Bog-Mire Towers. With his task complete, he went downstairs to the drawing-room and poured a large glass of brandy. Filling his pipe with beech-leaf tobacco, he sat in his armchair by the fireside, and waited for the arrival of the Harbinger.

CHAPTER THIRTY-NINE

At the crux of his nightmare, Dragon Slayer Twelve Seven Two woke with a start. Even with his eyes open, the haunting image of being chased for his life through the forest by the giant black monster refused to dissipate. Rising from the bed, he walked over to the window. It was dark outside, and all was quiet. Shivering, as much at the recollection of the nightmare as at the chill of the room, he moved to the fireplace.

Placing a log on the smouldering fire, he waited as the embers sparked to life. As he watched the flames dance, his fingers settled on the identification tag around his neck. He'd worn it all his life, as was the tradition of his forebears. Was it a badge of honour or an emblem of the cursed? He wondered sometimes which was the more apt description.

He slipped the cord over his head and placed it on the wooden mantelpiece. He hoped the gesture wouldn't offend those who had gone before but he desperately felt the need to break the bonds, if only for a few hours. Maybe then, he would manage to sleep.

Climbing back into bed, he gazed fondly at the woman lying asleep next to him. At least his troubled dreams hadn't disturbed her. Tracing his fingers across the identification brand adorning her shoulder, he marvelled at the softness of her skin.

As she murmured softly in response to his touch, Twelve Seven Two closed his eyes. He yearned for trouble-free sleep.

Again, he hoped in vain.

CHAPTER FORTY

'Rugen! Finally! I've been trying to reach you for over an hour.'

Thrown by the urgency in Mitchell Egberts' voice, Hans Rugen offered his response grudgingly. 'I just got back, Mitch. I've been out for a walk.'

'In the forest? Next to your cottage?'

'Yes.'

'Listen, I don't know how that novel of yours is coming along but if you're looking for inspiration you need to get down to Greenhill Forest. There's definitely something strange going on in there.'

Rugen rolled his eyes. 'Yes, Mitch, you've told me all this already, and I've told you that I've shelved my novel about the walker in the woods. It wasn't working. I've accepted that, why can't you?'

After a moment of hesitation, Egbert's tone darkened.

'Hans, I'm telling you, your answers lie in Greenhill Forest. Something strange is happening in there. I've heard voices coming from below the cliffs near the old loggers' cabin. I'm sure it all ties in with your novel. I've just got to figure out how to get down there, find out who they are, and what they are up to.'

Rugen shook his head. He'd received several calls from Egberts in the last few days; the conversation had followed the same pattern each time. Rugen tried, once again, to present the voice of reason.

'Mitch, I'll tell you again, there is nothing strange going on in the woods. You're just letting your imagination run wild. I wish I'd never put this idea in your head. You need to forget about the whole thing and stay away from those cliffs. It's dangerous up there.'

He waited for a response, but none came.

Mitchell Egberts had hung up on him again.

CHAPTER FORTY-ONE

Waking to the sound of birdsong, Sanna opened her eyes and sat up in the bed. She scanned the unfurnished room for clues to her whereabouts. The marble floor felt cold beneath her bare feet as she crossed the room towards the sunlight.

The glass doors opened on to a balcony with a stunning view of a steep-sided gorge. A succession of waterfalls tumbled noisily down to the winding river far below. The sun felt good on her skin. Revived by the gentle breeze, she turned her thoughts to what had happened. How had she come to be here?

Drawing away from the view, she moved back into the room, pulled on her boots, and went looking for answers.

A sweeping staircase led down to the ground floor. A quick search of the rooms found no sign of life. Finding her way to the front entrance, she went out into a large area of gardens awash with colour. At the centre of the grounds, the grand building's white turreted towers stood tall amidst the swaying larch trees. Crawling ivies clung vigorously to the garden walls, covering the marble with a flush of green.

'I see you are up and about.'

The voice caught her unawares. She turned to see a white-robed woman approaching. The woman's smile put her at ease.

'I trust you are feeling better?'

'I feel fine.' Sanna replied cautiously. 'Where am I? I lost my way whilst searching for a friend.'

The woman's pale skin radiated in the sunlight as she flicked her blonde hair behind her ear. 'Your friend, the Woodsman?'

'How do you know about him?'

'You mentioned him several times on your arrival here.'

'And how did I come to be here?'

The woman studied her carefully. 'You don't remember?'

Sanna shook her head. Her recollections of what had happened after she'd left Scaraven at the pinnacles were vague at best. She remembered entering a house and going up the stairs; she thought she'd heard voices, people talking, but had found the house to be empty. And as for what had happened after that... nothing. 'No, I don't remember.'

'I found you at the edge of the forest. You were tired and disorientated; I brought you here. You spoke of your search for the Woodsman, I assured you that I would offer my assistance when you had rested.'

'Then I am in your debt.'

'There is no need for you to thank me, Sanna Vrai. You are welcome here.'

'You know my name? How can that be?'

The woman smiled. 'Our mutual friend Scaraven talks fondly of you.'

'Scaraven? You know him? Is he here?'

'He waits for you not far from here, but first you must deal with the task at hand. Your search for the man of the woods is almost over. All that remains is for you to have a little patience.

Walk with me a while for the roses need my attention and the gardens of Kar-Bysdell will not tend to themselves.'

Sanna met the words with a look of astonishment. 'This is Kar-Bysdell? The gorge…' Stopping mid-sentence she moved quickly to the wall. Her gaze followed the course of the river to an unmistakable rock formation in the distance.

'The gorge leads south to the Enchanted Pass.' She said the words aloud as if for confirmation. From the head of the Pass of TorisDuan, she had, on several occasions, looked towards the crumbling ruins of Kar-Bysdell. Her mind raced. Crumbling ruins? This couldn't be right. She spun round. 'This place looks so different…'

Whilst her attentions had been focused elsewhere, the woman in white had descended to a lower level of the terraced garden. Sanna watched as she disappeared through an arched doorway. She looked around in disbelief. It appeared she had the answer to her location.

The where seemed beyond doubt; the when? That was another matter entirely. In pursuit of answers she hurried across the garden, went down the steps, and followed through the doorway.

She found herself in a small stone-walled room bereft of furniture. Spears of daylight glanced through a spider-webbed window, drawing her attention to the bottom of a narrow stairway. Easing her body into the tight space, she began to climb.

Confined to a rounded tower, the spiral stone stairway overlooked the sprawling gardens. After passing a third arrow-slit window the stairs came to a sudden end. She found her progress barred by an old wooden door. The rusted door handle broke free in her hand. Throwing it aside she pushed at the door. It held firm. Years of abandonment had taken its toll.

Puzzled by the woman's disappearance she vented her frustrations by shoving repeatedly against the door with her shoulder. Despite its initial stubborn reluctance, her determination prevailed and with a loud crack of protest the door lurched open. Walking into the sunshine, she stared ahead in bewilderment.

The gardens of Kar-Bysdell now lay in a bad state of neglect. Moss and fungi covered the dilapidated ornamental walls, the rose bushes were ragged and bare, and the flower beds lay hidden from view, suffocated under a blanket of weeds and long grass.

As she struggled with the sudden change in her surroundings, a noise from the far end of the gardens caught her attention. With her curiosity aroused, she moved towards the sound of voices.

The path came to an end just short of an imposing hedge. Her grip tightened on the handle of her longsword as she waited in anticipation. Hearing footsteps on the far side of the hedge, she braced herself for possible confrontation, and stepped forward to meet the approaching threat.

CHAPTER FORTY-TWO

'And so it was, that on the thirty-third day of the seventh moon, in the twelfth cycle of the two suns, the Life Companionship Ceremony of Procrastinator Vardoger and Kalina Tronn took place in the grand hall of Craton City Chambers. And what an event it was, my friends. Cheering crowds lined the streets, desperate for a view of the happy couple, whilst in the inner sanctum of the Chambers, the rich and powerful of Craton filled their bellies with the finest foods and drank their fill of the finest wines in all the Eight States. Although the merriment continued long into the night, official documentation of the time recorded that Vardoger and Kalina left the celebrations long before the chiming of the twelve bells.'

The storyteller paused to appease his thirst. Eyeing his captive audience he gulped down his ale, wiped his mouth with his tattered sleeve, and continued his tale.

'It was said that the Procrastinator had appeared somewhat preoccupied during the whole ceremony. Of course, history makes reference to his unusual behaviour in the period leading up to his betrothal and the events surrounding perhaps the greatest achievement of his illustrious career. Whilst some claimed he was merely displaying pre-ceremony nerves, there were others who believed that mysterious forces were at work, prompting suggestions that the Procrastinator had developed the gift of second sight.'

Letting his words hang, the storyteller studied his listeners. Four and three he counted, seated around the wooden table; young and old among them. He sensed several others, lurking unseen in the shadows. The fire cracked in the open hearth at the far end of the table. Wisps of pipe-smoke drifted lazily up towards the wooden rafters. The black and white dog lying by his feet on the flag-stoned floor yawned, stretched, scratched impatiently at his hind quarters for a moment, then closed his eyes again. Content that he had his company's full attention, the storyteller continued.

'Now, in my defence, let me say that I am merely a teller of tales. Myth and legend grow from history, and who amongst us can know for certain where one ends and the other begins. However, of one thing there can be no doubt, the tale I am about to share cannot be found anywhere in the libraries of New Craton City.'

Pausing for effect, allowing his narrative to breathe and grow, he leaned forward in his chair and, lowering his voice, lured his audience further into his confidence.

'Craton, in Vardoger's time, was a rich and powerful society. It was a world with little room for superstition and folklore. And yet word spread; whispers that have echoed down through the centuries. Following his return from the lands of the Dead Lakes, rumours of the Procrastinator's uncharacteristic behaviour resonated through the halls of power, filtering down into the taverns, ale houses and the backstreet houses of ill-repute.

Speculation was rife as to the cause of his strange behaviour. Some said the heat of the desert sun had affected his mind. Many suggested that his plan to desalinate the Dead Lakes was a sure enough sign that the man had lost his rationale. However, there were others who believed that the Procrastinator had gained knowledge beyond the normal comprehension, and the events of the days following his union ceremony only further added to this speculation.
After slipping unseen from the celebrations, Vardoger and Kalina remained hidden from the public eye until three days later, when it was officially announced that they were to undertake a state visit in commemoration of their union. It was to be a voyage to Khensu, the capital city of the Dead Lakes State. Excitement grew as speculation mounted over the choice of their destination. But, as the day of their departure drew ever closer, events took a sudden and even stranger twist...'

A fist thumped down on the table, instantly silencing the storyteller. Startled from their attentive state, his listeners jumped with surprise whilst the dog, none too pleased at having his snooze disturbed, lurched to his feet, a low growl rumbling in his throat.

'Find yourselves a seat elsewhere or leave.' The Innkeeper snarled his disapproval at the folk gathered around the table. 'I'll not have you giving this old clown any further encouragement.' He loomed ominously over the storyteller's shoulder as they dispersed. 'Look here, Teller, I've warned you before about sharing your tall tales in here. Any more of it an' I'll be throwing you outside, snow or no snow. And shut that flea-bitten mutt of yours up too. I'll not have him growling in my direction.' With his commands issued, the Innkeeper stomped back across the room and returned to his duties.

Left with only his dog for company, the storyteller quietly supped his ale. Casting an eye to the far end of the table he saw two figures emerge from the shadows. Silhouetted by the fire beyond, they took a seat, one on either side of the table. He reckoned them to be of small stature and though their faces were hidden, the shadows failed to conceal the pointed ears protruding from under their hats. The figure on the left leaned forward. Resting his chin on his cupped hands, he spoke in a hushed, mischievous tone.

'Pray continue, Teller,' he squawked, 'for us loves a good story, we truly does.'

His companion let out a high-pitched cackle and clasped his long, spindly fingers together in anticipation.

The storyteller glanced over his shoulder. The Innkeeper was nowhere to be seen and if anyone in the room was aware of his new companions, they were choosing not to show it. Beside him, the dog suddenly lifted his head to the side, his attentions following an unseen source of distraction. Quickly becoming aware that he too was being watched, the dog looked guiltily in his master's direction, yawned, scratched again at his hind quarters, and lay down, resting his head on an outstretched paw. Turning his attention back to his new audience, the storyteller took another mouthful of ale. In his time he had told tales of old to all kinds of strange creatures. Ears were ears; it didn't matter to him whether they were pointed or not. Taking one last quick glance over his shoulder, he addressed his new listeners.

'So, little friends, you wish to hear the tale of Vardoger, the Procrastinator with the gift of second sight? Can I assume you have been paying attention thus far?'

The two figures at the far end of the table nodded their agreement and cackled with delight, eagerly bidding him to continue.

'Excellent! Then I shall delay no further. The day of the voyage had arrived, and all appeared to be going to plan. However, events took a sudden twist when a somewhat agitated Vardoger announced to his entourage that he had changed his mind. He and his partner would not be taking the trip to Khensu after all. When asked for his reason he declined to comment but sent word to the captain of the ship asking him to consider cancelling the voyage altogether. When his request was rejected by the port authority it is said he became very alarmed, stating that it may be a decision they would come to regret. But, as the Procrastinator was unable to offer any reasoning to substantiate his strange demands, the voyage went ahead as planned.'

The storyteller wagged a pointed finger towards the fire as he continued. 'The official documents of the time clearly state that Procrastinator Vardoger and his companion did not sail on the ill-fated voyage that day, my friends. Yet, as events unfolded, the speculation and the questions surrounding his bizarre prediction grew. Six days later, on its return voyage from Khensu, the ocean ship on which Vardoger had been due to sail was hit by a terrible storm. Huge waves crushed the ship, condemning it and everyone on board to a watery grave. None survived.'

Gasps of wonder came from the shadows at the far end of the table. The tell-tale sound of long fingernails scratching on the wooden table told him all he needed to know. With his listeners hooked, buoyed by their reaction, the storyteller continued his account with fresh vigour.

'Well, you can imagine the furore that surrounded the Procrastinator in the aftermath of such an event. Strangely, having been seen to have returned to his usual indecisive self in the days prior to the tragedy, Vardoger was said to have had no recollection of his request to the port authority that fateful day, or indeed of his ghastly premonition, and this only added to the general consternation. Eventually, after much fuss, and appeals for calm from the Supreme Assembly, things returned to normal for him. But wait, my pointed-eared friends, for the strangest part of my tale is yet to be shared. Another version of these events has endured throughout the centuries. Which is the true account, I hear you ask? Fear not, for I will let you, my trusted listeners, judge for yourselves.'

As the storyteller continued, captivated by the images conjured to life by his lilting words, his audience pictured the events unfolding around them as if they themselves had been thrust into the very midst of the tale.

'It is believed by many that the Procrastinator and his companion did indeed undertake the voyage to Khensu and that furthermore they undertook a journey far into the desert lands.'

Procrastinator Vardoger and Kalina Tronn watched from the viewing deck of the ocean ship *Titan* as the sparkling city of Craton merged with the hazy horizon far behind them. Vardoger pulled his companion close. Sensing his anxiety, Kalina kissed him on the cheek and offered her whispered reassurance before returning her gaze to the vast open sea.

Vardoger's behaviour in recent weeks had become increasingly worrying and, according to Jarl Sere, it was putting his political future in jeopardy. It wasn't only the Supreme Assembly that was concerned. Kalina Tronn missed her bumbling, indecisive Vardoger. She hoped, for her own sake as well as his, that whatever was troubling him would be resolved in the stifling heat of the desert.

Ta-nish watched on in quiet anticipation as they disembarked at the dock. The man from government and his companion had contacted her several days before, requesting that she meet with them on their arrival in Khensu. If their terms were agreeable she was to escort them into the desert, to the settlement of Kiva, visiting the Pyramids of Saa on the way. She found the statesman's manner unnerving, but he paid handsomely for her services as a guide. Recalling his previous visit to the pyramids, which had clearly unsettled him at the time, she couldn't help but wonder why he wished to return there so soon. Perhaps he merely wanted his companion to gaze upon the wondrous creations with her own eyes.

Waving a hand in greeting, she made her way through the bustling crowd towards them.

A short while later, as they sipped chilled wine in a quiet corner of a quayside tavern, she listened intently as the Procrastinator's companion took control of the conversation.

'Ta-nish, we have already discussed our wish to visit the Pyramids of Saa. As to our reason for requesting a return trip to Kiva, the Procrastinator takes with him a surprise for his newfound friends there. A convoy of trucks will accompany us on our journey; tankers filled with safe drinking water. The convoy heralds the dawning of a new age. The desalination of the Dead Lakes will soon begin.'

Ta-nish took a moment before responding. 'Can this really be true?' She eyed Vardoger cautiously. 'You've made this happen?'

'Yes,' his companion replied forcefully. 'The Procrastinator has made it all happen.'

Ta-nish tipped her glass in Vardoger's direction. 'Then I must apologise to you, man of government. I would not have believed it possible for anyone to achieve such a feat in so short a time, far less a man of your indecisive nature. I was wrong to doubt you.'

The guide's words played over in Vardoger's mind as he waited for sleep later that night. Safe in the privacy of his own thoughts he had to admit he agreed with her; he too found it inconceivable that he had managed to make it all happen.

A troubled sleep was followed by an early start the following morning. Vardoger watched as the convoy of trucks bound for Kiva snaked its way through the outskirts of Khensu and out into the searing heat of the desert.

Several hours and an uncomfortable jeep ride later, he found himself standing once more inside the great chamber of the central pyramid. A nervous excitement grew within him. After weeks of waiting he was finally back. His eyes shifted constantly from his companions to the small opening in the far corner of the chamber. Beads of sweat formed on his forehead as he wondered how to manage a moment to himself in which to explore the tunnel.

Kalina was engrossed by the hieroglyphics on the chamber walls. She studied them closely, paying great attention to the detail. 'These are incredible, Ta-nish. Have they all been deciphered?'

'Generations of scholars have dedicated their lives to the study of the symbols,' replied the guide, 'yet little is known about them. Some have simple meanings which can be easily understood but the majority of them remain a mystery.'

Vardoger watched on impatiently as their conversation continued.

'Look, here.' Kalina tapped the wall inquisitively. 'This is so strange; these symbols look like trees. Don't you think that is unusual for these surroundings?'

'Unusual indeed,' Ta-nish nodded, 'and there, next to the trees, there are symbols depicting a great flood of water.' She shook her head. 'Trees and water, the last things you would expect to find in this burning wasteland. At times, the Ancient Ones appear to make no sense at all. Perhaps it is only our ignorance that hides the true meanings from us.'

Vardoger felt his patience wane. He eyed the small tunnel entrance again anxiously. Feeling the guide's gaze land on him he shifted uneasily. The woman made him feel very uncomfortable. It was as if she was trying to get inside his mind. When she spoke, her words unnerved him further. It was as if she had read his thoughts.

'There are some interesting hieroglyphs in the entrance chamber of the adjacent pyramid. Would you like me to take your companion to see them?'

'Yes, that would be good,' Vardoger responded eagerly, 'if that's okay with you, Kalina?'

'Yes,' she smiled. 'I'd like that. But come and join us soon, don't hang around in here too long, Vardoger.'

'I agree.' Ta-nish eyed him warily as she led Kalina from the chamber.

Vardoger could scarcely believe his good fortune. Hurrying down the steps, he made his way across to the tunnel entrance and crouched down to peer inside. It was pitch dark. Was his memory playing tricks on him? Hadn't there been a flicker of daylight the last time? He was certain of it. With a shrug, he took the small torch from his jacket. The beam of light cut a fine line through the darkness as he pushed himself into the tunnel and slowly made his way forward.

Reaching the end of the tunnel he stood upright. He remembered being here before, but something was different. Holding his breath in expectation, he switched the torch off and waited in the darkness. After several minutes he switched on the torch to examine the stone wall. It was completely intact. He slapped his palm against it in frustration.

Why was everything different? On his previous visit the stones had been displaced. Some of them had fallen forward, revealing glimpses of daylight from beyond. A wave of despair washed over him. What was he waiting for? What was he expecting to happen?

Slapping the wall again, he turned the torch's beam around and made his way back along the tunnel. Emerging from the cramped passageway into the inner chamber of the pyramid, he found their guide standing over him, her arms crossed and an impatient look on her face.

She stared at him questioningly as he struggled to his feet. 'Your companion waits for us in the jeep, man of government.'

Vardoger shook his head despondently. 'We can continue on our journey, Ta-nish. I failed to find what I was looking for.'

'What were you doing?' she asked suspiciously. 'What were you looking for?'

Shaking his head in response, Vardoger sighed as he brushed past her. He had no answer.

'The Procrastinator offered no explanation, and no clues to what he had been hoping to find in the pyramid. And so his peculiar behaviour continued as their journey took them further into the burning wastelands…'

'Another ale, Teller.' The Innkeeper interrupted the flow of his tale as he placed a full tankard on the table. 'Glad to see you took my advice and kept your tales to yourself.' Snorting his amusement, the man lumbered back across the room.

The storyteller's gaze searched the far end of the table. His pointy-eared listeners were gone. Raising his ale, he offered a hushed toast to his absent audience. 'Let our paths cross again soon, my friends, so that you may hear the end of my tale.' Breaking into a smile, he surmised that the Innkeeper might have intervened at just the right moment. For some folk, truth seemed harder to believe than fiction.

The storyteller eased back in his chair and watched the flames of the fire as they waned, their rhythmic dance signalling the passing of another day. On the floor by his side the dog watched as yet another invisible friend passed by only a few feet away from his outstretched paws. Moments later both the storyteller and his four-legged friend were sound asleep.

They were wakened early the next morning by the Innkeeper's wife. She placed a plate of eggs and sausages in front of the storyteller, who offered his sincere thanks and apologies for sleeping through the night. The dog munched greedily on his bowl of scraps from the previous evening as the woman raked the ashes of the fire.

'No need to apologise,' she said. 'It was a foul night and my husband, grumpy as he is, was easily persuaded to let you snooze by the fire. It's a fine morn though, the sun is warm and most of the snow has melted. Enjoy your breakfast, Teller.'

A short while later, having settled his payment for the food and ale, the storyteller stepped into the bright sunshine. With his faithful companion by his side, he walked down the cobbled streets leading to the docks. Passing the busy boatyards, he pondered the sight of the great ocean ships.

'Perhaps, old friend, we should take a voyage one day. Just like Vardoger. What say you? Strange new lands filled to the brim with folk; keen ears poised, ready to hear the tales of old.'

The idea was an appealing one. Perhaps one day he would take a voyage to new worlds. Perhaps he wouldn't. Either way, there was no need to rush into making a decision.

CHAPTER FORTY-THREE

As they journeyed further into the desert, Vardoger's frustrations deepened. Certain that the answers to his dilemma lay in the pyramid, he became resigned to the fact he would have to stop there again on the return journey from Kiva. He had only a few hours to come up with a believable excuse; a tangible argument to convince his companions to agree.

Kalina's concerns for Vardoger's troubled state of mind intensified as she desperately sought answers on how best to help him.

Their guide Ta-nish had thoughts of her own. Her curiosity had been further stirred by the man of government's actions in the pyramid. What had he been up to in the chamber? Despite her better judgement, she was beginning to let herself wonder if there was actually some element of truth behind the people of Kiva's beliefs. Was the man of government really some kind of messenger of the Gods? As unlikely a possibility as it seemed, it could explain the sudden, incredible turn of events. And if true, was he somehow able to make contact with the Sky Gods?
Was that what he had been doing in the pyramid? She eyed him warily as she drove the jeep harder across the endless sands.

Their arrival at Kiva was met with great excitement among the settlement's inhabitants who had already gathered around the convoy of water trucks.

Following a flurry of activity, and a frenzied discussion to arrange preparations for the water distribution studiously translated by Ta-nish, Vardoger felt his mood lift as a familiar face broke free from the crowd and ran towards him. Crouching down to greet her, he caught the little girl in his arms as she threw herself at him in a warm embrace.

'This is Ketoh,' he beamed, turning to his companion. 'Isn't she beautiful?'

Kalina Tronn detected a smile sweeping across the girl's disfigured face. 'Yes,' she replied, holding out her hand in greeting. 'I do believe she is.'

The girl clutched Kalina's hand warmly then raised Vardoger's arm in the air. The chattering crowd fell silent as the girl addressed them, speaking boldly in her strange tongue. Feeling ill at ease with being the apparent centre of attention, Vardoger turned quickly to his guide and translator.

'What did she say, Ta-nish?'

The dark-haired woman hesitated before answering.

'Her meaning was clear, man of government. It is as she had predicted. The messenger has returned with the gift of the Gods.'

An eerie silence followed as the people of Kiva contemplated Ketoh's words. With heads bowed, the crowd stood in hushed contemplation. To Vardoger it appeared as if time stood still. Even Kalina and Ta-nish appeared to be affected, held in the clutches of the strange trance-like state.

'You can put me down now.' whispered the girl.

Vardoger looked down at her in astonishment.

'You spoke my language? I didn't know you could.'

The girl smiled as she motioned him to follow her towards the underground entrance.

'You have changed the lives of many. Come with me, friend, I have a gift for you in return. You have been lost for some time,' she continued, 'the one who has been searching for you awaits your safe return. I will take you to her now.'

With an almost calming sense of inevitability, Vardoger followed her further into the underground caverns. She spoke softly, reassuring him that all would soon be well and whilst the implications of her words lay far beyond his comprehension it didn't seem to matter. As they came to a stop, he held his breath in anticipation.

'It is time,' the girl stepped away. 'Do not be afraid.'

A sudden breeze whipped through the cavern. Vardoger waited nervously as a tingling sensation washed over him. As the gust of wind receded, he felt a sense of release, as if a great burden lifted from his shoulders. Looking over his shoulder he saw the little girl waving to him.

'Why are we down here, Ketoh?' he glanced hesitantly around the cavern.

The girl called out in response, once more gesturing to him to follow. Confused and disorientated, he started back towards the surface. As they emerged from the shadows into the blazing heat of the desert sun, the crowd, revived from their peculiar trance, began to cheer loudly. Vardoger's gaze settled on his guide as she strode towards him.

'Ta-nish, you didn't tell me these people spoke Cratonese.'

'They do not.' Her expression stiffened.

'But the little girl, Ketoh, she spoke to me, underground. I understood her.'

The guide eyed him suspiciously as Kalina moved next to him.

'What are you talking about, Vardoger?' She took his arm in hers. 'You weren't underground. You were holding Ketoh. You just put her down a moment ago.'

'Perhaps the heat of the sun is playing tricks on you,' Ta-nish offered bluntly. 'It can happen.'

Vardoger shook his head in confusion. Looking down, he saw the little girl watching him closely, her admiration plainly evident, even on her horribly twisted features. They'd been underground; he was certain of it. The little girl had spoken to him and he had understood her words. At least, he thought he had. Had he imagined it? For a fleeting moment he contemplated pressing his point further, but Kalina's expression convinced him otherwise.

A shout from Ta-nish brought silence to the chattering crowd. Facing Vardoger, she addressed him directly.

'You would have us know you as a man of government, but these humble people are indebted to you and in their eyes, you are a messenger of the Sky Gods. Is there anything you would like to say to them? Speak now, let them hear your message.'

Vardoger swallowed uncomfortably.

'I don't know... I mean, I really wouldn't know what to say.'

‘You have brought the promise of life to a desolate land,’ continued the guide as she gestured towards the crowd. ‘You surely carry the message of the Gods. Speak the words, I will translate them.’

Vardoger turned anxiously to Kalina. His expression said it all. She felt a rush of relief. The Procrastinator finally appeared to be back to his old self. She smiled as she gripped his hand tighter.

‘What would you like to say to them, Vardoger?’

‘Oh, I don’t know, Kalina,’ he replied shakily. ‘You decide!’

CHAPTER FORTY-FOUR

Hans Rugen frowned at the ringing telephone.

The prospect of having to listen to more of Mitchell Egberts' ridiculous nonsense wasn't an appealing one. Egberts' obsession with Greenhill Forest was becoming almost as infuriating as his fixation with Rugen's abandoned storyline.

Rugen had heard enough. It was time to put an end to it all. Picking up, ready to vent his annoyance, his verbal onslaught was stopped in its tracks by the sound of a woman's voice.

'Hello, Hans? Is that you?'

'Yes… this is Hans Rugen.'

'Hi, this is Sonja. Mitchell Egberts' wife.'

'Oh… hello.' He felt the knot in his stomach tighten. 'What can I do for you?'

'Hans, I'm sorry to trouble you, but I'm so worried. I don't know what to do. It's Mitch…'

'What about him? Is he okay?'

'No, he's not okay, I think he's losing his mind. He's obsessed with some novel you're writing. He keeps talking about it. He says you let him read the first chapter but now you're being secretive about the rest of it.'

'Sonja, there is no novel,' Rugen sighed. 'I did let him see a few draft pages, but I shelved the project soon after. I've told him this repeatedly, but he doesn't seem to want to hear it.'

'He says it's about someone walking in the woods.' Egbert's wife persisted. 'Now he has taken to spending most of his time in Greenhill Forest. What is he doing in there?'

'I honestly don't know.'

'The night before last, he didn't come home until the early hours of the morning. His clothes were dirty, and when I challenged him, he mumbled some nonsense about voices he was hearing in the forest. He is convinced there are people in there, and that they are connected to your novel.'

Rugen's patience finally snapped. 'Sonja, believe me, there is no damned novel about people in the forest.' He drew a breath. 'I'm sorry, but...'

'I understand your frustration, Hans. I know it's a lot to ask but would you consider writing something, even just a few pages? Perhaps it would help Mitch regain some grip on reality.'

'I'd like to help, truly I would, but I am working on a crime novel and it's due with my agent in the next couple of weeks.'

'Please, Hans.' The concern was evident in her tone. 'I'd really appreciate anything you can do to help. I don't know what else to do.'

'Okay.' Rugen relented. He felt he had no other choice. 'I can't promise, but I will try to put something together. But like I said, I had hit the wall with that idea. I just didn't see it going anywhere.'

'Thank you, Hans. Thank you so much. It could be just what he needs.'

Rugen ended the call with a sigh of dejection. He feared it would take a lot more than a few pages to satisfy Mitchell Egberts' fascination with his failed storyline. That said, he couldn't shake the nagging feeling that he was partly responsible for Egberts' troubled state of mind. The least he could do was try to help resolve the situation.

Pouring a glass of wine, he eased himself into the armchair by the fireside to ponder his dilemma. The concept seemed straightforward enough. The theme of the walker in the forest was already in place. All he had to do was conjure something up to appeal to Mitchell Egberts' overactive imagination.

The voices... The voices in the forest.

Egberts' ramblings had already given him something to work with. Closing his eyes, Hans Rugen let his mind drift in search of further inspiration. Within minutes, he was sound asleep.

CHAPTER FORTY-FIVE

As he stumbled towards the light, Taro Brook heard the woman's voice echo all around. Spurred on by the words of reassurance, he reached the end of the passageway and stepped out into daylight. Glancing back over his shoulder, he saw a blonde-haired woman dressed in white, fade from view. Puzzled by her presence, he then turned away from the doorway and climbed a short flight of steps to gain a better view of his surroundings.

A ruined, white-stoned building stood at the centre of the overgrown grounds. Brook scratched his head in bemusement. Where was he? And how had he come to be here? And, more to the point, where were the pinnacles?

Walking through the long grass, he followed alongside a tall conifer hedge, until a gap in the greenery yawned invitingly. Stepping through, he found he was no longer alone.

'You!'

Startled by the shout, he wheeled round quickly. 'Sanna.'

'It is good to see you again, Taro Brook.' She stepped towards him. 'We thought you were lost.'

'Lost? I've only been gone a few minutes.'

'That is not how it appeared to us.'

Her expression troubled him. 'What do you mean? And where are we? Where are the pinnacles?'

'This place is known as Kar-Bysdell.'

'How did we come to be here?'

Sanna shook her head. 'I don't know. You disappeared back at the pinnacles. My search led me here. I know you must have questions; there are things I too do not comprehend. Scaraven can perhaps provide us with answers.'

'Messenger Two Cups? Is he here?'

'He waits for us at the Enchanted Pass. It's not far.'

Descending the moss-covered steps, they passed through the overgrown gateway of Kar-Bysdell and, with one final look back at the deserted ruins, began the tricky negotiation of the cliff-top track as it wound its way among the scattered birch and rowan trees. As they walked, Taro Brook thought about Sanna's strange reaction. Was it possible that he had been gone for longer than he realised?

'So, where are we in relation to Sumarren now?' he asked. It was becoming increasingly difficult to keep any sense of bearing. How far from home was he now?

'We must be getting closer,' she replied, 'though I am not certain. Tell me what happened to you at the Pinnacles of Sorrow.'

'I heard movement in the rocks, a scuffling sound, there didn't seem to be any danger, so I went to investigate. Then the shape of the rock appeared to distort, and everything went dark. Moments later I saw daylight, it led me into the gardens at the ruins, just before I saw you again.'

'How do you explain your arrival at Kar-Bysdell? Do you know how you got there?'

'No,' he replied blankly. 'I haven't a clue.'

'Do you remember seeing anything else?'

Brook hesitated. 'I heard a woman's voice in the darkness, telling me I didn't have far to go. Then, as I reached the daylight, I caught a glimpse of her.'

'What did she look like?'

'I saw her only from a distance. She had long blonde hair and was dressed in white.'

'She was watching over both of us, Taro Brook, for I saw her too. I was lucky enough to talk with her, if only for a moment. She told me my search for you was almost over.'

'Who was she?'

'I don't know, but she said we share a common acquaintance. Perhaps he can tell us who she was.'

As they passed between two tall sandstone pillars flanking the track, a familiar voice drifted towards them in the breeze.

'Make haste, weary travellers. Tea's up!'

Sitting by a pool near a stand of birch trees, they updated Messenger Two Cups with their sketchy recollections.

'All very interesting,' he toyed with his whiskers. 'The gateways can be very unpredictable. You don't recall anything else, Sanna?'

'No, but perhaps something will come back to me.'

'How can we have such varying perceptions of the time we were apart?' Brook raised the question hesitantly.

Two Cups snorted his response. 'There is that word again. Time has no relevance here, Woodsman. You ask me to explain passages of time, you might as well ask me to define the present.'

Brook stared back. 'I'm not sure I understand.'

Two Cups grinned knowingly. 'Of course you don't. How could you? It's impossible. If you were to believe in such a concept, you would have to concede that were I to attempt such a definition, before I would be able to conclude my hypothesis, the point at which I started would be in the past. Agreed?' He frowned at Brook's blank expression, then continued. 'Your understanding would, no doubt, follow at some juncture further down the line.' Pausing for a second he then pointed skywards.

'For example, if the sun were to explode at this precise moment, we wouldn't know about it until the implications of such a catastrophe would reach us. Would you say that the sun died at the point of explosion, or when we became aware of it?'

'I don't know.' Brook conceded. 'But I think I get your meaning.'

'Excellent!' Two Cups chuckled. 'For your interest, there are those who suggest that eight of your so-called minutes would elapse between such an occurrence and everything on your world being obliterated.'

Brook took a moment to digest the information. 'How do you know such things?'

'Travel broadens the mind, my friend.' Two Cups poured another mug of tea. 'Every reality tries to comprehend things in its own unique way. It is only to be expected. Mankind has a tendency to feel insecure about his place in the order of all things so, when faced with the unknown, he tries to quantify things. However, there can be complications when attempting to chart the great unknown. Such are the perils of the explorer.'

He sipped a mouthful of tea before continuing enthusiastically.

'And this raises another issue; one which may help to answer some of your questions. You will have witnessed strange events on your recent travels. Let me give another example to aid my explanation.' Emptying his mug in two big gulps, he waved it animatedly in the air. 'If I were to throw a cup of inferior quality at that rock, it would most likely smash into pieces. Two different events; my throwing the cup being one, the other being the cup shattering on the rock. We would most likely see those two events happening in sequence as one was the direct result of another.'

He fixed them with a twitching eye. 'With me so far?'

Fully in his flow, he continued without waiting for their response. 'However, there are occasions when the order of events fails to concur with this basic logic. We must, therefore, not make the mistake of assuming that was the order in which they occurred. The past, present and future of all realities may for that reason appear to be very jumbled indeed.' He grinned. 'But fear not, fellow travellers. I wish not to confuse you. Suffice to say, if something appears to make no sense, don't worry about trying to comprehend it, for it may not always be possible. All I ask is that you keep an open mind and be prepared to accept the unacceptable.'

He got to his feet. 'I suggest you get some rest before we continue our journey through the pass. I must listen to the wind.'

Brook watched as Two Cups clambered onto a rock a short distance away. He turned to Sanna.

'You didn't ask him about the woman in white.'

'I didn't get the chance to.'

Nodding his agreement, Brook stretched out in the sunshine. Closing his eyes, his thoughts returned to home. How long had he been gone? Two days? Three? Or longer? He really couldn't say for sure. In this strange place, free from the restraints of everyday life, he began to wonder if Messenger Two Cups was right. Maybe time really was irrelevant. And as for the strange events and unusual surroundings, he wondered, not for the first time, if any of it was real. Perhaps he was dreaming the whole thing. Within minutes, he was fast asleep.

The visions of his dream unravelled again.

Walking in the moonlight, he approached the tall standing stones. The bearded figure appeared and beckoned him forward. The images jumped quickly, and once again he found himself in the grand banqueting hall, flanked by the two dogs. Snow flurried outside, offering glimpses of the white-clad mountain peaks. The stranger turned to him and offered his instruction before walking through the doorway. 'Make haste for Sumarren.'

Taro Brook followed cautiously until the sound of splashing water brought him to a sudden halt. Looking down he saw that the water level was rising steadily. Turning back towards the banquet hall, he heard another voice calling his name.

A woman's voice...

'Wake up, Taro Brook. Wake up!'

Stirred to life by the firm grip on his shoulder he opened his eyes to see Sanna leaning over him. 'On your feet, Taro Brook. We have company. A rider approaches.'

Getting to his feet with a yawn, Brook stretched as Messenger Two Cups greeted the rider. 'Who is that?'

Sanna's expression hardened. 'I don't know. For a moment I thought he looked familiar, but I was mistaken.'

Two Cups strode purposefully towards them, the black-cloaked man shadowing his every step.

'Now, my friends, let me introduce you to an old acquaintance of mine. Some say bad news follows him wherever he goes and while this may be true due to the calling of his profession, let not the nature of his work taint your judgement of the man, for he is of noble valour and his bank of courage knows no bounds. This is Harbinger Talus.'

The rider lumbered forward, hawked a spit to the ground, and raised a gloved finger to his forehead in greeting.

'The Woodsman and the Sun Warrior. I consider us well met.' His eyes wandered lazily from Sanna to Brook and back again. 'You can draw your own conclusions; I daresay your opinion will differ somewhat.' His gaze fixed again on Sanna. 'You have a look about you, woman. Would swear I'd run these hawk eyes over you someplace before.' He hesitated. 'And yet, I may be wrong.'

His attention then swung to Taro Brook as a scowl soured his hardened features. 'This one's a bit on the large side for a hobgoblin is he not?'

Two Cups snorted his agreement. 'That's exactly what I said when I first saw him and yet he is indeed a keeper of the forest.' Changing topic quickly, he showed his flask. 'Would you like some tea, Talus?'

'Thanks, but no thanks.' The Harbinger pulled a small hip flask from his cloak. 'I'll stick with what I know.'

Turning to Sanna, Brook lowered his voice. 'He called us the Woodsman and the Sun Warrior? What is that all about? Are you sure you haven't met him before?'

'I'm certain of it. Scaraven probably mentioned us in their previous discussion.'

Her expression left Brook feeling less than convinced.

The Harbinger cleared his throat as he put away the hip flask. 'Much obliged to you for the introductions, Messenger, but we must be about our business. I carry with me a scroll, from the Scribe of Bog-Mire Towers. It urgently requires your attention.'

Two Cups nodded. 'Read it aloud, Talus. I suspect I know the nature of its content and there is nothing to be gained by my being secretive amongst friends and allies.'

Talus frowned. 'These are the written words of the Scribe, meant only for the eyes of Scaraven.'

'There's no need to stand on ceremony here, Harbinger. Let's hear what Token ScriptScratcher has to say. What unspeakable acts have those fools in the High Council committed. Read, my friend. Read!'

'Very well.' Visibly unsettled by the unexpected change in protocol, Harbinger Talus fumbled at the scroll. 'It reads as follows,' he cleared his throat. 'Scaraven, my old friend. Let me apologise in advance for this hastily prepared scrawl, but I fear the fate of Enntonia now hangs in the balance. My investigations have uncovered startling revelations. I hereby state the facts to the best of my knowledge in the hope that it will save us valuable moments upon your arrival here. You will note that I save from requesting your presence, my assumption being that having read this, you will know what must be done.

Having previously informed you of my part in proceedings, I will waste no further ink on the matter. By now, the orders of the High Council will have reached their destination high in the Basilisik Mountain. Written by my own hand, the summons is as simple as it is ghastly. The High Council will grant Osfilian his pardon and freedom on one condition alone. He must summon the dragons! The return of the Black Wing is imminent!

The fools, in their despair they lose what little sanity they had left. According to my confidante, the High Council are on the brink of financial ruin. Rumours now spread like wildfire. There are reported sightings of an approaching army, bearing the banners of Ergmire, marching under the command of General TrollGatten. It transpires Ergmire is owed a fortune in unpaid mining operations, and their patience is running out.

And so, faced with the threat of invasion, the High Council's desperation plummets to new depths. When TrollGatten's force reaches Enntonia, it may well find Osfilian's Black Wing waiting for them. And what of those fools in the High Council? They have plans in place to leave by ship, under cover of darkness, leaving the rest of Enntonia to its fate.

So, having shared the facts as best I can amid this confusion, I bring this scrawl to an end and await the arrival of the Harbinger. I pray he finds you without delay, and that you may be able to offer us some small measure of hope in this our darkest hour.

Yours, in friendship, T.S.'

Taro Brook watched on as the Harbinger rolled the parchment. As the Messenger paced a circle anxiously, Sanna broke the awkward silence.

'The events the Scribe foretells…'

'Yes?' Two Cups interrupted. 'What is it, Sanna?'

'They sound familiar.' Her gaze darted fleetingly to the Harbinger. 'It's as if I've seen them for myself.'

'Incredible!' Two Cups snapped his fingers. 'I must go. My presence is urgently needed in Enntonia. With luck, I will arrive there before it is too late.'

'Wait.' Taro Brook found his voice. 'This doesn't make any sense. How could Sanna possibly recall seeing things that haven't yet happened?'

Two Cups fixed him with a wry smile. 'Perhaps this was what I meant when I asked you to keep an open mind, Woodsman. Be prepared to accept the unacceptable, for everything is not always as it appears. I will try to explain further upon my return but for now I must ask you both to continue the journey through the Enchanted Pass. Mount up, Talus. Make haste for Enntonia.'

The Harbinger fixed Brook with a cold stare. 'We're well met, Woodsman.' Brook nodded as Talus turned his attention to

Sanna. 'Should our paths ever have cause to cross again, Sun Warrior, I will be sure to remember you.'

Sanna watched impassively as the Harbinger turned his mount and galloped into the distance.

'My word.' Two Cups grinned. 'I do believe the big fellow just paid you a compliment. Very unusual.'

'Are you not going with him?' Brook cut in. 'I thought you were going to Enntonia?'

'I am, indeed, Master Brook, but I never did take to horses; always found them a particularly uncomfortable way to travel.' His hand fumbled in the pocket of his faded coat. 'I much prefer my own method of transportation. Take care in the Pass. I will re-join you as soon as I can.'

Glancing ahead towards the towering rocks, Brook heard the Messenger's footsteps in the gravel. When he turned round, Two Cups had vanished from sight.

'What the…? Where did he go?'

'Enntonia.' Sanna replied.

'But he just disappeared!'

'Have you already forgotten your first meeting with Scaraven?'

Brook nodded. Having witnessed the Messenger's strange abilities on more than one occasion he shouldn't have been surprised by the sudden disappearance. 'So, the Enchanted Pass, what lies ahead next I wonder?'

'Expect the unexpected, Taro Brook,' she called back freely. 'Isn't that what Scaraven would say?'

As they wound their way up the narrowing track towards the sand-coloured escarpment, Brook's thoughts strayed back to his recurring dream.

CHAPTER FORTY-SIX

Reaching out blindly, he knocked the bedside lamp crashing to the floor. Tybor Barkal sat up and rubbed the sleep from his eyes. Where was his damned phone? Stumbling from the bed, he picked his jacket up from the floor. Throwing himself back down on the crumpled covers, he pulled the phone from the jacket pocket and answered the call gruffly.

'Barkal!' Sobek's voice sent the familiar shudder down his spine. 'About time! I told you to stay alert. I called you earlier, you didn't answer.'

'Didn't hear it, Senator. I must have been asleep.'

'Late night was it?' Sobek droned sarcastically. 'You'd best not have a hangover, Barkal, you are already running behind schedule. Instructions for today are waiting at the usual place. Get your act together, and make sure you answer the phone next time I call.'

Barkal lay in the silence of the half-lit room contemplating his horrid predicament. Would he ever be able to sever his ties with Senator Sobek?

Dragging himself from the bed, he pulled open the blinds. Daylight flooded the room. Shielding his eyes from the sudden glare of the morning, he turned to the mirror. Inspecting his tired reflection he quickly dismissed the notion of shaving. The time

saved would be better spent having a cold beer in the Ice Bar and, as he had to go there anyway, it made perfect sense.
Stepping into the shower, he wondered how he had missed Sobek's earlier call. He was a light sleeper. How had he not heard the phone ringing?

CHAPTER FORTY-SEVEN

... Troubled yet again with the unnerving sensation of being watched, he glanced repeatedly over his shoulder, each time expecting to see someone emerging from the trees behind. There seemed little doubt about it. He was being watched. He was being followed.

Tapping the desk impatiently, Hans Rugen stared blankly at his laptop screen. Mesmerised by the blinking cursor he waited in vain for inspiration. It was useless. None was coming. Following Sonja Egberts' call for help he'd tried for two days, without success, to add something to the failed storyline.

It was hopeless. His thoughts turned to Mitchell Egberts. It had now been three days since he'd heard from him. His initial sense of relief that the phone calls had stopped had now turned to concern at the lack of contact.

Focusing on the task at hand, Rugen conceded enough was enough. He had a crime thriller to finish; his deadline was looming ever closer, and his agent was getting restless. He would just have to call Sonja and make his apologies. He'd tried his best, she would understand; too bad if she didn't. At the same time, he could enquire about Mitch. Perhaps things had returned to normal, maybe that was why he had heard nothing.

With his decision made, he rose from the chair, picked up his empty coffee cup, and went through to the kitchen. Behind him the cursor blinked impatiently, eagerly awaiting his return.

After preparing another coffee, he went out into the backyard to fetch logs for the fire. As he neared the shed where he stored his firewood he came to a sudden halt. His eyes were drawn to the trees beyond the picket fence. Unable to shake the feeling he was being watched, he became lost, engrossed by the movement of the branches as they swayed hypnotically in the breeze.

Moments later, scolding his lapse in concentration, he picked up an armful of logs and marched back along the garden path. There was no time for daydreaming; he had work to do.

Back once again in the living room, he placed two logs on the fire and sat down in front of the laptop. Taking a mouthful of coffee he held the cup at arm's length, eyeing it dubiously for a few seconds before placing it down on the table. It just didn't taste right. With a shake of his head he returned his attention to the dancing cursor. Scanning the short passage of text on the screen, he nodded his acknowledgement, flexed his fingers, and began typing.

Becoming engrossed in his work, he paid no heed to the passing of time. When he eventually lifted his attention away from the screen, he saw that the sun had dipped below the treetops and was casting ghostly shafts of light into the darker recesses of the forest. Satisfied with what he'd written, he eased back in the chair. He needed a drink. Picking up the discarded coffee, he rose from the desk and went back into the kitchen.

Pouring the cold coffee away, he rinsed the cup clean and took a box of tea leaves from the cupboard. Placing the kettle on the stove, he stared out of the window and let his mind wander.

The whistling of the boiling kettle brought him to attention. Dismissing the notion of tea, he made a fresh cup of coffee and made his way back to the living room. He picked up the phone. He had a call to make; there was no point in putting it off any longer. Sitting down in front of the laptop, his gaze met with the flashing cursor. His jaw dopped open in astonishment.

Leaning forward in the chair, he stared at the screen in disbelief. He scrolled back through the text. Page after page after page. He didn't remember writing any of this. Exasperated by its sudden inexplicable appearance, he scrolled to his starting point and, in a desperate effort to reconcile himself with the words on the screen, began to read.

By the time he'd finished reading, the last throws of twilight had surrendered to darkness. Though far from complete it was a fascinating tale, yet its very existence troubled Rugen greatly.
He had no recollection of writing it.
Rising from the chair, he flicked on the light switch and paced the room. Pouring a glass of red wine, he drained it quickly. As he refilled the glass, he eyed the laptop suspiciously. The cursor taunted him with unanswerable questions.
When had he written this, and why could he not remember doing so? Why did he not feel any familiarity to the characters, or recognise any part of the storyline?
Was he experiencing some form of memory loss?

He didn't think so. Apart from the obvious feelings of unease, which were understandable given the circumstances, he felt fine. And yet, it was the only conceivable explanation.
So, where had the inspiration for this storyline come from?
He'd abandoned the idea of the walker in the woods, only returning to it following Sonja Egberts' plea for help. Even then he'd been forced to concede that the story was doomed to failure and resigned to the fact, he'd been about to call Sonja.
And then this had happened.

Sonja. He should call her now. An explanation to his situation clearly wasn't about to present itself but perhaps he could do some good in the meantime. With his eyes fixed on the screen, he picked up the phone and dialled the number. In his eagerness to pass on his startling news, he failed to notice her muted response.

'Hello, Sonja, this is Hans Rugen. I'm not quite sure how I've managed it, but I've come up with some more on that storyline you asked me about, quite a lot more actually. It's not finished, but there is plenty to keep Mitch occupied if he wanted to read some of it. Is he there?' He waited for a response, but none came.

'Sonja, is Mitch there?' Still no response. 'Sonja, are you there?'

'Yes, Hans... I am here.'

Rugen held his breath in anticipation. Something was wrong, very wrong.

'Hans... I was going to call you...' Her speech was slow and measured. 'Mitchell's body was found earlier today at the foot of the cliffs in Greenhill Forest. He'd been missing for three days.

They said he must have slipped and fallen over the edge… He didn't survive the fall.'

Rugen searched for the right words. Any words. None came. He swallowed uncomfortably as Sonja Egberts continued.

'I'm really happy for you that your story has sprung to life, Hans.' The words stung him to the core. 'Unfortunately,' she continued, 'it's come too late to help Mitch.'

As she ended the call, he stared at the computer screen in disbelief. The plot he had struggled with for so long had suddenly appeared from nowhere, written this afternoon without his knowledge, only hours after Mitchell Egberts' obsession with the damned thing had driven him, quite literally, over the edge.

Rugen hovered over the edit menu. He wanted to delete it all. And yet, as his eyes wandered over the newly discovered story, he knew he wasn't ready to dispose of it. There were far too many unanswered questions. Saving his decision for another day, Hans Rugen shut down his laptop.

Easing himself gently into the chair by the fire, with the wine bottle for company, he drained and filled his glass three times in quick succession. As the numbing effects of the wine took hold, he closed his eyes in a futile attempt to dispel the bizarre and distressing events of the day.

CHAPTER FORTY-EIGHT

As the track steepened, the overhanging cliffs loomed dauntingly over the pass leaving much of it hidden in shadow. Feeling less than enthusiastic about the prospect of what might lie ahead, Taro Brook looked back to the white ruins of Kar-Bysdell far in the distance.

'Stay close, Woodsman.' Sanna's voice focused his attention. 'You know what can happen when we separate.'

'Have you been through the Pass before?' He quickened his pace.

'That is not an easy question to answer. I've been here several times, but the path offers many differing destinations.'

Brook noted the caution in her words. 'You mean there are gateways here?'

'There are gateways everywhere, Taro Brook.'

As they walked, her voice echoed among the crags. 'This was once known as the Robber's Pass. It was a favoured hangout for thieves. Many travellers who ventured here were never heard of again. It became infamous, a place to avoid for fear of ambush.'

'Is it safe now?'

'Yes, ever since the Magicker came and cast an enchantment, placing the Pass and the surrounding area under his protection.'

Brook let the reference to magic pass without comment. 'I can't imagine this place being a prosperous haunt for thieves,' he countered. 'I haven't seen much sign of life these last few days. It seems few journey this way.'

'Appearances can be deceptive. Many now travel through the Pass and besides, the thieves I mentioned were not interested in monetary gain. The stone ghouls had their sights set on a bounty of a very different nature.'

'Stone ghouls?'

'Foul creatures, remnants of what were once men. Scaraven could tell their story better than I, but this much I know, they feed on fear and draw strength by draining the souls of others. Luckily, the threat of stone ghouls is long gone from this place.'

Overhead, the sound of ruffling feathers and whispered chattering carried eerily among the rocks. Hidden from view, a winged guard of honour followed their progress from above. A loud, raspy 'kraa' did more than just startle Brook; it betrayed the identity of the watchers from above. He knew the signature call of the crow and raven well.

'What do you make of the Harbinger's words?' he asked.

'It is grave news for the people of Enntonia,' she replied. 'Perhaps Scaraven can do something to help them.'

'But you said you recognised the events he described. How do you explain that?'

'I don't know, and it troubles me. Scaraven would have us keep an open mind, but I find it easier to allow such things no further consideration.'

Acknowledging her words, he changed the subject.

'Have you been to Sumarren before?'

'No. But I've heard much about it. I look forward to seeing it.'

As the track levelled, the steep sides of the pass took on a dark, foreboding feel as the rock changed in colour and appearance. Brook paused for refreshment at a falling stream of crystal-clear water. Cupping the water in his hands, he jumped back in surprise as a face formed in the rock in front of him. Empty eyes stared back at him; an open mouth gaped its silent greeting.

'Taro Brook.' A whisper came from above.

Looking up, he saw another of the faces appear in the rock. Stepping back in alarm, he saw yet another, then another. The wall twisted animatedly with a multitude of the yawning faces. The whispers increased in number; a cacophony of voices, each with their own warning, each issuing their own command.

'Go back, Taro Brook.' whispered one.

'Go home, Taro Brook.' hissed another.

'Trust no one, Taro Brook.' warned the next.

'Your end is coming, Taro Brook.'

'Taro Brook... Taro Brook...'

'Taro Brook, what are you doing?' Her voice cut through the melee. Turning, he saw Sanna striding towards him. 'We have to stay close. It's too dangerous to become separated here. What were you looking at?'

'Faces,' he replied hesitantly. 'Faces in the rock. They were calling my name, warning me. They're gone now. Did you see them?'

She shook her head. 'I saw nothing, but that is understandable.'

'Why? What do you mean?'

'This is an enchanted place. I too have seen things here that no one else could see.'

'Are you suggesting that I imagined them?'

'Some say there is little difference between imagination and perception, Taro Brook. You saw what you say you saw; I do not question your word.'

'But what would they have been? Were they stone ghouls?'

'I doubt that. Perhaps your mind projected your interpretation of them, and that is what you saw. We should keep moving. Keep your thoughts clear and your eyes fixed straight ahead.'

As the Pass widened again, the track led down a gentle slope and followed alongside a large pool of water churned into a white frothed frenzy by a series of waterfalls cascading down the mountainside. Brook marvelled at the rock sculptures carved intricately over time by the falling water. Mesmerised by the noise and motion of the water, he became lost in his thoughts.

'Thinking of home?' she asked.

'Yes, and I was thinking about all the strange things that have happened recently. It's like a work of fiction; it would make an interesting read.'

'Are you a writer, Taro Brook?'

'Can't say I've ever tried,' he replied. 'Probably not.'

'Do you carry writing implements with you?'

'No. Why?'

'Then I suggest you give it no further consideration. You will remember nothing of this on your return. As for your thoughts of home, perhaps you get nearer with every step you take.'

'Do you think so?'

'I don't know,' she shrugged. 'But it's a possibility worth considering.'

The path flanked the swirling water's edge, clinging tightly to the jagged contours of the eroded rock. At the crest of a short incline, an impressive structure came into view on the far side of the water. The lower half of the building, constructed from grey-coloured stone, was lined with an array of narrow windows. The timber upper level led to a wide balcony covered by an elaborate, overhanging roof. Despite its impressive construction, it appeared that an important detail had been omitted. Taro Brook could determine no means of access, and no point of entry. Perched high in its rocky lair, the building seemed completely impenetrable.

'Interesting place. What is it?'

'I don't know,' she replied. 'I've never seen it before. It appears we are both now in uncharted territory.'

Troubled by her unexpected response, he followed quietly as she led the way. The terrain steepened sharply again and as they gained further height a green-washed meadowland dotted with scattered trees stretched out before them.

Directing his gaze away from the scene, Sanna gestured ahead.

'We must ignore the tempting distractions of the Enchanted Pass, Woodsman. Our path leads that way.'

CHAPTER FORTY-NINE

Easing himself into a sitting position high in the upper branches of the tree, Elfin Fingle pulled his spyglass from the inside pocket of his cloak and focused on the dust cloud in the distance.
His lofty vantage point offered a clear view. As his eyes focused on the cause of the disturbance, he let out a gasp of disbelief.

An army, bearing black banners emblazoned with a streak of gold, was marching towards Enntonia.

A keen student of heraldry, Elfin had no further need of the spyglass. Pushing it back inside his cloak, he clambered hurriedly down the tree. Jumping to the ground, he landed awkwardly and rolled forward, coming to rest against an old fencepost.
Scrambling to his feet, he dusted himself down. His afternoon ramble in the forest had taken an unexpected twist, and there was no time to waste. He followed the rickety fence down past the abandoned watchtower. There was no need to climb for further confirmation and besides, there was no time. He had to inform Token ScriptScratcher at once. He had to get back to Bog-Mire Towers.

Running as fast as his short legs would carry him, Elfin hurried through the ancient oak wood and crossed the corn fields, pushing the long stalks aside dismissively as they waved gently in the breeze.

As he jumped the fence at the end of Oak Lane, he heard the sound of a horse approaching. Instinctively, he took cover amongst the branches of the whispering fir trees and held his breath as the horse and rider galloped by. Under normal circumstances there would be no need to use such caution. Elfin had the feeling things were far from normal.

Catching a fleeting glimpse of the hooded rider, he thought for a moment of Harbinger Talus before dismissing the notion. The Harbinger always wore black gloves when riding.

The pallid, bony hands gripping the reins sent an unsettling shiver down Elfin's back. Relieved at his decision to take cover, he reluctantly left his hiding place and hurried on his way.

An eerie silence accompanied him as he made his way along Shadow Lane. The dark, brooding trees closed in suspiciously. Glancing over his shoulder, he broke into a run. The sooner he was back at Bog-Mire the better.

At the first glimpse of the familiar grey-stoned turrets poking above the treetops, he stopped for breath. 'Nearly there.' He puffed his satisfaction. A few moments later, he opened the front door of Bog-Mire Towers and entered the grand hallway. He was about to climb the stairs to the Scribe's study when a shout from the drawing room stopped him in his tracks.

'In here, Elfin!'

He tapped gently on the door and entered the room. Token ScriptScratcher was standing by the fire, a cup of tea in one hand, his pipe in the other.

'Come in, Elfin. We have a visitor. Let me make the introductions.'

Elfin's gaze shifted to the armchair on the far side of the fireplace. A wily looking character, dressed in a faded overcoat and strange yellow hat, greeted him with a cheery smile as he rose energetically from the chair.

'No need for introductions, Master Scribe,' he snorted as he bounded towards Elfin. 'Delighted to make your acquaintance, Master Fingle.' He thrust out a hand in greeting. 'Messenger Two Cups at your service. Come join us by the fireside, we are having a cup of Mrs Burrows' tea, and a fine brew it is.'

Warming instantly to the stranger's jovial manner, Elfin almost forgot the pressing business that had curtailed his visit to the woods. He glanced towards the Scribe.

'I apologise for the interruption, but I have worrying news. I saw something when I was up by the old watchtower; something bad.'

Token ScriptScratcher responded with a worried frown. 'Take a seat and tell us this news.'

Elfin quickly relayed the details of what he'd seen. 'The army,' he summed up nervously, 'they bore the banners of Ergmire.'

Token ScriptScratcher rose from his chair and tapped his pipe repeatedly on the mantelpiece. 'So, it appears our worst fears are confirmed. Your news is not altogether unexpected, Elfin, but I am troubled by the pace of events. I had hoped we might have had more time.'

'Time is of no relevance, old friend.' The Messenger placed his cup firmly down on the saucer. 'Ergmire's force will soon be upon us. We must make haste.'

'And what do you suggest we do?' Token ScriptScratcher sighed. 'I had hoped for more opportunity to prepare.'

'We must face the task head on. We must ride out to meet with TrollGatten.'

'What about Scaraven?' asked Elfin, taken aback by their lack of surprise to his news. 'Did Harbinger Talus find Scaraven? Will he be coming to help?'

'Yes, yes, the Harbinger found him.' Waving Elfin's concerns aside, the Messenger took control of the conversation. 'Scaraven is already playing his part and will arrive if and when he needs to. Now, as to our present dilemma.' He toyed with his whiskers. 'Perhaps we can provide some kind of smokescreen, an illusion, a little something to keep our impending foe at bay.' A grin flashed across his face. 'And I think I might have an idea.'
He clapped his hands together. 'My friends, ready your horses whilst I make some last-minute preparations. We must meet with TrollGatten before he descends from the foothills of the Hogback Mountains.'

The mention of horses triggered Elfin's recollection of his close encounter with the hooded rider. 'That reminds me,' he burst out excitedly, 'there was something else I had to tell you.'

'Yes?' Token prompted. 'What was it?'

'On my way back here I saw a strange rider in the woods at Oak Lane. There was something very sinister about it. It was cloaked and hooded. I hid in the trees but caught a glimpse of its hands as it passed. The fingers... they were skeletal.'

Messenger Two Cups held a finger to his lips in a silencing motion. 'Say no more about it, Master Fingle.' He turned to the

Scribe. 'It appears things may be worse than we thought, Token. Much worse!'

'What is it?' Elfin asked edgily. 'Who was the rider?'

'I will not speak of it here. And I suggest you try to put it from your thoughts.' As if sensing Elfin's growing bewilderment, Messenger Two Cups flashed him a reassuring smile. 'Worry not, young fellow, perhaps we can still turn things in our favour.' Lowering his gaze, his smile was quickly replaced by a worried frown. Reaching out suddenly, he swiped at the sleeve of Elfin's green cloak. Elfin looked down to see a small black insect wriggling in desperation on the floor.

'Curses on you, Tickbus Tard.' The Messenger hissed his annoyance as his boot brought the insect's struggle to a swift end.

'What is it?' Elfin eyed the squashed remains. 'I've never seen one like that before.'

'There are few in these parts that have, Master Fingle.'

'I don't understand. Where could it have come from?'

'Did you come through long grass on your way here?'

'Yes, but I often take that shortcut and I've never seen...'

'It matters not, it is here now.' Messenger Two Cups shook his head in disgust. 'Despite its small stature, its appearance is unwelcome. It is a servant of an undesirable creature, a tormented soul with a twisted mind.' He glanced at his two companions. 'We will speak more of this later. It appears our situation is bleak, but we must delay no longer. TrollGatten and his army await. My friends, I must beg your assistance. I would face this task alone and spare you from any involvement if I could, but I fear the challenge is too great.'

'Of course, Messenger,' Token ScriptScratcher nodded. 'You do not need to ask. I will do all that I can.'

'I would never doubt it, old friend.' The Messenger smiled as he turned towards Elfin. 'And so, Master Fingle, fate has decreed that you too have a part to play in the unfolding events, but I must offer a word of warning. You may encounter things that make little, or no sense, and it would be fair to say that some things might never appear the same again. I would not presume to force such things upon you without your assent. What say you?'

With no real thought or consideration to what he was agreeing to, Elfin's sense of adventure took control. 'Yes, Messenger,' he said excitedly. 'You can count on me.'

Messenger Two Cups smiled with satisfaction.

'So be it. Perhaps we can yet salvage some hope in the days ahead. This latest twist,' he glanced at the squashed remains on the floor, 'requires my urgent attention. There is something I must attend to before we deal with TrollGatten.' He fixed his willing accomplices with a determined grin. 'Prepare your horses. I will meet you soon at the Western Gate.'

CHAPTER FIFTY

As they continued their progress through the Pass, Taro Brook pondered the striking similarities between the structure in the cliffs and the building in his dreams. As unlikely as it seemed, the resemblances were undeniable.

Stopping him in his tracks with a gesture of her hand, Sanna held a finger to her lips, prompting him to silence. As he followed her gaze to the rocks above, she moved closer and whispered her warning. 'We are being followed.'

'Followed? How do you know?'

'I saw movement in the rocks further back. They're tracking us from above.'

'I don't see anything. There were birds further back, ravens or crows...'

'These are no ravens, Taro Brook,' she hissed. 'I think I can tell the difference...'

Her response stalled as a figure jumped into view a short distance ahead. Dressed only in grey leggings, his bare upper torso was almost covered in dark blue markings. His long dark hair was tied back from his face. Waving a broadsword in their direction, he watched them closely.

Sanna took hold of Brook's arm. 'No sudden movements, Woodsman. There are more of them. Their archers have us firmly in their sights.'

As if prompted by her words, a shout came from behind as more of the blue-marked strangers emerged from the cover of the rocks.

Brook shot her a look of dismay. 'We are surrounded. What do we do?'

'For now, we do nothing.'

As one of the painted men moved towards them, he snapped his commands to his fellow warriors.

'Bind them! Blindfold them. Take them to the stronghold.'

CHAPTER FIFTY-ONE

Huddled in the lee of the ancient oak tree, Token ScriptScratcher and Elfin Fingle watched on anxiously as the group of riders approached. Trembling with fear, Elfin glanced up at the Scribe. Token placed a reassuring hand on his shoulder.

'Easy, Elfin,' he said, trying to disguise the shake in his voice. 'I'm certain the Messenger will be here soon. He will know what to do.'

'But what is taking him so long? I thought he would have been here by now.'

On their arrival at the Western Gate they'd found a hastily written note pinned to the door of the old sentry post. Clutching it tightly, Elfin hurriedly scanned the words again.

Friends,
Forgive my delay. I will be with you as soon as my preparations allow. In the meantime, I implore you to continue on your way. TrollGatten's army has come to a halt at the foot of the Hogback Mountains; he now leads a small scouting party towards the city. Make haste, my friends. I will meet with you at the fork in the trail, by the Old Great Oak.

Elfin crumpled the note back into his pocket and watched nervously as the horsemen came to a halt. Three riders, one bearing a black and gold banner, broke rank and dismounted. An ominous sound carried across the glade as the armoured warriors lumbered towards them.

'The big fellow in the middle,' whispered Token. 'I think that could be General TrollGatten himself.' Clearing his throat, he straightened himself in an attempt to not appear intimidated and delivered his greeting boldly. 'Welcome, TrollGatten of Ergmire. Enntonia is honoured by your arrival.'

Elfin Fingle drew a sharp intake of breath as the leader removed his helm, revealing his haggard features. The rough-textured skin stretched tightly over an elongated jawbone set beneath an accentuated snout. Stubby pointed ears sprouted from a closely cropped mane of wiry black hair. Towering over them, his huge claw-like hands hovering worryingly close to his sword, he gave a short growl and addressed his welcoming party bluntly.

'Enntonia's honour is of no interest to me. Your words are well meant, but my business is with the High Council. Do you speak for them? If not, then stand aside.'

Elfin shuddered uncomfortably as Token ScriptScratcher fumbled for a suitable response. To their relief, a shout from the trees came to their rescue.

'Hail, TrollGatten of Ergmire.' A dark-haired figure, cloaked in red, entered the glade and strode towards them. 'Enntonia's High Council has fallen. I will speak with you in their stead.'

'Who is that?' Elfin whispered. 'What's he talking about?'

Token ScriptScratcher's stare scolded him to silence.

'Who are you?' TrollGatten scowled his response. 'Announce yourself. Under what authority do you address Ergmire's envoy?'

The new arrival stood his ground boldly. 'The High Council no longer holds power in Enntonia. I am well aware of Ergmire's trials and tribulations with the fools who ruled here until recently, but your arrival is in vain.'

Elfin glanced up at the Scribe in confusion. Token ScriptScratcher shook his head in response.

TrollGatten of Ergmire wasn't ready to be so easily dissuaded. His fist hovered over the handle of his sword as he responded to the stranger.

'Enough talk. Give me your name. I tire of your ramblings.'

'There is no need to reach for your blade, TrollGatten. It has long been my calling to protect these lands and its people and for my failures I now carry a heavy burden. In the absence of King and High Council, it is my duty to deal with matters as best I can. You are speaking with the Defender of all Enntonia.'

Elfin Fingle gasped his astonishment. How was this possible? The Defender belonged in myth and folklore. Glancing sideways he was relieved to see his thoughts mirrored on the Scribe's face.

'Your name is known to me, Defender,' growled TrollGatten. 'That is, if you are who you claim to be.'

'It cannot be so,' sneered the standard-bearer. 'The one you mention left these lands to their fate centuries ago.'

'Silence!' TrollGatten roared his annoyance. 'Hold your tongue, soldier.' He turned his attention once more to the newcomer. 'Tell me, Defender, what proof do you offer to support your claim and, more importantly, what is this news you would have us believe? What fate has suddenly befallen this wretched land?'

'As for my identity, it doesn't matter whether you believe me or not. It is irrelevant. But, as you have marched many long days and nights through inhospitable terrain, you should at least consider heeding my warnings. I don't expect you to take my word alone for what has happened here but perhaps I can dispel your doubts in other ways. I will lead you to the evidence you desire. Let your own eyes succeed where my words fail.'

In response to his shrill whistle, a grey horse cantered into the clearing. 'Make your preparations, TrollGatten, we ride for town. I will accompany six of your riders, no more.'

He then turned his attention to Token and Elfin. 'The Messenger sends his apologies. Events have taken a dramatic turn which is why he called for my assistance. You will ride with us; he will meet you in town. Say nothing on our journey. Though your questions be many, I bid you… say nothing!'

Elfin joined the Scribe in quickly nodding their consent. Coupled with the daunting presence of Ergmire's show of force, the stranger's sudden appearance and grim warning was more than enough to quell Elfin's usually vocal enthusiasm. As they left the clearing, flanked by the riders of Ergmire, Elfin wondered with trepidation what lay ahead. Straining his ears as best he could, he listened in as TrollGatten questioned the red-cloaked stranger further.

'Tell me more of what you claim has happened here. When last I heard from these lands, the High Council still held power.'

'And tell me, when did you last receive word from Enntonia?'

'It has been some time…' The warrior hesitated. 'Enntonia has been negligent in its correspondence.'

'And is that why your armed force is now at large in our lands?'

'My homeland expects their debtors to pay up,' roared TrollGatten, riled by the questioning of his motives. 'We have tried to claim what is owed by peaceful means, but our patience is at an end.'

'I am well aware of the debts due to Ergmire, but you will find none here in a position to set things right. A dark evil has returned to this land, a land held tightly in the firm grip of chaos.'

'What evil? What trickery is this?'

'It is no trickery. I speak of the wizard Osfilian, and the return of the Black Wing dragons.'

'More lies,' snapped the standard-bearer. 'Dragons live only in myth and legend.'

'Silence, you fool,' TrollGatten spat his command. 'Or I will cut that loose tongue from your mouth.'

'As your banner man rightly says, these cursed beasts should live only in legend. But their threat is all too real and present. Osfilian's dark agents are afoot in Enntonia. Word of the impending arrival of the Black Wing was enough; panic spread like wildfire. The cowards in the High Council were among the first to flee. The city has fallen into disorder, blighted by looting and riots. To escape the anarchy, many have fled to take shelter in the hills. Few now remain, waiting in fear, hoping that the dark days will pass, praying that the Black Wing do not return.'

Elfin and Token ScriptScratcher exchanged glances. They now understood the stranger's request for silence.

'I will hear no more of your talk.' TrollGatten spurred his steed into a gallop. 'I will see this for myself. Let's find what truth lies behind your veil of deception.'

A strange mist greeted them as they rode into town. Elfin gasped in astonishment at the scene of destruction. The deserted streets offered no sign of life. Smoke rose from the blackened shells of burnt-out buildings. Merging with the mist, it blocked all view of the sky. Elfin found some comfort in Token ScriptScratcher's troubled expression. The Scribe's confusion clearly matched his own. What had happened here? When had it happened? And how had they not heard about it until now?

The group rode along the eerily quiet main thoroughfare until TrollGatten's raised fist brought them to a halt outside the chambers of Enntonia's High Council.

'What has happened here?'

'The Black Wizard's mist hangs over this place like a curse. What you see before you is the result of fear and desperation.'

'So be it.' TrollGatten snarled his contempt. 'In exchange for the debt owed, we will search this place and take what we find. Dismount!' His command was met by silence. 'Dismount!' He repeated the order. 'There's work to be done.'

'Something is wrong here, General.' The standard-bearer aired the boar-men's doubts. 'There is sorcery at work here. We should leave this place.'

TrollGatten shook his head in annoyance. 'Superstitious cowards.' His unnerving glare settled on Elfin Fingle. 'What say you, little one? Is there witchcraft at work here?'

'Yes,' Elfin struggled to find the nerve to respond. 'I think so.'

TrollGatten picked at his pointed teeth as he considered his options. 'Very well, I see little point in pushing my faint-hearted comrades against their will. We will ride back and re-join our brothers in the foothills, but heed my words, we will remain in position until I am convinced that things here truly are as you claim them to be. My scouting parties will uncover the truth. Ergmire will not be denied.'

'A fair compromise, TrollGatten.' The Defender nodded his agreement. 'I will accompany you back to the forest.' He then turned to Token ScriptScratcher and Elfin.

'Farewell for now. Urgent matters call me elsewhere. But I expect the Messenger will be here soon.'

They watched as the riders disappeared into the mist. As the sound of the horses faded, a bemused Elfin Fingle was finally able to raise his concerns.

'What has happened here, Scribe? I just don't understand it.'

Token ScriptScratcher shook his head in response. 'This is far beyond my reckoning, Elfin. We must wait for the Messenger to arrive, perhaps he can throw some light on it all. He did say something about a diversion of sorts. But this?'

'Where will we wait for him?'

'I know the very place. Let's go, I swear this confounded mist is getting thicker by the minute.'

Picking their route through the debris, they turned down a narrow side-street and entered a tearoom often frequented by the Scribe of Bog-Mire on his visits to town. Aside from an overturned table and a couple of scattered chairs, it remained largely unaffected by the chaos outside.

'Get the kettle on, Elfin. I think we could do with a brew.'

Elfin busied himself in the kitchen, preparing a large pot of steaming hot tea. Searching the cupboards, he quickly assembled a plate of cream buns and oat biscuits and re-joined the Scribe who was preparing his pipe for a smoke. As Elfin began pouring their tea, they heard the sound of footsteps and whistling from outside.

'You'd best find another cup, Elfin.' Token grinned. 'It sounds like we have company.'

The tuneless whistle stopped abruptly as the door of the tearoom swung open and Messenger Two Cups stepped inside.

'Aha! Excellent timing. Recharge the pot, young Elfin. I'm parched.'

Messenger Two Cups drained his third cup of tea and offered his appreciation. 'An excellent brew, Master Fingle, excellent indeed.' He patted his stomach. 'Let me apologise for not being with you. I was delayed with other urgent business, but I take it TrollGatten fell for our little deception?'

The Scribe of Bog-Mire's eyebrows twitched inquisitively. 'It appears that way, but tell me, that deception as you call it, was it all your doing?'

Messenger Two Cups shrugged dismissively. 'I can take credit for the idea, but I had some assistance in its manifestation. Don't worry though, it is nothing more than an illusion.'

'An illusion?' Elfin jumped to the window. 'But… the mist is still out there.'

'Indeed it is, and I hope it remains there long enough to fully deceive our visitors from Ergmire.'

'I don't understand,' protested Elfin. 'How is it possible to create such an illusion?'

'Ah, well, in order to comprehend that, we must first ask what an illusion is. And the simple answer? A perception, representing something in a different way to how it appears in reality.'
He grinned widely. 'But which reality? There are many possible outcomes to any given scenario; we merely exchanged one of these outcomes for another. The sad truth, my friends, is this; our deception is not all that hard to imagine. If we fail in our efforts to thwart Osfilian's plans, the scenario you witnessed out there will indeed become our reality.'

'Who helped you?' Elfin asked eagerly. 'Was it Scaraven?'

'Indeed it was, Master Fingle.'

Token ScriptScratcher tapped his pipe gently on the table. 'And the Defender? Was he part of the illusion?'

'No illusion there, the Defender played his part in bringing my scheme to fruition. His role in dealing with TrollGatten was vital.'

'But that's impossible.' Elfin voiced his doubts. 'How could it really be the Defender? He was last seen in Enntonia centuries ago.'

The Messenger eyed him with a hint of disapproval. 'My recollections of Enntonian folklore suggest that the Defender was a wizard of great renown. You'd have to concede that it would be a bold claim on your part to question his abilities and limitations.'

'Bold or foolish!' Token scolded. 'Really, Elfin, you must try to consider your words more carefully, especially in these troubled times.'

Elfin quickly offered his apologies. He had never quite mastered the art of thinking before speaking; his randomly shared thoughts were often a source of embarrassment.

With that, the Messenger rose abruptly from his chair. 'There are dark days ahead, my friends. We must act swiftly. Whilst I fear the illusion will not hold TrollGatten at bay for long, it is of little consequence. If we do not stop Osfilian in his tracks, our fate will be sealed. I sense that he may already be on his way, I have seen signs which may herald his arrival.' He frowned deeply. 'I have to leave you now. I have other friends in need of my help. Return to Bog-Mire, my trusted allies, and await my further instruction.'

Elfin Fingle watched the door close and waited until the sound of whistling faded. He turned to the Scribe. 'Do you think it's possible that Scaraven is the Defender?'

Token ScriptScratcher eyed him suspiciously. 'What do you mean?'

'Well,' he hesitated, 'they are both said to be wizards... Aren't they?'

'I have no idea, Elfin,' Token puffed his pipe dismissively. 'Can't say I've ever given the matter any thought.' He frowned at his young assistant. 'And neither should you. Wizards' business is business best left alone.' He rose from the table. 'Come, let's

get back to Bog-Mire before the mist clears. Put the rest of those cream buns and biscuits in a bag. We'll take them with us.'
He gave a mischievous wink. 'It would be a shame to let them go to waste, wouldn't it?'

CHAPTER FIFTY-TWO

Taro Brook watched from the window as daylight crept across the sky bringing with it the promise of another fine day. He wondered for a fleeting moment if it ever rained in this strange land then turned his attention to the room.

The hours had passed slowly since their abduction in the Pass. Having undone their bonds, the blue-marked warriors had left without explanation, locking the door from the outside.

Sanna sat cross-legged on one of the beds, her eyes shut in quiet contemplation. She'd said little since their imprisonment and when he'd commented on her laid-back approach to their predicament, she'd suggested that they reserve judgement until their captors' motives became clear.

He stifled a yawn. He hadn't slept well. Seemed he held a strong aversion to being locked up against his will.

'You worry too much, Taro Brook.' Sanna opened her eyes.

'I don't like being held prisoner.'

She shrugged. 'At least they are not hostile, and they left us with food and drink. Things could be worse.' As she got to her feet, the sound of footsteps came from beyond the locked door. 'Don't say or do anything hasty,' she cautioned. 'Let's hear their intentions before we act.'

They waited in anticipation as the lock clicked back loudly. The door swung open as the keyholder entered the room.

'Two Cups?' Taro Brook couldn't contain his surprise at the unexpected twist. 'How did you find us?'

The Messenger chuckled as he marched to the table and helped himself to some bread and cheese. 'It is good to see you both again. I trust you were looked after sufficiently?'

'Looked after?' Brook frowned as he glanced towards the open door. 'Shouldn't we get going before they discover you're here?'

Two Cups grinned widely. 'There's no need to worry, Woodsman. We won't be disturbed, nor will you be detained any longer. My painted warrior friends were merely looking after you until I made my return.'

'What? You mean to say you arranged our capture?'

Sanna laughed at Brook's reaction. He turned to her.

'Did you know about this? Is that why you appeared so calm?'

'I knew nothing of this,' she shook her head. 'But it makes sense. They showed no hostility towards us.'

'But why did you have to do it that way?' Brook turned to Two Cups. 'Could you not have had them explain it to us?'

The Messenger dismissed the notion as he poured a mug of tea from his flask. 'I fear communication between you would have been difficult. Besides, even if you had been able to understand what they were saying, would you have believed them? Would you have let yourself be imprisoned?'

Taro Brook took a moment to consider his answer before reluctantly conceding the point. 'No, I suppose not.'

'Why was such action necessary?' quizzed Sanna. 'We were making good progress through the Pass. What happened?'

Two Cups drained his tea mug noisily. 'I apologise for your ordeal. I'm sure it must have come as a shock, but I'm afraid it was unavoidable. I could think of no other way to ensure your safety at such short notice. The Black Wizard's servants are on the move, I have seen the signs of their stirring. I fear the Enchanted Pass no longer offers us safe passage. We must take a diversion.'

'Where would you have us go, Scaraven?'

'We must make for the coast and descend the sea-cliff steps. With good fortune and a low tide, we can pass under the sea arch. From there, the coastal path will lead us to the headland overlooking the Firth and our final crossing to Sumarren.' He grinned widely at Taro Brook. 'What say you, Woodsman? Does that sound like a plan?'

Brook frowned. 'Do we have any option?'

Two Cups snorted. 'An excellent answer, my friend. I do declare you are learning fast.' He gestured towards the open door. 'Let's be on our way.'

As they descended the stairs, Brook glanced behind, half expecting their captors to appear at any moment, but he saw no one. The Messenger spurred them on through an unfurnished hallway at the foot of the stairs. Pushing open a timber door, he then led them along a dimly lit passageway, through a second doorway, and out into bright daylight.

A precariously positioned footbridge led them across a deep-sided gully to a grassy ledge where they picked up a track winding its way amongst the colourful rhododendron. Looking back, Brook wondered if the building was the same one they'd seen earlier in the Pass. From this angle it was difficult to tell. He then turned to the Messenger.

'Does this diversion mean I am now further away from home?'

'Fear not, Woodsman. As promised, I will ensure you return safely to the Harlequin Forest at the earliest opportunity.'

Sanna changed the flow of the conversation. 'Tell me of the painted warriors who took us captive, Scaraven.'

'Ah, interesting fellows, don't you think? Descendants of a once noble tribe; guards of honour to an ancient line. Bad luck found them banished to the wilds. They now drift between worlds, and can often be found by the gateways surrounding the Enchanted Pass. I've found them to be very helpful on several occasions.'

'I sensed their honour,' she grinned. 'Taro Brook seemed less convinced.'

Brook quickly changed the subject. 'You said you were going to Enntonia with the Harbinger. You weren't gone for long. Were things there better than you had expected them to be?'

'The situation in Enntonia is grave.' Two Cups replied with a frown. 'I did what I could with limited resources, but I fear dark days lie ahead. Perhaps, on our arrival at Sumarren, I can find answers to help.'

'You didn't seem to be gone long enough to have achieved anything.' Brook was puzzled by the Messenger's response.

'Perception is everything, Woodsman. And therein lies the fundamental problem with the need to quantify things. Your perception may be quite different to that of the next person.' He waved a finger to emphasise his point. 'Perceptions of everything around you, perhaps of your own very existence. For example, this strange land you find yourself in, you are probably wondering if it is real, if this is all actually happening to you. Am I right?'

Brook nodded his agreement. 'That sums it up pretty well.'

'Then you must ask yourself, is anything real? Where does reality end and imagination begin? Is your very existence anything more than a product of your own imagination?' He paused as if measuring Brook's blank expression. 'The truth of the matter is that everything exists in your own mind, for were you not a conscious entity there would be nothing for you to be aware of.' He stroked his whiskers and grinned contentedly.

'It could be worse,' Sanna interrupted dryly. 'You could exist only in someone else's imagination.'

Two Cups chuckled. 'Now there is a thought to truly bend the mind.'

Whilst a full understanding of the Messenger's profound words lay a long way off, Taro Brook felt his mood lighten.

'I sense an awakening, Woodsman.' Two Cups grinned. 'A novel idea, isn't it? To question the fundamental essence of everything you've ever taken for granted. Let me articulate further, my friend. Before the Harbinger arrived we were discussing sequences of events and how perceptions of them may differ. Allow me to tell you a tale as we walk. A tale concerning the people of a distant star constellation, an advanced race who, among other things, had mastered space travel. Despite all their great achievements they were an arrogant people who believed that no other life existed in their star system, or in the infinite number of galaxies that lay far beyond their knowledge.'

He snorted his amusement. 'And so, they sent their people out into the great unknown. Many years passed, contact between the ships and the home world ceased and the people feared them lost. They believed the mission to be a failure but took solace from their loss, believing it to be proof that no other worlds existed and, as it offered no safe return, space travel was useless. The fools lived their lives happy in their ignorance.'

'Why do you call them fools?' asked Brook.

Messenger Two Cups turned to fix him with a steely grin. 'Because their assumptions were completely wrong. Their people did return, bringing with them proof of life from far dimensions in space.'

'I don't understand. How was that not accepted as proof?'

'Because they didn't return to the same point of origin. As far as they were aware, they had landed on a strange, uninhabited planet. Not recognising their own world, concluding that their search for their homeland was in vain, they settled there, thus becoming their own ancestors.'

Brook eyed him dubiously. 'Did that really happen?'

The Messenger shrugged. 'There is a sprinkling of truth in all the best tales. I merely share it to illustrate how easily the order of events can be misinterpreted.'

Taro Brook's mind wandered as he considered the endless possibilities. A silence descended on them as they followed the overgrown track through the long grass.

CHAPTER FIFTY-THREE

Deep in the bowels of the Castle of Spite, Tickbus Tard the Arachgnome wakened from another restless sleep.

Yawning widely he scratched at the crusty skin beneath his broken shell. Bitter frustration gnawed constantly inside his head. An incessant itch plagued his waking hours; his only relief coming in sporadic spells of hibernation.

Stretching his deformed body to the best of his stunted ability, he clambered awkwardly from the wooden pallet he'd come to call his bed. The thin layer of straw strewn across it offered scant comfort; tragically, comfort was a concept Tickbus Tard had long since forgotten about. He waddled across the damp stone floor and emptied his bladder. He watched as the fluid meandered along the rusty trough. A trickle disappearing down a drainpipe appeared to be a fitting analogy for his wretched existence.

From the far recesses of his memory, flickering glimpses of happier times taunted him; ghostly recollections of scenes from a past existence when he had lived amongst the fair folk in the world far above.

Distracted from his reverie, he slapped at the small insect crawling on his forearm and examined its crushed remains for a moment before placing it on his tongue and swallowing.

Dragging his twisted body across the room, he held a flickering flame to the large black candle standing amidst the clutter on the old wooden bench. It spluttered lazily to life, casting shadows across the wax-covered surface and to the wall beyond.

Cracking his stumpy fingers together, he shuffled his way around the bench as he made his preparations. It was time to send another battalion of his foot soldiers out into the world above. Soon there would be little time for him to spend on his latest creation.

The Dark One was coming; he could sense it. His master would have other work for him to do and he wouldn't dare defy him. The consequences of such an action were unthinkable.

Shuddering at the thought, he pulled the leather-bound grimoire towards him. A twisted grin stretched across his tortured features. His only pleasure in life now was inflicting pain and torment on others. In his eyes it was only fair. Why should he be the only one to suffer? His cursed allegiance with the Dark One had offered Tickbus Tard this one small measure of contentment.

Leafing studiously through the time-worn pages, he methodically prepared his workspace whilst at the same time scratching the troublesome itch in his neck. Although he was still unable to properly coordinate his extra appendages, he would readily concede that there were advantages to having three pairs of hands.

Despite his limited natural abilities, his obsessive determination, coupled with countless long days and nights of practice, had enabled him to perfect the creation of his insect army, his very own legion of the damned. He cackled with delight as he imagined them roaming loose, causing suffering to the very ones who had so cruelly shunned him, forcing him to flee far beneath the ruins of his once grand home.

Tickbus selected the black oval-shaped bottle from the shelf, pulled out the stopper, and poured a measure of the foul-smelling contents into a bowl. Adding the other necessary ingredients, he placed the bowl above the burning flame. Stirring the bubbling contents diligently, his knarred finger traced the words on the page of the old book as he muttered the strange incantation.

Almost immediately he heard the familiar scuffling noise coming from within the stone walls of his dark hideaway.

His army was on the move. A smile crept across his tortured face. He gave a shriek of delight. His mind danced in warped ecstasy and for a few blissful moments he felt alive again.

But the sense of elation was short-lived. The overwhelming despair of his pain and loneliness quickly returned.

Consumed with rage, Tickbus Tard screamed in anguish and threw the bowl and its contents onto the floor.

Extinguishing the candle flame, he shuffled slowly back to his pallet. Lying in the darkness, he listened to his army of thousands as they scurried towards the daylight above.

CHAPTER FIFTY-FOUR

Stepping clear of the long grass, Taro Brook looked down and saw the black horde of insects crawling on his legs.

Sanna snarled her annoyance as she slapped at her arms and legs. 'Curses on them!'

Messenger Two Cups scowled his displeasure as he patted animatedly at his jacket. 'Do your best to remove them all,' he instructed. 'The little devils will clamp themselves to your skin and feed from your blood. They are fiercely toxic and could make you feel quite ill.'

'Their bite nips!' growled Sanna. 'What are they?'

'Parasites,' he hissed, 'and they are afoot in many places. I saw them recently on my travels. We must stay clear of the long grass, for it is their favoured habitat. The little fiends are the work of Tickbus Tard.'

'Who? I've not heard that name before.'

'A most unfortunate fellow,' replied Two Cups. 'He dwells in a distant realm, in the remains of what was once a great palace but is now known only as the Castle of Spite.'

He paused for a moment to adjust his whiskers. 'The fate of Tickbus Tard is a sorry tale indeed. He was born of noble blood. His father, a well-liked gent of fine standing, always saw the best in everyone and was generous to a fault. Young Tickbus, however, was quite the opposite. He was known to be impatient, short-tempered, and even nasty at times, in truth a thoroughly disagreeable individual. I believe he was known by another name back then, but I can't quite recall what it was. Not that it matters anyway.'

He puffed out his cheeks and continued. 'Young Tickbus had no time for his studies and wished his youth away, longing for the day when he would replace his father as lord of the valley. His only interest lay in alchemy and wizardry, and he spent most of his time locked away in his private quarters deep beneath the castle. Concentrating all his efforts towards mastering the skills of the dark arts, he abandoned all attention to his other studies, and this I'm afraid would turn out to be his downfall.'

The Messenger tutted his disapproval. 'As the years passed, his father succumbed rapidly to the trials of old age, something which troubled Tickbus greatly. He didn't want to ever suffer the indignities accompanying such a condition and thus, a foul plan hatched in his mind. Using his acquired knowledge of sorcery he attempted to summon agents of the dark side which he hoped would grant him the gift of unnatural long life.'

Two Cups drew to a halt. 'And here, my friends, is where the story takes its most sinister turn. His grand conjuration was a success. He invoked a powerful dark force and, in return for his oath of service and loyalty, it promised him his heart's desire. With no thought for the consequences, foolish Tickbus accepted the offer without hesitation. All that remained was for him to read aloud the incantation it presented to him.'

'What happened?' asked Brook.

'Well now, as I've already mentioned, Tickbus had neglected his studies and I'm afraid his reading skills left a lot to be desired. Unable to fully comprehend the wording of the incantation, he was oblivious to the fact he was being deceived. To make things worse, he made grave errors in the reading of the spell and to further compound his misery, in his frustration, he broke a jar containing dozens of harvestmen, an order of arachnid. Breaking free at a critical moment they became entwined in the fabric of the spell. Instead of gaining the gift of long life, the alchemist condemned himself to a living nightmare. His fate was to suffer eternity as an Arachgnome.'

'A what?' Sanna frowned. 'I've never heard of such a thing.'

'An Arachgnome; a bitter creation spawned from the transmutation of man and insect. The dark force ignored his desperate pleas for help, instead vowing to hold him to his pledge. His new grotesque appearance did not go down well. Believing that the castle and its inhabitants were cursed, the people of the surrounding lands severed all contact. With his aging father driven to madness and a swift end by his offspring's fate, Tickbus became the last of his line. Shunned by those he had sought to rule, he retreated far beneath the castle where it is said he festers in his misery to this day.'

Taro Brook considered the words of the Messenger carefully. 'What part does this creature have to play in all of this?'

Two Cups met his gaze. 'I honestly don't know, Woodsman. Perhaps none, but his threat is real, nonetheless. If it is meant to be, his role in things will become clear soon enough.'

With a grin, he gestured ahead. 'Despite all obstacles, I feel we are making excellent progress. Let's make for the coastline.'

CHAPTER FIFTY-FIVE

Mickey Spades lit a cigar and watched on as the paramedics zipped up the body bag. Above the sound of the incessant rain he heard footsteps drawing to a halt close behind.

'So, another case successfully wrapped up, Detective?'

Spades took a long draw on his cigar and turned reluctantly to greet the new arrival. Forensic Pathologist Amy Coda shot him a warm smile. Spades frowned defiantly in response. He found her company difficult at the best of times, right now, in the pouring rain as the clock approached midnight, she was the last person he wanted to see. He blew a wisp of smoke in her direction.

'Yes, far as I'm concerned the case is closed. There's no need for you to even be here, Coda.'

'Oh, come now,' she smiled, 'everyone is entitled to my services. You know that as well as anyone.'

Spades grimaced at her reaction. What was it about her that got under his skin? She was beautiful, that much he would readily concede. Her shoulder-length auburn hair perfectly framed her movie-star face, and she had all the right curves in all the right places. Her appearance could hardly be the reason for his irritation. Spades drew again on his cigar as he met her gaze. There was more to her than just good looks. As well as being known for her brilliant mind, Coda was a genuine, considerate person who was always willing to put the needs of others before her own. Maybe that was it. Maybe she was just too nice. Maybe that was why she unsettled him so much.

He flicked the half-smoked cigar to the ground and crushed it with his boot. 'This low-life doesn't have any rights, Coda. Gave them up the day he took his first victim. Five at last count. Who knows how many more he's responsible for?' He cast a judgemental look over the body bag. 'Guess we'll never know now. He isn't going to be giving a confession any time soon.'

Amy Coda frowned. 'So, what happened here? I'm going to hear about it anyway, so how about you get me up to speed.'

'There's not much to tell,' he shrugged. 'I followed him here from the bar he's been hanging out at. Judging by his reaction he knew I was on his tail. He ran up the fire escape stairs; he'd reached the third floor when he slipped.' Spades looked up into the night. 'Down he came. Hit the ground at a fair rate of knots. Show over! No encore!'

He held his breath, hoping for some semblance of annoyance in her reaction. But he was to be disappointed. She stepped closer and placed a hand on his arm.

'Don't blame yourself, Spades. It was an accident. You were just doing your job.' She smiled again. 'Why don't you go home? I'll take care of things here.'

He turned away quickly to hide his frustration. Offering a grudged mumble of thanks, he pulled his collar up against the driving rain and made his way along the alleyway. Stopping to light another cigar, he watched from a safe distance as she went about her duties.

Spades shook his head and carried on walking. As irritable as she was, Amy Coda was only partly responsible for his current discontent.

He'd come to the realisation, some time ago, that something was amiss. He'd long suspected things weren't the way they were meant to be. He was trapped in a thankless, dead-end existence, chasing down low-life scum, bringing them to account in the hope that a hopelessly inept justice system unfit for purpose would lock them up and throw away the key. But lately, things had seemed more out of sync than ever and, whilst working on one of his recent cases, he'd stumbled upon evidence suggesting that none of this was real.

Detective Mickey Spades was nothing more than a figment of someone's imagination.

Difficult as it was to believe, far less accept, the compelling evidence seemed beyond doubt, and he was finding it hard to come to terms with its ramifications. His world had been turned upside down.

Boots splashing in the rain pools, he replayed the final moments of his latest case over and over in his head. He hoped whoever was behind the great deception had something more rewarding lined up for him in the future. It had been a raw deal so far. Maybe when he had found out more, he could take control of his own destiny.

He allowed himself a grin of satisfaction at the thought. As he pushed his way into the crowded bar, he felt lifted by the prospect of better times ahead.

A short while later as he drained his first bottle of beer, his mood changed as he wondered if any of his thoughts were really his own. Was his creator playing games with him?

He ordered another drink, lit another cigar, and resigned himself to the fact that, for the time being, he would just have to wait to find out.

CHAPTER FIFTY-SIX

'I like it, Hans! It's quite possibly your best yet. I'll get things moving without further delay. Tell me though, what took you so long? You normally make the whole process appear effortless.'

Hans Rugen shifted uncomfortably as the large-framed man took another mouthful of cream cake. It appeared their meeting had gone well; his agent was happy. Rugen's mood remained downbeat. 'Let's just say I had a few distractions.'

'Uh huh… right, well, no matter, it's done now, just in time to meet the deadline. Probably best to stick with what you know, Hans.' Larry Taskin flicked the cake crumbs from his shirt. 'If it ain't broke and all that. I assume you scrapped the other one, the story based in the forest?'

Rugen chose not to respond. Sensing his reluctance, his agent continued cagily.

'Well, if you ask me, I think you should get rid of it. I've never seen you so out of sorts. If something isn't working, you just leave it and move on. Am I right?'

'That's usually the case, Larry, but there's more to it. There were other factors involved. I'm sure you heard about Mitchell Egberts?'

'Yeah, I heard. But what has that got to do with you? You two weren't all that close… were you?'

'No, we weren't, but...' Rugen hesitated. 'Thing is, I let him see the beginnings of that story and he got carried away with the idea. I feel partly responsible.'

'Oh, come on, you don't honestly think that what you'd written had anything to do with his accident? Really, Hans, that's absurd. The guy was obviously overworked at the newspaper and went a bit crazy. You don't go wandering around the forest in the middle of the night for hours on end if the cuckoo train hasn't already left the station.' Removing his spectacles, Taskin tapped a finger to his forehead as if to emphasise his point.

Hans Rugen remained unconvinced but chose not to argue the point further. 'I guess not.'

'Exactly! What was the outcome of the investigation anyway? No suspicious circumstances?'

'No, I don't think so. I heard they'd concluded that he must have slipped, and fell from the cliffs.'

'There you go then, just a terrible accident. Think no more about it.' Taskin rose from his chair and offered his hand, almost knocking his coffee cup over in the process. 'Leave everything to me, I'll get the ball rolling. Why don't you go take a break and recharge the old batteries?'

Rugen nodded silently as he shook the clammy hand and made for the door.

'Just go relax, Hans,' his agent bellowed enthusiastically. 'I've got a good feeling about this one.'

Hans Rugen descended the stairs from the third-floor office. His thoughts were still troubled. It would take more than a few well-meant words from his agent to dispel his concerns surrounding the untimely demise of Mitchell Egberts.

As he left the building and waited to cross the busy street, he heard a woman's voice calling his name. He turned to see Sonja Egberts approaching.

'I'm glad I caught you, Hans. I saw you go in there earlier. I hope you don't mind me waiting for you. I've been meaning to call you but there has been such a lot to deal with.'

Rugen's trepidation eased quickly. 'Of course, Sonja, it must be an awful time for you. I came to the funeral service but didn't get a chance to talk to you.'

She smiled. 'I understand. Hans, I feel I owe you an apology.'

'You do? Whatever for?'

'For the way I spoke to you on the telephone that day when all you were trying to do was help. I am so sorry. That was despicable of me. It was all just such a shock.'

'There is no need to apologise, Sonja. I just wish there were more I could have said or done to help.'

'Thank you, it's done now, there's no point in regret. It changes nothing. I just have to move on, that's why I insisted that the forensic investigators closed the case.'

'I'm not sure I follow,' Rugen frowned. 'I thought they knew what had happened. What were they investigating?'

'It was probably nothing.' She raised a hand dismissively. 'They found a strange wound on Mitch's chest; one they didn't think was a result of the impact from the fall. The woman who was leading the investigation was doing a lot of digging, but I just felt they were dragging it on too long. And besides, it was just a theory, and she'd admitted to me that the chances of proving it were slim at best.'

'Sonja? What was her theory?'

'It was ridiculous. She said the wound appeared to have been caused by an arrow. I told her it was nonsense. I mean, no one is wandering around Greenhill Forest these days with a bow and arrow.'

Rugen could barely believe what he was hearing.

'I'm sorry, Hans.' She took a breath. 'I didn't mean to burden you with this. The reason I wanted to talk to you was something else entirely.' Reaching into her coat pocket, she handed him a sealed envelope. 'I found this in Mitch's things, it's addressed to you.'

Rugen eyed the handwritten envelope tentatively.

She smiled apologetically. 'I know it must be unexpected, but I felt I had to pass it on to you.'

Rugen stared back at her. 'Do you not want to know what's in it?'

She frowned. 'No, Hans, I really don't. I must go now. There is still so much to deal with.'

'Take care, Sonja. If there's anything I can do, just let me know.' They exchanged a parting wave as she disappeared into the crowd.

Hans Rugen found a quiet coffee shop and sat in the corner of the room. Taking a cautious sip from his cappuccino, he nervously tore open the sealed envelope and held the tattered scrap of notepaper in his trembling fingers.

Filled with an unexplainable dread, his eyes wandered over the dead man's message.

Rugen!
If you are reading this, I've been proved right. They know I'm watching them. I've heard them talking.
I think they are coming for me!

Rugen glanced warily round the room; his heart thumped loudly as he read the ghostly words again. His mind raced as he tried to make sense of their meaning. A few hours earlier, he would have dismissed the note as nothing more than the last ramblings of a troubled mind. That was before he had spoken to Sonja Egberts. A chill ran down his spine as he recalled the detail of their conversation. He shivered as a shocking thought presented itself.

Maybe Mitchell Egberts hadn't been talking nonsense after all.

CHAPTER FIFTY-SEVEN

Sitting in the corner of the busy bar, Mickey Spades felt further detached from reality than ever. The smoke from his cigar drifted lazily towards the ceiling as he contemplated the swirling concept of reality. Just what was real anyway?

Shaking the dregs of beer round the bottom of the bottle, he lifted his stare to greet the newcomer.

Amy Coda stood a few feet away holding a beer bottle in each hand. 'Mind if I join you, Detective?'

Making her wait for a response, he straightened himself in the chair and drained his bottle. 'It's a free country, Coda, and it's Spades now. I'm off duty.'

With a nod, she placed one of the beers on the table in front of him and pulled up a chair.

Spades drew slowly on his cigar. 'Want a smoke?'

She shook her head. 'No thanks. It's a disgusting habit.'

Her response was no surprise. He'd only wanted to provoke a reaction. 'It sure is. I've many bad habits. I'll tell you all about them sometime... if you're interested?'

'I bet you do.' She took a mouthful of beer and pouted her lips mockingly. 'How the women must hang on your every word.'

Spades shifted uncomfortably. Not quite the reaction he'd hoped for.

'Mickey Spades,' she smiled. 'Why don't you drop the bad guy act? Yes?'

Spades shrugged. It appeared his efforts to repel her attention were failing badly. 'Fair enough.'

'Good!' She quickly got to her feet. 'I'll go get us something a little stronger to help melt the ice.'

Spades watched as she crossed the room. She was a fine-looking woman, but something about her had him on his guard. He followed her progress closely as she returned, armed with a bottle of Firewater liquor and two shot glasses. Coda poured a generous helping into each of the glasses and pushed one towards him.

'Here's to us, Spades.' She drained her glass in one mouthful. 'Keep up,' she grinned. 'You're hanging with the big guns now.'

Spades forced his drink down in one gulp and watched as she emptied her glass for the second time. It might only have been the effect of the Firewater, but he felt he was warming to her company. 'So, Coda, what's the news from the dead zone?'

'It's been busy.' She re-filled the glasses. 'Always will be in my line of work. It's never gonna go out of fashion.'

Spades offered a wry grin. 'Don't suppose it is.'

'Lots of cases,' she continued, 'most of them routine, the usual thing, but I had one recently, there was something very strange going on there. I was doing a lot of digging; you know what I'm like…'

'Sure do.'

'I was making progress when they pulled the plug. Case closed.'

'Not good for your success rates.'

With a knowing grin, she leaned forward. 'Just because they call time on it, doesn't mean I give up. I just need to be more discreet with my enquiries. I'll figure it out, and when I do, it may help answer other questions I have.'

'You reckon?' Spades wondered where all this was leading.

'Absolutely. The game is easier to play once you realise how it works.' She fixed him with a grin as she raised her glass. 'But you've already figured that much out, haven't you?'

He eyed her warily. 'Figured what out?'

'You don't have to play coy with me, Spades. I know you've stumbled onto something.'

Spades held her stare. Was she bluffing? Was she trying to trick him? 'Enlighten me.'

Amy Coda glanced around the room. 'Okay, I won't go into detail, you never know who is listening.' Her voice was little more than a whisper. 'I reckon you've figured out that someone might be pulling all the strings.' Lifting the glass to her lips, she raised an eyebrow inquisitively, inviting his response.

Spades considered his reaction carefully. There seemed little point in playing the denial card. There might be more to be gained by being honest with her. At least, he hoped there was.

'Okay, let's say I know what you might be suggesting. Go on, I'm listening.'

'Good, I'm glad we're on the same wavelength. Question is, what are you going to do with this knowledge? You know that someone is behind it all, but who is it? Do you try to find out? Or do you just accept things for what they are?'

Spades leaned forward. 'Coda, you need to level with me. What do you know?'

'Probably not much more than you, but I've had a bit longer to adjust to it. But here's the thing, unless you are prepared to carry on as normal…'

'I can't!' His snapped response was harsher than he intended it to be. 'Can you?'

'I've already made my decision, but here's a word of warning. You need to work through it slowly, step by step, to try to come to terms with it, and believe me, things are going to seem a little crazy for a while.'

'How come you know so much about it?'

'I realised something was amiss, same as you did. I just got there sooner. I've been searching for answers ever since.' Coda shot him a look of resignation. 'I can see you are not going to let this go and I don't blame you, my reaction was the same. Put your detective skills to work if you must, but beware, if you dig too deep you never know what might happen.'

She hesitated for a second. 'But there's one thing you must understand; no matter how much you detest the idea, until you fully figure it out, someone has to be in control.'

He waved his hand in denial. 'I don't accept that. I don't want to be controlled…'

'Someone has to be in control, Spades. They have to be… otherwise…'

'Otherwise what? What do you mean?'

Amy Coda held his stare. 'You could become lost… with no way back.'

CHAPTER FIFTY-EIGHT

Hans Rugen reversed his car as far along the overgrown track as the gorse bushes would allow. When the steering started to struggle, he switched off the headlights and turned the key in the ignition. As he waited for his eyes to adjust to the darkness, he pondered the folly of his actions. It would have been easier to do this in daylight, but he couldn't put it off any longer. Aware that his resolve might desert him at any moment, he forced himself into action.

Following the overgrown track once used by the horse-drawn carts that had been the lifeline of the old logging operations, he made his way into the forest. Two generations had passed since the last of the workforce had left the mill and Greenhill Forest had reclaimed its silent solitude.

Glimpses of moonlight appeared from behind the clouds, teasing him with brief moments of illumination. Rugen moved quickly, hoping his nerve would hold long enough to complete his task. With every step he ventured further into the forest.

A disturbing thought brought him to a sudden halt. A shiver ran down his spine as he considered the striking similarities to his storyline of the walker in the woods. Despite the obvious difference between night and day, it felt as if he was re-enacting the lines of a script.

Glancing around nervously, he rubbed a sweating palm across his face. What was he doing here? Wandering through the forest in the dead of night. Had he lost his mind?

His heart jumped as an owl hooted from the branches high above. Glad of the distraction, he reigned in his imagination. He had to carry on, he had to know if there was any truth in what Mitchell Egberts had told him.

Were there really people hiding in the forest near the old timber mill? If so, who were they? And what were they doing there?

It had been almost a decade since the great storm had raged for several days; the torrential rain causing the river running through Greenhill Forest to burst its banks and tear a huge rift in the landscape. Some parts of the forest had become inaccessible and now the only place to see the disused mill was from the cliff tops.

Moving on, he considered the daunting prospect of what might lie ahead. If there were people down there, what part, if any, had they played in Mitchell Egberts' tragic fate?

At the second bend in the trail he left the track, and the memories came flooding back. He hadn't been here since his teens, but the route was familiar. Before the storm, it had led to a popular viewpoint but the resulting landslide had left it a neglected part of the forest where few now ventured. Rugen wondered just what had drawn Mitchell Egberts here.

The trees thinned as he gained height and, spurred on by the increased visibility, he clambered hurriedly up the last stretch to reach his vantage point.

From high above, the waning moon cast ghostly shadows across the vast expanse of the forest. Rugen scanned the scene as he caught his breath.

Only a few moments had passed when his eye settled on a light moving through the trees far below. He crouched himself low to the ground. As he followed its progress he realised it was no ordinary torch light; it was a burning flame. He contemplated his next move. He needed to get closer, he had to know who was down there. There could be a rational explanation. One thing was certain; if he was going to talk to anyone about this, he needed to present a more creditable case than the one Egberts had offered to him.

Eyes fixed on the flame, he tried to judge the distance. He needed to get closer, but how? Dangerously high and steep, the cliffs were no place for the novice. In years gone by they'd been a favourite haunt of experienced rock climbers who came to hone their skills. The collapse of the access track and the erection of the warning signs had seen the climbers move their activities elsewhere. He was about to call a halt to his plan when the moonlight drew his attention to a narrow ledge running at a steep angle down the rock-face not far ahead. With racing pulse he moved towards it expectantly. It might just work. It might just lead him closer to the light-bearers below.

With a deep breath he stepped out onto the ledge. It was just wide enough for him to stand upright. With his heart thumping loudly in his chest, and his face only inches away from the rock, his fingers gripped on tightly as he shuffled his way slowly but surely down the jagged shelf. Glancing back, he assessed his progress. He was dropping height steadily. As the ledge widened, grateful for the reprieve, he stopped to catch his breath. Easing himself down onto his stomach, he peered over the edge.

The flame had come to a standstill. He listened as the sound of voices carried upwards in the breeze. Was it a foreign language? If so, it was one he had never heard before. Rugen could scarcely believe it. Mitchell Egberts had been right all along.

There were people here. But who were they? He had to get closer. Pulling back from the edge, he scrambled to his feet. Moments later, his precarious descent ended abruptly as the ledge came to a sudden stop. Cursing his luck, he looked down.

Some distance below, an outcrop of rock beckoned invitingly. He tried to gauge the drop. Could he jump it? Suddenly it seemed as if all sense of reason abandoned him. There appeared no need for debate. The decision was an easy one. He had to try.

As he readied himself to cross the void, he saw that the flame was on the move again. It was now or never. Taking a deep breath, he launched himself into the air.

He made the jump with room to spare but lost his balance as he landed. Throwing out an arm in desperation, he caught hold of a jagged slither of rock. His fleeting moment of relief turned to horror as the rock came loose.

Scrabbling for salvation, arms flailing wildly, he fell backwards over the edge. Closing his eyes, he held his breath, and braced himself for the impending impact.

CHAPTER FIFTY-NINE

Morusk of DunTreggan stepped from the cover of the trees as his companions came into view.

'What news?' he asked. 'Was it a Raider?'

'Don't know.' Stuc shook his head. 'Eldir's aim was true; he found his target. We saw the watcher fall. We searched but found no trace of a body.'

'The forest is too dense.' The Northman added his thoughts.

Morusk nodded. He didn't think it likely that the Raiders would be tracking their progress from the cliffs, but someone had been watching them from above for several days and nights. 'The body is probably hanging in the upper branches. It matters not who it was. We know the Raiders are still on our trail. At least you've solved the problem of the watcher from above.'

'There was another,' Stuc offered hesitantly. 'It appeared sometime after the first, and from the same place. We'd given up the search and were on our way to re-join you when it appeared.'

'What happened? Did you…?'

'No,' the Northman replied. 'They also fell, but not by my hand.'

Morusk sighed. The threat of a solitary watcher was one thing, but another? How many more might there be? And who were they? The Raiders' relentless pursuit was enough to worry about. He scratched at his beard as he considered the fate of the second watcher. If the Northman wasn't responsible for its demise, then who was? 'Perhaps he just slipped and fell,' he said, thinking aloud. 'Did you search for the second body?'

'Yes,' replied Eldir. 'But with the same result.'

'It makes no sense,' added Stuc. 'There's something not right about it. He fell from the same place as the first, yet we didn't find either of them.'

'Perhaps both are lodged in the treetops?'

Stuc appeared unconvinced. 'We searched the area well. I'd have expected to find one of them at least. Maybe we should go back and look again to be certain?'

'No, we can't waste any more time. Whatever happened to them, one thing is certain. We have two fewer followers to worry about. Let's go, the others will be waiting for us.'

Morusk had much to consider as they made their way quietly through the forest. Following the attack on their settlement, DunTreggan's survivors had begun the journey north under the leadership of Juuk but, after succumbing to a sudden fever, their much-loved elder had passed away. The group's choice for a successor was unanimous and, despite his protests, the responsibilities of leadership had fallen on Morusk.

It had proved to be an inspired choice. Not long after they'd said their farewells to Juuk, a group of riders had entered their camp at sundown demanding to know why they'd come to the lands of the Brochen Eyne. Their aggressive manner had changed quickly when they saw Ava and recognised her as one of their kin.

Since the tragedy that had brought them together, Morusk and Ava had grown inseparable, and when she'd introduced Morusk as her companion, the Northmen rallied to their cause. A union was forged, with the Brochen Eyne pledging to help guide them to safety and to help eradicate the threat of the Raiders who had tracked them all the way from DunTreggan.

Morusk smiled as his thoughts turned to Ava. They rarely talked about the cruel twist of fate that had drawn them together, yet neither could deny the feeling that for some unknown reason they were bound to one another.

'The terrain grows ever harsher, my friend.' Eldir's words brought him to attention. 'The Raiders' mounts will fare poorly on the rocky ground beyond the great forest.'

'That is good news, Eldir. Their pursuit is incessant, and our group grows weary. How long will it take us to reach the pass?'

The Northman considered his response carefully. 'Three days and nights will take us to the edge of the forest; from there, we will see seven sunsets before we reach our destination.'

'Do you really think this whole ambush thing is a good idea, Morusk?' Stuc asked hesitantly. 'If we can put more distance between us and the Raiders on the harsher terrain, would it not be better to keep moving?'

'We can't go on like this, Stuc. We must make a stand, there will be no respite until we do.'

'They are in for a surprise when they find out where we are leading them,' scoffed Eldir. 'The Blackheart Pass is the perfect place for an ambush. Provided we get there with sufficient time to prepare, believe me, they will bother you no more.'

Morusk found himself grinning in Stuc's direction. 'Doesn't that sound like a good plan to you?'

'I suppose it does,' Stuc agreed hesitantly. 'Just seems a bit dangerous to me.'

The Northman laughed out loud. 'The greater the danger, the sweeter the taste of success when it comes.'

Nodding his approval, Morusk slowed his pace as they neared camp. The responsibility for the group's safety weighed heavily on his shoulders. The ambush was a brave plan. He hoped he was making the right decision.

As he entered the clearing he saw someone stepping from the entrance of the old mineshaft. He smiled as Ava moved towards him in the moonlight.

'You look troubled, Morusk of DunTreggan,' she said softly. 'Want some company?'

Without answering, he took her in his arms and held her close. Sometimes words were unnecessary.

CHAPTER SIXTY

'You appear troubled, Woodsman!'

Taro Brook shifted his focus from the sky to the Messenger and offered his response. 'It could be that my eyes are playing tricks on me, but the sun dipped beyond the horizon some time ago and yet I'd swear it isn't getting any darker.'

'An excellent observation. I do like that inquisitive nature of yours, a most endearing quality. A true thirst for knowledge is never quenched, eh?'

'So,' Brook rolled his eyes, 'should it not be dark by now?'

Two Cups snorted his amusement. 'There is no deception, my friend. The suns of two different worlds hold council over this part of the Krechan-Bhann and when one fades from view, the distant light of another holds the dark at bay. And believe me, it is just as well; our progress would become a much more difficult proposition under cover of darkness.' He grinned reassuringly. 'Onward, friends, it's not far now to the coast.'

The sound of the waves crashing on the rocks far below heralded their arrival at the edge of the sea cliffs. Twilight cast an eerie spell on the landscape as they began their hasty descent down narrow steps forged from the rock-face. Brook marvelled at the craftsmanship of the rugged stairway, built in such a precarious setting. The long drop down focused his attention.

Proceeding with caution, he tried his best to keep up with his sure-footed companions.

Overhead, a swirling mass of inquisitive seabirds took flight from their rocky outposts and hovered high above, monitoring the progress of their uninvited guests. A raven settled on a ledge just a few feet away and eyed them suspiciously. For a fleeting moment Brook recalled a dream concerning ravens then pushed the memory from his mind. So many strange things had happened lately, it was becoming difficult to differentiate between dream and reality.

The steps zig-zagged relentlessly down towards the sea. Brook became aware of the continued presence of the raven as it flew ahead of them, every now and again settling on a ledge, as if waiting for them to catch up. It stayed with them for the duration of the descent, leaving only when they reached a small stony beach at the foot of the cliffs. He watched as it flew from sight and was about to comment on its unusual behaviour when Two Cups gave a shout.

'Luck is with us!' The Messenger strode along the pebbled shoreline. 'The tide is low; if we hurry, we will be able to pass through the sea-arch without delay.'

The winged guardians cried their shrill warnings from above as they patrolled the skies in ever-increasing circles. Brook gazed up at the towering cliff-face as his boots crunched in the stones. As the shoreline narrowed, a series of jagged shelves of sea-worn rock slowed their progress. Leading the climb, Two Cups hurried them into a narrow cleft in the foot of the cliffs.

With the hypnotic sound of the waves fading behind, Brook followed into the darkness. Guided only by the sound of their footsteps up ahead, moments later, he emerged back into the half-light. A short distance away, a yawning arch, gouged from the rock by the relentless surge of the sea, beckoned them onwards.

'Hurry!' urged Two Cups. 'The tides can be unpredictable. We could quickly become trapped. Beyond the arch, another stone staircase will lead us to safety.'

The advancing waves seemed intent on bringing his warning to fruition as they passed under the arch. Taro Brook stared up at the timeless creation of the sea; his sense of wonder spoiled only by the continuous drip of ice-cold water.

Suddenly, from nowhere, a black object flew past him in a blur. The raven was back. Coming to rest atop a boulder, it fluttered its wings and studied them closely before taking flight again. Circling high above, it watched their movements as they left the rapidly receding shoreline and began their ascent of another stairway.

As they neared the top, and as daylight began to regain control of the sky, a mist rolled in from the sea. Messenger Two Cups brought them to a halt.

'We should rest here for a short while.' He poured a mug of tea. 'It's not far now to the Firth of the Last Crossing,' he grinned. 'And your first view of Sumarren.' Taking the bread from his pack, he handed it to Brook. 'Look behind you. It appears our guide may be hungry.'

Perched on the ledge only a few feet away, the raven eyed them closely. Taro Brook broke a small piece of the bread and tossed it to the ground. The raven hopped forward and scoffed the offering without hesitation.

'Perhaps he will come closer.' Following Sanna's suggestion, Brook dropped another piece of the bread. The raven came closer and took the reward readily.

'Remarkable,' chirped Two Cups. 'I do declare the little fellow would take the bread from your hand if you offered it.'

Brook was about to try when the raven took to the sky.

'That's odd!' Two Cups scrambled hurriedly to his feet. 'Looks like something's caught his attention. Come, let's get to the top to find out.'

Sanna was next to move, shadowing the Messenger's steps. Brook followed hesitantly, wondering what latest peril awaited them.

Reaching the top of the stone staircase, Two Cups gave an excited shout. 'Great news, fellow adventurers,' he bellowed. 'The Plain of Elsor! Exactly where I'd hoped we would be. And what a wondrous sight awaits you.'

Grinning widely, he greeted them as they joined him. 'Behold!' he rolled an arm for effect. 'One of the rarest sights in all the known worlds. The Nomads of Aaskrid and their legendary herd!'

Taro Brook took in the scene with a growing sense of awe. A wide expanse of rolling grassland stretched as far as the eye could see. Moving slowly across the landscape, a long procession of men, women, and children, bare-footed and garbed in tan-brown cloaks, marched in regimental fashion flanking a large group of elk-like creatures. Despite their size, the dark-furred creatures moved gracefully, their great antlers swaying gently.

'Those creatures. They're magnificent!'

'They are called the Seyk.' Two Cups was struggling to contain his delight. 'Isn't this just the most wonderful sight?'

'Shouldn't we be worried they will see us?'

'No, Woodsman, there is no chance of that at all. The Seyk and their guardians occupy a plane of existence far removed from ours. It is only thanks to the intricacies of the Krechan-Bhann that we can marvel at this sight. And believe me, the opportunity is rare indeed.' He snorted his appreciation. 'But we must be on the move again.'

'Shouldn't we wait until they are clear of our path?' Brook asked warily.

'There's no need, my friend. But take a further moment to feast on the vision if you must, for I'm afraid their image will fade and disappear long before we reach them.'

Taro Brook continued to watch the procession in wonder but was dismayed to find that, just as the Messenger had predicted, the image of the herd and their guard of honour began to dissipate as he started to move towards them. 'Why are they fading now? I could still see them, even when you began walking.'

Two Cups was quick to offer his response. 'Perception, Taro Brook,' he snorted. 'Perception is everything. And being able to harness its power, that there is the true gift of the Drifter.'

Brook considered the vagueness of the response as he strode to close the distance between him and his companions. Up ahead, the Messenger came to a sudden halt at the top of a gentle slope.

'We are here,' he shouted back excitedly. 'We've made it. We have arrived at the Firth of the Last Crossing.'

On the far side of the firth, a lone figure watched from the centre of a circle of ancient standing stones as the three companions began the short descent down to the water's edge.

The Man of the Trees' arrival grew ever closer.

Troubled by the sudden appearance of a fourth figure, limping awkwardly, some distance behind the others, the bearded stranger followed its progress for a few moments until it disappeared. Satisfied that it was gone, he retraced his steps among the ancient stones, and entered the ruins of Sumarren.

CHAPTER SIXTY-ONE

Pushing his way through the crowded city centre plaza, Tybor Barkal despaired at the flock mentality of Sahropa's citizens as they pressed and harried, desperately trying to get the best view of the procession of foreign dignitaries. Their eagerness to catch a fleeting glimpse of the men of power made him think of puppets dancing to the tune of their masters. The arrival of the World Peace Convention and its surrounding pomp and ceremony appeared to have the city of Sahropa bursting at the seams. Barkal couldn't wait until the whole thing was over.

Having made his visit to the Ice Bar, he'd quenched his thirst and acquired his instructions for the first task of the day. Arriving at the designated meeting point, he took a seat on the bench and awaited the arrival of Senator Sobek's contact. Shaking his head at the fevered frenzy, he braced himself as a blonde-haired woman appeared from the crowd and walked towards him.

'Do you mind if I sit here?' she motioned to the far end of the bench.

'I guess not,' he replied. 'Probably makes sense.'

She threw him a puzzled look. 'Sorry?'

Realising his mistake, he offered his apology. It wasn't the first time he'd made a wrong assumption about the identity of an unknown contact. He found the tiresome process uncomfortable and wondered if all the secrecy was really necessary.

'It's a beautiful day.'

Her voice brought him back to the present. 'Yes, it is. Sorry, I was miles away.' Her smile offered a welcome distraction from his thoughts of Sobek's laborious machinations.

'This city of yours is quite a sight,' she gazed up at the mirror-like skyscrapers. 'I don't think I'd like to live here though, it's far too busy. I prefer the quiet life.'

'I hate it here,' Barkal responded matter-of-factly. 'It looks bright and shiny, but it has its dark side. I would gladly leave it if I could. You live in the countryside?'

'Yes, a small place, hundred miles or so east. You probably won't have heard of it.'

He guessed not. 'Sounds nice. I'm envious. It's a dream of mine to live somewhere like that.'

'If you don't like living in the city, why don't you just move? Why not follow your dreams?'

'Maybe one day,' he frowned. 'Maybe when the time is right, but for now I'm afraid my circumstances dictate otherwise.'

'Caught in the rat race?'

'That sums it up perfectly.' Barkal regrouped his thoughts. 'Are you in the city for business? Are you part of this peace convention circus?'

'No, no,' she scoffed. 'Politics definitely isn't my thing. I'm just here for a short visit,' she hesitated as she glanced at her wristwatch. 'And I catch my train home in a few hours.' She rose from the bench. 'I should get going; I have a few things to do before I leave.'

Barkal nodded. 'If you work up a thirst whilst waiting for your train, I can recommend the Boneyard Bar. It's not far from the terminal.'

'Okay, thanks. Next time I'm in the city, I'll look it up. Maybe I'll see you in there?'

Barkal grinned. 'That's more than a distinct possibility.'

'Okay, then!' she smiled her farewell. 'Until next we meet.'

'I'll have the beers lined up waiting.'

As he watched her merge with the crowd, a skulking figure with an altogether less favourable appearance moved towards the bench.

'Are you Barkal?'

'Yeah, that's me.'

'I don't appreciate being kept waiting. Who was the woman?'

'I have no idea who she was. I've never seen her before.'

'What were you talking about?'

'Nothing of any importance.'

'The Senator is a busy man. He doesn't like to be kept waiting either.' He handed an envelope to Barkal. 'This is for you.'

'What's in it?'

'I don't ask,' glowered the man. 'Anything you need to know will be in there.' Rising from the bench, he fired Barkal a sneering look of disapproval. 'If we are to meet again, you'd best not keep me waiting. I'm not known for my patience.'

Barkal watched him leave. 'And not for your manners either.' With a scowl, he tore open the envelope.

The instructions were vague; a time, a location, and a warning that it was imperative that he be there. Tybor Barkal did a quick time-check. He had nearly five hours to wait.
Rising from the bench, he began walking in the direction of the Boneyard Bar.

CHAPTER SIXTY-TWO

Waking from his troubled slumber with a start, Tickbus Tard the Arachgnome immediately sensed the dark presence in the shadows. A shiver ran down his twisted spine as the sound of footsteps came to a stop only a few paces away from his pallet. Fear coursed through his veins. The Master had returned.

He shut his eyes in the hope it was just a bad dream. But he hoped in vain.

'I know you are awake, Tickbus Tard. Get up! I have work for you to do.'

The voice sounded different somehow, not as chilling as before, not as disturbing. Or had time merely clouded his recollections? Either way, his sense of desperation was the same. He wondered if it was time to start believing in the power of prayer. Was there a god watching over wretched souls like him? He doubted it. If there was, it was a god with a very twisted sense of humour. Resigning himself to the fact there was no help coming his way, he rolled over awkwardly and scrambled to his feet. The long-extinguished sconces on the damp stone walls flickered with life, the flames bringing light to the gloom. Tickbus braced himself as the dark figure standing over him pulled back the hood of its cloak.

He stared up in surprise at the smooth complexion of the fresh-faced, elegantly dressed young man.

'You... You look different!'

'Apologies if my appearance confuses you,' the new arrival grinned. 'You would have been expecting me to look the same as when we last met, but I quickly grew tired of the scaly-skinned, horned, and tortured look. Painfully stereotypical I've always thought.' He raised an eyebrow. 'Appearances can be deceiving, Tickbus Tard. You of all people should be aware of that. But, if you would prefer, I can easily change back.'

'No!' Tickbus panicked. 'That won't be necessary.'

'Very well. Prepare yourself, I have an errand for you to carry out.'

'What kind of errand?'

'Something infinitely more important than playing with childish transmutation spells.' The Master picked a potion bottle from the workbench and studied it for a moment before shaking his head in disapproval.

'Please be careful with that.' Tickbus pleaded nervously.

'Is this really the best you can do? You sad little creature, I would have thought, even with your limited skills, that you would be able to produce something more. I fear, as apprentices go, I find you to be a crushing disappointment.' The scowl darkened. 'This pitiful creation of yours, this little insect army, and your efforts to inflict misery on others, forgive the expression, but I do believe your spite is stunting your growth.' As he grasped the Arachgnome's shoulder, a wicked grin curled the corners of his mouth. 'Perhaps I can help widen your horizons.'

Tickbus squirmed in the grip of the unnaturally cold hand. 'What do you mean? What do you want from me?'

'A simple task, my ugly little friend. And it will do you good to leave this disgusting hole you hide in, even if it is only for a short while.'

'But I can't go into the world above, not looking the way I do.'

'You are not going to the world you know. I am sending you somewhere else. Somewhere you will appear less... how can I say this? Odd!'

'Where are you sending me?' Tickbus frowned. 'And how will I look different? How is that possible?'

'All things are possible, faithful servant. Perception is the key to transformation. Does the possibility not intrigue you?' He motioned him to follow.

Tickbus fumbled nervously at the ragged remains of his shirt as he waddled across the damp floor. 'I think I'd rather stay here.'

The Master turned on him quickly. 'Your wishes are no concern of mine, Tickbus Tard. Have you forgotten our agreement?'

'No,' he whimpered, lowering his gaze away from the piercing glare. 'I have not.'

'Good! I didn't come here for debate. And you shouldn't be so dismissive. Perhaps you may even enjoy the experience.'

With a growing sense of trepidation, Tickbus watched as the Master moved towards the far corner of the room, gesturing animatedly, reciting whispered verses of a haunting incantation. In response to his words, a peculiar oval shape, translucent in appearance, began to take form. Beyond the blurring oddity, Tickbus saw the detail on the stone wall ripple.

He swallowed uncomfortably. 'What is that?'

'You should think of it as a doorway,' the response was cold and measured. 'A doorway to another world.'

The burning sensation in Tickbus Tard's bladder became too much to bear. With a sharp wail, he stumbled across the room to the trough.

The Master laughed aloud. 'On the bright side, while you are gone you won't have to endure the troubling ailments related to your current form. Imagine that.'

'I don't understand,' mumbled Tickbus. 'I don't see how that can be possible.' With his bladder drained, he simultaneously fumbled with his torn trousers and scratched nervously at the loose scabs of skin on his neck.

'When we open our minds to the impossible we sometimes find the truth, Tickbus Tard. With an open mind there are no limitations and no boundaries.' The Master shook his head in feigned disappointment. 'You were once an aspiring alchemist. Tell me, when did you stop believing?'

Tickbus' frustration grew. 'I still don't understand.'

The Master's patience was starting to wane. 'It's a simple concept. The realisation and acceptance that there is more than one of everything. Do you not wish to explore the possibility?'

Tickbus edged forward nervously. 'But... how do I get to this other world? And what is it you want me to do when I get there?'

'All will become apparent. Do not concern yourself with details. You will know exactly what you must do when you get there. Come now, let us waste no more time.'

Waddling towards the strange anomaly, despite his fears, Tickbus began to wonder about the prospect of visiting another reality. Was such a thing possible? Was it possible to find a new world where he wasn't cursed by this hellish appearance? A glimmer of excitement tugged at his imagination but as he got closer to his target the image started to fade. He was only a few paces away when the Master clapped his hands together and the distorted image disappeared completely.

'What happened?' shrieked Tickbus, staring at the bare stone wall. His eyes flitted around the room in dismay. He was still here; still trapped in his grotesque body, hidden away in his self-imposed prison. 'I… I don't understand. Why am I still here?' He spun round angrily. 'What happened? You said I was leaving.'

The Master's face twisted with a ghoulish grin.

'You must forgive me, my unfortunate little friend, I may have been a little disingenuous. I'm afraid you can't ever leave this place.' He rubbed his hands together slowly. 'But take some comfort from my words, for I speak some truth. In another reality, another version of you will carry out my commands.'

'I don't care.' Tickbus snapped his fiery response. 'I don't understand, and I don't care.'

'Oh, don't be like that. Not when I can offer you further consolation. Although all worlds appear the same, all must differ in some form or another. Imagine for a moment the possibility that, in one of those realities, your attempt at summoning me was successful and it is I who serve you.' He paused for a moment as though considering the implications of such a scenario before continuing. 'However, the balance of all things must be maintained and in this reality you are condemned, as much by your own stupidity and ignorance as anything else, to remain in this prison, in that hideous shell, until I see fit to release you from your bonds.'

Tickbus clenched his misshapen fists in anguish. 'You lied! You said I was going to be able to leave.'

The Master shook his head. 'To be able to shift from one reality to another whilst at the same time keeping control of one's senses is a talent far beyond your stunted capabilities. But surely you can see things from my point of view. What's the point in being a wicked demon if you can't visit your slaves to torment them every now and again? And on the subject of torment, you should know that in some realities you are dashingly handsome, obscenely laden with riches beyond your comprehension, with a beautiful wife or perhaps an entire harem of beautiful women at your beck and call, each one eager to fulfil your deepest, darkest desires.'

Tickbus had heard enough. Crestfallen, he shuffled slowly across the stone floor and threw himself down on the wooden pallet. He felt the bitter sting of tear on his crusty face.

'Carry out your orders, Tickbus Tard.' Laughter echoed round the room. 'Your Master commands it.'

The sconce flames flickered violently and as the macabre laugh faded, the room plunged into darkness leaving Tickbus Tard with only his torment and despair for company.

As his eyes adjusted to the gloom, his mind raced with the possibility of leaving his dungeon and experiencing another reality.

Sleep came quickly, and with it came the dream.

The sound of their voices carried in the light breeze. Seemingly unaware of his presence, the three figures chatted excitedly as they walked towards the water's edge. He needed to get closer; he had to hear what they were saying. He had to follow.
Looking down in wonder at his legs, he realised that he was standing upright. He took a tentative step forward, and another; and then another. A feeling of elation rushed through his body. He was walking again. There was still an undeniable trace of a limp, but he was walking. His joy was short-lived. Lifting his head, he stared in horror and disbelief as the image of the three figures suddenly faded from view.

He screamed with frustration as he opened his eyes.
Leaning on a twisted elbow, he listened for the voices, but the deafening silence offered no solace. It had only been a dream.
Dragging himself from the bed, he stumbled across the room. Disorientated by sleep he lost his balance and, as he fell to the floor, his head smacked against the leg of his workbench. With a screech, he punched at the bench. A horrendous pain shot up his arm and racked through his twisted spine.

He lay on the floor sobbing uncontrollably until the pain subsided. Taking hold of his rage, fuelled by anger and an overwhelming sense of injustice, he pulled his wretched body up from the floor. Grabbing hold of the workbench, he lit the candles next to his potion bottles.

Flicking through the pages of his book of conjurations, he tapped the bench impatiently. Finding his place, he wiped the dripping snot from his beaked nose with his ragged sleeve and set to work on raising another battalion of his parasitic insect army.

CHAPTER SIXTY-THREE

Sunlight sparkled brilliantly on the water. A frenzy of gannets dived repeatedly at the white-tipped waves whipped to life by the sea breeze. On the far side of the firth, set against a backdrop of pine trees, Taro Brook saw the remains of a white-marbled structure, its towers glinting in the sunshine.

A circle of stone monoliths stood guard over the entrance to the ruins, like ancient custodians holding court over all before them. Above the pine, a blanket of spruce and fir trees coloured the lower slopes of the mountains. Higher still, a succession of jagged peaks and precipitous ridges speared the lingering wisps of cloud.

'Myth and legend do this place no justice, Scaraven.' Sanna began the short walk down to the water's edge. 'Its beauty is beyond words.'

Grinning widely, Messenger Two Cups turned to Taro Brook. 'And what say you of the wonder of Sumarren, Woodsman?'

'She's right.' Brook nodded his agreement as his eyes scanned the land on both sides of the water. 'But how do we get across? I see no boat and no jetty.'

'Fear not.' Two Cups boldly hurried on. 'If I remember rightly, all we have to do is ring the bell and wait.'

Buoyed by the sight of their destination and sensing that his strange journey might at last be nearing an end, Brook followed them eagerly down to the shoreline.

'So, the bell we must ring… where is it?'

Messenger Two Cups chuckled his amusement as he pulled a tarnished handbell, no more than two inches in size, from inside his jacket. Holding it up to the sun, he shook it four times then placed it back inside his jacket.

'It didn't work,' frowned Brook. 'I didn't hear it ring.'

'I wasn't hailing you,' grinned the Messenger. 'There was no need for you to hear it.'

'Then who were you hailing? What do we do now?'

'Now, Taro Brook, we wait.' He fixed them with a wry grin. 'Anyone for tea?'

Declining the offer, unsure of quite what it was they were waiting for, Brook gazed longingly across the water to Sumarren. They were within touching distance; he was so close to his answers. But, after having come this far, were they to be denied? If they couldn't get across the water, their journey would have been in vain. What then? Would he still be able to find a way home? With the moments passing slowly, his impatience got the better of him.

'Nothing is happening. What exactly are we waiting for?'

Messenger Two Cups raised a finger and pointed out into the firth. 'There, Woodsman. There is your answer. That's what we are waiting for.'

Ghostly trails of vapour began forming on the water's surface. Within minutes, a thick blanket of mist had obscured all view of

Sumarren and as they watched in wonder, a narrow wooden craft came eerily into view. A hooded figure stood statuesque at its stern guiding the craft's progress through the calm water.

'Incredible!' Brook struggled to come to terms with the strange apparition. 'Where did that come from?' As the craft drew closer, the swirling mist reached the shoreline enveloping them in its silent hold. To Brook's astonishment, a wooden jetty appeared only a few feet away from where they stood.

'Splendid!' Two Cups grinned as the craft came to rest, bumping gently against the weathered uprights of the jetty. Turning to them, he motioned them forward. 'Shall we embark, fellow travellers? One final push for Sumarren.'

Clambering aboard, Taro Brook moved to the front of the craft and looked back at the imposing boatman. The hood of the dark-grey cloak was pulled forward revealing only a glimpse of a white jawbone. Making no acknowledgement of their presence, the figure pushed the craft away from the jetty. Guiding them effortlessly, his long oar cut silently through the water. Shuddering at the sight of the oarsman's hands, the pale-white skin stretched thinly over bony fingers, Taro Brook shifted his gaze back to the shoreline. As the distance between them and dry land widened, the image of the jetty faded from sight. Turning again, he shared his unease with a whisper.

'Doesn't say much, does he?'

'Who?' Two Cups followed his stare. 'Oh, him! You won't hear anything from him. The old fellow is completely unaware of the fact we are here.' He clapped his hands noisily. The hooded figure made no movement. 'Our ferryman is an

Indentation,' he grinned, 'forever sailing his craft across the Firth of the Last Crossing, only ever becoming visible to those who ring the bell.'

'I take it there are other bells then?'

'I imagine there must be.' Two Cups hesitated. 'I'd never thought about it before.'

'And he doesn't know we are here?'

'He hasn't got a clue. Just like our old friend you saw in the forest that day.'

Brook pondered the Messenger's response as the short voyage across the water continued. The sea breeze snapped, invigorating his sense of wonder. The unfolding landscape filled him with awe. In the distance, an endless serrated ridge of mountain peaks rose dramatically from the sea and reached for the clouds. On the coast beyond Sumarren, a sweeping bay merged with the land in a glorious stretch of white sand.

'Why is this called the Firth of the Last Crossing?'

'It is the journey's end, Woodsman,' replied the Messenger. 'And besides, look around you. Having set eyes on this magical place, why would you possibly want to go anywhere else?'

Taro Brook found it hard to disagree. A short while later, as the craft nudged once more against a jetty, he felt a pang of disappointment that the crossing was over. As they disembarked, Two Cups took a small silver coin from his pocket and tossed it into the floor of the boat. It rolled noisily several times before coming to rest at the feet of the ferryman who, without even acknowledging the gesture, pushed away from the jetty. Brook watched spellbound as the strange craft and its ghostly occupant drifted from view, enveloped by the returning mist. He turned to the Messenger.

'Why did you throw him a coin when he wasn't even aware of us?'

'Always pay the ferryman for a safe crossing,' Two Cups replied firmly. 'I am a great believer in tradition and I certainly wouldn't like to upset that fellow. I don't mind admitting, he gives me the creeps.' With a grin he motioned ahead. 'Sanna is almost at the standing stones. Let's not delay.'

Taro Brook had seen ancient remnants like these before but had never heard a satisfactory explanation of either their purpose or meaning. Standing within the circle, he felt an overwhelming sense of inadequacy. Several of the stones stood more than twice his height. The weathered surfaces were adorned with symbols, both strange and indecipherable. Brook studied them with wonder. 'What do all these markings mean?'

'Some tell of prophecies; others are accounts of events.' Two Cups ran his fingers fondly over the stones. 'Some of the writings have been interpreted, some have not. Some of them I remember,' he hesitated, 'some I don't. But, if I'm right, one of these stones bears mention of the Days of Thunder prophecy.'

Two Cups muttered quietly to himself as he wandered among the stones, every now and again sharing his recollections loudly. None of it made sense to Taro Brook and he was relieved when the Messenger announced that they should enter the ruins to further continue their search for answers. Leaving the stone circle, Brook raised his concerns.

'What answers are you looking for? And how does all this relate to me getting back home? We're now at Sumarren and I understand less about this journey than I did when I started it. You said you needed my help and in return you would ensure that I found my way home.' He hesitated. 'I'm not even sure I want to know, but I have to ask, what is it you need my help with?'

Two Cups stopped mid-stride and turned to face him.

'I honestly don't know.' A look of concern flashed across his face. 'That is what I hope to find out. You recall me telling you about the prophecy?'

'You mean the prophecy about the Woodsman from the Harlequin Forest? You honestly still think it's me?'

'Yes, Taro Brook. I really do. We must figure out what part you are destined to play. I believe the scrolls in the hidden chambers here at Sumarren may hold some of the answers to the mystery. And let's not forget the visitor from Nallevarr, perhaps further clues lie hidden in the scroll he wants us to translate.'

'The man from the frozen lands.' Brook looked to Sanna. 'You said he was waiting here for us.' She nodded her agreement. Brook turned again to Two Cups. 'So, where is he?'

The Messenger toyed with his whiskers. 'He is here, I can sense it. I expect he will appear when he is ready. He's probably waiting for us inside. Shall we go and find out?'

As they followed his lead the grass underfoot gave way to a white marbled surface, cracked in places and under attack from the encroaching moss and weeds. 'The gardeners have been lazy,' muttered Two Cups as they ascended a flight of steps leading through an arched gateway. Standing wide open, the intricately decorated iron guardians were themselves fighting a losing battle with brambles and ivy. 'We are now in the main courtyard.' Two Cups' voice was hushed. It seemed not even he wanted to disturb the peaceful surroundings.

From somewhere close by, a blackbird's call let them know they were not alone. Reaching the edge of the courtyard, flanked on either side by an impressive row of stone pillars, they came to a yawning stone archway.

'The West Entrance of Sumarren.' Two Cups frowned as he looked up. 'Not quite as grand as it once was, I'm afraid.' His tone softened as they walked under the arch. 'Great oak doors bearing the carvings of the finest craftsmen in all the lands once filled this void.'

For all its wonder, Sumarren was in an undeniable state of disrepair. The dilapidated walls reached for the open skies; sporadic wooden beams were all that remained of a long-departed roof. The walls were littered with a host of blank spaces, the ghosts of long-forgotten windows. Long-dormant doorways, their wooden remnants lying rotting on the ground, offered further glimpses of the never-ending intricate architecture. Here and there, small sections of stone stairways led teasingly up from ground level only to come to an abrupt stop.

'It's like walking in a stone maze.' Brook marvelled at the sheer scale of the structure.

'I only wish you could have seen the old place in its former glory,' lamented Two Cups as he examined a cryptic message on a sun-bleached wall. 'On the face of it, the structure of Sumarren is little more than a shell, but I believe its underground treasure should still be mostly intact.' He chuckled at their expressions. 'Not treasures in the usual manner of gold and jewels, my friends, but in the many scrolls and parchments stored below, the contents of which hold value beyond words.' He smiled at Brook. 'I suspect the learned men of your world would refer to such documentation as history and although the repetitive foolish actions of mankind would suggest otherwise, much can be learned from history for it has an uncanny habit of repeating itself. So, whilst most think that it is merely a record of things that have passed, never to happen again, I believe the best way to predict the so-called future is to study what some scholars would regard as the past.'

'And you think these prophecies of the Seer Magister may be recordings of things that have already happened?'

'It's possible that certain events which have already taken place, and others that are yet to happen, will recur again and again.' Two Cups eyed him intently. 'Remember, my friend, time is irrelevant. There is no past or present, there is no structured order to things, all we can do is look for clues in the writings and try to learn from the events already documented.' He waved a finger to emphasise his point. 'So, taking this hypothesis further, I believe that the repetition of some events can be avoided and, in some instances, it may be possible to prevent them from ever happening.'

'So, you think that I have some part to play in something that is yet to happen.' Brook hesitated. 'It can't be something that has happened before. Surely I would remember it?'

Two Cups gave a snort. 'You wouldn't recall anything about it. Remember, we are talking about infinite numbers; infinite worlds and realities, and infinite versions of you.'

'So, assuming something happens involving my participation, it may not even happen in this reality?'

'I would think that to be the most likely scenario.'

'If and when it happens, I may not even be aware of it?'

'Exactly!' Two Cups smiled. 'I do believe you sound almost disappointed at the prospect.'

Taro Brook wasn't sure how he felt. His continued confusion was playing havoc with his sense of judgement.

'As I've already intimated,' Two Cups continued, 'on your return to your own world it will seem as though you have never been away. You will remember nothing of this entire experience.'

'Nothing at all?' He looked at them both in turn. 'Will I not remember either of you?'

'I would like to say yes, but the truth is, I very much doubt it.'

'Not in my experience.' Sanna agreed.

'But if it's any consolation, Taro Brook,' Two Cups continued with a smile, 'you can rest assured that we will remember you.' As Sanna nodded, Two Cups changed the subject excitedly. 'You know, I think I remember how to find the entrance to the vaults. Quickly, follow me.'

Entering one of the many archways, they moved along a darkened corridor. Looking up through the gaping holes in the timber roof, Brook caught glimpses of the ruined white towers. Sporadic recesses in the walls hinted at further possibilities of hidden rooms and secret passageways.

The corridor led them through another ghostly doorway into an open-roofed, paved enclosure. At its centre, a solitary standing stone covered with symbols and inscriptions beckoned them forward.

Two Cups studied it excitedly. 'It's on here somewhere, I'm certain of it.'

'What are you looking for?'

'Aha! Here it is.' he tapped the stone vigorously. 'Look, this inscription here. The instructions on how to gain access to the chambers below. Let me see now…' He pulled at his whiskers. 'It shouldn't be too difficult… Yes… Ahaa! It is just as I thought.' He turned to the others gleefully. 'The entrance is hidden from view.'

Sanna's expression soured. 'Then how do we gain entry?'

'According to this inscription it is not far from here.' Two Cups mused loudly. 'I just translate this other verse…' He clicked his fingers. 'That's it. Follow me!' As he began walking, a doorway appeared from nowhere in the stone wall directly ahead.

'Just like the jetty,' groaned Brook. 'How does that happen? How do these things appear from nowhere?'

'They don't, Woodsman.' Two Cups hurried towards the door. 'These objects are there all along. Training the eye to see them, that is the secret. Much is hidden from our view by ignorance and a lack of awareness. Follow me, friends.'

They pushed the door open and stepped inside. As they descended the stone stairway the wall-mounted sconces flickered to light, illuminating their entry into the hidden chamber. Their discovery was a sight to behold.

Running the full length of the walls, a succession of large bookcases were filled to over-flowing with books and journals. Row upon row of wooden chests and crates were crammed full of rolled-up parchments. Two large wooden benches in the centre of the chamber were laden with piled up maps, scrolls and manuscripts. Barely able to conceal his excitement, Two Cups dashed to the nearest bench to admire the heaped scrolls.

'What a place,' he beamed. 'Isn't it just fantastic?'

Taro Brook was more than a little puzzled by the Messenger's reaction. 'You're acting as though you're seeing all this for the first time. I thought you'd been here before?'

'I have been, Woodsman, on many occasions. Unfortunately, my last visit here was long ago and I'm afraid my old memory is not quite what it once was.' He paused as if considering his words. 'I may have already told you that; apologies if I am repeating myself.' Clearing his throat, he cast an eye over the manuscripts on the desk. 'Now, what was I saying?'

Sanna had begun leafing through the scrolls. Taro Brook could scarcely believe the task ahead of them.

'There's so much. Where do we start? Do you know what you are looking for?'

Two Cups fixed him with a determined stare. 'What we really need to do is find the visitor from the frozen lands. He is here somewhere; I can sense his presence. The man from Nallevarr carries a scroll that I am meant to decipher; it says so in the prophecy.' He gestured towards the stairs. 'He must still be wandering in the grounds. Find him, Woodsman. Find him and bring him below. I will ensure that the door remains open until you return.'

'Very well,' Brook felt almost relieved to escape the task of scouring the contents of the chamber. 'I will go and look for him.'

Sanna watched him leave. 'Should I go with him?'

'No,' Two Cups brushed her concerns aside. 'I need your assistance. No harm will come to him here, and I sense that the man from Nallevarr is close by. They will return soon.' He hurried to a large wooden chest. 'There is something else we need to look at while he is gone. I think it's in here. Help me with this.' They dragged the chest towards the desk, pulled back the rusted catches, and prised the lid open. Leaning over the chest, Two Cups began rummaging through its contents.

'What is it you're looking for?'

'Patience, Sanna.' He pulled free a handful of rolled-up papers and quickly scanned them one by one. 'No! Not these.'
He dropped them to the floor and turned again to the contents of the chest. 'Maybe this one!' He pulled another scroll from the chest. 'Yes, this is it! This is the one I'm looking for.'
Unrolling the parchment quickly, he spread it out on the bench. 'It's true, the man from Nallevarr does carry a scroll of great importance but this,' he pointed animatedly at the text, 'this is the part of the prophecy already in our possession. We were aware of the prediction that the Woodsman would come from the Harlequin Forest, but I didn't manage to translate this section before.' Two Cups tapped thoughtfully on the bench. 'I have the nagging feeling I am missing something… something obvious.'

He glanced warily to Sanna. 'And I think it would be better to find out what it is whilst he is not here.'

'What is it you expect to find?'

Two Cups looked at her worriedly. 'I honestly don't know, but my instincts tell me it's not going to be good.'

CHAPTER SIXTY-FOUR

Standing on the deserted platform, Ashrynn Fala watched in disbelief as the last eastbound train of the day, her intended passage home, picked up speed and slipped from view beyond a bend in the track. Confused by her decision not to board the train, she replayed the events of the last hour over in her mind.
Arriving early at the terminal she'd reserved a window seat for the journey home and had passed the time in a quiet corner of the cafe, armed with a large coffee and a trashy magazine brimming with inane gossip concerning fake people with plastic smiles.
Even as the crowd of expectant travellers began to swell for the arrival of the train there had been no hint of her impending change of mind. But at the last minute, as the carriage doors slid open to welcome the passengers on board, gripped by a sudden unexpected change of heart, she'd stepped back from the edge and, for reasons beyond her comprehension, had watched the train depart without her.

Unable to fathom an explanation, she concluded there was little use in thinking about it any longer. Casting one last wistful look along the track, she gathered her belongings together and marched back along the platform towards the terminal exit. Catching her reflection in the glass as she passed the ticket office, she paused to flick a loose strand of blonde hair behind her ear.

Smiling at the vacant-faced attendant, she pushed through the barrier and walked into the warm evening sunshine, and the bustling streets of Sahropa.

CHAPTER SIXTY-FIVE

As he emerged from the shadows of the passageway, Taro Brook saw a tall figure step into view from within the circle of standing stones. He held his breath in expectation as the bearded stranger moved towards him.

'Welcome to Sumarren, Man of the Trees. I've been awaiting your arrival.'

Brook's surprise quickly gave way to astonishment. 'You?'

The stranger hesitated. 'You recognise me?' With a shake of his head he dismissed the notion. 'That can't be possible.'

As unlikely as it seemed, Brook was certain of it.

'I do recognise you,' he countered. 'I had dreams…' he hesitated, knowing how ridiculous his claims sounded. 'Strange, vivid dreams, and you were in them. Who are you?'

'I come from the land of Nallevarr.' The stranger began cautiously. 'I have in my possession an ancient scroll, to be translated by one called Scaraven. Is he here with you?'

'Yes, Scaraven is here, inside the ruins. He sent me to find you. I will take you to him now.'

'Wait, I must speak with you first.'

'You'll not find me much help.' Brook frowned.

'I'll judge that for myself.' The stranger had a commanding presence. 'These dreams you had, tell me more about them.'

'They don't make much sense.'

'Is that not the nature of dreams?'

'I suppose so. They didn't make sense, but they had a recurring theme.'

'And what was it?'

'A land blanketed in snow and ice.' Brook paused. 'Was it Nallevarr?'

'I don't know, it was your dream. What else?'

'There was a building in the mountains. You... the man in the dream, referred to it as the chambers of a king. You spoke of ravens and days of thunder.' The bearded man drew a breath. Taro Brook sensed the change in his mood. 'I see you are familiar with this. Messenger Two Cups... Scaraven refers to it as a prophecy.'

'I know of all these things.' The stranger's expression hardened. 'What troubles me is how you know about them.'

'The dreams... and Scaraven.'

'What else did you dream about?'

Brook felt the weight of the stranger's stare. Shifting his gaze to avoid eye contact, his attention settled on the standing stones. 'The stone circle, I remember it clearly from the dreams and I remember you telling me to make haste for Sumarren.'

'The man in the dreams, you say it was me. Are you certain of this?'

'Yes,' Brook pondered his answer. 'As certain as I can be of anything.'

'Did anything else happen in your dreams?'

Brook recalled the moment Sanna had wakened him just before the Harbinger's arrival. 'I was standing in water. It was shallow at first, but it began rising steadily.'

The stranger's expression darkened. 'I've heard enough.'

'What is it?' Brook fired. 'What does it mean?'

'I am no expert in these things, but it seems your dreams carry a warning. And perhaps their purpose is to be a reminder.'

'A reminder of what?'

'The news I must share with you and your companions. I didn't think I would have the opportunity to speak with you directly and I regret there is no easy way to say what must be said.'

'What news?' urged Brook. 'What have you to say?'

'A great tragedy is imminent. My warning will do nothing to avert it but perhaps, with the help of the dreams, you will remember my words and find the knowledge useful.'

'What tragedy?' Brook's mind raced. 'What is going to happen?'

'I am unsure of the cause, let's call it a natural phenomenon brought about by the forces of nature.' The stranger hesitated; his stare fixed on Brook as if gauging his reaction. 'A massive shift in the oceans will change your world forever. Vast areas of land will become lost beneath the waves.'

Staring blankly at the stranger, Taro Brook took a moment to process the bizarre prediction before responding. 'How can you possibly claim to know this? You know nothing of my world.' He shook his head defiantly. 'I refuse to believe it. If this were really going to happen, I think Scaraven would have warned me about it before now.'

'It may be that he hasn't told you because he doesn't know.'

The stranger's words sent a chill down his spine. 'What do you mean?'

'If my suspicions are correct, Scaraven has not yet been able to translate that part of the prophecy.'

'I don't believe in prophecies,' Brook snapped. 'I just don't accept that anyone can predict the future.'

'It doesn't matter whether you believe it or not. The flood will happen. It is inevitable.'

'Then we should inform Scaraven of everything you know. He will be able to help.'

'No one can help with this, Woodsman. The fate of your world is decided. There is nothing you can do to change it.'

Brook felt his tolerance wane. 'If it is destined to happen, then surely you would expect me to return home and warn people. This terrible flood, when will it happen? How long do we have to prepare?'

An awkward silence followed as the stranger picked his words carefully. 'In truth, I don't know. It may have already happened.'

'That's impossible! I've only been gone for...' His words drew to a crashing halt. He had no idea how long he'd been gone from his home world. How many days and nights had passed since he'd lost his way in Farnwaar?

The stranger seized on his doubts. 'Your concept of time means nothing to me. I can't say when this tragedy will strike. Past, present and future are difficult to define here.'

Two Cups' lectures about the irrelevance of time rang clearly in Taro Brook's head. 'This is absurd. You make it sound like you are from my future.'

'Perhaps not as absurd a conclusion as you might think.'

Thrown by the peculiar response, Brook took a moment before countering. 'If this flood is inevitable and if there's nothing I can do to prevent it, why travel all this way to warn me? It makes no sense.'

The stranger frowned at this. 'Must everything make sense? I find it easier to accept things for what they are.' He raised his hand in appeasement. 'But let us talk no more of it. It's possible you will remember nothing of what I have told you, but I will feel better for having tried to warn you. Where is Scaraven? There is much I need to discuss with him.'

Brook nodded. His patience with everything was almost at an end. The stranger from the frozen lands, with his incredulous predictions of impending disaster, wasn't the only one needing to talk to Scaraven. 'Follow me, I'll take you to him. He is in a chamber beneath the ruins. We can discuss things further there.'

The stranger calmly dismissed the invitation. 'I must talk with Scaraven alone.'

Brook's frustration jumped another notch. 'Why? Surely it's only fair that I hear what needs to be said and have my say in the discussions.'

'You misunderstand me, it's not that I don't want you to be involved, it's just…' he hesitated, 'I fear it may not be possible for both of us to talk with Scaraven.'

Brook stood his ground. 'Nonsense. Let's go. This way, it's not far.'

With a sense of knowing, the bearded man followed a short distance behind. A wry grin flashed across his weathered features as, halfway along the corridor, Taro Brook halted suddenly, stepped inquisitively into one of the recesses, and disappeared.

CHAPTER SIXTY-SIX

'This is not good.' Messenger Two Cups looked up from the scroll. 'This is not good at all.'

'What is it?' asked Sanna, moving quickly to his side. 'What have you discovered?'

Two Cups directed her attention to a line of symbols near the bottom of the parchment. 'This may be the missing link in the prophecy,' he sighed. 'And if I'm right in my translation, I think the Woodsman's world is in grave danger.'

Sanna studied the inscription. 'These symbols, they look familiar. Could I have seen them somewhere before?'

'All things are possible, Sanna, you know that as well as I.' He pulled at his whiskers. 'Do you recall where you may have seen them?'

She studied them carefully for a few moments before shaking her head. 'I don't remember where or when, but I have seen these symbols before. I'm certain of it. What do you think they mean?'

'Given what we already know about the Woodsman from the Harlequin Forest and the arrival of the traveller from the ice-lands,' he hesitated, 'if we add my translation of this manuscript, I'm afraid all my theories lead to the same conclusion.'

'And that is?'

'The destiny of Taro Brook's world seems likely to lie beneath the ocean.'

Sanna held her breath for a moment before answering. 'I don't understand. What do you mean?'

'By my reckoning,' he puffed out his cheeks, 'a great flood, the result of some catastrophic event which triggers the oceans to rise. The cause is unclear,' he tapped the manuscript, 'but the outcome seems beyond doubt. Much of his world will be submerged under water.'

'When will this happen?' She fixed him with a determined stare. 'There must be something we can do.'

Two Cups shook his head. 'I honestly don't know. Much still needs to be understood. The Woodsman's appearance must relate to these events, but why?' He scratched his forehead. 'What purpose can be served by his being here?'

'We need to tell him, Scaraven.'

'Yes, you're right. We do.' He clapped his hands together energetically. 'And we must examine the scroll from the land of Nallevarr. It may hold further answers. We may be able to figure out when this disaster will unfold, and how long he has to warn his world.'

A voice came from the shadows, taking them both by surprise.

'Surely that would depend on when he returned there.' A bearded figure stepped into view. 'I apologise for my unannounced arrival,' he glanced around the chamber with interest, 'but my guide vanished in the ruins above.'

Sanna's hand reached for her longsword. 'Who are you?'

The stranger held his arms open in welcome. 'I am a messenger, from the frozen lands of Nallevarr. I have come to speak with Scaraven.' He held out a rolled parchment. 'And to present this scroll for translation.'

'Splendid!' Two Cups' excited reaction filled the room. 'A messenger, just like myself.' As he bounded towards the new arrival, Sanna relaxed and drew her hand away from her blade. 'Delighted to meet you.' Two Cups grasped the stranger's hand. 'Deeelighted! We are honoured to welcome one from such a distant world.'

'I have travelled long and far to meet with you, Scaraven.' The stranger bowed. 'The honour is mine.'

'Where is the Woodsman?' Sanna challenged. 'Where is Taro Brook?'

'I don't know.' The stranger's expression gave nothing away. 'It may sound odd but, he just disappeared.'

'No, it doesn't sound odd at all.' Two Cups rubbed at his chin. 'In fact, it seems to have become quite a regular occurrence. Very frustrating, I thought we would be more in control of the phenomenon here at Sumarren. It appears I was mistaken.'

'We need to find him.' Sanna moved towards the stairway. 'There is much we need to tell him.'

The new arrival's words stopped her in mid-stride. 'The fate of the Woodsman's world is preordained. There is nothing he can do to change it.'

Two Cups gasped his surprise. 'What? You know about the impending disaster?'

'Impossible!' Sanna snapped. 'How would you know such a thing?'

'Why or how I know is irrelevant. There is nothing he can do to avoid the inevitable fate awaiting his world, but I believe he may have a part to play in other scenarios.' He passed the scroll to Two Cups. 'And that is why we must translate this.'

'Indeed!' Quickly voicing his agreement, Two Cups unrolled the parchment and laid it on the bench. His eyes widened with interest. 'This is incredible!' His excitement plainly obvious, his fingers traced quickly over the contents of the parchment. 'These writings, some of them are the same as the scroll we were just poring over.' Tapping his finger animatedly, he prompted Sanna to make the comparison for herself as he lifted his gaze to the new arrival. 'Tell me, man of Nallevarr, how did your people come by this scroll?'

The bearded man offered his explanation willingly. 'In recent years, as a result of rising temperatures, parts of our ancient world have emerged from their ice prison. At the edge of what was believed to have once been a great forest, we found the remains of a large settlement. In caves beneath the ruins, our archaeological teams discovered a maze of sealed chambers containing countless relics and artefacts. This scroll was one of many that were found.'

'Remarkable!' chimed Two Cups. 'There were others like this?'

'Yes, we managed to translate some of them but without knowing their true origins or purpose, much of what we uncovered is still a mystery. Are they recorded events from our ancestors' history? Elements of the writings hint at this. Some of our more imaginative elders declared them as prophecies, but most discounted them merely as works of fiction.'

'The very fact you made this journey suggests you don't conform to the latter school of thought.' Two Cups grinned.

'Your existence proves my journey was not in vain. The name Scaraven is mentioned several times in the writings. Scaraven, the wise one, a follower of the great Seer. It also mentioned that you could be found here at Sumarren.'

'The wise one!' Two Cups snorted his delight. 'I like that.'

Despite her shared amazement at the turn of events, Sanna's focus was fixed firmly on her current dilemma. 'This is all very enlightening,' she hissed, 'but what does it have to do with Taro Brook?'

'The Woodsman is also mentioned many times in the scripts,' the stranger replied forcefully. 'But this part of the scroll is beyond our reckoning.' He pointed at the parchment. 'We were unable to translate it. It belongs to a different language; one we have not encountered before.'

'Yes,' Two Cups mumbled his agreement. 'I don't recall seeing this one before either. It is most likely an ancient text, long fallen out of use.'

Casting a half-hearted glance at the script, Sanna drew a sharp intake of breath.

'What is it?' Two Cups was quick to notice her reaction.

She took a moment to confirm her suspicions. 'I recognise this language.'

'Really?' Two Cups struggled to contain his excitement. 'Are you certain?'

'It is as you say, Scaraven,' she nodded. 'It is an old text, an archaic language used long ago by the high priests of the Ra-Taegan.'

'Can you translate it?' the bearded man pressed eagerly.

'I think so.' She moved closer. 'Perhaps not completely, but here.' Her finger traced over the script. 'It mentions a man of the forest… a man of the trees.'

'What else?' Two Cups prompted. 'What else does it say?'

'It mentions puppets… and masters. The downfall of the puppet masters.' She looked up from the scroll. 'I'm not sure it makes any sense.'

'Just because something appears to make no sense, it should not undermine its relevance or importance. Continue as best you can,' urged Two Cups. 'What else can you see?'

Sanna returned her attention to the writings. 'Reflections… I think it relates to mirrors… a land of mirrors… and…' Stopping mid-sentence, she lifted her eyes from the scroll. A haunted look flashed across her face.

'What is it, Sanna?' Two Cups pressed. 'What have you found?'

Her voice wavered slightly. 'I think I understand why this form of text has been used here.'

'Why? What does it say? We have the Man of the Trees, puppet masters, a land of mirrors. What else?'

She forced the words from her mouth with an air of resignation. 'It tells of the Sun Warrior.'

'You?' Messenger Two Cups thumped a fist into the palm of his hand. 'Of course. It's all falling into place.'

'It is?' Sanna returned his stare blankly. 'The Harbinger used these words, Scaraven. How would he know of this? What does it all mean?'

'It means, Sanna, that our suspicions were correct all along.' He rubbed his hands together in delight. 'Despite his appearance, Harbinger Talus is a learned fellow whose readings of the old texts obviously led him to the same conclusion. The opportunity for you and the Woodsman to fulfil your destinies has arrived.' He smiled almost apologetically. 'Events are unfolding, Sanna. It is imperative that you go now. You must go and find him.'

'But what about him?' she gestured to the bearded man. 'He still hasn't told us how he knows about the fate of Taro Brook's world.'

'I will discuss things with him further,' Two Cups replied dismissively. 'You have my word. Please, you must go. The Woodsman needs your help.'

Turning towards the stairs, she hesitated. 'What is it I must do when I find him?'

'Do what you always do, Sanna. Use your intuition.'

CHAPTER SIXTY-SEVEN

Somewhere in the sprawling bustle of the Sahropan subway metropolis, Tybor Barkal had lost all sense of awareness.
The alarming realisation came as his foot caught the top of the escalator, sending him tumbling forward. The impact with the burly man's travel case was a precursor to the crack of his fist landing on Barkal's chin. Reeling back to catch his balance, Barkal mumbled his half-hearted apologies. Dismissing them with a barrage of obscenities and an array of hand gestures, the man stormed into the crowd.

Barkal hissed his annoyance. Some people just couldn't keep things in perspective. It had been an accident; he hadn't done it on purpose. In a grand gesture of defiance, and much to the amusement of a group of teenagers standing nearby, he offered an offensive gesture of his own, then turned to face the sea of travellers swelling between him and the subway exit.

Pushing his way through the melee, it began to feel like he was invisible. A steady flow of bodies blocked his way, shoving him, barging into him, knocking him both sideways and backwards. The only break in the onslaught came in the form of an awkward moment immediately following eye contact with a huge-framed man sporting a ridiculous moustache.

Following the inevitable shifting of feet and the guessing game to determine who would step aside, moustache-man lunged forward, knocking Barkal into the surging torrent of people.
Feeling bruised, battered, and disturbingly out of sorts, he managed to escape the madness via an emergency exit leading to a quiet side street. As he wandered slowly back towards the crowd, he fumbled in his pocket for his cigarettes. Perhaps a smoke would help. Pausing to strike a match, he changed his mind. Without lighting the cigarette, he threw it to the ground and continued walking.
Reaching the busy main street, he re-joined the maelstrom, thoroughly convinced that all was not right in Sahropa. Everything seemed strangely out of sync. Or was it just him?
Was the pressure of Senator Sobek's attentions finally becoming too much? He certainly felt on edge, but maybe he was just overthinking it all. Perhaps it was just one of those days; a day you feel you just don't fit in with your surroundings.

A short time later as he approached his destination, a shabbily dressed figure broke from the crowd, appeared to trip mid-stride, and stumbled into his path.

Barkal cursed as he threw his arms up to deflect the inevitable collision. As the tramp's head struck his chest, Barkal shoved him back into the throng.

'A thousand pardons, Sir,' the beggar snivelled. 'I lost my footing on the uneven surface.'

'Get a bath!' Barkal hollered his sarcastic response as he brushed through the sniggering bystanders. Moments later, he arrived at the doorway to his sanctuary.

Glancing at his phone, he reached for the cigarette packet. Staring at it blankly for a few seconds, he threw it in the garbage bin and made his way inside the Boneyard Bar.

CHAPTER SIXTY-EIGHT

Gabrat Sobek glanced up from his journal as the telephone began to ring. The call was right on cue, just as he knew it would be. Lighting a cigar, he puffed a circle of smoke towards the ceiling and eased himself back in the chair.

'I trust everything is organised, Senator?' The voice was direct as always.

'Yes,' Sobek replied guardedly. 'All good to go.'

'Excellent. Everything is proceeding as planned. I've just been informed that the drop-off has been made, the location is as discussed previously. The package is ready for collection and should be delivered to the convention banquet later this evening. I assume there are no last-minute changes that we need to know about?'

'No.' Sobek lied convincingly. 'No changes.' He paused to draw on the cigar. 'But I still need the name of our recipient. I need to ensure that it gets delivered to the right person.'

'Have no fear, Senator, someone will be waiting. They will make sure it gets all the necessary attention.'

The response was evasive, as he expected. Sobek wasn't the kind to give up easily. 'So, do I get a name?'

A dry laugh greeted his request. 'You're a determined man, Senator. A fine quality. Very well, I suppose it's late enough in the day to do no damage. Tell your envoy to look out for Rhea Midder. As I said, she will be waiting.'

'Rhea Midder?' Sobek raised an eyebrow. 'The vice president's press officer?'

'Yes, that's right. Do you know her?'

Sobek leaned forward in the chair. 'Not personally, but I have to say I'm surprised. I thought we were keeping this under the radar?'

'That was the plan but, to cut a long story short, Midder found out that something was brewing, and she wants to be involved. But there's no cause for concern; although she is a late addition to our plans, she is going to prove invaluable. I've been impressed with her. Very ambitious woman, wants to get to the top, and isn't too worried about a little collateral damage.'

Sobek flicked the cigar above the ashtray. 'And what does she bring to the table?'

'Quite a lot. Turns out the VP has some tasty skeletons in the closet.'

Sobek drew slowly on the cigar. If the VP's press officer was involved it meant things were moving faster than he'd been led to believe. A wry grin crept across his face. His plans to intercept the delivery and inspect the contents for himself had just proved to be an inspired move. Disguising the satisfaction in his voice, he pushed for further information.

'So, the vice president is in our sights too?'

'Definitely. It's too good an opportunity to miss.'

Sobek wheeled his chair away from the desk. He didn't like the way the conversation was unfolding. This sudden change reeked of recklessness. He didn't like surprises, he liked being in control. He needed to change things around. 'I was under the impression our plan was to bring change slowly, inconspicuously, one small step at a time?'

'Why wait?' The eagerness in the voice was obvious. 'We have an opportunity to go for radical change, and for it to happen quickly. We'd be fools not to seize it. Surely your ambition can let you see the attraction in that?'

Sobek hesitated. The thought was an appealing one, but he had his concerns. 'I think we need to slow down here; review the situation. Are you sure you have enough evidence to carry this through? Maybe I should run my eyes over the dossier before we deliver it tonight?'

'Senator,' the tone hardened. 'We've been through this already, several times. The less you know at this stage, the better. What you don't know can't come back to haunt you further down the line.' It made sense, Sobek chose not to admit it. 'Our paymasters are happy, Sobek, and they're keen to proceed quickly. Relax, let them do their worst, then when the dust settles, you and I step into the limelight. Believe me, when Rhea Midder gets a hold of this, the whole system is going to be shaken to the core. All you have to do is ensure that package gets to her tonight at the convention.'

Sobek had heard enough. 'Consider it done.' He ended the call abruptly.

Leaning back in the chair, he puffed on the cigar and reflected on the exchange. His decision to intervene, to have the package taken here without his contact's knowledge, was proving a wise one. It was vital he reviewed its contents. He had to get back in control of the situation. He was dealing with dangerous, powerful people; figures lurking unseen, pulling strings from the shadows. Despite this, they were people he had considered sound allies... but now, he wasn't so sure. He would have to be diligent; he'd have to stay one step ahead of them or could all too easily find himself being their next target. Placing the cigar in the ashtray, he picked up the phone and dialled the number.

'That you, Scar?'

'Yes,' wheezed the response. 'Go ahead, Senator.'

'The package we were waiting for, you have it now?'

'Yes, it's here. A small briefcase. It was delivered a short time ago. Do you want me to proceed as planned?'

'Yes. Have it sent here to my office, leave it at reception.'

'I'll see that it gets to you as quickly as possible. Do you have someone in mind to take it to its final destination or would you like me to arrange that too?'

'No, that's already taken care of. You'd best lie low for a couple of days, Scar.'

Sobek hung up and dialled down to reception. 'A package will be delivered shortly. Let me know the minute it arrives.'

He put down the phone and set flame to the cigar. The audacity of people never failed to amaze. The idea had been his in the first place, yet somehow, somewhere along the line, others had managed to seize control and were now hiding things from him. It was totally unacceptable. He wouldn't let it pass. When things had settled down, he would take steps to exact his revenge. He'd find out who they were, and he would make them pay.

With his anger slowly subsiding, he slouched back in the chair. The package would be here soon. Once he had familiarised himself with its contents and evaluated their worth, taking copies if necessary, his messenger, the drunkard Tybor Barkal, would deliver it to the convention banquet.

Blowing another ring of smoke, Sobek reached for the television remote control. The large screen on the wall burst into life, sharing the live coverage from the peace convention as it prepared for its big opening ceremony.

Glancing at his watch, he settled back in the chair, and waited for the drama of the next few hours to unfold.

CHAPTER SIXTY-NINE

Sanna Vrai hurried to the top of the stairway and stepped out into the sunlight. The sudden transformation from dark to light stopped her in her tracks. Shielding her eyes from the glare, she saw a group of figures gathered under a crumbling archway. As she began walking towards them, the ruins of Sumarren faded quickly from view.

Caught in the midst of the bustling crowd, she watched as they boarded a strange looking carriage, dark grey in colour and unlike anything she had ever seen before. All along the side of the strange contraption a succession of windows filled rapidly with bemused faces staring back at her. With no horses to pull it and no trace of smoke from an engine's fire, she was amazed when, following several shouts from an unseen source, the doorways slid closed and the carriage lurched forward noisily. Gaining speed rapidly, it was gone from sight in a matter of seconds.

She was alone. And the ruins of Sumarren were nowhere to be seen. Where was she? And Taro Brook? Was he here? Had she drifted to the right place? Scaraven's words rang clearly in her mind. She had to find the Woodsman, and she had to do it quickly. As she walked alongside the track, her focus began to waver. Strange images flashed through her mind; vivid memories that weren't her own. Trusting in her intuition, she ceased the futile attempts to block all thoughts other than her own.

Knowing she would remember little, if anything, of what was about to happen, that she would barely even be aware of her actions as events played out, she clung to the hope that she would find Taro Brook before it was too late.

Stealing a moment by a window, she checked her reflection. As she flicked her blonde hair, the face behind the glass changed. An expressionless man returned her smile with indifference.

Moments later, she found herself once more in the midst of a jostling crowd. Grasping every precious second of clarity, Sanna took in her surroundings. Looking up, she gasped at the sight of the huge structures towering high into the sky.

The sunlight danced and sparkled on the shining buildings, sending colourful flashes of reflected light in every direction. Forcing her way through the crowds, she felt her pace quicken. She was in the right place; she was certain of it. The endless procession of shining towers left little room for doubt. She had arrived in the land of mirrors.

Her mind quickly became a jumbled mass of mixed thoughts and emotions. Accepting she was no longer in control of the situation, she focused on the one thing she knew for certain.

She had to find Taro Brook.

CHAPTER SEVENTY

Wandering slowly along the alley, Wartimer Oldomor prodded at the litter with his makeshift wooden crutch. Though hindered by his troublesome limp, he didn't have much need for the walking aid; its main purpose was to add effect whilst begging. He despised the necessity to play the role of downtrodden vagabond, scrounging felt so beneath him, and he wondered if it was even worth the effort. Everyone in this wretched place seemed too concerned with their own troubles to care about those less fortunate. He hadn't raised a coin worth of mention in two miserable days.

He threw the crutch onto a pile of discarded boxes in disgust. It was no great loss; a replacement could easily be assembled if the need arose. Removing his eyepatch, he put it in the pocket of his tattered overcoat. As well as being an integral part of his beggar's disguise, the patch had another useful purpose; deflecting the blinding glare when the sun danced on the shining buildings. He abhorred being stranded in this strange futuristic world with no way home and no understanding of how he'd come to be here. At first, he thought his visits here were nothing more than dreams, but he had long since reached the conclusion he was trapped in a living nightmare.

He often thought longingly of home. Moribor might be a gloomy and drab world, lit only by candlelight and the glow of the fireside but it was where he belonged, and where he had a true purpose. Back home, he was an important member of society. In the hours before midnight, he used to patrol the town square and its adjoining lanes and alleyways, extinguishing all unnecessary candlelight thus signalling the end of another day.

He cursed his rotten predicament. This dazzling land was no place for him. There was no need for a candle snuffer here. He had to make ends meet as best he could, and sometimes that meant begging on street corners, putting himself at the mercy of these uncouth Sahropans; miserable sods, every one of them.

Dodging the motorized carriages as he crossed the busy street, he heard the strange contraption in his pocket buzz noisily. Pulling it from his jacket, he fumbled with the buttons and placed it against his ear.

'Where are you?'

The wheezing voice belonged to the man who'd given him the device.

'I will be there soon.'

'Good, be quick about it. Your assignment is waiting, and it's important.'

Prompted by the sudden silence, Wartimer pressed the buttons again and slipped the gadget back into his pocket. He didn't think he'd ever feel comfortable using it. He considered it an unnecessary invasion of privacy and a very odd form of communication. He usually preferred to see someone's face whilst talking to them, but the thought of Scar's face made him shudder. Surmising that the device might have some benefit after all, he proceeded towards his rendezvous.

So, the task ahead was important; it seemed they all were. Scar knew a lot of important people, at least, that was what he told Wartimer. Funny how appearances could be deceptive. The facial features of his accomplice left a lot to be desired. They were similar to those of a farmer from the borders of the old town back home who'd suffered the misfortune of being gored by a wild boar. Wartimer had refrained from asking him if he'd suffered the same fate.

Suspecting that Scar's connections were, at best, unsavoury, Wartimer kept their contact minimal, an arrangement that suited them both. The task of running errands was simple and financially rewarding. Wartimer didn't ask questions, he always did as he was asked, and carried out his instructions meticulously. Scar regularly commended him on this. 'Reliability, Wart,' he would wheeze. 'Reliability is everything in this game.'

He hated it when he called him Wart, considering it a sign of ignorance and laziness. In truth, there was little he liked about his disfigured associate but until his dream of returning home became reality, the financial benefits of keeping on good terms with Scar far outweighed the need to share his opinions.

Navigating the crowded streets, he frowned disapprovingly at the people in their bizarre attire. He just couldn't imagine himself dressing the way these clowns did. Being viewed as the odd one out filled him with a warming sense of self-importance, and he was used to the looks of disgust and derogatory comments which were hurled in his direction on a daily basis. Much to his amusement, his personal hygiene and limited wardrobe seemed to be an endless source of annoyance to those around him.

He passed through the crowded market stalls, so different to the street markets of Moribor where he'd spent hours browsing the wares of the countless candlemakers. The majority of candles here, with their bright colours and unpleasant aromas, bore little resemblance to those of his homeland. He found them irritating. Candles were meant to provide light and warmth, nothing else.

The sunlight sparkled on the tall buildings. This wretched place was so bright. He fumbled in his pocket for the eyepatch. Perhaps he should get a pair of those ridiculous blackened eye-glass frames everyone seemed to wear. Shuddering at the thought of how stupid he would look, he put the patch in place and pushed on towards his designated meeting place. Once there, he would be able to get away from the bright sunshine, even if only for a short while. The incessant glare was giving him a blinding headache.

He stumbled as a sudden wave of nausea surged through his body. His face twisted as a sharp pain shot down his jaw. Staggering backwards he fell against a wall. As he waited for the dizziness to pass, the blurred shapes of passers-by filled his vision but none stopped to offer assistance. A moment later, certain that the worst was over, he lurched forwards. He had to get out of the sunlight, it was making him feel quite ill.

With his judgement impaired, his torn boot caught in the paving, sending him tumbling forward into the crowd. Shoved back aggressively, he offered his apologies but was left wishing he hadn't bothered. The angry response suggesting that he bathe hardly seemed relevant.

Arriving at his destination feeling disorientated and physically drained, he removed the eye-patch and knocked three times on the barred wooden doors. Content that no one was watching, he made his way down the alleyway next to the dilapidated building. As he neared the end, a rusted metal door swung open and Scar's head appeared, inviting him to enter quickly. Following into the vast dimly lit storage area, Wartimer revelled in the refreshing cool air. He liked his sporadic visits here; the half-light reminded him of home. Picking their way among the precariously stacked boxes and containers, they came to the small storeroom Scar called his centre of operations. Stepping inside, Scar motioned to a black case on the desk.

'This is your task,' he said dryly, handing him a scrap of paper. 'Deliver the case to this address.'

As Wartimer studied the handwritten note, a hooded man pushed his way into room and closed the door. Scar turned in surprise then fired a disgusted glare towards Wartimer.

'You fool! You were followed.'

'No!' Wartimer jumped to his own defence. 'I didn't see him. I followed procedure.'

With a snarl, Scar turned his fury on the new arrival.

'Who are you? What do you want?'

'No concern of yours,' he nodded towards Wartimer. 'My business is with him.'

'What do you mean?' Scar glared Wartimer's way. 'What are you up to, Wart?'

'I don't know what he's talking about. I've never seen him before.'

'This is private property,' snapped Scar, turning his attention back to the imposter. 'I suggest you leave; any business the two of you have can be carried out elsewhere.'

The man shook his head defiantly. 'No, here will do fine.' With a fleeting movement he pulled an object from inside his jacket and flung it across the room. The short-handled blade came to a sudden halt as it struck Scar in the neck.

Watching on in horror as his accomplice slid lifelessly to the floor, Wartimer's stare fixed on the hooded man as he bent to retrieve the knife.

'Please don't kill me.'

The assassin turned to face him. 'Why would I want to kill you?'

'I… I don't know. Just… please don't.'

'Relax, friend.' The man eased a pack from his shoulder. 'You and me, we are on the same side.'

'I don't understand.'

'It doesn't matter.' The man pulled a small case from his pack. 'Listen carefully, there is a change to the plan. There are now two cases to deliver, and it's imperative you don't get them confused.' Picking the case up from Scar's desk, he opened it and thumbed quickly through the papers. Satisfied, he closed it again and handed it to Wartimer. 'You must present this case to the receptionist at your designated location. It will be taken away for inspection. You must wait until it is returned. Do your best to appear inconspicuous.' He pulled a wad of notes from his pocket. 'Acquire some new clothing on the way there. Your appearance draws too much attention.'

Taking the money, Wartimer nodded as the man continued.

'When the case returns, you'll need to distract the receptionist and swap the cases, leaving the other one in its place.' He tapped the case he had taken from his pack. 'Is that clear?'

Wartimer nodded nervously. 'What will I do with the first case?'

'Get rid of it, destroy it, discard it in any way you like. It will have no further use.' He handed him the backpack. 'You can use this to carry them but remember, don't get the cases confused.' He fixed him with a chilling stare. 'It would end badly for you. The Master does not tolerate mistakes.'

Wartimer felt a shiver run down his spine. 'Who is the Master?'

'Judging by your reaction, I think you know more than you realise.' Taking a small container from his jacket pocket, the man removed the lid and began dousing the contents of the storeroom with a foul-smelling liquid.

'What is that?' Wartimer edged closer to the door.

'Just a little something flammable to help cover our tracks. Fire cleanses best of all, wouldn't you agree?'

'You're a fire-raiser?'

'Amongst other things. You should be on your way. You have important work to do. I'll take care of things here.'

Needing no further invitation, Wartimer pulled the backpack over his shoulder and made his exit. Stumbling among the storage boxes, he charged through the rusted door and moved hurriedly along the alleyway. As he mingled with the crowd on the main thoroughfare, he heard the first shouts of panic and alarm ringing

out. Turning to watch the unfolding drama, he quickly became captivated by the flames as they engulfed the building.
The sound of sirens brought him to his senses. He had to get away from here. Resisting the urge to discard the backpack and escape his disturbing predicament, he instead found the courage to adhere to the stranger's directive. Scar's untimely demise didn't change anything. A delivery still had to be made, and he must carry out his orders.

As he pushed his way through the crowd, the pain in his legs intensified. A sudden burning sensation in his bladder forced him into an alley. A side entrance to a disused building offered an opportunity for relief, but it was short-lived.
What was happening to him?
Thrown by the disturbing turn of events, he pushed on stubbornly as a host of conflicting opinions began to rage inside his head.

CHAPTER SEVENTY-ONE

'Hey, Tybor. Want a beer?'

Thrown by the woman's beaming smile and enthusiastic welcome, Tybor Barkal's attempt at a response faltered. Her face seemed familiar enough but, for some strange reason, he couldn't remember her name. 'Yeah. A beer would be good.' His eye settled on an empty booth in the far corner of the barroom. 'I'll be over there when you're ready, thanks.'

Making his way across the room, he ignored several offers to join company. With his current troubled state of mind, conversation was the last thing he needed. Arriving a few moments behind him, the woman shot him a look of concern as she placed his beer on the table.

'Is everything okay, Tybor?'

'Just one of those days.' Shrugging his shoulders, he picked up the beer. 'This'll help.'

'Okay.' She seemed less than convinced. 'Give a shout when you need a re-fill.'

'Will do.' Nodding his appreciation, he watched her leave. Why could he not remember her name? He took a mouthful of beer. It lacked its usual refreshing bite. He shifted restlessly in the seat. He was finding it difficult to think straight. The music was far too loud. It seemed like it was bouncing off the walls and reverberating through the floor. Was it always like this?

He didn't think so. He gripped the bottle tightly. The waiting was obviously starting to get to him. The sooner his association with Senator Sobek came to an end the better. He checked the time and put his phone on the table.
The flashing images on the giant television screen were starting to give him a headache. The music seemed to be getting louder by the minute. He had to get out of here. He needed fresh air. As he rose from the seat, he knocked the phone from the table. Cursing, he bent to retrieve it from the floor.

'Mind if I join you?'

A woman's voice startled him. Looking up quickly, he caught his head on the corner of the table.

'Sorry,' she offered a smile. 'Didn't mean for that to happen. Are you okay?'

'Yeah, I'll be fine.' He rubbed the palm of his hand on his forehead. 'Don't worry about it. I'm having one of those days.' Their eyes met. He recognised her face. Maybe his memory hadn't abandoned him after all. 'It's you! We met today, didn't we? At the main plaza?'

'Yes,' she smiled again. 'We did.'

'You said you were on your way to the train terminal. Were you not leaving the city today?'

'Yes,' she hesitated, 'that was the plan.'

'So, what happened? Did you miss your train?'

'Yes, and no.' She glanced towards the seat. 'Do you mind if I sit down? Or were you just about to leave?'

'Yeah! I mean, sure, have a seat. Do you want a drink?'

'Thanks, I'll have a beer.'

'Okay.' He signalled his order towards the bar. 'I was just going to get some air, but I'm fine now.' He glanced at his phone as she sat down.

'I hope I'm not keeping you back. Is there somewhere you need to be?'

'Yeah, but I don't have to go yet. There's time for a drink. So, what happened with your train?'

'I don't really know what happened,' she hesitated. 'I got there early, then when it came time to board, for some unknown reason, I decided not to.'

'That's strange. Any idea why?'

'None at all, I can't figure it out. I didn't even wait at the terminal, I…' She stopped mid-sentence.

'What is it?'

'I came looking for this place. You told me about it earlier.'

'Yes,' he nodded. 'I remember.'

'Why would I do that? Just completely change my plans at the last minute?'

Tybor Barkal gave a shrug. 'I don't know, but if it helps, I've been feeling really out of sorts today. Maybe there's something in the air.'

'Maybe there is,' she pursed her lips. 'Maybe it was our meeting that sparked it.'

Was her comment made in jest? He didn't know for sure. The bar attendant arrived with their drinks. She flashed a grin towards Barkal as she left. He shook his head as he watched her go.

'There's another weird thing, I come in here all the time but today, for some reason, I can't remember her name.'

As if prompted by his words, she reached across the table. 'Well, my name is Ashrynn.'

'I'm Tybor,' he shook her hand. 'Good to meet you, again, and properly this time.'

Warming to her company, Barkal felt his mood lighten and all thoughts of Sobek slipped from his mind. Losing all concept of time, he listened enviously as she talked about her home in the countryside. With all thoughts of his prior commitments forgotten, she took him by surprise when she brought up the subject of his earlier distraction.

'Do you realise how long we've been talking? I hope I haven't made you late.'

'Sorry?'

'Were you not meant to be going somewhere?'

Glancing at his phone, he felt his stomach knot. He was running late. Lifting his jacket he offered his apologies as he rose from the table. 'I'm really sorry, but I have to get going.'

'Wait, do you have to go?'

Her response took him by surprise. 'Well... yes, I don't want to. I'd much rather stay and talk to you, but I really don't have a choice.'

'Don't go!'

'What?'

'Don't go,' she repeated firmly. 'Stay with me.'

'I... I have to.' He stared at her questioningly. 'Why would you say that?'

'I think there is always a choice,' she continued. 'And I don't think you should go.'

Why was he hesitating? He knew he had to go, yet he felt inexplicably drawn to her. His phone burst into life, causing him to jump. Glancing at the display, he mouthed the words loathingly as he silenced the call. 'It's Sobek.'

'Is that who you are meant to be meeting?'

'Yes. Well, truth is, I don't even know who I'm supposed to be meeting, but he's the one calling the shots. And he's not someone I should keep waiting.'

'I don't think you should go. I have a bad feeling about this.'

The phone rang again. Silencing it, he sat back down. 'What's going on here, Ashrynn? Tell me what you're thinking.'

'I don't know, but I have this feeling you shouldn't go. I can't explain it, but you have to admit that something strange is happening here. For some reason I didn't get on that train, I don't know why…' she hesitated, as if searching for the right words, 'at least, I didn't know at the time, but now…'

'But now?'

'I don't know why, I don't know what made me do it, but I just had to come and find you.'

He stared back blankly as her words steered him further away from his plans. 'You really think so?'

'It's the only thing that makes any sense. Why else would we have met earlier? Everything seems to fit into place.' Her hand reached for his wrist. 'I know it's hard to believe, but I think I've been sent to stop you from making a terrible mistake.' She tightened her grip. 'Don't go! I won't let you.'

Barkal was left speechless. As unlikely as it seemed, she was right. It made sense; it was the only thing that did. Her eyes drew him closer, deeper into her confidence. The moment ended as the phone rang again. Picking it up, he held the power key firmly until the screen went blank. Seemed like he'd made his decision. It was an action certain to incur grave consequence but, for now, the implications could wait.

'Will he come looking for you?' she asked quietly.

'Probably.'

'Does he know you come here?'

'Yeah, he probably knows everything about me.'

'Then we need to go. Your home won't be safe either.' She rose from the table. 'We can go to the hotel I was staying at. They still had rooms available. It will be safe there.'

'Are you sure you want to be in my company? You maybe don't realise what you are getting involved with. Sobek is a very powerful individual. Powerful and dangerous.'

She appeared unfazed by his concerns. 'Then we'd better get moving. Let's go, the hotel is not far from here.'

Struggling to keep up with the sudden twist in circumstances, Tybor Barkal followed her towards the exit.

CHAPTER SEVENTY-TWO

Wartimer Oldomor glanced nervously over his shoulder as he relieved his aching bladder. He wasn't happy having to do so in public but had no option. Perhaps the shock of all that had happened was finally sinking in and the vivid recollection of Scar's horrific demise wasn't the only cause for concern.
His inner turmoil was becoming increasingly difficult to ignore. Why were two voices, with two extreme opinions, waging a war inside his head? His sense of self-preservation nagged constantly, urging him to drop the backpack and flee but, for some unknown reason, he seemed determined to resist and to persevere with his orders. He had to ensure that he delivered the two cases. His determination might well be founded in his unwavering diligence, but the fear of being tracked down by the assassin and meeting the same fate as Scar was proving to be a more likely incentive.

Arriving at his destination, he checked the street nameplate for confirmation and followed the bend in the road. A sweeping flight of marble steps led him to the entrance of an enormous glass-fronted building. He eyed the peculiar revolving door with trepidation. He'd never seen anything like it before. As he pushed against it the door spun round quickly. Struggling to maintain his balance, he fell forward and hit his forehead against the glass. His jacket got caught in the struggle. Tugging it free with a wail of frustration, he stumbled unceremoniously into the bright high-ceilinged reception area. A smartly dressed woman cast him a look of revulsion as she walked past and exited the building.

'No beggars!' A harsh voice carried across the foyer. A woman was gesturing animatedly from behind a polished marble desk. 'This is a respectable establishment.'

Wartimer shuffled towards her determinedly, suddenly aware he'd forgotten the instruction to change his clothing on the way. He shook his head and scolded himself. Follow instructions at all times. Simple rule. It wasn't like him to forget.

'I am here on business,' he countered defiantly. 'I have an important delivery.' He reached inside the backpack. Ensuring he selected the correct case, he placed it on the desktop. 'There, dispatched. Now, if you don't mind, I need to use your facilities.'

The woman gave him a look of scorn as she lifted a telephone receiver to her ear. 'Second door on the left, down that corridor,' she pointed. 'The facilities are not usually for public use, but I suppose on this occasion we can make an exception.'

He didn't care about the reason for the concession, his bladder was on the point of bursting. As he neared the corridor, a man, puffing on a large cigar, emerged suddenly from between two sliding doors which opened at the prompt of a high-pitched bell.

'Hold the elevator.' Cigar-man bellowed his instruction as he strode across the foyer. Picking the case up from the desk, he quickly retraced his steps and stepped back behind the sliding doors. Wartimer watched as the doors closed. Things were moving just as his instructions had dictated they would. He had to move quickly; the opportunity to swap the cases might present itself very soon.

After emptying his bladder, this time in more suitable surroundings, he paused to inspect his reflection. Back home in Moribor, mirrors were a luxury for the upper class and, for Wartimer, the novelty of seeing himself was still fresh. But today, something about his appearance troubled him and he quickly shied away from the looking glass. Picking up the backpack, he thought, just for a second, about leaving it where it was and walking away. Shaking his head at such negligent thoughts he flung the pack over his shoulder and walked back out into the corridor.

He scanned the foyer. The woman wasn't behind her desk. Where had she gone? Had the first case been returned? He cursed his bladder; he should have been more attentive. As he moved forward warily, the sliding doors opened again.

A uniformed man stepped from the doors and crossed the room. Wartimer held his breath as the woman emerged from a doorway behind the desk.

'Mr Sobek said to leave this with you,' the young man sounded nervous. 'He said to inform you that someone will be here to collect it soon.'

'Okay,' the woman frowned her indifference. 'Leave it there on the desktop. I'll let him know when it's gone.'

The young man did as he was asked, then retreated quickly and disappeared behind the sliding doors. Wartimer watched on, waiting for his chance to act. The woman seemed oblivious to his presence.

To his relief, he didn't have long to wait. His pulse quickened as she left her desk again.
Seizing his opportunity he moved quickly, eyes fixed firmly on his target. Taking the second case from the pack, he approached the desk and hurriedly made the exchange. The second case felt slightly heavier, but the difference was marginal. No one would notice.
As he fumbled with the ties on the backpack, the sound of voices from beyond the door behind the desk ushered him towards the exit. Not daring to look back, he heard the woman's sarcastic farewell as he focused his attention on the perils of the revolving door.

With heart thumping loudly in his chest, he made his way towards the river. It would be the best place to dispose of the incriminating baggage. Taking a diversion down a cobbled side street he came upon a group of vagrants gathered round a fire burning in an old steel drum. It was an opportunity too good to miss. To their whoops of delight, he tossed the backpack into the flames.

Glancing back over his shoulder, ensuring his task was complete, Wartimer quietly congratulated himself on a job well done.

A sudden stab of pain in his legs brought his self-appraisal to an abrupt halt. His limbs burned in agony. What was happening?

As the pain subsided, a wave of steely determination fired him into action. Someone, somewhere, held the answers to his dilemma, and he intended to find them. But who was it? And where would he find them?

His new-found determination didn't yet have all the answers. And so, confused, limping awkwardly, trying desperately to silence the conflicting voices in his head, Wartimer Oldomor wandered aimlessly back in the direction in which he had come.

CHAPTER SEVENTY-THREE

Elfin Fingle silently cursed his troublesome curiosity. It didn't mix well with his over-active sense of adventure. The combination had a habit of landing him in awkward situations and his current predicament was, by a long stretch, the most precarious to date.

Having ignored Token ScriptScratcher's warning to the contrary, Elfin had decided to see if the peculiar mist was still enveloping the town. To save time, he had taken a shortcut through the old forest. He wished now that he hadn't. He stood at the edge of the clearing, transfixed by the horror that lay before him.

A dozen or more wooden cages hung from the branches of the old beech trees. The contents of the cages made him feel sick to the pit of his stomach. Mutilated bodies; their entrails hanging loose, and their blood dripping onto the forest floor. As he crept forward to investigate further, a groan from one of the cages stopped him in his tracks. One of them was still alive.

His heart thumped loudly. As he edged closer and the identity of the casualties became clear, his jaw dropped in shock. The corpses were TrollGatten of Ergmire's soldiers. He couldn't believe his eyes. What could have done this to these giants?

The sound of approaching riders sent him scurrying for cover. Hiding behind the juniper bushes, he held his breath and watched as a group of riders entered the clearing. Boar-men of Ergmire.

Elfin swallowed uncomfortably as he watched General TrollGatten jump from his horse and stride towards the cages.

'In the name of the Gods,' he roared, 'what has happened here?'

'It's like I told you, General,' offered one of his riders. 'It's the scouting party. I found them like this.'

A dying gasp came from a cage at the far edge of the clearing. Elfin's pulse quickened. The last survivor was gone.

General TrollGatten swore his vengeance as he inspected the cages. 'By all the Gods, the perpetrators of this cowardice will pay. I will tear their beating hearts from their chests and feed them to the hounds.' His rage subsided as quickly as it had appeared. 'Send a rider,' his voice echoed chillingly across the clearing. 'Find Red Cloak, bring him to me. If this is more of his trickery, it will be his entrails flying in the wind.'

'It is no deception, General,' growled another rider. 'A group of hooded riders was seen nearby; a war party.'

'A war party belonging to whom?' TrollGatten scowled. 'What banners?'

'They bore no banners, General.'

'Then let's find them.' With a snarl, he bared his pointed teeth. 'Hunt them down, run the fiends into the ground. Mount up!'

They rode from the clearing with a volley of roars and curses. Waiting a few moments, Elfin stepped gingerly from his hiding place. With his inquisitiveness quelled by the gruesome discovery, his appetite for adventure was gone. He had to get back to Bog-Mire as quickly as possible. The sound of an approaching rider caught him off guard. Spinning round to face the threat, he saw a dark-robed figure bearing down on him. There was no time to escape. Lifted from his feet by the rider, Elfin's fear turned to surprise as he recognised his assailant.

'Harbinger Talus! What are you doing?'

Talus offered no response as they rode at break-neck speed through the forest.

'What is going on?' Elfin repeated his cry. 'Who did that to TrollGatten's men?'

'There's no time for explanations,' snapped the Harbinger. 'We need to get away from here quickly. We're making for higher ground. There are riders on my tail, and they weren't far behind.'

'What riders? Who are they?'

'Most likely the ones who put the boar-men in those cages.'

Elfin's stomach lurched. The image of the clearing moved him to silence. They gained height quickly and, as the trees thinned, the Harbinger slowed his horse to a halt. Dismounting, they found cover among the scattered stone tors.

'Down there.' Talus pointed. 'We managed to lose them.'

A group of hooded riders, a score of them, maybe more, galloped by in the gully below.

'Who are they?' Elfin asked quietly. 'I saw one of them in the forest near Shadow Lane.'

'Raiders, Master Tingle.'

'It's Fingle!'

The Harbinger shot him a look of disinterest. 'And now there's trouble ahead.' He pointed towards the grassland beyond the edge of the forest.

Elfin saw another group of riders converging at the edge of the trees. 'Is that TrollGatten's group? They were going looking for the riders who attacked his scouting party.'

Talus pulled his spyglass from his cloak. 'Looks like they found them. And I don't imagine it's going to end well.'

They watched as the mayhem unfolded. The clash of steel, the braying of the horses, and the cries of the fallen echoed loudly through the forest. And it wasn't going well for the riders of Ergmire. The Raiders cleaved through them savagely. Elfin watched in horror as the hooded riders cut and hacked their quarry to pieces.

It was over quickly. Moments later, when the last survivors of Ergmire's war party laid down their swords to offer surrender, a lone Raider urged his black steed forward, raised his blade high in the air, and beheaded them one by one.

Elfin felt the bile rise in his stomach. 'Why? Why did they do that?' He fought back tears. 'They were offering their surrender.'

'The Raiders don't recognise the folly of surrender.' Talus shrugged. 'The boar-men must have had a Drifter in their midst; only explanation for such a brutal annihilation.' He hawked a spit to the ground. 'That's what would have attracted those Raiders; that's what would have driven them to that carnage.'

'What do you mean?' Elfin looked up quizzically. 'What is a Drifter?'

The Harbinger scowled as he mounted up. 'I'll leave such explanations to those better qualified. Perhaps the Scribe can help you, or the Messenger when he makes his next appearance.' Offering a hand to Elfin, he pulled him up on to the horse. They watched as the hooded Raiders rode from sight, leaving the remains of their victims to the gathering crows.

'I'll get you back to Bog-Mire. These woods won't be safe for some time. But one thing is sure,' Talus hawked another spit. 'Enntonia is no longer under siege, not from Ergmire, at least.'

Elfin shuddered. The Raiders. As daunting as TrollGatten and the boar-men from Ergmire had seemed, he couldn't help thinking Enntonia now faced a far greater threat.

CHAPTER SEVENTY-FOUR

Token ScriptScratcher took one last look out into the night before closing the wooden shutters. He was worried. Elfin Fingle was never late for supper and with the weather taking a horrible turn for the worse, his concern for his apprentice was growing. Extinguishing the candles, he pulled the study door closed behind him and went downstairs to the drawing room.

Pouring himself a glass of brandy, Token took a seat by the fire. The flames danced merrily; their energy fuelled by the wind in the chimney. Sipping his brandy, he listened to the hypnotic ticking of the clock on the mantelpiece and with each passing minute his sense of unease grew. He'd waited long enough; the time had come to take action. As he rose from the chair, he heard the front door closing.

'Elfin! You're late. What kept you out on a night like this?' He waited for an answer, but none came. 'Elfin, is that you?'

Token moved to the drawing room door and stepped into the hallway. His eyes were drawn immediately to the wet footprints on the flag-stoned floor; footprints too big to belong to Elfin Fingle. He followed them tentatively along the corridor leading to the old banqueting room. The west wing of Bog-Mire, housing the banquet hall and library, was rarely used these days; Token ScriptScratcher himself restricted his visits there to those of absolute necessity.

The door to the banqueting hall stood slightly ajar. As he drew closer, Token saw that it had been it forced open. Sounds of movement from inside the room prompted him forward boldly.

'Elfin? Are you in here? Is someone with you?'

A dull grating noise came from the far end of the room. A burst of flame suddenly appeared in the disused fireplace. As if prompted by the fire, the candles on the wall sconces flickered energetically to life. Token shivered. What trickery was afoot here? What was happening?

Then he sensed it, the presence. He shivered again. With a growing sense of alarm he watched as the robed figure stepped in front of the fire. Summoning all his courage, Token challenged the imposter.

'This is private property. You must leave at once.'

The dark form remained motionless.

'Who are you?' Token demanded. 'State your business here.'

The figure raised an arm towards him.

'My identity and business here are no concern of yours, Scribe. You look tired, ScriptScratcher; perhaps you should get some rest.'

Token felt a vice-like grip close around his neck. As his breathing began to toil, his blurring vision saw the figure raise a clenched fist high in the air. Panicking, clutching at straws for means of escape, Token spluttered a desperate verse of protection. In response, a burst of mocking laughter echoed round the room.

'You fool; your pathetic incantations are useless against me. Sleep, old man. Sleep!'

Token ScriptScratcher felt the grip around his neck tighten further. Gasping for air, he fell to his knees and slipped from consciousness.

CHAPTER SEVENTY-FIVE

The Central News Agency's special correspondent Fara Lane fell silent as Senator Gabrat Sobek muted the television, picked up his telephone, and dialled the number again. The outcome was the same. No response. Where was that fool Barkal? What was he playing at? Sobek cancelled the call and dialled down to reception.

'Has anyone been in to collect the case yet?'

'No, Senator. It's still here.'

Sobek ended the call and tried the number again. This time it went straight to answerphone. He felt the fury rise from deep inside. Barkal had just turned his phone off. Sobek's clenched fist struck the desk in anger. He picked up the crystal glass and hurled it across the room. It shattered against the wall, only inches away from Fara Lane's muted broadcast. With a growl, he dialled reception again.

'Get me the Boneyard Bar.'

He slumped back in the chair. Why was everything suddenly going wrong? After months of planning, his success was now hanging in the balance. All because some drunken idiot couldn't carry out simple orders. It had all being going so well, even allowing for this afternoon's unexpected change in plan and the inclusion of the vice president's aide. He'd checked the contents of the dispatch case and had been impressed. The dossier of incriminating evidence, much of it fabricated but nonetheless compelling, would help bring Sobek and his co-conspirators' plan to fruition. He now questioned his judgement, and the folly of entrusting such an integral part of the process to a waste-of-space like Barkal. His telephone rang. He answered it hurriedly.

'I have the number you wanted, Senator. I'm putting you through now.'

Sobek waited as the line connected.

'Boneyard Bar. Sina speaking.'

'Is Barkal in there?'

'Sorry? You'll have to speak up.'

'Tybor Barkal!' Sobek shouted. 'Is he there?'

'No, he isn't here. He was in earlier, but he left some time ago with a woman. Do you want me to give him a message if he comes back in?'

Sobek hung up without responding. What was Barkal doing? Was he finally on his way? He called him again, with no success. It went straight to answerphone. He glanced at the clock. He was running out of time. He had to change his plans. He scrolled through his list of contacts. Scar would have to arrange an alternative courier.

The call to Scar's number didn't even connect. The line went dead. He tried it again with the same result. What was happening? Where in damnation was everyone tonight? Sobek's blood boiled. Months of preparation were falling apart before his eyes. His focus wandered again to the clock. Was he going to have to deliver the case himself? No, that would be far too risky. The chances of him being noticed at the banquet were too high.

It could cause suspicion as events unfolded. And could he trust his fellow conspirators to back him up if the need arose?

The recent turn of events suggested not.

He picked up the phone and called down to reception.

'Is the case still there?'

'Yes, Senator, it's still here.'

'No one has called in?'

'No,' she hesitated, 'but the weird character who dropped the case off earlier…'

'Yes? What about him?'

'He passed by outside, about five minutes ago.'

'Go after him. Find him, and bring him back here. Call me when you do.' He re-lit a cigar and threw himself back in the chair. He might just have found a solution, but was it going to be too late? What were the repercussions going to be? Someone would have to pay for this. His receptionist's call came quicker than he expected.

'Did you find him?' he demanded. 'Where are you?'

'I'm outside.' She sounded confused. 'I followed him as you instructed. I caught sight of him, four, maybe five hundred metres along Quay Street. I shouted to him, I told him to wait, but he kept going, so I ran after him.'

'And? What happened?'

'He turned down a side alley,' she continued. 'I followed and then…'

'Then what? What happened?'

'He just vanished!'

Sobek's bizarre evening was becoming stranger by the minute.

'He what? That's not possible. People don't just disappear.'

'This one did! He disappeared, right in front of my eyes.'

The tone in her voice left little room for discussion, and there was no time to waste. 'Where are you now? Still in the alleyway?'

'Yes.'

'Okay. Just come back. I need you to deliver the case.'

Sobek rose from his chair, stubbed the cigar on the ashtray, and picked up the television remote control. Intending to turn it off, he pressed the mute button by mistake, bringing Fara Lane's coverage from the convention banquet back to life.

'The President is about to begin his speech. This is without doubt a momentous event...'

Her words were the last thing Senator Gabrat Sobek heard.

CHAPTER SEVENTY-SIX

'That's it! I regret to say, I can do no more.'

Messenger Two Cups sighed as he looked up at the bearded stranger. 'I have translated your scroll to the best of my ability. In truth, I would not have been able to do it without Sanna's contribution. I'm afraid the archaic text would have had me stumped. So, there we have it,' he tapped the parchment. 'As far as we can tell, the Woodsman has gone to this so-called land of mirrors, thus fulfilling part of his destiny.'

'But what part does he play? Good or evil?'

'Taro Brook is a man of honour, my friend. With Sanna's help, I'm certain only good could come from his involvement.'

'That's assuming she is able to find him. What if she fails?'

Two Cups dismissed the notion with a grin. 'She is a determined individual. She will find him, have no fear of that.' Stretching, he stifled a yawn. 'I could do with some fresh air. Come, let us wander a while in the grounds of Sumarren.'

Back once again in the sunshine, Messenger Two Cups sensed a change in the stranger's manner. The bearded man seemed less self-assured, and it appeared he was constantly reassessing his surroundings. He addressed Two Cups questioningly.

'Is there more to the Days of Thunder prophecy?'

'It's impossible to know for certain. There may still be undiscovered writings connected to the prophecy. Such is the nature of these things.'

'The Woodsman told me about dreams he'd been having, and he claimed that I featured in the dreams. Is that possible?'

'Now, that is interesting.' Two Cups raised an eyebrow. 'He mentioned the dreams on several occasions. Tell me, what is really behind your interest in Taro Brook?'

The stranger shrugged. 'We are merely trying to find out more about the history of our world, and the Woodsman is mentioned in our writings on numerous occasions.'

Two Cups grinned and nodded playfully. 'Yes, but we both know it is more than that, don't we? Tell me more of your world. The land of Nallevarr once fell victim to a great flood, didn't it? You told us of the archaeological finds; would it not be right to surmise that, at some point following the advance of the seas, an ice age covered your homeland in a ghostly frozen shell? Is this why you feel such an affiliation to the Woodsman and the fate of his world?'

Casting his gaze towards the firth, the stranger offered his concession willingly. 'It would be folly to attempt to deceive you, Scaraven. And you are correct in your assumptions; our historians would concur that Nallevarr did indeed suffer the same fate facing Taro Brook's world and yes, I do confess to having more than a passing interest in him. I believe that with our help, he can survive the terrible fate awaiting his world.' A knowing grin flashed across his face. 'In fact, I am certain of it, now that he knows it is going to happen.'

The disclosure took Two Cups by surprise. 'You told him?'

'Yes, I spoke with him before he drifted in the ruins. I'll admit our conversation came as a surprise to both of us.'

'How so?'

'The Woodsman would not have been expecting to meet with someone from his dreams and I certainly didn't think it would be possible to talk with him.'

Two Cups was finding it difficult to conceal his growing suspicions. 'Tell me, envoy of Nallevarr, why is it so important to you that he survives this catastrophe?'

'As I said, I am certain he will survive the tragedy but, given the importance of the Woodsman in our historical writings, I felt my intervention was essential. The scroll needed translating; we had to know more about the Woodsman and his part in this unfolding prophecy. I needed your help in finding the answers.'

Two Cups pulled thoughtfully at his whiskers. 'Intervention can be a dangerous thing.' He pondered the concept for a moment. 'And yet, at times, it is essential as you rightly say.' Adjusting his hat, he continued with his line of questioning. 'You are certain Taro Brook will survive the flood?'

'Yes.'

'What makes you so sure?' he waved an accusatory finger. 'What proof do you have?' With the lack of response further stoking his enthusiasm, Messenger Two Cups continued his inquisition. 'I feel that you have me at a disadvantage, my friend. We've discussed many things. You seem to know a lot about me, but you haven't told me your name.' Two Cups detected a further change in the stranger's demeanour: an air of quiet resignation.

Sensing that he was getting closer to his answers, he probed further. 'What else did you tell the Woodsman? Did you tell him who you were?'

The stranger's expression broke into a grin. 'I think I had sufficiently tested the boundaries of Taro Brook's imagination with what I'd already told him, and besides, I didn't think it was really necessary for him to know.'

Two Cups was barely able to contain his satisfaction. 'I have another question for you. How old are you?'

The stranger scratched thoughtfully at his beard. 'I honestly don't know, but I once knew a wizard who told me repeatedly that time was irrelevant. Perhaps age should be viewed in the same way?'

'Excellent answer!' Two Cups grinned his delight. 'Isn't this just incredible?' He clasped his hands together. 'You need continue no further with your pretence, my friend.' Chuckling his amusement, he bounded forward enthusiastically. 'I am incredibly happy to see you again, Taro Brook. In fact, you might say I am deeelighted!'

Their handshake was firm and sincere. Two Cups cackled with excitement. 'Who would have thought it? The Woodsman and the man from Nallevarr. I hadn't even considered the possibility that they could be the same person; that they could both be you!'

'Imagine my surprise, old friend, having been drawn here to discover that the wise one Scaraven, mentioned so many times in our ancient texts, is none other than an old tea-drinking acquaintance.'

'You didn't remember that it would be me?'

'No, I didn't suspect for one minute that I would know you.'

'Hahaha! You know, it doesn't seem that long ago that I was telling you that very same thing. I suspected that it would be so. When did you start to remember? I must say you hid it well, you rascal.'

'Things started to come back to me as we talked; fleeting memories, recollections of things that had gone before. I regret to say I didn't remember Sanna at all. But after she left, when I realised who you were and that I remembered you, I wasn't sure if I should say or not. It's wonderful to see you again. How long is it since we have seen each other?'

Two Cups shook his hands in the air and tutted distastefully. 'Now, you should know better than to ask me such a question. Remember what I told you?'

'Time means nothing here.' They voiced the words in unison. Two Cups snorted his delight and fumbled with his pack.

'This calls for a celebration. Would you do me the honour of joining me in a cup of the old Silver Birch tea?'

'I thought you would never ask.'

Laughing heartily, Two Cups hurriedly grabbed the flask, poured two mugs of tea, and raised one in salute. 'It is so good to see you again, Woodsman. I must admit to finding this whole scenario fascinating. Tell me, how much do you remember? Do you recall anything of what happened when the tragedy struck your world? Do you remember how you survived?'

Taro Brook shook his head. 'I don't remember anything about it, and when I arrived here, I barely recognised myself.'

Two Cups nodded appreciatively. 'It must have been a very disconcerting concept. Do you have memories of any other worlds?'

'If you mean do I remember anything of when I drift, I'm afraid the answer is no. That's why I came looking for you, to find answers. I still can't get my head around the fact that I can shift from one time to another.'

Two Cups grinned widely. 'Tell me more about these dreams. Were you aware of what you were doing? Were you attempting to send a message?'

'I don't know. Possibly.'

'The building in the mountains, was there any significance to it?'

'Not really, I stay there sometimes, when the weather allows. Being in the mountains gives me a profound sense of peace, but I have no idea of the history of the place.'

'You suggested it was once the residence of royalty.'

'Only in jest, it makes it sound more impressive, don't you agree?'

'Indeed, and the two giant snow dogs?' Two Cups prompted excitedly. 'What of them?'

'It was in the aftermath of a snowstorm, I found them as pups, abandoned in a cave in the mountains. I watched the cave for several days, but no adult returned. Fearing for their chances of survival, I took it upon myself to rescue them. They have proved to be loyal and faithful companions.'

Two Cups smiled as he refuelled their tea mugs. 'So, tell me of Nallevarr. How much were you aware of there?'

'It's hard to say. I often had dreams and visions, but none that made much sense. I worked as a guide for the archaeological expedition groups, and many of their findings merely proved what I'd come to suspect. I had found traces of the old world emerging from the ice long before they arrived. What's your opinion on the dreams I was experiencing? Do you think they are messages? Or just recollections? Is it possible for someone to communicate with oneself from the past or the future?'

'I don't believe there is any definition between past, present and future, Woodsman. Remember, we are not talking about a past life or existence, you are simply drifting from one presence to another. And as for the dreams, perhaps you were trying to communicate, trying to deliver a message.' He grinned broadly. 'And let's be honest, it worked, didn't it?'

'It does seem that way. So, the knowledge I'd gained from the scrolls we'd uncovered gave me the will to seek out answers, but how did I know to come here, and to come now?'

'It's all down to synchronicity. Your presence here with Sanna and myself would have been a big pull, adding to your desire for answers surrounding your part in this otherworld prophecy.'

'But there is no way for us to know what I do there. What if I don't survive in that other world? How would that affect me? How do I find the answers to these questions?'

Two Cups patted his arm reassuringly. 'Relax, my friend, I may not hold all the answers, but I can assure you of one thing. The ability to drift from one place to another, from one world to another, or as you like to call it, one time to another, is in every one of us. It's in every living being. However, only a gifted few ever become aware of it. We refer to them as Drifters, and the good news for you, Taro Brook, is that a Drifter can never die.'

'Really? But what if I were to die in another world?'

'Any incarnation of you may well cease to exist, but you are a conscious entity for whom the journey will never end.'

'You are talking about immortality?'

'No, for you there is no such thing. Mortality is a very real concept for those inhabiting the earthly plane, but you now exist on a much higher level.' A worried expression suddenly replaced his smile. 'Curses! It is happening again.'

'What is it? What's wrong?'

'Look there, by the standing stones.' Two Cups pointed. 'Do you see the blurring of the shapes?'

'Yes, I do. What does it mean?'

'It means I must leave you again, my old friend.' Two Cups sighed as he hurriedly packed away the flask.

'But I still have many things to ask you. There is so much I need to know.'

'Fear not, Woodsman, the answers will present themselves to you when they are meant to.' He grasped Brook's hand firmly. 'Believe me, I would dearly like to stay and talk more, for I feel there is much we could learn from each other.' He gave a broad smile. 'But we will meet again soon. You can rest assured of that.'

'But what will happen to me now? Where will I go?'

'There truly is no need to concern yourself, Taro Brook. You are here, there, and everywhere. Your very presence is forever entwined in the fabric of the here and now.' He raised an eyebrow suggestively. 'Wherever that may be!'

As he neared the strange phenomenon floating amidst the standing stones, Messenger Two Cups turned to see the bearded man's image fade from view.

'Farewell, Taro Brook,' he whispered.

The distorting shapes enveloped him quickly, and the warm sunshine and idyllic setting of Sumarren were soon left behind. The temperature dropped rapidly. The air turned cold and damp. As the blurring images settled, he studied his surroundings with a sense of recognition.

'Night-time in Bog-Mire Forest.' He braced himself against the chill air. 'I wonder what draws me here?'

Following the track towards Bog-Mire Towers, he sensed that, whatever the reason, it wasn't going to be good.

CHAPTER SEVENTY-SEVEN

High above the Blackheart Pass, the late afternoon sky darkened as a bank of cloud gathered menacingly. Spurred on by a sense of impending gloom, Morusk of DunTreggan scrambled up the steep slope. Reaching the top of the climb, he crouched in the cover of the tors, and scanned the landscape for sign of their pursuers. It was as he suspected. The hooded riders were gaining ground. It now seemed certain the skeletal warriors would be upon them by nightfall.

He pondered their desperate dilemma. The Northman Eldir's plan to ambush the Raiders was a brave one; the harsh reality was that it was their best hope of survival. It was a courageous plot, but Morusk feared for its success. Having witnessed the Raiders' brutality with his own eyes, even with the element of surprise on their side, he feared their casualties would be many. Their numbers had been bolstered by the arrival of further riders of the Brochen Eyne but, despite being bred specifically for the harsh terrain of the northlands, the horses were now restricting their options and slowing their progress. They desperately needed something to help swing the odds of survival in their favour. Something. Anything.

With a growing sense of urgency, he studied his surroundings in search of inspiration. And looking skywards, near the top of the cliffs, he saw something that might offer a glimmer of hope.

A rough track wound its way precariously up the side of the ravine. Near the top of the track, a huge boulder blocked its progress. The great rock loomed ominously over the pass, and a stack of dead, fallen trees appeared to be the only obstruction holding it in place.

Morusk's mind raced as he quickly played out the possible scenario. If the fallen trees were dislodged, the boulder would be free to begin its rapid descent of the steep ravine, taking everything in its path with it. If its journey to the bottom of the gorge ended in a collision with some of the hooded riders, Morusk and his allies might stand a better chance of surviving the night. Jumping to his feet, he descended the loose scree quickly, to where his friends waited quietly with the horses.

'How close are they now?' quizzed Stuc.

'My guess is they will be with us not long after dark.'

'We can't keep moving all night, Morusk, the horses are tired. The rocky ground and fast pace are a bad combination.'

'I know,' he nodded. 'Eldir, how much further to where you planned to execute the ambush?'

The Northman gestured ahead. 'Not far. Another two, maybe three turns in the trail. We are almost at the heart of the Pass. The trail narrows before widening again, and that's where I plan to make our stand. There are caves for shelter, and the steep slopes on either side of the trail offer many positions for our bowmen.'

Morusk nodded his approval then shared his thoughts.

'The Raiders are savage killers; we have all seen what they are capable of. We need to gain some kind of advantage, and I think

I may have an idea. Eldir, I saw a track in the cliff-face high above. Do you know of it?'

'Yes,' nodded the Northman. 'But it is steep and dangerous… and unsuitable for horses. I don't think we should attempt it.'

'It doesn't sound like a wise idea.' Stuc cautioned.

Morusk brushed aside their concerns as he mounted up.

'We will risk only one horse. Stuc, send the others ahead with Eldir's people. They will show them where to find shelter and prepare. Eldir, how far is it to this track?'

'It begins its ascent just around the next bend.'

'Good! Go, both of you. Relay the orders and meet me there and, Eldir, bring several of your bowmen.'

'What are you thinking, Morusk?' Stuc challenged. 'What's your idea?'

'There's no time to waste,' replied Morusk. 'The Raiders will soon be upon us. Go! Pass on the instructions and meet me at the foot of the track. I'll tell you the plan as we climb.'

CHAPTER SEVENTY-EIGHT

Messenger Two Cups closed the front door of Bog-Mire Towers quietly behind him and moved through the half-light towards the drawing room, Token ScriptScratcher's favoured place for his evening pipe and brandy.

The fire sparked invitingly as he peered round the door, but the room was empty. A half-filled glass waited on the table next to the Scribe's armchair. With his suspicion that all was not well further fuelled, Two Cups turned back into the hallway.

As he made towards the stairs, a glimmer of light from beyond the door of the old banqueting room caught his eye. Moving quickly along the corridor, he pushed the door open wide and entered the room.

In the dim glow of candlelight, he saw his old friend's body slumped on the floor. With a gasp, Two Cups hurried to the Scribe's side where a quick examination dispelled his worst fears. Token ScriptScratcher was unconscious, but alive. At the sound of footsteps behind him, he spun round to see a dark-robed figure stepping from the shadows.

'Well, look who has come to Bog-Mire in its hour of need,' sneered the gravelly voice. 'Welcome, old man, it has been a while since last we met.'

Two Cups jumped to his feet. 'Osfilian!' The stranger's face was unfamiliar, but he'd know that voice and recognise that evil presence anywhere. 'What are you doing here? This is hallowed ground. What have you done to the Scribe?'

Osfilian shrugged his indifference. 'Fear not, he will suffer no long-term harm. I merely put him to sleep whilst I attend to my business.' He scowled. 'You, however, are a different proposition altogether. I'm afraid I must employ more extreme methods to hold your attention.'

Sensing the danger, Messenger Two Cups threw himself to one side, but he was too slow. A flash of light flared across the room and struck him on the shoulder. Almost immediately he felt a numbing sensation creeping round his neck, down his lower arm, and into his hands and fingers. Unable to move a muscle, he was trapped in suspended animation. 'Curses on you, Osfilian.' His speech, at least, seemed unaffected. 'Release me at once. You shouldn't have come here. You should have stayed in your mountain prison.'

Ignoring his demands, Osfilian moved towards the fire and lifted a burning candle from the mantelpiece. Cupping the flickering flame, he whispered a short verse, and threw the candle across the room. Unable to move, the Messenger watched on as the candle came to a sudden halt only inches from his face, before erupting into a luminous ball of flame. Surrounded by the glowing sphere, Two Cups watched on helplessly as Osfilian sat on the arm of the chair and glared mockingly.

'Now that I have your full attention, Scaraven, we can talk. You should have taken care of things properly when last we met. You know it was never my destiny to remain in that pathetic mountain lair, the foolishness of man would never allow it. Your actions were borne out of weakness and your weakness will be your downfall.'

'You know full well that I could do no more,' rallied Two Cups. 'You know the nature of balance, good and evil, if I could have destroyed you once and for all that night, I would have. But your fate awaits you, Dark One, and when it comes you will not escape it.'

'Some of your words hold true, Scaraven, but I am bored with the old laws and I tire of the need for balance.'

'I see you have changed your appearance. It fools no one. Your evil ways cannot be concealed.'

'I have no need to hide the nature of my intentions. As for my appearance, it serves my purpose well, it keeps the mind fresh. I suggest you try it, old man,' he taunted. 'That old coat and hat appear very jaded.' He leaned forward menacingly. 'But, as much as I enjoy your idle chatter, my business here in this confounded place calls for haste.'

'What business?' quizzed Two Cups. 'Why are you here?'

Osfilian steepled his fingers as he crafted his response.

'I've been experimenting. As I've said, I'm tired of the constant ebb and flow in our long-standing battle and I must confess to taking steps to gain some modicum of advantage.' He paused momentarily before continuing. 'These agents of yours, these so-called Drifters, I'm sure you are aware of my continued efforts to eradicate them completely. I find them troublesome. However, my servants in this cause, my skeletal warriors, have enjoyed only meagre measures of success.'

'Shame on you!' Two Cups' anger boiled over. 'You are letting them run amok. They are now crossing between worlds. They are an abomination.'

'Yes, they truly are,' purred Osfilian. 'An abomination I am immensely proud of. You see, it had occurred to me that these Drifters and their talents could be deployed to a more fitting cause. Unfortunately, they seem unwilling to swap allegiances. So, instead of trying to sway them, I now continue with my efforts to destroy them whilst simultaneously proceeding with my new creation.'

'What new creation? What evil do you plan to unleash now?'

'A new variant of Drifter, one with a very different purpose to yours.'

'You already have your agents of random chaos. They create more than enough havoc as it stands. They are your agents, and the Drifters are their adversary. That is the way of it. The natural balance.'

'And I am tired of the balance,' roared Ophidian angrily. 'The agents of random chaos can only exist in their own worlds. They are unable to drift from one reality to another.' His expression calmed instantly, and his voice dropped to a whisper. 'You must see, you have me at a disadvantage.'

'Nonsense!' Two Cups fired his response. 'Tell me, what you have done?'

'It's quite a simple procedure really,' a grin of contentment flashed across his rival's face. 'A form of transportation, similar to the one deployed by the Drifters, but instead of being a naturally occurring phenomenon, they are created by joining the personalities of those yet to discover their capabilities with characters of my own choosing.'

Two Cups shook his head in disgust. His long-standing antagonist had gone too far this time.

'It is an evolving process,' Osfilian continued. 'And, if I'm honest, I have yet to perfect my creation. And that is why I am here. Believe me,' he glanced loathingly around the room. 'Only desperate measures would drag me here to this wretched place, but there may be writings held within these walls, ancient scripts that would assist me in my quest.'

'You will find nothing here to aid you in such dark works,' snapped Two Cups. 'Nothing stored within these walls would ever be of help to you. I know of no such scripts. Stop this folly now, release me from my binds and leave while you still can.'

Osfilian shook his head calmly. 'I think not. Your arrogance surprises me, Scaraven. Your knowledge has boundaries which you seem unable to accept. I don't believe your claims, I think these writings exist and it stands to reason that they would be here. When I have found them, well, perhaps I will release you, perhaps I won't, at least not for a while.' He grinned. 'Your continued incarceration would give me the chance to perfect my creation which would then present you with the opportunity to raise your game. What say you? Can you rise to the challenge?'

'Never!' Two Cups fired defiantly. 'I absolutely refuse to take part in your foolish games.'

'You have become an incredible bore, Scaraven. I'm merely trying to make things more interesting for both of us. You see, unlike you, I can accept that we need each other. Good and Evil, the perfect partners, waging war on each other endlessly down through the ages.' He pointed animatedly. 'Deep down, you know that one has no real cause to exist without the other. Admit it.'

'I will make no such concessions. I strive for the day when we can rid all worlds of your evil ways.' He hesitated. 'The dragons... What do you intend to do with the Black Wing? Are you going to carry out the orders of the High Council? Would you condemn Enntonia to such a fate?'

Osfilian snorted his disgust. 'At least credit me with being a wizard of honour. I cannot renege on the bargain struck with those fools. After all, they did release me from the Basilisik Mountain.' He jabbed a pointed finger. 'I'm not usually one for holding grudges, but what you did there really annoyed me.' An indignant scowl settled on his features. 'A deal is a deal; I must repay the debt and do as they bid.'

'Don't do it,' implored Two Cups. 'For pity's sake, don't do it. The fools in the High Council are all gone; they fled like the spineless cowards they are. Only the innocent remain. The army the High Council so feared is now camped at the edge of town. I have held council with the riders of Ergmire, and I believe they will settle their differences peacefully. Let them take what is owed to them and leave Enntonia alone.'

'Your information is outdated,' Osfilian sneered. 'I know you tricked those boar-men with your deception, but they are no longer an issue.'

'What do you mean?'

'A group of Raiders wiped them out.'

Two Cups drew a breath of despair. 'All of them?'

'Perhaps a few stragglers were allowed to escape. It's a damned clever tactic, they form an excellent bait.' Osfilian dismissed the subject with a wave of his arm. 'The Black Wing is the least of your worries, Scaraven. You must try harder to keep up, to move with the times. Mankind throws me no end of opportunities to spread havoc. Truly, have you set eyes upon the many wonders? The glorious weapons of destruction? The war planes?'

'I have seen the ruin caused by your steel dragons.' Two Cups responded angrily. His patience was almost at breaking point. Desperate to break free from his quandary, his mind raced. If he could just regain the feeling in his hands he might be able to escape the sphere.

'I sense you are tiring, old man.' Osfilian rose from the chair purposefully. 'And I must tend to business. Things are unravelling quickly.'

'What do you mean?'

'I have under my influence an undesirable creature who has unwittingly put himself at my disposal. He is my trial case and is, hopefully, carrying out my orders as we speak. As my creation is not yet perfected and, what with him being a rather unbalanced individual, I am slightly apprehensive about how it all may unfold. His judgement cannot truly be trusted. Do you know, the fool actually once tried to summon me, to have me do his bidding.'

'What happened?'

'His futile attempt ended badly for him. He bungled his incantation. Can you believe it? Such a basic error.'

Though Osfilian's disclosure held a familiar ring, Two Cups kept his suspicions to himself and instead questioned his rival further. 'And this individual, what is it you have planned for him?'

'A simple task, in truth. To meddle with a routine delivery. I have successfully merged him with one of your Drifters. Imagine that, a combination of both our talents, a creation to transcend all boundaries. Does that not fill you with pride?' He roared with laughter at the lack of response. 'No, I thought not.' Clasping his hands in delight, he continued, nonetheless.

'But listen to my tale, for it is a sumptuous example of greed and corruption. I stumbled upon a plot, a tame one in all honesty, to undermine a regime from within. The rogue element had in their possession, information which they intended to use against their government. Their aim was to bring about fundamental change in both policy and personnel, and their plan was to use the staging of a conference of nations to set things in motion.' Osfilian groaned his delight, a low guttural sound rattled in his throat. 'Even you would have to appreciate the irony, Scaraven. It's a summit to promote peace amongst nations and I, having managed to infiltrate their plans, am on the cusp of creating carnage on a massive scale.' Pursing his lips, he grinned his satisfaction. 'The consequences could be colossal. Worldwide condemnation should, I imagine, quickly lead to all-out war. Magnificent! Even if I say so myself; it's downright magnificent.'

'What have you done?' Two Cups' voice trembled.

'It's all been so simple. My agent's task was to intercept and exchange two dispatch cases. One case contains the incriminating evidence, the other is fitted with an explosive device big enough to destroy a large building, obliterating everyone in it.'

Left reeling by the shocking divulgence and all its intricacies, Two Cups could only manage one word in response. 'Where?'

'You may have heard of it. It is mentioned in an old prophecy. The place in question is known as Sahropa, but the prophecy refers to it as the Land of Mirrors.'

'No!' Two Cups' horror intensified. Osfilian pounced on his reaction.

'I see that you are familiar with it.' He paced menacingly in front of the fire. 'I'll be honest, the prophecy troubles me. Has it happened before and is history merely repeating itself? Or was it meant to happen but didn't for some unknown reason. Perhaps, on a previous attempt my erroneous agent bungled the plan. This is why I am determined to ensure it doesn't happen again. I am certain my enhancing his persona with your Drifter will suffice, but I must take further actions to ensure future successes. I'm sure you can appreciate my attention to detail, what with you being a perfectionist yourself.'

He flashed a sarcastic smile. 'But listen to me rambling on. Apologies, old friend, I expect you have things on your mind too. The prophecy also mentions the Woodsman and the Sun Warrior.' His expression darkened.

'I believe they are acquaintances of yours, Scaraven. Good friends even? For your sake, I hope they are not where I think they are.'

CHAPTER SEVENTY-NINE

As Elfin Fingle and the Harbinger rode towards Bog-Mire Towers, the failing light heralded the arrival of night and with it came an unwelcome change in the weather. By the time they entered the cobbled courtyard, the rain was falling heavily.

As they drew to a halt, a black object flew past their heads. Elfin watched the raven circle several times before it came to rest on the wooden handle of an old plough. Flapping its wings vigorously in defiance of the weather, it eyed them closely.

Harbinger Talus dismounted. His boots splashed noisily as he helped Elfin down from the horse. Removing his glove, he put his fingers to his mouth and gave a short, high-pitched whistle. The raven took flight instantly and landed on his outstretched arm. Wiping the rain from his face, Elfin watched on as Talus removed a small parchment from the bird's leg.

'Duty calls. I must go.' Talus mounted up quickly. 'Inform the Scribe of all that has happened, Master Fingle.'

The Harbinger galloped into the darkness, leaving Elfin speechless. Talus had finally got his name right.

As he moved towards Bog-Mire's front entrance, a glimmer of light from one of the stables caught his attention. Shielding his face from the driving rain, he hurried across the courtyard to investigate. Pushing the door open warily, he looked inside but saw no sign of the light. The stable was in darkness.

As he turned to leave, he sensed someone, or something, brushing against him. Shaken by the strange sensation, he waved his arms wildly, as if fending off his invisible assailant.

When he was sure the moment had passed, Elfin closed the stable door and bolted it. He could come back in the morning to make a further inspection.

Marching quickly across the courtyard, he climbed the steps to the front door, and made his way inside.

CHAPTER EIGHTY

Tybor Barkal woke with a start and sat upright in the chair. At the far end of the room he saw Ashrynn sitting by the window, her face illuminated by the bright lights of the city. He got to his feet and stretched.

'That noise, was it thunder?'

'Not thunder,' she replied solemnly. 'You'd best come and see for yourself.'

'I didn't mean to fall asleep. You should have wakened me.'

'Don't worry about it, you weren't asleep for long. You need to see this. It's awful.'

He was ill-prepared for the shocking sight that awaited him. To his astonishment, he saw that the city skyline was ablaze.

'What's going on? What happened?'

'I can't believe it. A building just burst into flames.'

'An explosion? Really? You saw it happen?'

'Yes, there was to be a firework display tonight at the peace convention banquet. I was watching for it when that happened.'

Tybor Barkal watched the scene in disbelief. Drawing his eyes from the sight of the burning building, he started pinpointing the city landmarks and, as he ran the scenario through his head, the pieces of the puzzle tumbled into place. The conclusion hit him like a train. With a gasp he turned away, clasping his hands behind his head. She was quick to pick up on his reaction.

'Is that where you were meant to go tonight?'

Barkal nodded. 'My rendezvous point would have been right there, somewhere in the middle of that.' He paced the room for a moment before sitting down on the bed. 'How could you have known?'

'Known what?'

'You said earlier that you had a bad feeling about tonight. How could you have known something like that was going to happen?'

'I didn't know. Why would you say such a thing?'

'Well, how do you explain it? Only hours after we meet for the first time, you come to find me in the Boneyard, you completely alter my plans for the evening, and you… you…'

'I save your life. Is that what you're trying to say?'

Stung by the truth in her words, Barkal was quick to offer his apology. 'I'm really sorry. That came out wrong. I didn't mean it to sound like that. It's just so…'

'Hard to explain? You think it's strange? How do you think I feel? I'm the one who changed her plans at the very last minute to go looking for a total stranger, so I could save his life? And I have no idea why I did it.' She held his stare. 'How am I supposed to make sense of it?'

Spurred by her response, Barkal moved from the bed and knelt down next to her. 'Don't think about it, I don't understand it either. We could spend forever trying to figure it out and not come up with an explanation. How about we just agree to accept it? I know one thing for sure, whatever happened, whatever the reason, you probably saved my life.' He took her by the hand.

'How does someone even start to say thanks for something like that?'

'I don't know,' her frustration eased quickly. 'Maybe you don't need to thank me. Maybe I'm your guardian angel.'

'Maybe that's it.' With a grin, he got to his feet again. 'Sounds like the perfect explanation. Thank you for convincing me to change my plans.'

'I don't know what made me do it.' She rose from the chair. 'I guess I'll never know, but I'm glad I found you in time. I dread to think what would have happened to you. Can I ask what it is you were meant to do when you got there?'

'I don't know,' he sighed. 'My instructions were vague, they always are. Just a time and a place.'

Watching him closely, she raised an eyebrow questioningly. 'So, the place you were meant to be gets blown up? Coincidence?'

Barkal found the alternative hard to believe. 'It has to be. I'm not a likely target for an assassination attempt. I mean, I'm just not that important... to anyone.'

'What about the man who was calling you? You said he was dangerous.'

'Sobek? Yes, he is, but...' He paused to consider the notion. Why would Sobek want him dead? It didn't add up. 'No, it's just a coincidence. I'm not even sure how close I would have been to it all. I may have been several blocks away from the explosion.'

Accepting his reasoning with a smile, she moved towards the window. 'You're probably right. I've seen enough of this now.'

He watched as she pulled the curtains.

'Your tattoo,' he said the words without thinking.

'Yes?' Turning to him, she pulled up the sleeve of her tee shirt. 'Do you like it?'

'It's beautiful.' He hesitated. 'I know this will sound strange, but it looks familiar. I think I may have seen something like it before… I just don't remember where.'

She laughed out loud. 'Definitely not. It's my own design, and the only place you'll find it is on my arm or in my sketchbook.'

'Really?' He looked at it again. She was right. His moment of recognition had passed. Had he imagined it? How could he have recognised it? Opting to say no more about it, he made his way back to the bed. His mind raced. So much had happened in such a short time. Tomorrow he would have to face the wrath of Senator Sobek, but for now he wanted to live in the moment; to find out all he could about this beautiful stranger to whom he felt so connected. She refilled their wine glasses and curled up next to him on the bed.

'Well, if this is fate,' she smiled, 'I suppose we should get to know each other better.'

Ignoring the sound of sirens from the streets below they talked long into the night until, as the early morning light began to invade the room, they finally surrendered to sleep.

CHAPTER EIGHTY-ONE

Suspended in a trance-like state, Tickbus Tard felt his grip on reality diminishing rapidly. Was he dreaming? Or was all this really happening? The figures and voices in his initial dream had been replaced by all manner of strange and disturbing images.
He felt inexplicably torn but, as troubling as the visions were, the last thing he wanted to do was open his eyes to discover he was still trapped in his dismal dungeon. The dreams had become his only means of escaping his prison.

Trapped like a voyeur, aware his thoughts and actions were not all his own, he stepped into the heavy rain and crossed the cobbled courtyard towards the imposing structure. Its grey towers spiked the darkening sky. It was a scene so different to the crowded cityscape with its tall shining buildings where he had watched the scar-faced man meet with his grisly end.
The ghastly scene had become all the more disturbing at the mention of the Master and at being told once again to carry out his orders. Why was the Master in his dreams? Was the Dark One so deeply entrenched in his fears?
Resisting the urge to run, he'd done as he was told. Swapping the black cases, he'd danced to the Master's tune like a puppet on invisible strings. But, as unpleasant as the whole experience had become, the most disturbing moment of all had been gazing into the looking glass to see a stranger staring back at him.

Who had stolen his reflection?
His initial shock had quickly turned to intrigue and, as the visions continued, Tickbus began to suspect that their origins were not confined merely to dreams. Could it be that he had somehow infiltrated another's presence?
The stranger's reflection, paired with the bizarre feeling of not being in control of his own thoughts and actions, supported this theory. Was this what the Master had meant when he talked about sending him to another world? Had the Master sent him here after all? Was he finally free from his nightmare existence as an Arachgnome? Excitement coursed through him at the prospect.
If he had infiltrated another's presence, could he take control and become the stronger willed of the two?
He had to try. The voice in his head was constantly questioning his every thought, his every movement, and try as he might, he couldn't make it stop.

As he pushed the door open, a sensation of dread screamed caution. Was he walking into a trap? Was the Master here? In spite of his fears, some small part of him hoped so. He wanted answers and he needed help silencing the voice in his head.

At the far end of the dimly lit corridor, a glimmer of light beckoned him forward. Although he was still hindered by a troublesome limp, this rare feeling of freedom, far from the hideous torment of his castle dungeon and the cursed constraints of his arachnid body, was almost too good to be true. Glancing down at his legs as if for confirmation, he reached the source of the light. Pressing his ear against the door, he heard the sound of voices from the room beyond. Excitement and alarm coursed through him in equal measure.

The Master was here.

A wave of panic set in. He had to get away before the Master caught him and punished him. But the voice in his head disagreed; worse still, it completely ignored him. Wracked by fear, Tickbus looked down helplessly as his hand grasped the bronze handle and pushed the door open. Gasping in amazement, his eyes settled on a large sphere of flame hovering in the centre of the room. Trapped within the flame, a small figure in a faded grey coat and yellow hat bellowed commandingly in his direction.

'No, Master Fingle. It is not safe. Do not enter this room!'

Ignoring the pleas, transfixed by the wondrous sight, Tickbus strode towards the ball of flame. Despite its undeniable beauty such a flame should not be burning freely. Not indoors, and certainly not at this late hour. Such extravagance made his blood boil. It must be extinguished immediately.

'Stay away from the flame.' The venomous roar of the Master's voice stopped him in his tracks. 'Who are you? What are you doing here?'

Frightened and confused, Tickbus was on the point of turning heel and running when the voice in his head intervened. Fuelled by a sudden surge of rage, he launched his scathing retaliation.

'You fiend, you pretend not to know me? Does my lack of appendages confuse you?' He screeched wildly. 'Do you not recall taunting me with false promises in my dungeon prison?'

The voice in his head screamed at him to put out the flame. Turning his attentions away from the Master, he pulled his cloak from his shoulders and moved towards the flame, at the same time bellowing his defiance and contempt. 'Remember taunting me with the notion that in some other world it would be I who command you? Well, here I am, and I defy you.' Gripping the cloak tightly, he threw himself at the ball of flame. 'I defy you!'

'Tickbus Tard!' The Master moved towards him angrily. 'You should not be here! Get away from the flame.'

Ignoring the order, Tickbus beat repeatedly at the flame with the cloak. 'It must be extinguished,' he shouted. 'All candlelight must be extinguished!' His spirit danced with elation. Oh, how he had missed this.

A sudden searing pain shot down his arm. Dropping the cloak to the floor, his feeling of euphoria came to a shuddering halt.

What was he doing? Why was he beating at a flame like a lunatic? What was this madness coursing through him? He barely recognised the sound of his own voice. With his mind reeling, a shout refocused his attention. No longer held captive by the flame, the figure in the yellow hat gestured animatedly in his direction.

'Listen to me, Tickbus Tard. The pain in your arm, it is your Master's sorcery. You must recite the last four lines of the Black Transmutation verse. Direct them towards him. You will be freed from his ties for evermore. The last four lines, say them now!'

Tickbus spun round to see the Master bearing down on him and shrieked the incantation. A flash of bright light struck the Master squarely in the chest, hurling him across the room. Colliding with the far wall, he fell to the floor.

'Well done, Tickbus Tard.' Yellow Hat struggled to his feet. 'You did it. But he will only be stunned. You must restrain him further.'

'How?' Tickbus asked frantically. 'What should I do?'

'You must perform the Banishment Ritual. The fifth verse should suffice.'

'The fifth verse?' Tickbus felt his insides lurch.

'Yes, the fifth verse. You must know it? It's the most basic of conjurations. Quickly, before he regains his strength.'

With a sinking feeling, Tickbus knew all hope was gone. It was useless. If only he had spent more time on his studies. Time was against him, there was no point in pretence. Trembling with fear, he openly admitted his failings. 'I'm not sure of the wording. Help me!'

'I'm afraid I can't.' Yellow Hat shook his head ruefully. 'You alone must carry out the ritual. If I were to do it, you would simply be exchanging one master for another. You don't want that, do you?'

Tickbus' dilemma was getting worse by the second. He certainly didn't wish for such an outcome, yet he knew if he got the incantation wrong the consequences would be unimaginable.

'Hurry!' urged Yellow Hat. 'Your Master is beginning to stir.'

It was now or never; he had to seize the opportunity and hope he delivered the wording correctly. Edging forward nervously, he raised a trembling hand in the air and began his recital.

Tickbus had only delivered the first few words of his ill-fated attempt when he saw the figures and shapes in the room begin to twist and distort.

The blurred image of Yellow Hat faded from view in a haze and was replaced by a vision from his worst nightmare.

He woke screaming in anguish at the sight of the damp stone walls of his dungeon. The dream was over, his foray into freedom cruelly ended. He was trapped once more in his ghoulish shell, condemned to his self-imposed incarceration far beneath the Castle of Spite.

CHAPTER EIGHTY-TWO

Watching on as the madness unfolded, Messenger Two Cups felt the power of the flame begin to dissipate. As its vice-like grip relaxed, the feeling slowly began to return to his aching limbs. Summoning all his available strength, all power of mind and the will to change illusion, he stepped free from the binds of the flame and fell to his knees.

Though drained by his entrapment he knew he had to act quickly, and it was clear he was going to need assistance in foiling his adversary's foul plans. It appeared Osfilian's claims were true, Elfin Fingle was clearly being influenced by another's presence but judging by Osfilian's reaction, things had taken an unexpected twist. As Elfin's crazed attack on the flame came to a sudden halt, Two Cups swiftly seized his opportunity.

'Listen to me, Tickbus Tard. The pain in your arm, it is your Master's sorcery. You must recite the last four lines of the Black Transmutation verse. Direct them towards him. You will be freed from his ties for evermore. The last four lines, say them now!'

He watched on helplessly as Osfilian moved ominously towards the Scribe's young assistant. At the last minute, just as all seemed lost, Elfin spun round and, realising the danger, shrieked the incantation.

A sudden flash of bright light struck the Black Wizard squarely in the chest, hurling him across the room. As the body collided with the wall and slid to the floor, Two Cups clambered to his feet.

'Well done, Tickbus Tard. You did it. But he will only be stunned. You must restrain him further.'

'How?' Elfin Fingle begged desperately. 'What should I do?'

'You must perform the Banishment Ritual. The fifth verse should suffice.'

'The fifth verse?' struggled Elfin.

Two Cups knew this was his chance. His plan was working perfectly. 'Yes, the fifth verse. You must know it? It's the most basic of conjurations. Quickly, before he regains his strength.' It gave him no pleasure to watch the helpless Elfin writhe in desperation. He consoled himself with the knowledge that it wouldn't be for much longer. If his suspicions were right, it would be over within a matter of minutes.

'I'm not sure of the wording,' Elfin faltered. 'Help me!'

'I'm afraid I can't.' Two Cups shook his head. 'You alone must carry out the ritual. If I were to do it, you would simply be exchanging one master for another. You don't want that, do you?' He masked his feeling of elation. He had the flailing Tickbus Tard right where he wanted him. 'Hurry!' he urged one last time. 'Your Master is beginning to stir.'

The final prompting was enough. Elfin moved cautiously towards Ophidian and began his botched attempt at the ritual. The outcome was as Two Cups suspected it would be. In mid-sentence, Elfin Fingle fell silent and fell to the floor.

'What's happened to him?'

Two Cups wheeled round to see the Scribe of Bog-Mire struggling to his feet. 'Excellent timing, old friend,' he grinned. 'I'm glad you're back with us. Don't worry about young Master Fingle. He will be fine, I promise. I urgently need your help with another matter.' Pointing towards the large mirror on the wall above the fireplace, he bellowed his instructions. 'Remove everything from the mantelpiece, Token. There must be no obstruction.' With his attention drawn to the scuffling at the far side of the room, he saw Osfilian rising to his feet.

'So, the fool bungled his lines yet again?' He gave a chilling cackle. 'Hardly surprising though, given that no fifth verse exists.' He clapped his hands mockingly. 'Very clever, Scaraven, although I must say I'm surprised that you, of all people, would stoop to such devious tactics. Was such deception really necessary? The imbecile would have struggled with any of the actual four verses.'

'Desperate times call for desperate measures,' winced Two Cups. 'I couldn't take the chance. There was too much at stake.' Glancing over his shoulder, ensuring Token ScriptScratcher had fulfilled his task and was safely out of harm's way, Two Cups grabbed the poker from the fireside and struck the flag-stoned floor four times. 'I gave you the chance to leave Bog-Mire of your own free will, Osfilian, but you chose not to heed my warning. Now I must take matters into my own hands.'

'Oh, really? This should be good. What do you have in mind?'

Ignoring the sarcastic taunts, Two Cups stuck to his plan. Osfilian was a formidable foe, his only hope of success depended on catching his old enemy off guard. A momentary diversion was all he needed. Gathering his resolve, he set his plan in motion. Tapping the floor with a slow and steady rhythm he began the incantation.

'Banished to the Hidden Realm, no light or flame to guide...'

The Black Wizard roared his amusement. 'That won't work, Scaraven,' he sneered. 'Not when I am here, right in front of you, blocking your feeble efforts.'

'On the contrary, I suspect your defences have been breached quite badly.'

'Nonsense. The cockroach failed, and so will you.'

'Oh, I think you may be surprised.' Two Cups edged slowly towards him, all the while tapping the floor. 'You see, I think despite the obvious failings of our unfortunate friend, we might have to concede that Tickbus Tard actually does possess some element of talent.'

'What do you mean?' Osfilian's expression darkened. 'What talents could he possibly possess? What just happened was a lucky strike.' He pointed an accusing finger. 'And I suspect you were helping him.'

'Perhaps, but aside from the fact he was able to throw you across the room with words alone, it appears he might have been right. He may indeed have had some degree of power over you in this world.'

'Ridiculous!' Osfilian bared his teeth in anger. 'Why would you say such a thing?'

'Oh, it's just a hunch, just a sneaking suspicion.'

'Based on what, Scaraven?' The Black Wizard was growing more belligerent by the second. 'I tire of this game.'

'Your appearance.'

'What of my appearance?'

'It's changed,' toyed Two Cups, revelling in the gameplay. 'It has changed somewhat dramatically.'

'What do you mean?' Osfilian stalked the floor towards him.

'I suspect young Master Tard may have cast some kind of spell on you. Why don't you see for yourself?' Two Cups pointed a finger towards the mirror above the fireplace. 'But prepare yourself, the transformation is quite shocking.' Two Cups stepped aside as Osfilian lunged towards the fireplace.

'Curses on you, Tickbus Tard,' he snarled his rage. 'I will have my revenge...' His outburst came to a sudden halt as he examined his reflection. 'What are you talking about, Scaraven?' he hissed. 'There is no change.' His fingers traced across his pale complexion. 'My appearance has not changed.' His suspicion switched to shocking realisation as the horrendous stabbing pains began surging violently through his body. He'd been tricked. Unable to draw his gaze from the mirror, he watched in horror as his reflection began to distort.

'Perhaps not,' Two Cups purred with satisfaction. 'But it's just about to.' Pacing triumphantly, the Messenger tapped the bronze poker repeatedly on the floor as he recited the four verses of the Ritual of Banishment. With the hexing almost complete, he dropped the poker noisily at his feet.

'So, Osfilian, you would send my dear friends into grave danger in the Land of Mirrors would you?' He raised his hands above his head. 'Then let that be your fate. As you're so concerned with your appearance, let your vanity be your bind. I banish you, Dark One. Be gone!'

Trapped by his reflection, unable to move, Osfilian screamed his desperation. 'Not this, Scaraven! No! Not like this!'

Token ScriptScratcher looked on in astonishment as the Black Wizard's body twisted and convulsed. Deformed wing-like arms appeared from the black mass, beating frantically as it tried to escape its plight. Failing desperately in its efforts, the macabre shape faded abruptly and vanished.

The Scribe could scarcely believe his eyes.

'Incredible! What happened, Scaraven? Where did he go?'

Two Cups gathered his breath. 'Look in the mirror, Token. You will see.'

Peering warily into the mirror, the Scribe watched in disbelief as Osfilian's anguished expression slowly materialised, silently mouthing his torment and despair. Moments later, the image blurred and faded from view. It was over. The Black Wizard was gone.

Token ScriptScratcher shook his head at the sudden appearance of his own bewildered reflection.

The Messenger's voice brought his thoughts back into focus.

'Aha! It appears young Master Fingle is back with us.'

'Are you all right, Elfin?' The Scribe hurried to his apprentice's side.

'Who are you?' Scrambling to his feet, Elfin eyed them both suspiciously as he scanned the room. 'What is this place? Where am I? And what happened to the flame?'

'Curses on the fiend,' reacted Token angrily. 'What has he done to Elfin?'

'Fear not,' replied Two Cups reassuringly. 'This is not Osfilian's doing. Help me with him, I think we need to get him outside.'

'Outside? In the rain? Whatever for?'

'We need to help our friend here find his way home.'

Arm in arm, they huddled together against the driving rain as they crossed the courtyard and entered the stables. Shaking the rain from their jackets, Two Cups placed a friendly arm on Elfin Fingle's shoulder.

'Not much longer now, my friend. We will soon have you on your way. Tell me, what is your name?'

'My name is Wartimer Oldomor.' Elfin replied boldly.

'And your home world,' pressed Two Cups. 'What is it called?'

'Moribor,' Elfin hesitated. 'Though many days and nights have passed since I gazed on my beloved homeland. Try as I might, I can't seem to find my way back there.'

'Perhaps this time.' Two Cups sniffed the air as he toyed with his whiskers. 'Follow me, it's this way.'

Leading them further into the stable, Two Cups sat Elfin down, resting him against a bundle of straw.

'Relax and close your eyes, friend, and may you find your way home safely.'

'Just one thing,' Elfin Fingle's eyes rolled open suddenly. 'That beautiful flame, did I manage to extinguish it?'

'Yes, you did,' enthused Two Cups. 'And we are very much in your debt for doing so. Farewell, Wartimer Oldomor.'

A contented smile settled on Elfin's face as he closed his eyes.

'I've no doubt you have questions, Token,' Two Cups grinned. 'But we'd best wait a few moments before we take him back indoors. He will be asleep for a while; we can talk freely. And, I don't know about you, old friend, but after all this drama, I find myself in desperate need of a refreshing cup of tea.'

CHAPTER EIGHTY-THREE

Tybor Barkal slept late into the morning. When he finally woke, he found that Ashrynn Fala was gone. Stretching the sleep from his body, he pondered the striking effect of her absence.
How was it possible to become so attached to someone in such a short space of time? He wondered why she hadn't wakened him before she left. The events of the previous evening came flooding back as he crossed the room to the window. Almost doubting what he might see, he pulled open the curtains.

Dominating the city skyline, the smouldering remains pushed all doubt from his mind. A large cloud of ash and smoke hovered above the scene of the disaster, its presence darkening the already grey mid-morning sky.

Shaking his head at his lucky escape, he wondered what would have happened to him if Ashrynn hadn't intervened? Would he still be alive? Again, he wondered how she could have possibly known that something so bad was about to happen?
A premonition? Did he even believe in such a thing?

Dismissing the need for explanation, he went into the bathroom. As he splashed water on his face, his reflection returned his stare blankly. He barely recognised himself in the mirror. Was he in shock?

Back in the bedroom, he straightened the covers and sat down on the bed. There was no point delaying the inevitable aftermath of his actions. There were going to be repercussions. The sooner he faced them the better. As he pulled his phone from his jacket pocket, a piece of paper fell to the floor. Turning the phone on, he picked up the handwritten note.

Didn't want to wake you
Come find me on the other side. xxx

Ashrynn. Puzzled by the message, and its possible meaning, he read it several times. Startled by the phone as it started ringing, he eyed the screen warily. He slipped the note into his pocket and answered the call. Jeb's tone put him even more on edge.

'Ty, I've been trying to catch you all morning. Where are you? You need to get down here soon as you can.'

'What's up, Jeb? Are you okay?'

'I'm at the bar. It's serious, Tybor. Just get here quick as you can. We can talk then.'

'Okay, I'm on my way.'

Barkal ended the call and checked his messages. Sobek didn't usually leave messages; didn't like leaving a trail as he put it, but then Barkal didn't usually avoid answering his calls. To his relief, there were only two messages, both from Jeb, both reiterating the urgent need for his presence at the Ice Bar. With the unnerving lack of contact from Sobek and the uncertainty of what was happening with Jeb, there was much to consider as he made his way downstairs.

'All taken care of,' announced the woman at reception, much louder than was necessary. 'The blonde woman settled the bill.'

Barkal nodded and went outside.

The streets of Sahropa buzzed with intrigue and suspicion. In crude attempts to sell their broadsheets, the street vendors hollered their take on the night's events with claims ranging from the sublime to the ridiculous, their theories hinting at everything from global terrorism to an attack by an invading alien force. Tybor Barkal marvelled at how the truth sometimes just got in the way of a good story. Pondering the thought for a moment, he conceded that the visitor-from-another-world theory didn't seem quite as far-fetched today as it normally would.

A short while later, he arrived at his destination to find the doors of the Ice Bar closed. A grim-faced security guard ushered him swiftly inside. He found his friend behind the bar, frantically sifting through a bundle of papers.

'What's going on, Jeb?' He glanced round the empty room. 'Why is the bar closed?'

'You're incredible, Tybor. You don't know what happened last night?'

'You mean the explosion?'

'Yeah,' Jeb rolled his eyes sarcastically. 'The explosion.'

'Yes, well I saw it, right after it happened actually, but I don't get the connection. What's it got to do with the Ice Bar?'

'The connection is simple. The building that was destroyed belonged to Gabrat Sobek. It was HQ for Sobek International Industries.'

Barkal's eyes widened in astonishment. 'Really?'

'Sobek's missing, Ty, he's presumed dead. His secretary left the building only moments before the explosion. According to her, Sobek was still inside at the time and the authorities have found no trace of him since.'

Reaching into his pocket, Barkal took out the envelope with Sobek's instructions. 'Is this the address, Jeb?' He tapped a finger on the paper. 'Sobek's HQ, was this the address?' A shiver ran down his spine as Jeb confirmed his suspicions.

'Yes. That's it. Why do you have that?'

'I was meant to go there yesterday.' Scrunching up the paper, he let it drop to the floor. 'Sobek's orders.'

'To do what? Why were you meant to go there?'

'I don't know. That was all the instruction I had. You know how mysterious Sobek can be.'

With a shake of his head, Jeb opened two bottles of beer. 'I think we need these!'

Tybor Barkal swirled a mouthful of beer as he digested this latest dramatic twist. Things weren't becoming any clearer. 'I was meant to be there several hours before it happened, but I don't know long would I have been there. What was Sobek up to? The explosion, was it planned or just an accident? None of it makes any sense.'

'What happened? Why didn't you go?'

'I got side-tracked,' he replied elusively. 'I didn't make it to the rendezvous.'

'Risky, Ty. Sobek would take a very dim view of that. Luckily for you, it looks like he isn't going to be around to deal out any recriminations. But, for what it's worth, I'm glad you got side-tracked. It could have ended very badly. It could still end badly for some of us.'

'What do you mean?'

'Whatever happened at Sobek's HQ, whether accident or something more sinister, the authorities are going to be all over it. What with the whole peace convention thing going on, if this was an attack of some kind, if they find any sliver of connection, the whole city is going to be in lockdown.' He slapped a hand on the bar top. 'Which is why I asked you to get down here so quickly.' Taking a brown envelope from behind the counter, he pushed it in front of Barkal.

'What's that?'

'It's yours. One of Sobek's drones dropped it in here yesterday afternoon, said to ensure you got it today.'

Barkal eyed the envelope suspiciously. 'What is it?'

'If I had to hazard a guess, I'd say it's your last payment from Senator Sobek.'

Barkal put down his bottle, tore open the envelope, and inspected the contents. It was packed full of new banknotes. Thumbing quickly through one of the bundles, he drew a breath. 'I can't take this, Jeb, there's a fortune in here. I'm not due all this. In fact, I'm not entitled to any of it. I didn't complete the task yesterday, so I shouldn't get paid.'

'Take it! Sobek's not in a position to debate it. Dead men don't worry about such technicalities.'

'No. You keep it.'

'Absolutely not. The authorities are going to be digging into all of Sobek's affairs, investigating all his connections. You know he has an involvement with the Ice Bar. It's only a matter of time before they come here and turn the place upside down.

Everything has to be in order. I can't have that amount of cash lying around. It's yours, take it.' He gripped Barkal by the wrist. 'You're free, Ty. Free from Sobek's clutches. Take the money, get away for a while. Take a holiday, I'll get in touch when the dust settles.'

'What about you though?'

'I can't disappear, it would look bad. I'll be okay though. Sobek's involvement with the Ice Bar is all legal and above board, at least, I have legal documentation that suggests so. Don't worry, Tybor. I'll be fine.'

Having made their farewells, Barkal emerged from the gloom of the bar, wishing the security guard a pleasant day as he brushed past. He felt the cash-filled envelope pressing against his chest. Unable to resist a grin of contentment, he pondered his sudden upturn in fortune. The empowering feeling of wealth was quickly dwarfed by an exhilarating rush of freedom. Free from Sobek's restraints he would be able to think for himself again and to make his own decisions. Hit by the moment of clarity, he drew to a halt. He pulled Ashrynn's note from his pocket and read the message again.

Didn't want to wake you
Come find me on the other side. xxx

It seemed so obvious now. Why hadn't he worked it out earlier? Flipping the paper over, he saw the phone number written on the reverse side. With a grin, he pulled his phone from his jacket pocket and dialled the number.

Waiting on the platform, Ashrynn Fala took her phone from her bag and answered the call.

'Ashrynn? Is that you?'

The sound of his voice brought a smile to her face. 'Hi, Tybor.'

'Sorry I didn't call sooner. I was a bit slow to get going this morning. You should have wakened me before you left.'

'I didn't want to disturb you, so I thought I'd leave you my number. I'm glad you called.'

'Ashrynn, I need to talk to you. I need to thank you properly. And there's things I'd like to tell you about.' He hesitated. 'Where are you?'

'I'm at the train terminal.'

'When do you leave? I want to see you again. Can we meet up before you go?'

'I'd like that, but I'm leaving in fifteen minutes.' She took a breath. She wanted to choose her words carefully. 'This may sound a bit direct but, how would you feel about taking a trip to the countryside? Would you like to come with me?'

His response came immediately. 'Sounds like a great idea. I'd really like that. And the timing couldn't be better.'

'Then hurry up and get here, Tybor Barkal. I'm not going to let you make me miss my train home for a second time.'

CHAPTER EIGHTY-FOUR

Replenished by fresh kindling, the fire in the drawing room of Bog-Mire Towers sparked to life as Messenger Two Cups and Token ScriptScratcher supped their tea and discussed the evening's dramatic events.

The bustling Mrs Burrows, none too pleased at being summoned to prepare a midnight brew, had bid them goodnight, her tone leaving them in no doubt about her feelings on the matter. No good would come of late-night whispers in the drawing room, she'd warned them. Her suspicions had been further fuelled by Elfin Fingle lying fast asleep on the couch.

'What of Osfilian?' Token peered warily over his spectacles. 'Will the mirror prove to be a secure prison?'

'In the short term, it will suffice,' surmised Two Cups. 'When I have further arrangements in place, and when it is safe to do so, I will return and remove it.'

'And what do you have in mind for a long-term confinement? His banishment to the Basilisik Mountain proved somewhat unsuccessful.'

'I know, my friend, I know. And that is why I must consult with the Wise Ones. It is a precarious situation. Dangerous though he is, Osfilian is only a pawn in the game, a servant to a greater evil. We incur its wrath at our peril.'

Token sat forward in his chair, his voice dropping to a whisper. 'Is that why you chose not to destroy him?'

'For now, banishment is the best option,' Two Cups nodded. 'Our actions tonight will not have gone unnoticed, but by keeping Osfilian alive, albeit imprisoned, we might escape the attentions of something far worse.'

'Better the devil you know?'

'Very apt indeed.' Two Cups winked.

'But this greater power, won't it take some form of action?'

'Very possibly, and that is what we must prepare for. That's why we must be on our guard, to ensure we are not tricked into letting him escape again.'

The fire cracked loudly. Token ScriptScratcher cast his eye towards the couch. The night's events suggested there might be more to his young assistant than met the eye. 'Will Elfin be okay after what happened tonight?'

'Yes, he'll be fine. He'll probably be blissfully unaware of it. I strongly suggest we mention nothing of it to him.'

Token nodded his agreement. 'So, that Wartimer fellow. Is it safe to assume he was a Drifter?'

'That would seem the most likely explanation.'

Token drained his cup and began preparing his pipe for a smoke. 'And the other presence, what was happening there? I only caught the very end of your exchange with Osfilian, and what I heard made little sense. Did my ears deceive me? Were two Drifters present? I didn't think such a thing was possible.'

'It was no deception, Token, you heard correctly, and you are right. Such a thing should never have happened. It shouldn't be possible.' Two Cups shook his head in disgust. 'What you saw as you regained your wits, was the result of Osfilian's meddling. The fiend told me what he'd been up to. He's been experimenting, creating new agents of havoc. He told me he had achieved the unthinkable and, to be honest, I didn't believe it until I saw it tonight with my own eyes.'

'Despicable! But why was he here? What brought him to Bog-Mire?'

Two Cups refilled his cup. 'He believed he would find writings here in the archives that would help him perfect his creation.'

Token's expression poured scorn on the very suggestion. 'He would find no such evil here, Scaraven. If anything like that had found its way into Bog-Mire, I'd know about it. I've catalogued everything myself.'

'I don't doubt your word or your dedication to your work,' Two Cups smiled. 'But he was looking for something, and he was convinced he'd find it here. Perhaps we can carry out some further investigations when I return. But until then, the banqueting hall must remain strictly out of bounds. Open it for no one.'

Nodding his agreement, Token ScriptScratcher puffed heartily on his pipe. 'So, do you think Wartimer Oldomor will find his way home?'

'It's difficult to say. Some of them do but, sadly, for many it simply isn't possible. For some, their ability to drift only becomes apparent when tragedy strikes their own reality. In the case of

Wartimer Oldomor, it could be that the world he misses so much no longer exists.'

'Really? I hadn't considered such an eventuality.'

'Yes, I'm sad to say such an outcome is all too common. Indeed, it may well be the fate facing Taro Brook's world.'

'Ah, the Woodsman. Have you been able to translate the remainder of the prophecy?'

'Up to a point. Unfortunately, my visit to Sumarren was cut short yet again. I'm certain the answers I seek are to be found there, and I had good reason to believe the long-term prospects for Taro Brook were favourable. However, as we know, destinies can be interfered with and thus altered.' He pulled thoughtfully on his whiskers. 'I just hope Osfilian's meddling hasn't changed the Woodsman's fate. We can only hope, and wait to find out.'

Movement from the direction of the couch caught his attention. 'Aha, it appears our young friend is back with us.'

Elfin Fingle heard them chatting as he stirred from his sleep. None of what he heard made any sense.

'What happened?' He eased himself up into a sitting position. Token ScriptScratcher and Messenger Two Cups smiled warmly.

'You fainted, Master Fingle.' The Messenger was quick to respond. 'It was most peculiar. You came in from the rain, said your hellos, and then dropped to the floor. Out like a light you went. Do you not remember?'

'No,' struggled Elfin. 'I don't remember anything.'

'You were probably just light-headed from missing supper,' chimed Token. 'Where were you? What kept you out so late on such a foul night?'

'Here, young fellow,' Messenger Two Cups handed him a cup of tea. 'This should help jog your memory. Always works for me.'

Elfin eyed the table hungrily. 'Are those scones warm?'

'Still warm enough,' smiled Token, handing him the plate. 'Help yourself.'

As he sipped his tea and munched the buttered scones, Elfin told them of his encounter with Harbinger Talus. He relayed the news of the Raiders' attack, and of TrollGatten's subsequent demise. His memory appeared to be fine up until the point Talus had left him in the courtyard. He'd no recollection of what had happened after that.

Messenger Two Cups poured another cup of tea. 'Very interesting indeed. Well done, Master Fingle, your scouting foray has proved very useful. How are you feeling now?'

'Better, thanks,' replied Elfin, stifling a yawn. 'Still tired though.'

'You should get some more rest, a good sleep in a comfortable bed. The Scribe and I have things to discuss regarding Ergmire. Boring politics, I promise you won't be missing out on anything.'

'But what about the Raiders? They could strike Enntonia at any moment.'

'Ah, don't you be worrying about that,' replied Two Cups. 'There were some developments whilst you were asleep. Any imminent threat from the Raiders has been nullified.'

'Really? Was I asleep that long? Was it the Defender?'

'I suppose you could say that.'

'Is the strange mist still enveloping the town?' quizzed Elfin.

'Hmmm, I'd forgotten about that.' Two Cups tugged again at his whiskers. 'I expect everything will be back to normal by morning. In fact,' he snapped his fingers, 'I am certain of it.'

'But what about the dragons?' Elfin pressed. 'What if Osfilian brings back the Black Wing?'

'I can assure you no such thing will happen.' Two Cups grinned widely. 'I give you my word. Go and get some sleep. We must deal with this TrollGatten business. Ergmire must be informed of the tragic news.'

With his avenue of questioning firmly closed, Elfin accepted defeat. 'Very well. Will you be here in the morning, Messenger?'

'It's unlikely, Master Fingle.' Two Cups grasped him warmly by the hand. 'We shall meet again soon though. I am certain of it. Sleep well and pleasant dreams.'

Reaching the drawing room door, Elfin stopped and turned.

'Was there anything else, Elfin?' Token eyed him impatiently.

'Just one other thing. What is a Drifter?'

'A what?' The Scribe frowned.

'Harbinger Talus told me there must have been a Drifter in TrollGatten's group, and that would be why the Raiders attacked them so brutally. He said I should ask either of you to explain what a Drifter is.'

'Talus!' Token gave a snort of disgust. 'Pay no heed, Elfin, I've warned you before about his tall tales.'

'If I might interrupt,' Two Cups waved a hand in the air. 'Perhaps we shouldn't be too hasty in dismissing young Elfin's question. He has played an important role in our cause, proving himself worthy, and perhaps it's right that some information is shared with him.'

'Perhaps.' The Scribe nodded grudgingly. 'I will bow to your judgement on that.'

'I judge it to be so,' asserted Two Cups, 'but not tonight.'

Elfin didn't try to hide his disappointment. 'Why not tonight?'

'The sharing of such information should not be rushed, Master Fingle, and as I've already stated, we have pressing business to attend to. However, I will delay my departure, and first thing tomorrow, over a hearty breakfast, we will share with you all we know about the Drifters.'

Content with the compromise, Elfin said his goodnights and hurried upstairs to bed. The prospect of hearing all about the so-called Drifters was so enthralling he even dismissed the notion of eavesdropping at the drawing room door. Truth was, having already had more than enough adventure for one day, he was just too tired.

Waiting a few moments for his assistant to be safely out of earshot, Token ScriptScratcher voiced his concerns.

'How much are you going to tell him? Are you going to tell him that you are Scaraven? And are you going to mention what happened to him?'

'No, no,' Two Cups snorted. 'Fear not, I will be prudent with how much we tell him. He's a very inquisitive young fellow. You must ensure he doesn't gain access to the banqueting room while

I'm gone, Token. I dread to think what might happen if his mischief were to lead him in there.'

'I couldn't agree more.' The Scribe nodded. 'I have another thought,' he added warily. 'Is there a chance that the other presence could return? That Wartimer Oldomor seemed like a decent chap, a bit eccentric perhaps, but likeable enough. The other one seemed a rather unsavoury character. I'd prefer not to have him roaming the halls of Bog-Mire.'

'You raise a valid point and although I think his return is unlikely, I will endeavour to make certain of it. Despite the fact his actions tonight actually helped us, you are right. Tickbus Tard must not be allowed to wander freely.'

Pleased with the assurance, Token puffed contentedly on his pipe. 'I thought I recognised the name. Imagine that, the Black Wizard and the fool who summoned him, both here in Bog-Mire. The very thought of it chills me to the bone.'

Two Cups nodded gravely. 'Dark days, my friend. An invading army camped on our borders, the threat of fire-breathing devils from our worst nightmares hanging over us, our leaders in the High Council abandoning us to our fate, and the Black Wizard Osfilian stalking the sacred halls of Bog-Mire Towers. Dark days, indeed.'

'Perhaps the worst is behind us for the time being.' Token drew on his pipe. 'And with that hope in mind, what plans do you have for Enntonia in the short term? How are we to restore order and normality?'

'With the news that the Black Wing's return was nothing more than scaremongering by the cowards in the High Council, and the knowledge that Ergmire's force is gone, things will soon return to normal. But there will be an urgent need for law enforcement and some form of leadership until a new High Council can be elected.' Two Cups settled back in his chair as a wry grin flashed across his face. 'I think the moment has come for the Order of the Dragon Slayers to return once more to noble ways.'

'An excellent motion, Scaraven,' commended Token. 'And who will put these plans in place?'

Two Cups raised an eyebrow in pretence. 'I have it on good authority that the Defender himself is due in town tomorrow to make the announcement in person.'

'That is very reassuring.' Token ScriptScratcher nodded his appreciation before raising another concern. 'And you are certain the Raiders' threat is no longer an issue?'

'Absolutely! Without Osfilian's malice driving them, their purpose will quickly diminish. Unfortunately, such a twist has come too late for TrollGatten and his riders.'

'You didn't seem surprised by Elfin's news of the attack. You were already aware of it?'

'I had only just received the dreadful news from Osfilian himself. The fiend took great delight knowing I could do nothing about it whilst I was trapped in the flame.'

Token nodded solemnly and let a few moments pass before discussing the task in hand. 'And so, regarding TrollGatten. How do we break the news to Ergmire?'

'I must ask you to prepare a parchment, but first send a raven. Summon the Harbinger, he will ride to Ergmire to deliver the news.'

'Of course. And the parchment, what would you have me say?'

Two Cups rose from the chair and paced in front of the fire. 'Inform them that the esteemed General TrollGatten and his riders came to the rescue of Enntonia in its darkest hour, and that they fell in battle whilst playing their part in the defeat of an evil invader. Inform Ergmire that Enntonia will see to it that all debts will be settled in due course. They have the word of the Defender of all Enntonia. He will see to it personally.' Two Cups smacked his lips in satisfaction. 'That should suffice, Token. Enhance it as you see fit. Your gift for the prose is far greater than mine.'

Token ScriptScratcher tapped his pipe on the arm of the chair. 'Very fitting. Do you think they'll accept it?'

'They'll have to. And if they don't, we will deal with their response appropriately. It's a long journey for the Harbinger, so there is no immediate cause for worry.'

'Very well.' Token rose from the armchair and drained his brandy glass. 'I will get to work immediately. Nothing better for calming the old nerves than scratching the ink across the paper. I find it most therapeutic and, after all, doesn't everyone need their guilty pleasures?'

'Indeed.' Two Cups picked up the empty teapot. 'I know exactly what you mean. I'll take this little fellow to the kitchen for a refill and join you in your study shortly.'

CHAPTER EIGHTY-FIVE

Twilight crept stealthily through the Blackheart Pass. High above the trail, Morusk of DunTreggan tethered the horse and re-joined Stuc and Eldir in their silent vigil. Having bound the rope to the trees obstructing the giant boulder, there was now nothing else to do but wait. Their steep ascent of the eroded track had been slow and arduous but, with time against them and the threat of the imminent arrival of the Raiders, they had reached their destination buoyed by the prospect that luck might not yet have deserted them.

'Everything ready?' whispered Stuc tentatively.

'Yes,' replied Morusk. 'All we can do now is wait and hope for success.'

'It is a good plan,' Eldir offered. 'It will work.'

'How long do you think it will be until they get here?' The apprehension was etched on Stuc's face.

'They could arrive at any moment.'

'The archers are in position,' added Eldir. 'And the lookouts are ready, watching the trail.'

'With luck, their signal will give us enough time to free the boulder.' The temperature at their vantage point was dropping steadily. Morusk pulled his fur tightly around his shoulders. 'Now we wait.'

Watching the trail below, his attention shifted some distance ahead to where the others had taken shelter in the caves. He still struggled with the concept that some of them may not survive to see the dawn.

'Will they be safe there?' Stuc followed his gaze. 'If the Raiders break through?'

'If the Raiders avoid the falling rocks and Eldir's archers, no one will be safe tonight.'

'They are a formidable foe, Stuc of DunTreggan,' agreed Eldir. 'But Morusk's plan is good, and the bowmen of the Brochen Eyne are among the finest in all the lands. Maybe all is not yet lost.'

Morusk nodded. 'That's the hope we cling to.'

The hours passed slowly. Dusk heralded the appearance of a ghostly pale moon, illuminating the pass with its ethereal glow. From nearby, an owl's hunting call broke the silence, followed soon after by the sound of a horse galloping in the pass below.

'Someone's coming!' Morusk scrambled to his feet.

'There's the signal,' pointed Stuc. 'One rider is approaching.'

'A solitary rider?' Eldir looked puzzled. 'That makes no sense. What are the demons up to?'

Morusk hesitated. 'If it's a Raider, where's the rest of them?'

'Is it one of them?' echoed Stuc anxiously.

Eldir followed the rider's progress with his spyglass. 'It is difficult to say for certain in the moonlight. The rider is hooded, but his hands are gloved.' Dropping the spyglass from his face, he turned to them. 'I caught a glimpse of the rider's face. That is no Raider, Morusk. Do you want to see for yourself?'

'Your assessment is good enough for me, Eldir, but if it's not a Raider, who is it? And what do they want?'

'He's riding straight towards the others,' exclaimed Stuc. 'Should we not stop him?'

Eldir turned the spyglass to his archers far below. 'My bowmen await your signal, Morusk. Will they take the rider down?'

'No, let him through. It may be a trap; a diversion to attract our attention away from the trail. Let him ride into camp and state his business.'

From high above the Blackheart Pass, they watched on as the unknown rider galloped at full pace towards the encampment.

Ava watched the black-garbed rider approach. Pulling his horse to a halt, he threw his huge frame to the ground and bellowed commandingly. 'I bear news for Morusk of DunTreggan. Take me to him immediately.'

'He is not here.' replied one of the men tending to the horses.

'Then where can he be found? I carry news which I must convey to him in person.'

'He's not here.' Ava repeated calmly as she walked towards the rider. 'Share the news with me, I will see that he hears it.'

The rider's expression turned from one of determination to recognition. Nodding a greeting in her direction, he pushed a gloved finger to his brow. 'We meet again. It appears my memory may not be as bad as I feared.'

His reaction took her by surprise. 'Have we met before? I don't recall…'

'It matters not.' he interrupted. 'Where will I find Morusk? I must speak with him.'

'It's not possible. Tell me this news. I will take it to him.'

The rider fell silent for a moment, then cleared his throat with a growl. 'I see little point in debating with you. I'm Harbinger Talus.' He pulled a scroll from his cloak and handed it to her. 'And this is for Morusk of DunTreggan. Ensure that he reads it before the first light of dawn.'

'The Harbinger?' She began to open the scroll.

'Stop! That is not for your eyes.'

Ignoring his warning, Ava quickly scanned the parchment. Looking up, she met his stare. 'Is this for certain?'

'It is,' he nodded sombrely. 'Fate waits for no man, but not all receive the luxury of having time to prepare. Some consider advance warning a blessing.'

'More like a curse… Is there nothing that can be done?'

The Harbinger snorted unsympathetically. 'A summons of this nature is unnegotiable.' He studied her closely, as if guessing her thoughts. 'Intervention is sometimes possible, but not in this instance.' He shook his head as he grasped the reins of his horse. 'Nothing can alter this summons. I sense you are close to him. Do as you see fit, for my part in this is done.'

Ava watched as the rider's black cloak merged with the night. Scrunching the parchment up tightly, she walked to the campfire and threw it into the flames. As she watched it burn, she heard footsteps approaching from behind.

'What did he want, Ava?' Rovan stood next to her. 'What business did he have with Morusk?'

'Nothing important,' she replied quietly. 'The Raiders are camped a short distance back along the trail. He wanted to warn us. I told him I would pass the information to Morusk myself.'

'Do you think it's a trap?'

'No, Rovan,' she forced a smile. 'I think he spoke the truth. I must take the news to Morusk and the others.'

'Shall I prepare a horse?'

'No, I will go on foot, less chance of being seen. Be safe,' she clasped his hand. 'Look after the others.'

'And you, Ava. With luck, we'll all watch the sunrise together.'

'When the Raiders strike, you must find Stuc. If he is not with Morusk, send him to find me.'

'But why…?'

'Please, Rovan, just promise you will try your best.'

'Of course. I will do as you ask… I give you my word.'

Biting her lip, she nodded her gratitude and slipped into the night without once looking back.

High above the pass, Stuc's patience was waning.

'Where is he? Where did he go?'

'I don't know,' Morusk scanned for sign of the rider. 'I've lost sight of him.'

'Perhaps he rode past camp without stopping?' offered Eldir.

'Maybe,' agreed Morusk. 'It's possible he came across the Raiders and was trying to outrun them.'

'And talking of the Raiders,' Stuc sighed. 'Where are they? You said they would be here by nightfall.'

Morusk offered no response. Stuc raised a good point.

Where were the Raiders? What were they doing?

The time passed slowly, and the night grew steadily colder. The long wait changed their plans. Morusk now watched alone as Eldir and Stuc snoozed restlessly close by. He pondered the Raiders non-appearance. The hooded savages had obviously suspected something. Why else would their relentless pursuit suddenly cease? Would they now come at first light, expecting to catch their quarry unawares and tired from a sleepless night?

The sound of footsteps in the scree focused his thoughts, but before he had a chance to move, a hand settled on his shoulder.

'What the…?' As he spun round, the hand covered his mouth, muting his startled reaction.

'Sssh! Don't wake them.' she whispered. 'I just came to join you for a while.'

'Ava, what are you doing here? You're supposed to be at the camp with the others.'

Sitting down next to him, she pressed her forehead against his. 'We are bound to one another, Morusk of DunTreggan. Where you go, I go.'

He smiled as he flicked her hair away from her face. 'And I suppose I would be wasting my breath if I asked you to return to the camp?'

She squeezed his hand. 'I will not spend another moment of this life without you.'

'Nor I you.' He held her gaze then pulled her closer. 'We saw a rider. What did he want?'

'He didn't stop, he slowed only to give warning of the hooded riders.'

It was as he suspected. Satisfied with her explanation, Morusk nodded quietly. Huddled together against the night's chill, they watched the trail below in silence.

Several hours later, not long after Stuc and Eldir had wakened, and just as the first glimpses of dawn pierced the sky, the moment they had been dreading finally arrived. The sound of approaching horses echoed among the rocks and crags of the Pass.

The Raiders were coming.

'Move quickly, Morusk,' Eldir pointed. 'There is the watcher's signal.'

Sprinting to the horse, Morusk mounted up. Ava followed. Jumping into position behind him, she wrapped her arms around his waist.

'Ava! What are you doing? It's too dangerous.'

Ignoring his words, she tightened her grip. 'Ride!'

There was no time for debate. Morusk spurred the horse forward. It struggled in the loose rocks. He pushed it harder and seconds later, he felt the rope pull taut. With Stuc and Eldir frantically adding leverage with lengths of timber, the cracking of dry wood heralded the first sudden lurch of the boulder.

'It's moving!' yelled Stuc.

'Morusk!' Eldir shouted. 'I think it will free.'

Feeling Ava's grip tighten around his waist, Morusk doubled his efforts and, to shouts of triumph from Stuc and Eldir, he felt the strain in the rope dissipate as the stacked timber began to pull apart. Freed from its restraints, the boulder rolled forward and began its rapid descent of the mountain. The feeling of elation swiftly turned to one of despair as the rope snagged on a jagged edge of the boulder and pulled the horse off balance.

'Dismount!' screamed Stuc. 'It will pull you down with it.'

The warning came too late. Having relaxed her hold, Ava was thrown from the horse. Clinging desperately to the reins, Morusk tried to stop the rate of descent, but it was a futile effort. As he hurtled down the mountainside, he tried to reach for his dagger. He knew he had to cut the rope, but everything was happening too fast. Everything became a blur.

An excruciating pain followed a loud crack as his leg became trapped beneath the horse. Pulling free as the horse rolled again, he released his grip on the reins and braced himself for impact. His tumble ended abruptly, brought to a shuddering halt by a stubborn slab of rock.

With his head spinning, he lay motionless and listened to the unfolding chaos. The thunderous roar of falling rocks echoed in the gully far below. He heard shouts, and the braying of horses. What was happening down there? Had his plan worked? Had the rockfall hit the Raiders?

Wiping blood from his face, he grabbed hold of the slab and tried to stand, but his leg gave way and he fell to the ground. His head pounded. Where was everyone? What was happening to them? Pulling himself up into a sitting position, he held his head in his hands. A shout from above brought both hope and alarm.

'They have crossbows. Take cover!'

Was that Stuc's voice? It was hard to tell in the commotion. Morusk tried to shout but his words fell silent in his throat. He had to move, he had to get closer to them. As he tried again to

clamber to his feet, a hooded figure appeared ominously from the dust cloud only a few feet away. The sinking feeling in his stomach dulled the ache in his head and the pain in his leg.
A Raider, bearing a crudely assembled crossbow, had him fixed firmly in its sights. There was no hope of escape. Morusk of DunTreggan grimaced as he sat upright and bravely faced his fate. There was nothing else he could do.

As the dust began to clear, it picked up the scent again, much stronger than before. Clutching the loaded weapon tightly, it dragged itself free from the fallen rocks and went in search of its prey. Following the trail of the Drifter, it moved effortlessly, almost ghostlike, up the steep slope. Pulling itself over the rocky ledge it came face to face with its quarry.
This one was badly injured. It didn't care. It had no empathy. It was nothing more than an empty shell, driven by an insatiable need to kill, a gift bestowed upon it by the Black Wizard. It raised the crossbow. Systematically checking the bolt, and the tautness of the string, it gripped the bow section firmly and released the trigger. The bolt flashed through the air and found its target.
Watching impassively as its victim slumped to the ground, it sniffed the air suspiciously. There was another, and it was close at hand. It began reloading the crossbow, a sequence it was unable to complete. The charging figure appeared from the dust without warning and collided with it at full force.
Caught off guard by the sudden attack, it stumbled back awkwardly and fell over the ledge. It felt nothing. No fear of falling, and no sense of ending.

As the steel bolt struck him in the chest, the force knocked the air from his lungs. Morusk fell forward. As he lay gasping for breath, he heard footsteps approaching hurriedly. Through his blurring vision, he saw the figure lean over him and he felt her familiar touch.

'I am here, Morusk,' she whispered. 'Where you go, I go.'

She'd found him. She was safe. Relief surged through his aching body. He felt her hand in his, gripping tightly as she applied gentle pressure to his chest. Able to draw a short intake of breath, he managed to lift his head.

Over her shoulder he saw another of the hooded skeletal warriors approaching, its deadly weapon raised and ready. His desperate attempts to warn her failed hopelessly, his shouts dying mutely in his throat. Unaware of the danger stalking her from behind, mistaking his gestures of panic as symptoms of his distress, Ava gently coaxed him back into a lying position. Morusk screamed silently as the bolt fired and struck her squarely between the shoulder blades. The strike was deadly. She fell into his arms. Fuelled by despair, tears stinging his bloodied face, Morusk held her as tightly as he could, in the desperate hope he'd feel her breath on his face.

The hooded figure stood over him. What was it doing? Why was it waiting? Why was it not dealing its final fatal blow? After several minutes, a wait that seemed like an eternity, it turned away and dropped from view over the ledge. Deprived of his swift end, Morusk closed his eyes. Slipping in and out of consciousness, he lay waiting, desperate for sleep to finally come.

Stuc found him some time later. Morusk heard his old friend's shout of anguish.

'Eldir. Help me move her body. He needs air.'

'No, Stuc,' Morusk rasped weakly. 'Leave her.'

'But we need to get you up.' Stuc protested.

Eldir clasped Stuc's shoulder. 'No, my friend, we must leave him as he is. He cannot be moved. Say your farewells, Stuc of DunTreggan, you don't have much time.' The Northman gently placed his hand on Ava's head and brushed his fingers through her hair. 'Fly with the eagles, Ava.' he whispered.

'Stuc,' Morusk croaked feebly. 'Did... our plan succeed?'

'Yes.' Stuc grasped him by the hand. 'The rockfall struck the Raiders, blocking the trail in the process. A few of them broke off and climbed...' His words faded to nothing.

'Did we lose... anyone... else?'

'No. Some of Eldir's bowmen were injured, but not seriously. And not long after the rocks blocked the trail, the surviving Raiders slowly started to withdraw.'

'It's... their tactic,' Morusk struggled with his words. 'To leave... some alive...'

'No, this was different. Our scouts followed them. They just kept riding, slowly, almost without purpose. They are gone, Morusk, their pursuit is over.'

A semblance of smile etched Morusk's face. 'Go north, Stuc,' he whispered. 'Find a new home... for our kin. Eldir and the Brochen Eyne will... guide you.'

'I will see that it happens, Morusk. I swear it.'

Releasing Stuc's hand, Morusk's grip tightened around Ava.

'I need to sleep, Stuc,' he whispered. 'It's getting... so cold. Build me a fire, old friend... and make it a good one.'

Stuc nodded silently. Tears stung his face as he watched his life-long friend, Morusk of DunTreggan, close his eyes one last time.

Standing by the funeral pyre several hours later, his thoughts lost in the flames, Stuc felt a firm grip on his shoulder.

'Let not your heart be heavy, Stuc of DunTreggan,' Eldir said quietly. 'The Brochen Eyne believe the soul never dies. The spirit lives on, my friend.'

Finding comfort in the words, Stuc turned from the blaze.

'Come,' Eldir nodded. 'Let us ride north. The lands of the Brochen Eyne are your home now, you and your kin, for as long as you wish it.'

A sudden call from above caught their attention. Looking up, they saw an eagle circling high overhead. Dipping from view beyond the tops of the towering spruce trees it reappeared seconds later with another close behind it. Stuc pointed excitedly.

'Look, Eldir, there are two of them.'

The Northman's face opened into a wide grin. 'Fly with the eagles, my friends. Let your spirits ever soar.' He turned to Stuc. 'Let's join the others. We'll break camp and ride for home.'

Stuc watched the eagles for several minutes, his heart warmed by the majestic sight, until the great birds disappeared once more beyond the trees. Casting one last look towards the pyre, he silently bid his old friend Morusk one final farewell and began his preparations for the journey north.

CHAPTER EIGHTY-SIX

Disorientated by the sudden change in her surroundings, Sanna stumbled unwittingly towards the oncoming danger. Brandishing clubs and axes, her attackers appeared from the half-light of dusk without warning. The first charged her side-on, knocking her to the ground. As she sprang to her feet, the wooden club landed with a sickening crack on the side of her knee. Dropping to a crouching position, she kicked out as her assailant moved in for his decisive strike. Her boot caught him right between his legs. With a howl, he dropped his axe and fell to his knees. Drawing her longsword, the blade sliced effortlessly across his throat. As the blood ran freely, he slumped forward lifelessly.

There was no time to catch her breath. The second was already on her. Grabbing her from behind, his arm tightened around her neck. As she wrestled to break free, she felt the point of his blade pierce the skin on her shoulder. Gasping for air, she threw a clenched fist backwards and connected with his jawbone. His grip tightened in defiance. She punched again. Another lucky strike, and this time his hold relaxed just enough for her to pull away. She dived forward, caught hold of the first attacker's axe, and swung round blindly. Her first attempt missed the target. Consumed by rage, she swung again, and heard the scream as the axe wedged itself in his leg. As his legs folded beneath him, she grasped hold of her blade and ran it through his chest.

It was over.

Pulling herself to her feet, she quickly examined the bodies. If they'd showed a less belligerent approach she might have been able to glean information about where she was. She cursed her luck; she'd walked straight into an ambush, and if there were two there may be more. As she began dragging the bodies towards cover, she heard voices approaching. There were others coming, and she was in no fit state to confront them.

Abandoning her efforts she hobbled among the gorse bushes and began to climb among the scattered saplings. Blanking out the pain in her leg, she struggled up the hillside as the shouts echoed from below. The new arrivals had discovered the bodies. She glanced down. They were climbing; they were coming after her. Lifting her gaze she saw a black notch in the cliffs above. She scrambled up the scree towards her target. The shouts were getting louder; they were gaining ground. There was no chance of outrunning them. She'd have to make her stand at the cave.

With her pursuers closing steadily, she reached the cave and moved inside. Surrendering to the gloom she edged forward warily, her hands gauging her progress on the dry rock. Onwards she pushed, half expecting every step to be her last. The shouts from behind came again; they were now in the cave. Picking up her pace, she felt the walls close in on either side. It gave a glimmer of hope. A tunnel might offer a chance of escape.

The hope quickly came to fruition. As the voices faded behind her, she pushed further into the dark recesses of the cavern. She'd lost them. As the ground gave way suddenly beneath her, she tumbled down through the darkness.

Her fall ended softly, on a blanket of moss. Catching her breath, she rolled onto her back and stared up at the night sky.
Moments later she was on the move again, staggering awkwardly through a stand of birch trees.
After what seemed like an eternity, she broke free once more into the open. Drained by her exertions, and the pain in her knee and shoulder, she fell to the ground exhausted.
The night offered no clue as to where she was, she didn't care. All she wanted to do was sleep. Feeling her way onto a flat slab of stone she closed her eyes.

As sleep took hold the pain subsided, and was replaced by the familiar invigorating sensation of hot sun on her skin. She was home again. The smiling faces of her loved ones, laughing and waving as she walked amongst them, invoked strong emotions and fond memories. She missed them all desperately and though she had long since accepted the grim reality that she would never see them again, the aching sense of loss remained as strong as ever.
Her pulse quickened at the sight of Asyllyar walking towards her, his hand held out invitingly. Smiling playfully, he laughed and turned to run, calling out her name, inviting her to follow as he merged with the crowd.
The dream unravelled as it always did. Failing in her efforts to find him, she became lost in the underground passageways. They had spent much of their time together exploring the vast expanses of the labyrinth, listening spellbound to the Oracle as he captivated them with his wondrous tales. The ancient one, known

by many names and rumoured to be older than time itself, lived the life of a recluse in the underground maze, devoting his existence to the painstaking deciphering of the ancient symbols adorning the tunnel walls. Proudly announcing his findings to any who cared to listen, he would often carve his own interpretations into the sacred stone, all the while quietly reciting his haunting chants and verses. It was he who'd told them about the gateways, the doorways to other worlds, and although dubious of his claims of knowing how future events would unravel, Sanna's imagination was fuelled by the endless possibilities for adventure within the labyrinth.

Imagination had become reality the day her life had changed forever. Even now, held captive in her dreams as she frantically searched the tunnels, she relived the events of that fateful day. The day they had become separated for the last time, the day she had stumbled unwittingly into the strange tree-covered landscape. Her initial sense of wonder and excitement had faded quickly. Symbols carved on the labyrinth walls, depicting a land of trees, had been translated by the Oracle as a foretelling of a great tragedy and he had warned them of the danger of entering such a world. Asyllyar would never ignore the warnings of the Oracle; she would not find him here. Leaving the quiet solitude of the forest behind, drawn towards distant cries for help, she had re-entered the intricate tunnel network.

Impelled towards the loud screams of anguish and despair, she had emerged into the hot desert sunshine to see the enormous ball of fire falling from the sky.

Unable to move, transfixed by the horror of the unfolding catastrophe that would yield such devastating consequences for her home world, it was the Oracle who had come to her rescue, appearing suddenly from the shadows to usher her back into the tunnels, where he told her to run; to run for her life, and to never look back. And so, she ran, tears stinging her eyes, crying out for her loved ones, calling out for Asyllyar… Where was he?

She woke with a start. The sun had climbed above the horizon. Her first thought was of the symbols. She shook the sleep from her head as she sat up. The symbols from the labyrinth wall depicting the land of trees matched the inscription on the parchment at Sumarren. That was where she had seen them before. That was why she had recognised them.
Rising gingerly, she assessed her injuries. Her knee felt fine, barely even a twinge of pain. Only a numb sensation remained in her shoulder and it would quickly subside. Her thoughts spun quickly to her drift. What had happened? She could remember nothing. Her memories of home were quickly replaced by a more pressing dilemma. Where was Taro Brook? What had happened to him? Had she been able to find him?

She took in her surroundings; the ruins of a long-abandoned hill fort overlooking the sea. The moss-covered remnants of the battlement walls offered the chance of an elevated viewpoint. Climbing to the top of a broken stairway, she caught sight of a familiar landscape.

Far in the distance, beyond countless leagues of rolling fertile plain dotted with sporadic scatterings of trees, the jagged quartzite peaks of Krechan-Bhann pierced a low-lying blanket of cloud. Lifted by the sight, she quickly descended the stairs.

Drawn towards the distant, serrated mountain ridge, Sanna Vrai left the coastline, and began the journey to the Cairn of Scaraven.

CHAPTER EIGHTY-SEVEN

Dragon Slayer Twelve Seven Two sniffed the air and gauged the change in the weather. The bursts of thunder, which had been distant and sporadic, were becoming louder and more frequent. It was time to leave before the inevitable downpour of rain arrived.

As he made his way back through the forest towards the Eastern Gate of Enntonia, it became obvious he was being followed by something far worse than bad weather.

A blood-chilling roar sent a shudder down his spine. The noises he had mistaken for thunder were coming from another source. And whatever it was, it was coming his way. The sound of trees being crushed and snapped sparked his sudden change of pace. Running as fast as he could, Twelve Seven Two relived the visions from his nightmares.

The deadly pursuit through the forest, chased for his life, the helpless prey of some demonic monster. Another frightening roar came again. The beast was gaining ground. He had to reach the gate and raise the alarm before it was too late.

Stumbling free from the treeline he came to a sudden halt. A thick blanket of mist shrouded the walls of the Eastern Gate. Only the tops of the sentry post towers pierced the ghostly veil. Struck by a moment of indecision, he thought about creating a diversion to lead the beast away from the gate and back into the forest. Shouts from within the mist made his decision for him. The others were waiting at the gate; he had to warn them.

The ground shook beneath his feet. Looking over his shoulder one last time, he ran towards the shouts of desperation. As he approached the wall and the mist began to disperse, he saw three figures waiting by the iron gates. As he drew closer he yelled his warning.

'Run! Run for your lives!'

They didn't move! Why weren't they running? He yelled again.

They stared at him blankly as he came to a halt beside them.

'Run from what?' asked one, his haggard features etched with contempt.

'Dragon!' Twelve Seven Two gasped for breath as he glanced nervously over his shoulder. 'At least... I think so.'

'There's no such thing as dragons,' sneered another, a scrawny individual in desperate need of a wash. 'There hasn't been for centuries,' he sniffed. 'And that's if there ever was.'

'You don't hear it?'

'Don't hear nothin',' the haggard-faced man scowled. 'Nothin' but the ramblings of a fool with an over-active imagination.'

Twelve Seven Two turned to the forest. They were right. All was quiet. The mist was gone, and the morning was bright and clear. As he struggled to comprehend the unbelievable change in circumstances, the third Slayer, a gaunt man with sunken eyes and a breath that reeked of wine, barked his instructions.

'Mount up! We've got other stragglers to track down. I don't know what you were up to in there, Twelve Seven Two, don't know, don't care. We've to report to the General. Word is there's important work lined up for us.'

'What kind of work?'

'Reckon we'll find out soon enough.'

Twelve Seven Two readied his horse. His early morning venture into the forest had taken a peculiar twist. The reaction of his three companions was troubling. Where were the others? The shouts from the mist, he'd heard them only a few moments ago. There sounded like a dozen Slayers or more. So, where were they now? And what of the sudden disappearance of his deadly pursuer?

'No time for daydreaming,' snapped Wine-Breath. 'Best not keep the General waiting.'

Dragon Slayer Twelve Seven Two nudged his horse forward and fell into line behind the others. Something was amiss. Something very strange was going on, and he seemed to be the only one aware of it.

CHAPTER EIGHTY-EIGHT

In a quiet corner of Farnwaar Forest, startled by the sound of an approaching threat, the grazing deer barked their alarm and dispersed like leaves in the breeze.

The man burst suddenly from the trees, tumbled down the embankment, and splashed his way across the shallow stream. Reaching the safety of the treeline at the far side of the clearing, gasping for breath, he dropped to his knees. He scanned his surroundings anxiously for sign of his pursuer but saw nothing. There was no movement, no sound. The forest lay silently still.

He watched and waited. The minutes passed slowly. Glancing nervously in all directions he moved warily from his hideout and walked along the overgrown track. The feeling of being chased was gone, but the sensation of being watched still lingered. Looking over his shoulder constantly, he followed the trail down a gentle slope. As the ground levelled and he came alongside a stream, he rounded a bend in the track, and there it was.

Relief surged through him at the sight of the wooden footbridge. His fears had been unfounded. He wasn't lost.

Taro Brook glanced tentatively at his watch. 1.59 pm.

It felt later, much later. Unsure of how, or why, he had lost his way so easily, he hurried past the bridge and followed the track down through the tall conifers. The birch trees signalled his arrival at the edge of the forest.

Less than fifteen minutes later he turned the key in the ignition of his pick-up truck and began the short journey home.
With a shake of his head, he reviewed his time in the forest. What had gone wrong? He knew the old place like the back of his hand. How could he have become so disorientated?
His thoughts turned to the strange sensation of being chased. Was it a panicked reaction to thinking he was lost?
The sudden appearance of the breakdown recovery truck heading straight for him, urgently focused his attention.

Speeding towards his last pickup of the day, the driver of the breakdown truck sang along tunelessly with the radio. Not much further now. He could almost taste the cold beer that waited at the end of his shift. Wouldn't be long now.
His task was being made considerably easier by the lack of traffic. The remote location meant he hadn't met another vehicle in over an hour. Snorting his amusement, he applied further pressure to the accelerator. What kind of ranger got lost in his own forest?
Missing for six weeks, with no sightings and no clues to his whereabouts, the search had been officially called off and the authorities had given the go-ahead to have his vehicle towed away.
The breakdown truck driver grinned. If the ranger showed up after today, he'd have a long walk back home. Tapping the steering wheel, he cranked the radio volume up to maximum and, with the deserted road stretching into the distance ahead, eased back in his seat.

Jumping instinctively on the footbrake, Taro Brook swerved to avoid the seemingly inevitable collision. Spinning on the loose gravel, his truck slid broadside and came to a sudden halt as it careered into the gorse bushes. In the rear-view mirror he saw the breakdown truck speeding into the distance. It showed no sign of slowing down. Had it not even seen him?

With a curse, he reversed free from the bushes and got out to inspect the damage. A small dent in the bumper and a cracked headlamp. It could have been worse; much worse.

His strange day had taken a further bizarre twist. Shaken by the near miss, he climbed back inside his truck and started the engine. He yawned widely. He couldn't recall ever feeling quite so tired. He needed to get home, he needed to put this unsettling day behind him. The desperate need for sleep spurred him homeward.

CHAPTER EIGHTY-NINE

Detective Mickey Spades eyed his inquisitor suspiciously. He'd been listening to the chief forensic pathologist drone on for more than ten minutes wondering if he'd ever get to the point. Now that he had, Spades wasn't sure he liked where the conversation was going.

'You want me to help?' he challenged bluntly. 'Why me? If one of your colleagues is missing, you need to contact the Missing Persons department.'

'I'm well aware of the correct procedure in such matters, Detective, but I wanted to talk to you first, to see if you could help. Like I said, Amy Coda hasn't been in contact for over a week now. It's very unusual. Even when she is out of town on her investigations, she always checks in with us.'

'Okay, but why ask me? I barely know the woman, and it's not my area of expertise.'

The man hesitated as he pulled a black book from his desk drawer. 'The reason I'm asking you is simple. This is Amy's work planner.' Opening the book, he placed it on the desk and tapped the page to emphasise his point. 'On the day she was last seen, Coda left this office around lunchtime. According to her schedule, she was on her way to meet with you.'

Thrown by the unexpected twist, Spades felt a rush of intrigue as he cast his eye over the handwritten entry.

Detective Spades - Black Rose Café, Windmill Lane – 2.30

He read it several times before pushing it back across the desk.

'This is news to me. I don't know what she meant by this but there was no meeting scheduled between the two of us, on that day or on any other.'

'You didn't see her that day?'

'No, I just said so.' Spades didn't appreciate what was being suggested. 'I hope you're not insinuating I know why she hasn't been in touch?'

'I'm not suggesting anything of the sort, absolutely not, but others might, if I had to produce this book to help their enquiries.' Spades shot him a look of disgust. The chief pathologist ignored it and continued his pitch. 'But I think it would be best if this were kept unofficial for now. Besides, Coda may turn up safe and well and, knowing her as I do, she probably wouldn't appreciate me getting the authorities involved. She abhors any unnecessary attention.'

Spades nodded his agreement, he detested the rigmarole and ceremony of official inquiries; he was even less enamoured with the concept of being blackmailed. 'Okay. So, what do you want from me?'

'I won't waste my words, Detective, you have a reputation for getting results. I'd appreciate it if you'd look into this for me, on the quiet. Of course, I don't expect you to work for nothing. Just name your fee.'

Spades found himself warming to the proposal.

'Okay, but we can discuss fees later, depending on what I find out. Let me take a note of that address.'

'Sure, does it mean anything to you?'

'No, I've never heard of it. Any idea where it is? Did anyone go check it out?'

'Apparently it's in the old market town district. One of our colleagues went down there a couple of days ago, they found the cafe, but it looked like it had been closed for some time.'

'Really? Sure they had the right place?'

'Sure as we can be. Why would Amy choose such an odd venue to supposedly meet with you? It makes no sense.'

'You've got that right.' Spades shrugged. Coda's false arrangements made no sense at all. He'd had no contact with her for several weeks. There was no plan to meet up. Why had she put that entry in her work planner? Was she trying to get him in trouble? No, that didn't add up. The more he thought about it the less convinced he was that Coda was actually missing. The whole thing seemed very calculated. What was she up to?
Was she trying to send him some kind of message? It was definitely worth checking out. 'I'll look into it right away. I'll be in touch.' They shook hands and Spades briskly made his exit.

Prying a street map from a rusting vending machine, he lit a cigar and boarded the cross-town train. The old market town area of the city was often referred to as the Circus District, so called for the large population of travelling performers who had chosen to settle there. Spades couldn't recall ever visiting the place; he'd never had any reason to. Why was Amy Coda leading him there?

Arriving at his destination, he stepped from the train, checked his route on the street map, and began the short walk to the Black Rose Café.

The old buildings leaned precariously over the cobblestoned lane. In an attempt to disguise their dilapidated state, the badly weathered wooden doors and window frames had been painted bright, garish colours. Further decoration came in the form of luminous coloured flags and pennants that flapped nosily in the breeze. Gaining suspicious glances from the oddly dressed passers-by, Spades gawped at the open-fronted shops and cafes, filled to overflowing with tea-drinkers and pipe-smokers. The pungent aroma of dubious tobacco leaf filled the air. Shaking his head at the injustice of his existence, part of him wondered cynically if any of these people had jobs to go to. Puzzled by the dramatic change in culture, he struggled to shake the feeling he'd arrived in some strange foreign land.

Stopping at an ornamental fountain depicting a host of embracing water nymphs he checked the map again. Turning right, he followed the lane down a gentle slope, past a group of snoozing beggars huddled together in the doorway of a derelict building. At a crossroads, a faded hand-painted sign pointed the way ahead. Windmill Lane. Folding the map, he began the final stretch of his search.

Windmill Lane, a muddled conglomeration of candle-makers and fortune-tellers; tea rooms, herbalist parlours and cluttered bookstores, had an unsettling effect on him. Ignoring the scurrying noises coming from the darkened alleyways, he picked up his pace. Narrowly avoiding collision with an unsavoury looking character who staggered drunkenly from the shadows, Spades came to a sudden stop. Dismissing the drunkard's expletives with a shrug, he swung his attention across the narrow street to where an old weatherworn sign swung idly in the gentle breeze. The Black Rose Café.

He shook his head. It appeared his journey had been a waste of time and effort. The cafe was closed. The windows were barred by shabby wooden shutters. Flaking paintwork screamed years of neglect. An unwelcoming grotesque held a silent vigil above the door. Spades frowned again. Why had Amy Coda led him here? He checked his watch. 1.38. Was there a hidden clue in Coda's message? He was here now. There seemed no harm in hanging around for an hour or so to find out.

Stepping from an alleyway to his right, a dark-haired woman called for his attention, her accent lilting, almost hypnotic.

'Hey, Mister, want to know your future?' She approached him confidently, her long skirt swishing provocatively. She drew a long, painted fingernail across his chest. 'What say you?'

Her eyes sparkled like diamonds.

Momentarily captivated, Spades agreed willingly. He could think of worse ways to pass the time.

'Okay,' he shrugged, 'why not?'

Sealing their agreement with a smile, she turned and, with bangles jingling, led him through an open doorway. 'Wait here one moment, I will prepare.' Disappearing behind a curtain, she left him in the gloom. Adjusting his eyes to the half-light, he saw that he was not alone. A burly, tattooed man sat in the far corner of the room.

As their eyes met, the man stood up and pulled back the curtain.

'You go in now.' he instructed gruffly.

Spades walked hesitantly beyond the curtain. The air hung thick with incense. In the corner of the room, an old woman sat tapping her gnarled fingers impatiently on a round wooden table.

'Take a seat.' she snapped, gesturing him forward.

Spades cast his eye around the room as he pulled up a chair. 'Where's the girl?'

The crone cackled with delight. 'The girl has long legs, an ample chest, and eyes that promise much, but she knows nothing of what the future holds.' Annoyed at being so easily duped, Spades watched as the old woman rolled a handful of small wooden dice marked with strange symbols. 'So,' she continued, 'you are looking for answers.'

'Isn't everyone?' He sighed at the predictable opening.

'Not everyone,' she replied, arranging the dice in a cryptic pattern. 'Most are content to spend their existence in ignorance, but not you… no, not you. The answers you seek…' With a whispered curse, she quickly gathered the dice together and fired him a look of scathing disapproval. 'I've seen enough. The answers you seek are close by. To find them you must pass through a doorway. But beware; do not enter unless you are prepared for the consequences.'

'What consequences?'

'I have told you all I can, it's time for you to leave.'

Spades was on the point of debating the issue when the tattooed man emerged silently from the shadows and held the curtain open.

'You leave now.' he grunted.

Spades reached into his pocket. 'Fair enough, how much do I owe you?'

'I don't want your money, Detective,' the old woman scowled. 'You will pay no heed to my warnings. I don't want your money.'

'What the…? How did you know…?'

'Out!' she snarled angrily. 'Out!'

Harried towards the exit by his tattooed escort, Spades came face to face with the woman who had lured him inside. She glowered at him as he passed. Sparing her his thoughts, he stepped out into the sunshine as the door slammed shut behind him. Shielding his eyes, adjusting to the glare, he looked across the street in astonishment.

The Black Rose Café was now open. The weathered shutters had been pulled back to reveal quaint latticed windows. The door stood open invitingly, as if waiting in expectation. Contemplating the unlikelihood of the crone's lucky guess, he crossed the cobbled street and entered under the grotesque's watchful stare.

The Black Rose Café had an almost otherworldly feel to it. The wooden furniture was basic and faded, almost sun-bleached in colour. The black and white tiled floor reminded him of a giant chessboard. The walls were cluttered with a myriad of framed paintings and photographs; black and white portraits of clowns, dancers, and performers, and scenes of places he didn't recognise. The fine aroma of fresh coffee filled the air. Spades felt his taste buds tingle as he caught his reflection in the large gold-framed mirror hanging on the wall above the ash-filled fireplace. The cafe was empty, save for the girl who watched him warily as he approached the service counter.

'Did you just re-open?' It seemed like the obvious question. The girl stared back blankly, her striking green eyes unnerving him. 'I was here earlier,' he continued, 'but you were closed.'

She glared at him. 'You want something?' Her tone was harsh and unwelcoming; her accent matched the woman from the fortune-teller's place. 'You want something? Tea? Coffee?'

Spades reckoned the Circus District could do with some lessons on good manners. Abandoning his plans for idle chat, he got straight to business. Taking the photo of Amy Coda from his wallet, he placed it on the counter. 'Have you seen this woman? Has she been in here?'

The girl dismissed his question without looking at the photo. 'We see a lot of people passing through here, Mister.'

'But do you remember seeing her?'

'I don't remember any of them.' she replied. 'Do you want something? Tea? Coffee?'

Spades had been in the detective game long enough to know when he was chasing a lost cause. Accepting the outcome, he ordered a coffee and retreated to a table by the window to plan his next move. He glanced at his watch. 2.42. It seemed like the time had flown by. What now? Should he wait to see if Coda would turn up? What if he'd missed her? What if she had been here at two thirty? Instead of wasting time listening to the old crone's nonsense he should have been here, watching and waiting.

As he waited for the coffee to arrive, he picked up a newspaper from the adjacent table and scanned the front page. It was obviously a Circus District publication. He didn't see anything familiar in either the layout or the content. Turning the pages idly, his attention centred on an intriguing headline.

NO CLUES IN MYSTERY OF MISSING CRIME WRITER

With his interest sparked, he pulled himself upright in the chair, and shook the newspaper into shape.

'Your coffee!' The girl thumped the cup down on the table. 'Want anything else?'

Lowering the newspaper, he shook his head. Good manners and service with a smile clearly weren't on the menu. 'No, thanks.' He turned his attention back to the newspaper.

Three weeks after his sudden disappearance, authorities yesterday confirmed that no progress has been made in determining the whereabouts of renowned crime novelist Hans Rugen. Anyone with any information or sightings of Mr Rugen should contact them immediately.

Mickey Spades took a mouthful of coffee and continued reading. The footnote was of particular interest.

Mr Rugen's agent, Larry Taskin, has offered a reward for any information leading to the safe return of his client.

Spades' eye drifted over the agent's contact details. This was good. He had a lead. Taking another gulp of coffee, he got to his feet. Marching to the service counter, he held out the folded newspaper and tapped the article. 'This address, do you know where it is?'

The girl glanced at it. 'Yes.'

'Is it far from here?'

'No, Mister, not far.'

'Could you give me some directions?'

'It's not far,' she repeated. 'Turn left at the first crossroads and follow the sound of the river. When you reach the clock tower, turn right.'

He waved the newspaper. 'Can I take this?'

'If you wish.' The girl shrugged her disinterest.

He pulled a bank note from his wallet. 'How much for the coffee?'

She eyed the note suspiciously. 'That will be sufficient.'

'Really? No change?' He guessed not. Placing the money on the counter, he turned and made towards the door.

'No!' Her abrasive shout stopped him in his tracks. 'Not that way!'

'What do you mean?'

'You must leave by the other door.' She gestured towards a recess at the far corner of the room. 'There is another door, through there.'

'Why?'

'The newspaper,' she hissed. 'The address you ask about. If you want to go there, you must leave by the other door.'

Stung by her reprimand Spades mumbled his thanks and made towards the recess. He felt the weight of her stare as he crossed the room. This place was strange, no doubt about it. The sooner he was back in familiar territory the better. The recess led into a dimly lit passageway. At the end of the passage he descended the short flight of steps, pushed open the door, and stepped outside.

The temperature had dropped considerably; the air held a distinctive chill. The streets he now walked seemed much wider than before, the architecture more pleasing on the eye. Following the girl's directions, he found himself a short time later standing under an impressive marble clock tower. The sculpting and the carvings were magnificent. Such grandeur, such attention to detail; such a pity the clock mechanism hadn't been given the same consideration. He checked his watch, the time on the clock tower was wrong by more than seven hours. Scoffing his amusement he glanced at the newspaper and continued on his way. He was nearly there. His expectations rose. Could this missing writer hold the answers Spades so desperately needed? Had Amy Coda followed this same trail? Had she been here?

He found the address easily. Tapping a finger on the brass nameplate by the doorway in confirmation, he went inside. Climbing the stairway to the third floor, he knocked on the wooden panelled door and entered without waiting for a response. A spectacled man placed a half-eaten muffin down on the cluttered desk. Wiping his chin, he flicked the crumbs from his shirt, pushed back his chair, and got to his feet.

'Hello. Name's Larry Taskin, literary agent extraordinaire. How can I help you?'

Spades placed the newspaper on top of a stack of papers.

'I'm here about the missing writer.'

'I see.' The man eyed him expectantly. 'Do you know something about where he might be?'

'No,' shrugged Spades, 'but I'd be interested in helping look for him. It's kind of my speciality.'

With a flash of disappointment, Larry Taskin dropped back into his chair. 'Is that so? Are you a private investigator?'

'Something like that.'

'Well, that could be a problem.' Taskin picked up the muffin. 'I'm not sure my financial incentive would stretch as far as paying for the services of a P.I.'

'No charge.'

'Really?'

'No charge.' repeated Spades.

'No charge?' Taskin eyed him suspiciously. 'Now why would you do that?'

'What can I say? I like a challenge. Let me look into it. I'll see what I can turn up for you. If I find anything useful you can remunerate me as you see fit.'

'Okay,' Taskin's expression lightened. 'It's a deal. Where do we start?' He bit into the muffin enthusiastically.

'The writer,' Spades pressed. 'Tell me about him.'

'Rugen's a good guy,' Taskin's mouth bulged. 'I've been his agent for twelve years now, and it's been a successful working relationship.'

'Has he ever gone to ground before?'

'No, this is a first.'

'Newspaper says he's been missing nearly three weeks. Anything strange happen to him before that? Anything unusual going on in his life?'

'Not that I know of.'

'Any idea where he might be?'

Swallowing the last of the muffin, Taskin smacked his lips. 'Nope, none at all.'

Spades continued with his questions. 'What kind of books does he write? Fiction?'

'Yeah, crime thrillers. They may not be in the top league of best-sellers, but Rugen has made a comfortable living from them.'

'How many has he written?'

'We have eight novels published. Most recent one was released shortly before he went missing. It's selling really well. Of course, the hype surrounding the author going missing helps add to the interest, but I'd prefer to have Rugen found safe and sound.'

'Of course.' Spades winced. 'So, these crime novels, any recurring themes and characters? Are they a series?'

'Yep, all part of a series. Main character's a ruthless detective; has his own way of getting things done.' Larry Taskin paused as a grin flashed across his face. 'You know, in a strange kind of way, you remind me of him. Very direct.'

'Really?' Spades smiled falsely. 'I hope I can take that as a compliment?'

'Yes… absolutely.'

Sensing he was making progress, Spades pressed further. 'This most recent novel, you don't happen to have a spare copy, do you? Be nice to give it a read. Maybe get inside Rugen's mind.'

'Sure thing, no problem,' beamed Taskin. 'I've got plenty to go around.' Lifting a book from the shelf behind his desk, he handed it to Spades. 'There you go.'

'Thanks, I'll get it back to you.'

'Keep it. Consider it an advance, your free copy. If you help to find Rugen, I'm sure he'll be happy to sign it for you.'

'Okay.' Spades turned the book tentatively. A fleeting glance at the back-cover blurb was all that was needed. There it was, right in front of his eyes; all the confirmation he needed. Flicking quickly through the pages, picking snippets at random, the scale of his discovery became apparent. Everything was in there. Or was it? What about his discussion with Amy Coda? He had to know if any of his thoughts and suspicions were truly his own, and there was only one way to find out. He had to read this book as soon as possible. His mind buzzed with the possibilities. Was there more? Was another book being written? Was the writer really missing, or had he gone into hiding to work on a follow-up novel? He suddenly became aware that Larry Taskin was talking. 'Sorry?'

'I was just saying,' Taskin seemed less at ease. Spades generally had that effect on people. 'There was something that just came to mind.'

'Yes?'

'You asked if Rugen had anything going on before he vanished.'

'Yes?'

'It's probably nothing, but he'd started preparatory work on a new novel.'

'Oh really?' Spades knew it. Gut instinct... right every time.

'Very different to his usual thing,' continued Taskin. 'Tale about a man walking in the forest. He hadn't got very far with it when he'd run out of inspiration. Anyway, thing is, he'd let the editor of the local newspaper read his first chapter, just a rough draft you understand, and the crazy fool got carried away with the idea. Went over to the dark side if you ask me, spent most of his time wandering about in the forest. Day or night, it didn't matter.'

'What happened?' Spades wondered where this was going.

'Well, he went missing; hadn't been seen for three days when they found his body in the woods. They reckon he'd fallen from the cliffs.'

'I don't get the connection.'

'Rugen was quite troubled by it all, said he felt responsible for what happened to Egberts. I told him the idea was ridiculous; told him there was no way he was to blame, but he didn't seem convinced.' Larry Taskin hesitated. 'Do you think that's what has happened to Rugen? Gone walkabout and got himself lost in Greenhill Forest?'

'It's a possibility.' Spades replied, thinking aloud.

'Should I call the authorities? Ask them to concentrate the search in there?'

'No, not yet. Let me look into it first, best not interfere until we have something solid to report.'

'Okay, if you think so. I'll bow to your experience.'

Spades nodded as he altered the flow of the conversation. 'Why do you think he changed the theme of this new novel? Do you think the same characters were going to be involved?'

'I don't know, he said the idea just came to him. He'd just bought a cottage at the edge of the forest; he'd only been there a few months. Maybe that was the inspiration behind it.'

'Maybe. It sounds interesting. You got a copy of that one?'

'No. Like I said, it was in the very early stages. It will be on his old laptop computer; he writes everything on there.'

Mickey Spades felt his pulse quicken. He had to see the new storyline, at all costs. It was time to throw caution to the wind.

'Rugen's cottage. Where is it?'

'I'll write the address down for you.' Taskin replied obligingly. He scribbled on a scrap of paper and handed to Spades. 'Do you need to get into the cottage? I could try and arrange entry for you if needs be.'

'No, that won't be necessary,' Spades lied convincingly. 'I probably won't even go down there. Just good to know where it is. Sometimes it's useful to check a place out; it helps get a feel for what was going on inside someone's head.'

Taskin nodded approvingly. 'Got to say, I'm impressed with your attention to detail.'

Spades grinned. It was time to leave. He'd learned enough here. There was a lot to be done. 'Well, I'd best get started.'

Larry Taskin offered a handshake as he rose from the chair. 'So, what's your name, fella?'

'I prefer to work anonymously,' replied Spades guardedly. 'Until I find anything of any worth. Just an old superstition of mine.'

'Right,' grinned Taskin. 'I like that, a private investigator with an element of mystery.'

'Something like that.' Spades smiled falsely and quickly made his exit.

Mickey Spades found a quiet café, one with a friendlier manner than the Black Rose Café, took a seat in the corner, and braced himself for what he was about to uncover.

Four strong coffees and a little over three hours later, he finished reading Rugen's novel. Tapping his fingers impatiently on the back cover, he struggled to come to terms with what he'd read. More than mere confirmation of his suspicions, the novel was a staggering disclosure. Almost everything that had happened in the last few months of his life was there, laid out before him in black and white. With a sinking feeling of despair, he considered the previous seven novels in the Mickey Spades saga. How was this possible? Was he expected to believe that everything that had happened in his life was all just the product of some stranger's imagination? Everything…?

Maybe not everything! There was no mention of his recent thoughts, his recent suspicions, and his conversation with Amy Coda. So, was he now in control of his own thoughts? Or was Hans Rugen still pulling the strings? Was Rugen writing this now? He put his head in his hands. This just couldn't be happening. His thoughts turned again to Amy Coda. Where was she? How much did she know? Had she figured out who Rugen was? He tried to clear his head; he had to think this through logically. Rugen's new storyline was the key; he had to read it. Taskin had told him it would be on the writer's laptop. If Rugen was still in control, he would have the laptop with him, meaning Spades would have to find him to get to it. But, if Rugen was genuinely missing, the laptop might still be in his cottage. There was only one way to find out, and it was the obvious place to start.

Mickey Spades settled his bill and went outside. Lighting a cigar, he quickly reviewed the scribbled address Taskin had given him, and hailed a taxicab.

CHAPTER NINETY

'Thanks for coming to visit me, Sonja. I really appreciate it. I don't like hospitals much.'

'Don't mention it, Hans, I'm glad you're going to be okay. But I just don't understand, what were you doing wandering there in the middle of the night?'

Hans Rugen shifted uneasily in the bed. 'I know it appears strange…'

'Strange?' She cut him off sharply. 'That's an understatement. Why were you copying Mitch's last movements? His bizarre behaviour was his undoing; you're just lucky to have survived. What were you trying to prove?'

'It was the note you gave me; the one he left for me. It fuelled my curiosity. I suppose I was just trying to make sense of it.'

'None of it made any sense, Hans. Mitch had lost the plot.'

Rugen shook his head. 'Maybe not, Sonja. I saw proof of the things he'd tried to tell me about. There were people down there in that remote part of the forest, just like he said. I saw them from above, I was tracking them when I fell.'

Sonja Egberts waved a hand in protest. 'And what exactly does that prove? People in the forest, so what? It's crazy talk and I'd rather not hear any more about it. Let it go, Hans. I told that pathologist woman the same thing. It's upsetting and it won't bring Mitch back.'

Rugen nodded apologetically. 'Of course, I'm sorry, but do you mind if I ask just one more thing?'

'What?'

'How was Mitch discovered? Who found him?'

'An old man found him whilst walking his dog.'

Rugen's expression darkened.

'Yes, Hans,' she continued, 'the same old man that found you. Striking similarities aren't they? Coincidence?'

Rugen brushed the notion aside. Coincidence or not, the old man had saved his life. The doctors said he'd been unconscious when the hermit had found him and taken him to his cabin. Rugen had apparently spent twelve days and nights there with head and leg injuries. He had to take their word for it, he didn't remember anything. After that time, satisfied that Rugen's condition was no longer critical, the old man had taken the two-day walk from his cabin to alert the authorities.

Sonja Egberts sighed. 'I don't know what drove you to such actions, to be honest, I'd rather not think about it. You'd be well advised to forget about it all. You've had the lucky escape Mitch was denied.' She touched a hand to his arm. 'I must go now, Hans. Take care of yourself.'

The door closed quietly behind her, leaving Hans Rugen alone with his thoughts. There were too many unanswered questions. Who were the flame-bearers in the forest? Had they played some part in Mitchell Egbert's untimely demise? Or had he just fallen, the same as Rugen had? One thing was certain, when he'd fully recovered, Hans Rugen was going to return to Greenhill Forest. He had to find the old man and thank him; he owed him his life. And perhaps the hermit could shed some light on things.

A sudden knock on the door heralded the entrance of the grinning Larry Taskin. 'Snack time, Hans.' Handing Rugen a bag of apples, the sweet-toothed agent made himself comfortable in the chair next to the bed and tore open a packet of chocolate chip cookies. 'I had a chat with the doctor on the way in. He reckons you're going to be fine. No long-term damage.'

'Yes, it looks that way. Should be home in a few weeks if all goes well. Lucky outcome, all things considered.'

'Now, there's an understatement.' Taskin's expression grew serious. 'What were you doing in the forest in the middle of the night, Hans? Same place Mitchell Egberts fell to his death. What were you thinking?'

Rugen really didn't want to discuss it. He had other things on his mind. 'Just something I had to do, no point in talking about it. You probably wouldn't understand.'

'I'm guessing not.' Taskin bit noisily into a cookie.

Rugen was keen to change the subject. 'I'm ready to get writing again.'

'Really?' Taskin chomped. 'So soon? There's no rush.'

Rugen shook his head. 'Doc says it will be fine, and besides, when the inspiration strikes, you've got to make the most of it.'

'Okay, what are you thinking? What's cooking in that head of yours?'

Rugen pitched his plans warily. 'Remember that story of the man walking in the forest?'

'Yeah, I remember, I thought you'd abandoned it?'

'I thought so too, but it's strange, I've been getting flashes of inspiration. Random thoughts, but they feel like recollections or memories. This may sound odd, but it feels like there is a story there just waiting to be told.'

Larry Taskin munched thoughtfully. 'You know my opinion on this, Hans. I reckon you're best sticking to your genre.' He hesitated for a moment. 'But what's the worst that can happen? Now might be the perfect time for you to thrash out some new ideas, whilst you're recuperating.'

'Good, that's agreed then. So, did you take my laptop in, as we discussed?'

Larry Taskin sat forward in the chair. 'No, I couldn't find it.'

'What do you mean?'

'It wasn't there, I looked everywhere in your cottage but couldn't find it.'

'I told you it was in the study.'

'Nope, it wasn't in there.' Taskin shook his head. 'I couldn't find it anywhere.'

'That's just not possible. Are you certain?'

'It's not there, Hans.'

'Something's not right, it should be there… has the cottage been broken into? Any signs of someone having been in there?'

'No, there's no evidence of that at all.'

'If that's the case, where is my laptop computer?'

'I don't know… are you sure you left it at home?'

'Yes, I'm sure.'

'Oh well, don't worry. I expect it will turn up.' Taskin pulled another cookie from the bag and took a bite.

'Everything is fine at the cottage,' he continued. 'And besides, the likelihood of you being burgled is slim. It's so remote, no one would know the cottage was there, nobody would ever go there… unless…'

Rugen immediately seized on his hesitation. 'What is it?'

'It's probably nothing, Hans, but there was someone asking about you… when you were still missing.'

'Who? Who was asking about me?'

'Well, you know I'd put an ad in the newspaper asking for information about you, just in the hope that it might help?'

'Yes, you mentioned it. Go on.'

'Well, this private investigator came to see me. I think it was just a couple of days before you were found. Anyway, he offered to help look for you, didn't even want paid full rate for his work. He seemed very thorough, total professional.'

Rugen's patience was wearing thin. 'And what happened?'

'I only saw him that one time. I gave him a copy of your latest book, and he went on his way. I never heard from him again. Figured he must have heard you'd been found.'

'You didn't tell him where I lived, did you?'

Taskin fidgeted nervously with the cookie bag. 'I might have.'

'What do you mean?' fumed Rugen. 'You might have?'

'Look, he said he didn't intend going there, just that he might want to see the location… to get inside your head, he said.'

Rugen couldn't believe what he was hearing. 'He wanted to get inside my head. Really? He said that. And you thought it was a good idea to tell him where I lived?' Taskin's face flushed with embarrassment as Rugen continued. 'Dammit, Larry, you need to put this right. We need to report him to the authorities. He is obviously the one who has stolen my laptop, makes sense doesn't it? You said he was very professional; stands to reason he'd be able to break in without leaving any sign of entry.'

The agent grimaced. 'Makes sense, I guess.'

'I need you to report this. What was his name?'

Taskin shifted uneasily. 'Umm... that could be a problem.'

'What do you mean?'

'I didn't get his name...'

'What?' Rugen's blood boiled. 'Are you serious? You give my home address to a complete stranger, a psycho who wants to get inside my head, and you don't even get his name?'

'I did try, Hans, honestly I did. But he said he wanted to act anonymously.'

'No prizes for guessing why.' Rugen couldn't believe it. Why was someone so interested in him? Interested enough to offer their detective services freely? Interested enough to break into his cottage and steal his laptop computer? An uneasy feeling crept over him. 'The private investigator; what did he look like?'

'Funny thing was, and I think I said it to him at the time, he reminded me of Mickey Spades.'

Rugen felt a chilling sensation travel down his spine. 'You say he was asking about me?'

'Yes.'

'And you let him know where I live?'

'Yes.'

'And you gave him a copy of my latest book?'

'Yes, I'm sorry, Hans. Who do you think he was?'

Hans Rugen didn't answer. Scrabbling desperately in the drawer of the bedside cabinet he retrieved his notebook and pen, and began writing frantically.

'What is it, Hans?' pressed Taskin, alarmed by Rugen's sudden anxiety. 'What's wrong?'

'You have to go, Larry,' Rugen responded without lifting his head. 'I need you to bring me another computer, and you need to get it here quickly.'

CHAPTER NINETY-ONE

Rising early, Taro Brook ate a hurried breakfast and began the short drive to town. The doubt and confusion compounded by several troubled nights filled with disturbing dreams had finally lifted, leaving him with a clear if somewhat bizarre purpose.

As he reached the outskirts of town his doubts began to return. He wondered if he was still asleep, trapped in some peculiar dreamscape. Everything looked very different. The street layout appeared for the most part unchanged, but several of the town's familiar landmarks and buildings had either gone or had changed almost beyond recognition.

The countless unrecognisable vehicles in the early morning traffic gave cause for further consternation. What was going on here? How could everything have changed so much in only a few days?

Pulling to a stop on Main Street, he jumped from his pick-up truck. At least the police station appeared reassuringly familiar.

Taking one last worried glance around, he braced himself for the task ahead and went inside.

Police Chief Sallow sighed lethargically and eased himself back in his creaking chair. Tapping the papers with his pen, he addressed the hard-faced man on the far side of his desk.

'Everything looks in order, Agent, but I'm puzzled. Why wasn't I informed of this prior to your arrival?'

'Not my place to comment, Chief. You know what they are like; lines of communication are poor at the best of times.'

Sallow nodded his agreement. 'You're not wrong there.' Sitting forward, he blew out his cheeks and held up his hands. 'Very well, as we're not going to waste our time questioning the way Central Command operate, what do you need from me?'

'Access to your files, and a bit of privacy; shouldn't take long, couple of days at the most.'

'Are you looking for anything in particular?'

'No, just a routine review, looking over some old cases, tying up loose ends.'

'Unsolved? Ongoing, long term; that sort of thing?'

'Yeah, something like that.'

'Well, it seems only fair to tell you that we cover a big area. There's plenty here to keep you busy.'

'That's good. I was hoping to find a comprehensive source of cases in the one place. It will save me time travelling around.'

Sallow eyed his visitor with no small measure of suspicion. 'If you don't mind me saying, you don't look the type to enjoy going through paperwork.'

The man's steely expression shifted slightly. 'You're a good judge of character, Chief. I loathe it, but I have my orders.'

Sallow broke into a grin. 'You've been assigned to desk duties? Nothing quite like paper-pushing to help keep the wayward ones in check. Am I right?'

'Got me again, Chief.'

'Yeah, well it's none of my business anyway. You have your clearance. You can start in the morning.'

He pushed the papers back across the desk. 'You can use one of the rooms through the back. Do you need anyone with you?'

'No, best if I don't...'

A knock on the door cut the response short.

'What is it?' Sallow snapped.

'Sorry for the interruption, Chief,' an officer entered the room hesitantly. 'We've got someone in the interview room demanding to speak to someone in charge.'

'What's the problem?'

'He's not making much sense. He keeps rambling on about an impending disaster heading our way.'

'Is he making threats?'

'No, Chief, it's nothing like that. He says a devastating flood is imminent, says he's been given this message and needs it to be heard by the higher authorities.'

Sallow scowled. 'Probably a religious freak. Send the crazy fool on his way.'

'I tried, Chief, but he's very insistent. He's been here for hours, determined that his message gets heard. I've taken his statement, gone over it all several times and...'

'Get to the point, Tarner,' encouraged Sallow dryly. 'I really don't have time for this. I'm already late for an appointment.'

'Thing is, Chief, I thought you might want to talk to him.'

'Now, why would I want to do that?'

'Well, he's been asking all day to talk to Chief Hayle.'

Sallow's expression changed instantly. 'Chief Hayle? Really?'

'Yes, and that's not all.' Officer Tarner placed a document on the desk. 'I had to get this file from the archives.'

Sallow eyed the file suspiciously. 'Why?'

'Because he claims to be this missing forest ranger, and the scary thing is… he looks exactly like him.'

Taro Brook tapped his fingers impatiently on the desk. Things were not going well. If, as he suspected, this was another of his bizarre dreams, now would be a really good time to wake up. He'd been here all morning, desperately trying to get them to listen to him and to take his warnings seriously.
He'd gone over it all several times with the duty officer who, after hours of stubborn denial, had finally agreed to his requests.
He'd left the room, promising to return with the Police Chief. Maybe then Brook would have more success.
The man was obviously new, Brook had never seen him before. New and incompetent; he had been gone for nearly an hour. What was taking him so long?
Whilst Brook was willing to accept his claims were unusual by any stretch of the imagination, time was of the essence. Why didn't they realise it?
With his patience diminishing rapidly, he tapped louder on the desk. What was taking them so long?

Police Chief Sallow skimmed quickly through the file. 'You say he looks just like the man in the file photograph?'

'Yes, Chief, a dead ringer.'

Sallow scoffed. 'He must be a son, a nephew, or some other relative. These religious nuts are always coming up with novel ways to give credence to their claims regarding doomsday. I'll tell you both, it's the end of the world for me if I don't get out of here in the next five minutes. Being late for an anniversary lunch with my wife isn't advisable. I'd rather face the apocalypse. Just get rid of him.'

'He says he won't leave, Chief, not until he talks to someone in charge.'

Sallow cursed. 'Then throw him in a cell for the night. I'll deal with him first thing in the morning.'

'Perhaps I can help?'

Sallow turned his attention to the government agent. 'You?'

'Yeah, why not? I've got some time before I can check in at the motel. Let me talk to him, I'm from Central Command. That should placate him. What's the story?'

Sallow pushed the file across the desk. 'This is a missing person's case. You'd probably have come across it in your review anyway.' Rising from his chair, he pulled on his jacket. 'Person in question, Taro Brook, a ranger who disappeared in his own forest. Strange one; never did get a satisfactory outcome. You want a few moments back in interrogation? Be my guest. Find out why this nutcase is trying to steal the unfortunate ranger's identity, then either lock him up for the night or send him on his way.'

'Okay, but if I'm going to quiz him I need to know what you're thinking. Aside from the ridiculous claims about impending disaster, shouldn't you check him out? He could be who he says he is; maybe he's suffering from shock or something?'

Stalling by the door, the Chief of Police replied dismissively. 'It isn't him, believe me, it simply isn't possible.'

'Why not?'

Sallow grinned knowingly. 'Tell the agent why, Tarner, then show him to the interview room.'

As the door swung closed, Duty Officer Tarner rolled his eyes by way of apology. 'Excuse the Chief, he's not usually so short-fused, but he's right on this one. We have a fake in our interview room. I'll admit the resemblance to the man in the photo is striking, but he can't be who he claims to be. It just isn't possible. Forest Ranger Taro Brook disappeared without trace forty-six years ago.'

Detective Mickey Spades was struggling to comprehend the magnitude of his good fortune. In his search for answers, his guise as a government agent reviewing old case files had succeeded beyond his wildest expectations.

Picking up the trail on leaving the writer's cottage, the track through the trees had led him to a small township where, following a brief but fruitful visit to the local law enforcement office, he'd helped himself to the identity papers of a recently deceased government agent. Spades always found it intriguing that the more remote the law enforcement outpost was, the more open to inducements the officers were. For a small fee, they'd been more than happy to share their information. Whilst the theft of the unfortunate agent's identity was all down to his own creativity and quick thinking, one odd detail had not escaped his notice. As willing as the officers had been to answer his questions, neither of them would admit to ever having heard of the author Hans Rugen.

He obviously wasn't as well-known as his agent would have liked to believe.

Served by his dogged determination and guided by his ever-reliable gut instinct, Spades' quest to uncover the truth had finally led him here, face to face with the man who held the answers he so desperately craved.

It had to be him. The opening lines of the bizarre statement he'd given to the duty officer matched the storyline Spades had found on the writer's laptop. Matched it almost word for word. He could scarcely believe it. His stomach knotted with anticipation. The more he listened to the conversation between the man and the increasingly beleaguered Officer Tarner, the more convinced he became that he'd found Hans Rugen.

Yet he knew he had to tread carefully. He couldn't let the writer know who he was, not until he'd got the answers he needed. If he was ever going to be fully in control of his own destiny, Rugen was an obstruction that would have to be removed, but first Spades needed answers. He needed to get Hans Rugen alone, and he had to do it quickly.

Tarner's patience was almost at an end. 'Look, we've been through all this already. I'm not listening to your wild claims anymore. Just tell me who you really are.'

'I've already told you who I am… countless times. My name is Taro Brook. Where is Chief Hayle? You said you were going to get him. I demand to see him. He will vouch for me.'

'Why do you keep asking for Chief Hayle?' Tarner snapped in desperation. 'How do you even know about him?'

'Of course I know him, he's the Chief of Police. Everyone in the district knows him.'

Tarner shook his head in resignation. 'I've had enough of this, if you don't start being straight with me, I'm going to have to charge you with wasting police time. You can't speak to Chief Hayle. He's dead; has been for the best part of twenty years.'

Taro Brook eyed the duty officer suspiciously. What was going on here? What were they up to? Something was very wrong.

'Chief Hayle is not dead,' he countered defiantly. 'I spoke to him only a few days ago. You're lying.'

'Forget about Hayle.' The officer placed a document on the desk. 'Let's concentrate on this.'

'What's that?' Brook eyed the papers warily.

'It's a missing person's file.' Pushing it towards him, the officer tapped a finger on the photograph on the document. 'Are you going to tell me who you are, and how you can have such a striking resemblance to this missing forest ranger? Are you a son? Or a nephew? What is the connection?'

Taro Brook stared at the photograph. 'It's me! It's a photo of me.' He glanced at the document's wording. 'I'm Taro Brook. Why do you have a missing person's file with my name and photo on it?'

The duty officer slapped the desk in frustration and pulled the file away. 'You can't be who you claim to be. It just isn't possible. Taro Brook's been missing for forty-six years.'

Taro Brook stared back in astonishment. What was going on? Why were they making such a ridiculous claim? The whole thing was an entire fabrication. False claims and fake documents. But why? Why had they gone to so much trouble? What were they hoping to achieve? Hit by a sudden flash of doubt, his thoughts drifted to the things he'd witnessed outside. How had they managed to make everything appear so different? The cars and the buildings, and the people. Why did he not recognise anyone? Where had everyone gone?

Having waited patiently for an opportune moment, sensing that his chance had finally arrived, Mickey Spades boldly seized the initiative. 'I reckon we could all do with some coffee. Could you arrange that, Officer?'

'Yeah, no problem,' Tarner sighed with an air of resignation. 'I could do with a break from this, and the Chief promised you some entertainment.' He tucked the document back under his arm. 'I'd best keep a hold of this. I'll give you ten minutes, then I'll come back with the coffee.'

As the door closed, Spades fixed the man with a cold stare. 'So, who are you really?'

'I'm Taro Brook.'

'I don't think so. According to that file and to everyone here, Taro Brook's been missing for more than forty years.'

'It's all lies. The file is a forgery. I'm Taro Brook. What has happened here? Why is everything different?'

Spades ignored the pleas. He had questions of his own. 'I had a quick read through your statement. It makes interesting reading. It's intriguing, it reminds me of something I've read somewhere before.' Pulling a folder from his borrowed briefcase, Spades leafed through the bundle of printed papers and placed one down on the desk. 'Does this look familiar?'

Taro Brook scanned the page in astonishment. The similarities to his statement were striking. The page was titled Chapter One. Who had done this, and why? 'Where did you get that?' He thumped the desk in annoyance. 'What are you all playing at? We don't have time for this game. Instead of trying to discredit me, you should be taking my claims seriously, and start making preparations. What the hell is wrong with all of you?'

Spades thumbed hurriedly through the papers. 'Oh yeah, the impending disaster. A flood? I've read through all of this several times but haven't come across it. Perhaps you haven't got that far yet?' He placed another printed sheet down on the desk. 'This seems to be as far as we get... on the laptop computer at least.' He tapped the page. 'Remember this part?'

Taro Brook scanned the text quickly. His name was mentioned again but the rest was unrecognisable. There was a woman with him; her name meant nothing to him. They were being held captive in a tower. It made no sense. He reached out for it, but it was snatched away quickly. 'Where did you get that?'

'Are you saying you don't recognise it?'

'Of course I don't. Someone copied my statement for the first page you showed me... the rest is all a total fabrication.'

'You can stop bluffing. It's obvious you wrote this. You've used this missing forest ranger's identity as inspiration for your lead character.'

'That's ridiculous. If I'm not who I claim to be how come I look just like him?'

'Maybe you're a relative, using his unfortunate circumstances to make money from a book you're writing. You can't be Taro Brook. He's been missing forty-six years, yet you don't look a day older than he does in the photograph.'

Taro Brook held his head in his hands. 'This is all wrong.'

Mickey Spades glanced at the clock. He was running out of time. The duty officer could return at any minute. He had to make his move. 'Look, I'm going to level with you,' he began cautiously. 'I know who you really are, and it just so happens I've been looking for you. I've got a lot of questions that need answering.' He waved the folder animatedly. 'I've been to your house, I helped myself to a copy of your manuscript. Apologies for your laptop computer, I had to dispose of it. Incriminating evidence of my wrongdoing, it had to be done.'

Taro Brook stared blankly. 'I have no idea what you are talking about. Who are you? Are you even with the police?'

Spades prodded the folder angrily. 'This obviously isn't finished, Rugen. Where is the rest of it? How much more have you written? What else is in it?'

'What did you call me?'

'Rugen. Your name is Hans Rugen.'

'That's not my name.'

'It might not be your real name, but it's the name you've been using to write your novels about...'

The door swung open suddenly. A small man in a pinstriped suit entered the room, holding a cup in each hand.

'I believe you ordered coffee, gentlemen.' Placing the cups down on the desk, he pointed a finger towards Taro Brook. 'Ahaa! There you are! I've been looking everywhere for you.'

'Who are you?' replied Brook.

'Get out!' Spades fired angrily. 'We're in the middle of an interrogation.'

'So I see, Detective.' The new arrival stroked his white whiskers. 'Detective Spades isn't it?'

'Sorry, old man. You're mistaken. You must be confusing me with someone else.'

'No. There's no need for your subterfuge with me, Detective. I know exactly who you are. Your friend told me.'

'What friend?'

'Attractive woman, very friendly too. Lovely smile, auburn-coloured hair, about shoulder length.'

Spades drew a sharp intake of breath. 'Coda? You've seen her? Where is she?'

'Yes, that's her name. She's waiting for you, Detective.'

'Where?'

'Interview room six.'

Fumbling the folder back into the briefcase, Spades made towards the door. 'Interview room six. Where is it?'

'Hmmm, let me see now… ah, yes, take a left at the end of the corridor, go down the stairs, follow another hallway to the end. It's the only door. Just go straight in.'

Spades hesitated. 'You wait here, Rugen. I'll be back in a few minutes with Coda. She's going to be pleased to see you. Then, rest assured, we'll all get the answers we want.'

As the door closed behind him, the new arrival turned his grin towards Taro Brook.

'Well, he was in a hurry, wasn't he? I hope I gave him the correct directions. Did I say left or right?' He clicked his fingers. 'No need to worry, I'm sure he'll figure it out.'

'Who are you?' Taro Brook eyed him suspiciously. 'Where did Officer Tarner go? Is he getting the Chief to come talk to me?'

'Relax, my friend.' The little man pulled up a chair. 'I'm sure you have a lot of questions; I am here to help as best I can.' He grinned playfully. 'I imagine we have a lot to talk about. Where would you like to begin?'

CHAPTER NINETY-TWO

Mickey Spades was in trouble. There was no point in denying it. For the first time in his life he had to admit he was out of his depth. Things were happening over which he had no control. Worse still, as he searched frantically to make sense of his new surroundings, he found himself having to surrender to an uncomfortable truth. He was lost.

For the first time in his life he experienced the cold sensation of fear. Panic surged through his body, pulling frantically at his nerve ends. He should never have come here. He should never have crossed worlds. He should have stayed where he was; safe in his own world where everything made sense, where he was always in control. And he should definitely not have broken into the writer's home and stolen his laptop.

Mickey Spades had to admit it; he'd gone too far this time.

Cursing his arrogance, lamenting his colossal lapse in judgement, he pushed his way through the crowd. He had to find his way to the hospital as quickly as possible. He had to talk to Hans Rugen before it was too late. He needed answers; Rugen would have to answer for all he had done. Rugen would have to help him find his way home.

A disturbing scenario suddenly clouded his thoughts. Even if he was able to find him in this strange town, what if Rugen refused to help? What would he do then?

He'd been so immersed in the search he'd paid little attention to where he was going and had given even less consideration to how he might find his way back.
Pushing forward determinedly, he vowed that Rugen would have to help; he would give him no option. Hans Rugen would know better than to refuse. Rugen had created him; he knew him better than anyone. He would know what Spades was capable of and what he might do if he thought he wasn't going to get his own way.
Lost in his thoughts, stepping out blindly to cross the busy street, Spades failed to notice the pedestrian crossing light change suddenly to red. The warning shout from the shocked onlookers came too late. Spades turned to see the grey delivery truck speeding ominously towards him. There was nothing he could do. Impact was inevitable.
Mickey Spades closed his eyes and cursed his arrogance one last time.

Larry Taskin placed the open notebook down on the bed.

Sitting in the chair by his hospital bed, Hans Rugen probed for a reaction. 'Well? What do you think?'

Taskin's assessment was short and to the point. 'I don't like it.'

'Really? Why not?'

The agent appeared genuinely troubled. 'Why do you want to kill off Mickey Spades?'

'I just think the time is right.' Rugen found himself quickly on the defensive. 'I accept it needs a lot of work, but as a skeleton idea, I think it works; maybe as a short story to bring the Spades saga to a conclusion.'

Larry Taskin shook his head dismissively. 'It's too far-fetched, Hans. If you're really serious about getting rid of Spades, which I think is a big mistake, you should at least keep it in context. Maybe a stake-out or a chase that goes wrong, or a shoot-out, but this? Mickey Spades is way too smart to let himself get hit by a delivery truck. It just doesn't add up, it's like you've rushed to a conclusion without thinking it through. And besides, it's too much of a jump. It needs to stay in genre. The whole Spades series is a crime thriller, yet you're wandering off on some kind of sci-fi tangent.'

'It gives it a fresh twist though, doesn't it?'

'Not in my opinion. And it's not very original either, is it? I mean, writer creates character who comes to life then goes after writer. It's all been done before, several times.' Taskin fired Rugen a look of bemusement. 'Where did this all come from, Hans? When I left you yesterday, to go get the other computer, I thought you were going to be thrashing out ideas for the walker in the woods story. What made you come up with this?'

'Just something you said,' Rugen replied uneasily, 'about the private investigator that came to see you, about him reminding you of Spades.'

'So what? It just so happens he did, but I didn't mean you to take it literally.'

Hans Rugen didn't try to hide his disappointment. 'I guess we are going to have to agree to disagree on this one, Larry.'

'Are you okay, Hans? You seem a bit on edge. A bit troubled.'

'I'm fine,' lied Rugen. 'Just tired.'

'You should get some rest. Tell you what, why don't we delay any decision for a couple of days? We can think it over and have a catch-up early next week, see what we both think then. I honestly think you'll change your mind, but if you're still determined to go through with Spades' demise, maybe we can come up with a compromise? Some adjustments to keep it in genre?'

Rugen agreed grudgingly. It wasn't quite the outcome he'd hoped for, but it was a start. The door closed behind Taskin, leaving Hans Rugen alone again with his thoughts.

Maybe his agent was right; maybe the idea was too far-fetched. Nonetheless, Rugen felt better for writing it. In the unlikely scenario that there was any truth in his suspicions regarding Mickey Spades he'd probably nullified any potential threat with what he had written. The idea may not even have to be taken any further. But then again, if Spades really was on the loose and no longer under his control, would what he had written make any difference?

Rugen rubbed his temples wearily. What was happening to him? He looked for reason in his confusion and found none. Did he honestly think that Mickey Spades had come to life? That he was alive in Rugen's world, and that he had broken into his home and stolen his computer? Of course he didn't. It was ridiculous... and yet for a short while the prospect had seemed frighteningly real. Despite their disagreement, his agent was right about one thing. He needed rest. His escapade in the forest had perhaps taken its toll in more than just a physical way.

Everything would seem better after a few days of rest.

An abrupt knock brought his session of self-analysis to a sudden halt as Larry Taskin's head peered round the door.

'Look lively, Hans, you have a visitor.' Pushing the door open, the agent ushered a woman into the room. 'I found this young lady in reception asking about you. Turns out she is with the pathology department, figured maybe you and her could discuss the Egberts case. Thought it might help clear some things up for you, maybe exorcise some demons.' He winked casually. 'I will leave you two alone.'

Rugen winced uncomfortably as Taskin clicked his tongue against his soft palate before closing the door behind him. It was an annoying habit his agent succumbed to whenever he saw an attractive woman; a habit which often led to Rugen's embarrassment. He watched as the woman approached the end of the bed. Larry Taskin's assessment was accurate. She was beautiful; stunningly beautiful. Rugen found himself captivated by her presence. Judging by her manner, it appeared she was equally fixated with him. Was this the woman Sonja Egberts had told him about? If so, would she be able to offer some insight into Egbert's sad demise? Shifting uneasily under her stare, he prompted her to share her thoughts.

'So, you are here to talk about Mitchell Egberts?'

'No.' she replied.

'Oh!' Taskin had been duped. Again. 'Then how can I help you?' he asked nervously.

She hesitated for a moment before answering.

'You are Hans Rugen?'

'Yes, that's me.' He began to wonder where this was going. He glanced at the buzzer on the bedside cabinet. Was he going to have to call for assistance?

'I apologise if I seem a little overawed,' she continued slowly. 'It's a huge moment for me to finally meet you. I can barely believe it's happening.'

Rugen swallowed uncomfortably. Was she a crazy fan? Why had Taskin let this woman into his room? An awkward silence followed. Rugen searched for the words to help push things along.

'So, what can I help you with?'

She fixed him with a determined stare. 'Initially I'd just wanted to find you. I'd thought it might be nice just to talk with you if it was possible. But now, there is something specific I really need to ask you.'

'Yes?' replied Rugen warily. 'And what would that be?'

'What have you done to Mickey Spades?'

Her response took him completely by surprise. 'What are you talking about?'

'What have you done to Mickey Spades?' she repeated.

Rugen couldn't believe it. How could she possibly know what he'd planned for Spades? He'd only just let Taskin read his rough proposal. 'I'm not sure what you mean...'

'I've been waiting for him for several days,' she continued. 'I left him clues; a trail he could easily follow, but he hasn't appeared. What have you done to him?'

Rugen's eye shifted nervously to the notebook lying open on the bed where Larry Taskin had left it.

Following his gaze, she bent to pick it up.

'Hey, that's private,' he snapped. 'Put it down.'

She couldn't help but wonder why he'd glanced towards the notebook. She had to see what was written in it. Ignoring his pleas, she quickly scanned the penned notes. Gasping inwardly, she lifted her gaze from the page.

'You've killed him!' Struck by a numbing sensation of both shock and fear, she moved towards him. 'How could you?' A tear spilled down her cheek. 'Why did you do it?'

'It's only... It's only a proposal.'

He was lying. She knew it. She could feel it deep inside. She finally had her answer; this was why Spades hadn't showed. 'When did you write this?'

'It's just a proposal.' he repeated anxiously.

'It's too late,' she hissed. 'It's written now. You can't undo something like this.'

His arm reached out suddenly for the bedside cabinet. She panicked. Without thinking, she dropped the notebook to the floor and threw herself at him. Colliding with his chest as he rose from the chair, she heard the dull thud as his head smacked against the metal bed frame. Stumbling backwards on to the bed, she watched as the dazed writer slid to the floor.

Watching him closely as he slowly pulled himself to his senses, a terrifying realisation chilled her to the core. If he was capable of dealing with Mickey Spades so callously, chances were she might well be facing the same fate. Everything was spiralling out of control. Everything was going horribly wrong.

'Who are you?' he wheezed.

'You don't recognise me?'

'No, I don't...' he shook his head. 'Should I?'

That hurt her, more than she could ever have imagined. She took a deep breath before answering.

'Does the name Amy Coda ring any bells?'

Amy Coda! He couldn't believe it. Was this really happening? Holding his hand to the back of his head, Hans Rugen stared up at the woman standing over him.

It was her; it really was Amy Coda, looking exactly the way he had imagined her. Only, he had never pictured her looking this angry.

Larry Taskin hadn't been duped; she was from the pathology department. Taskin would never have considered the possibility that it might be her, he had rubbished the notion that Spades could come to life, but Rugen should have known better. He shouldn't have let himself be so easily dissuaded. He cursed his naivety. He'd been so fixated with the prospect of Mickey Spades turning up, he had failed to consider the possibility that Amy Coda might also be roaming free.

What now? Should he try to reason with her? It really didn't look like she was in the mood to respond to reason. He glanced again at the notebook. Was there enough time to write something? And if so, would it have any effect? There was only one way to find out. He had to get his hands on the notebook and try.

The look of horror on his face answered her question. Reacting quickly, he made a sudden lunge towards the notebook. She caught him by the shoulders and grappled him to the floor. As they fell, a pen slipped from his hand. She gasped in disbelief. He really intended to do it. She had to stop him. She couldn't let him get his hands on the notebook. She had to end this; he had given her no choice. It was either him or her, a bitter battle for survival. In the struggle for supremacy, she clambered on top of him. Straddling his chest, she pulled a pillow down from the bed. Fighting back the tears that threatened to consume her, she closed her eyes and pushed the pillow down, smothering the writer's muffled cries for help.

It was over in a matter of seconds. She checked for a pulse. There was nothing. He was gone. As the reality of her actions struck home, her tears flowed freely. She hadn't meant for any of this to happen. This was not what she had wanted.

Sobbing uncontrollably she covered him with the bed sheet, not daring to move the pillow, not daring to look down on his face. It was more than she could have coped with. Moving towards the door, she whispered her regret to the empty room and stepped out into the corridor.

Avoiding the escalators she ran down the deserted stairway, jumping three steps at a time. Reaching the ground floor she made her exit via an unmanned service door.

The moment she was clear of the hospital grounds, with the tears stinging her face, Amy Coda started to run. She ran and never looked back.

CHAPTER NINETY-THREE

Taro Brook eyed the stranger suspiciously. 'Who are you?' he asked again.

'You don't recognise me?'

'No, should I?'

'Perhaps, although I must concede my appearance does differ considerably from when we last met. I took some advice from an old acquaintance; I upgraded my wardrobe. I believe it's called changing one's image, but to be honest I just don't see it lasting. I've never been a fan of suits… much too formal for my liking. And the shirt collars are so uncomfortable.'

'Are you my legal advisor?'

'I suppose you could say I was an advisor… of sorts.'

'Well, I'm beginning to think I need one. It feels like I've been here for days. Why am I being detained?'

'I'm not sure you are being detained. Have you tried to leave?'

Taro Brook eyed the door dubiously. 'No. I didn't think I could.'

'The door is unlocked, my friend. You are free to go whenever you wish.'

'Really? I thought I was being held here,' Brook frowned, 'like I was being interrogated. It felt like some kind of conspiracy. None of it made any sense.'

'In my opinion it's best not to overthink things, Master Brook. You have been through a lot. Your confusion is understandable. And besides, sometimes the truth is stranger than fiction.'

'You called me Brook.'

'That is your name, isn't it?'

'Yes, yes it is. But I've been having some difficulty convincing people of it lately.'

'Ah, now there is a folly; trying to convince the ignorant of simple truths they don't want to accept. Worry not, Taro Brook, your interrogation is over. There will be no trial, you have done nothing wrong and besides, there is no one left here to incriminate or judge you.'

'What do you mean? Where is everyone?'

'All gone, I'm afraid.'

'Gone? What do you mean? What happened to them all?'

The stranger shook his head gravely. 'There was a massive undersea earthquake. Subduction, I believe they call it, when one tectonic plate slides under another. It triggered a catalogue of catastrophic subsequent quakes and aftershocks, sending a series of devastating tidal waves landwards. I'm afraid much of what you once knew as your world now lies far beneath the ocean.'

Taro Brook struggled to find the words to respond. 'When?... When did this happen?'

'Several days ago.'

'Several days? How long have I been here? How was I not aware of anything? And if everyone is gone… how did I survive?'

'Relax, my friend. I know it is a lot to comprehend. Worry not about how long you have been here. It is irrelevant, much like the concept of time itself. The important thing is that you survived.'

'But how could this have happened without my knowing? And Tarner, the duty officer, he was here just a short while ago. He went to get the coffee.'

'Things are not always as they appear, Taro Brook. We now find ourselves immersed in surroundings where what you might call the normal laws of nature no longer apply.'

Taro Brook let the enormity of the stranger's words pass without comment. He was still struggling to come to terms with the chilling revelation that much of his world was now gone; lost far beneath the sea. His warnings had fallen on deaf ears. 'Then it was all true. Everything that happened in my dreams, everything I tried to tell them, everything I tried to warn them about.'

'Yes, it appears so. But don't be too hard on yourself, you tried your best. You did all you could; you came back and tried to warn them. It isn't your fault that they didn't listen. Even if they had, I doubt it would have made any difference.'

'What do you mean?' Brook challenged. 'You just said I came back. Back from where?'

'A journey of sorts... you might call it a voyage of discovery.'

'I don't remember going anywhere,' he replied dismissively. 'It all happened in my dreams.'

'Your reluctance to accept the truth in my words is understandable. I will not try to convince you further, but do not underestimate your commendable efforts to save your world. You did all you could, and for a novice to return from a journey such as yours, missing your point of origin by a mere forty-six years, is in itself nothing short of remarkable.'

Brook stared at him in astonishment. 'You mean it's true what they said? I'd really been gone that long?'

'Yes,' the whiskered man nodded. 'But in the grand scheme of all things, forty-six years is but a blink of an eye.'

'Then, I really did go somewhere?'

'Yes, indeed you did.'

'Then, if only I had come back sooner, perhaps...'

'Come now, supposing you had returned earlier, do you think they would have listened? Would they have given any more credence to your claims than they did on this occasion?'

'I suppose not.' Brook's head buzzed with questions. Where had he been all that time? Why did he not feel any different? None of it made sense. A startling thought suddenly came to him, one that put all other questions in the shade. He eyed the stranger warily. 'If my world is now under the ocean... then where are we?'

'Here and there,' came the chuckled response. 'Forgive me, I don't mean to make fun, but the infinite can be difficult to quantify with mere words alone. I suppose you might say we are between worlds, entangled, in what some refer to as The Eldormaar. Many find it daunting and intimidating, I prefer to think of the endless possibilities for exploration and adventure. Think of that door as a gateway... Who knows what wonders lie beyond? Why not walk through, and find out?'

'I'm free to go?'

'Free as a bird. Always have been. The only binds holding you here are the ones put in place by your own mind. Given the circumstances, feelings of guilt, loss and regret are only to be expected.' The stranger moved slowly towards the door. 'And now, I must take my leave. I do sincerely regret having to be the messenger of such grim news.'

'Wait!' Brook glanced down at the desk. 'You didn't drink the coffee.'

'Oh, I've always considered myself more of a tea drinker. Farewell, Taro Brook. Until we meet again.'

The door closed behind him.

Taro Brook stared at the two cups on the desk. Struck by a sudden moment of clarity, his jumbled thoughts swung into focus. They had met before; he remembered now. He hurried across the room and pulled the door open.

'Two Cups! Wait!'

The sun felt warm on his skin. The light breeze flicked at his senses. The song of the lone blackbird fell momentarily silent as the flapping of wings heralded a new arrival. Coming to land atop the tallest of the ancient standing stones of Sumarren, a raven ruffled its feathers as it eyed them inquisitively.

'Two Cups.' Taro Brook almost whispered the words.

Messenger Two Cups turned to face him quizzically.

'Ah, yes, what was I saying?'

Brook hesitated, as if finding his place. 'You were saying that any incarnation of me may well cease to exist in other worlds.'

'Yes, that's right,' beamed Two Cups. 'And that you were not to worry because you are a conscious entity for whom the journey will never end.'

'You are talking about immortality?'

'No, for you there is no such thing. Mortality is a very real concept for those inhabiting the earthly plane, but you now exist on a much higher level.'

Pausing to digest the Messenger's words, as the pieces of the puzzle began falling into place, Taro Brook's eyes drifted skywards. As the staggering implications of his fate finally dawned on him his gaze followed the jagged mountain ridge down through the trees, flitted among the ruins of Sumarren, and settled once again on Messenger Two Cups.

'The great flood,' his words tripped out slowly. 'I didn't survive it.'

Two Cups pursed his lips and sighed. 'I'm afraid to say that I very much doubt it. The scale of the disaster would have rendered such an outcome very unlikely, impossible even. But, by being aware of the impending tragedy, your very essence had the presence of mind to leave that plane of existence, and that is the true gift of the Drifter.'

'Then I am not Taro Brook?'

'Of course you are,' scoffed Two Cups, dismissing all notion of gloom. 'And after all, what is in a name? I myself hold claim to several of them.'

He snorted his amusement as he patted Brook fondly on the arm. 'We must part now; the images once again begin to blur.'

He took hold of Brook's hand and squeezed tightly. 'But we shall meet again soon, and remember,' he grinned, 'you may well be the man from Nallevarr, but to me, old friend, you will always be Taro Brook.'

CHAPTER NINETY-FOUR

Chasing the storm clouds across the leaden sky, the biting north wind gripped the landscape tightly in its chilling embrace. Sunlight pierced the clouds, offering fleeting glimpses of azure blue, whilst great spears of light tumbled from the sky like celestial stairways linking the rolling seas with the heavens high above. The waves crashed noisily on the rocky shoreline; their timeless chorus broken only by the harsh cries of the sea birds circling overhead.

Scanning the rugged coastline he caught sight once more of his follower clambering awkwardly over the eroded shelves of rock. Despite the fact they'd been tracking him for some time he remained untroubled, their presence was in no way threatening. With a shake of his head he continued on his way, all the while slowing his pace intentionally. Traversing a jutting prow of jagged rock, he jumped down onto the white shingle. A short distance ahead, in the rocks at the foot of the overhanging headland, he saw a narrow notch gouged out by the relentless surge of the sea.

Crouching in the cramped sanctuary, sheltered from the buffeting wind he waited patiently, listening spellbound to the hypnotic swell of the waves as they pounded incessantly against the rocks. Not long after, a sudden, frantic increase in the sea birds' activity heralded the imminent arrival of his follower.

Moments later they appeared into view at the side of the rocky prow. Holding his breath in anticipation, he waited as they made their hesitant descent. Falling awkwardly onto the shingle, his pursuer hurriedly scrambled to their feet and dusted themselves down.

'Don't be alarmed.' He called out as he stepped from his hiding place. 'Are you hurt?'

'No!' came the startled response.

'You've been following me for some time. Are you lost?'

As she pulled back the hood of her jacket, the wind whipped her hair across her face. 'I'm sorry,' she began nervously. 'I am not from here.'

'That much is obvious,' he replied lightly. 'You are poorly prepared for our climate.'

'It is cold…' she shivered. 'So cold.'

'The days are not the worst,' he cautioned. 'Believe me, it gets much colder at night.'

'I am lost,' she continued shakily. 'I don't know where I am, or how I came to be here. When I saw you, I had to follow.'

'You seem anxious, don't worry. There's nothing to harm you here.'

'You're not angry with me for following you?'

'No. I would have done the same if I were in your position.' He pointed along the scattered shoreline. 'If you wish, I can offer food and shelter for the time you are here.'

'That's very kind,' she hesitated. 'For the time I am here? What do you mean by that?'

He smiled reassuringly. 'If it's any consolation I too have found myself in strange places with no explanation of how I got there, and from what I remember things can change very quickly.' He paused for a moment before continuing.

'We may have a lot in common you and I, perhaps more than either of us will ever understand. My recollections of such experiences are somewhat limited so I won't pretend to know all the answers but I'll share with you what I can. Perhaps it will help.'

'Any help you can offer would be appreciated. Thank you.'

'Think nothing of it. We should get going. The sun drops rapidly here and with it, the temperature.'

Ascending the narrow ridge from the shoreline, he studied her expression closely as she scanned the desolate landscape in wonder.

'It's beautiful,' she said quietly, 'bleak, but beautiful.' She turned to face him. 'I have seen no other sign of life. Do you live here alone?'

'No, there are others. We occupy a small frontier settlement not far from here.'

'What is this place? Where are we?'

'I know you must have many questions but first, tell me, what is your name?'

She hesitated for a moment as if measuring the danger in divulging such information.

'Amy,' she replied, flicking her windswept hair from her face. 'My name is Amy Coda.'

With a nod, he pointed her gaze towards the barren expanse of rounded hills and valleys, and the snow-capped mountains far in the distance.

'Welcome to Nallevarr, Amy Coda. You will probably hear the inhabitants of the settlement refer to me by another name, but you can call me Taro. My name is Taro Brook.'

Printed in Great Britain
by Amazon